The Wild Innocent . . .

When he could contain his passion no longer, he undressed her completely and gazed in awe at her smooth, pale body with its full, creamy breasts and gently rounded hips bathed in the soft morning light. Her beauty stirred him immensely.

Sighing deeply, he said, "This is wrong, Micaela, but I can't help myself."

"I know," she replied, surprised by the huskiness of her own voice.

"It's you who must stop me now."

"I can't, Patrick." She pulled him close to her. "I can't."

His hands fondled the smooth, silky skin of her inner thighs, slowly moving higher and higher, until they reached her sex. Now her desire seemed boundless; she writhed and moaned, her lips parted, her breath coming in rapid little gasps.

Love's Fervent Fury

A HOT-BLOODED ROMANCE OF THE SOUTH—AND THE HEART'S DEFIANT DESTINY

Love's Fervent Fury

Robin Joseph

BALLANTINE BOOKS • NEW YORK

Library of Congress Catalog Card Number: 78-61544

ISBN 0-345-27435-0

Manufactured in the United States of America

First Edition: December 1978

Dedicated
to
MARY C. JOSEPH
who has more than a little in common
with the heroine of this book.

Prologue

1

Don Andrés Almonester tossed the flaming torch onto the pile of kindling logs and odd pieces of timber and watched the wood ignite. The flames grew quickly, leaping higher and higher, filling the sky with billows of thick, gray smoke. The heat became so intense that Don Andrés was forced to move back into the crowd of friends and onlookers that had gathered in the square. Smoothing his ruffled hair, still vibrantly red despite his advanced years, he looked on with eager anticipation as a yellow and maroon striped bag, suspended a safe distance above the fire, filled with hot air and slowly expanded.

A short distance away, at the Almonester home on St. Peter Street, Louise, the don's young wife, remained steadfast in her refusal to join the throng of boisterous merrymakers in the Place d'Armes, as the square was unofficially called by the French populace, who stubbornly declined to refer to it as their Spanish governor did: the Plaza de Armas. Two factors prevented Louise from participating in the event: her opinion that it was ridiculous and undignified as well as dangerous, and her preference for a quiet private life away from the public eye. Although thirty years younger than her husband, she shared none of his sense of fun and frivolity. In many ways he often seemed more youthful than she. For weeks she had been trying to persuade the self-made Spanish entrepreneur to forgo his plans for such an extravagant celebration.

"Please, Andrés, give up this madness," she had pleaded.

"It's not every day that a man of such humble origins as I, a poor notary from Andalusia, is honored by our gracious king," Don Andrés had argued. "I am about to become a Knight of the Order of Charles the Fourth. That's nothing to be sneered at."

"After all you've done for this city, that's the least he can do for you. No one has been more generous to the many charities than you, nor more philanthropic. He is only giving you what you have earned."

"That's no way to talk about his Majesty," Almonester had gently reproached.

"I don't care a whit about your Spanish king or his so-called honors," Louise had retorted, a flush spreading across her fair-skinned face. Like so many Creoles of a pure French descent, she refused to recognize the Spanish sovereignty over Louisiana.

"A man's king is his wife's king as well," Don Andrés had pointed out with a good-natured twinkle in his dark eyes. "You know that, my dear."

"I know no such thing," Louise had snapped. Her stubbornness and persistent unwillingness to be submissive had been a great trial to her distinguished family and a stumbling block in their success in arranging a suitable marriage for her. Until Don Andrés had appeared unexpectedly, matrimonial prospects for the twenty-nine-year-old Louise Delaronde had looked rather dim. At sixty, the don—a childless widower who had arrived in Louisiana twenty years earlier—had shocked all New Orleans by presenting her with a marriage proposal. Louise had accepted and the marriage had taken place; much to everyone's amazement, it proved to be a success. Don Andrés adored his young, attractive wife in spite of her shrewish nature and ill-tempered disposition. The local society was further astonished when the elderly don succeeded in making the peevish brunette a mother, not once, but twice. Two daughters, Andrea and Micaela, were born to the couple, and despite some ribald speculation, there was little doubt as to the girls' paternity, especially Micaela's. The younger daughter bore an uncanny resemblance to her father, having the same long face, the same dark, flashing eyes, the same flaming red hair.

"You must be mad to consider such a thing—flying off in a balloon filled with hot air," Louise had continued. "A man of your age should be ashamed."

"A man of my age can do what he likes. That's the only advantage of growing old."

Exasperated, Louise had declared, "Sometimes, Andrés, you are more than I can bear."

"Am I?" he had said with a chuckle. "You have to understand, Louise, that I want my investiture to be the finest celebration this city has ever seen. I want people to remember it for years to come."

Unable to endure the swarm of visitors any longer, and irritated by the noise from the square opposite the house, Louise excused herself, left the crowded patio, and retired to her room. She lay down on the daybed and agitatedly fanned herself with the jeweled Spanish fan Don Andrés had presented to her after the birth of their younger daughter. She was annoyed that her husband had thrown their home open to the citizenry at large and then gone off to his balloon, leaving her to entertain what she considered the local rabble. She hoped that her departure would prompt the guests to depart, but the din of voices floating up through the closed jalousied shutters from the patio below belied such a wish. Light from the blazing bonfire in the square filtered through the cracks in the jalousies and reflected onto the walls of the bedroom. The shouts and laughter of the enthusiastic crowd in the plaza punctuated the steady, droning cries of vendors hawking fruit, ices, candy, and chicory-laced coffee.

"He's making a fool of himself," Louise muttered to herself. "Well, I'm glad the girls are asleep in their room and not witnessing this nonsense of their father's."

Her thoughts were suddenly interrupted by the appearance of Flore, the middle-aged black slave who had been part of Louise's dowry when she married Don Andrés.

"How dare you come in here without knocking first?" Louise cried.

"I'm sorry, Miss Louise," the woman apologized. "I thought you went out there with Master Andrés."

"You knew perfectly well I had no intention of participating in my husband's foolishness," Louise said in a mollified tone. "How are the girls? I hope all the commotion around here today hasn't upset them too much."

"They is all right, I guess. I ain't heard nothin' from them since I put them to bed," Flore replied. "There is so many folks downstairs to feed, I ain't had no time to look in on them. Miss Micaela sure was disappointed you wouldn't let her go with her daddy."

"Out of the question," Louise snapped.

"I had a terrible time gettin' her to bed," the slave added, shaking her head.

"Have they started to leave yet?" Louise asked.

"Who you talkin' 'bout?"

"All that rabble down in the patio who are trampling my running roses and newly blooming flags."

"They ain't leavin'," Flore informed her. "They is still comin'. That's why I is here lookin' for you, Miss Louise. Your cousin's done come."

Louise frowned. "Cousin? What cousin?" She paused. "You mean my brother and Miss Eulalie from Versailles?" Intermarriage among Creole families made nearly everyone along the Mississippi River relatives in one way or another and resulted in the term "cousin" being applied rather loosely.

"No, Miss Louise," Flore answered. "The baron."

Raising her eyebrows ever so slightly, Louise displayed the first glimmer of interest she had exhibited all day. "You mean the Baron de Pontalba?" She said the name carefully.

The slave nodded. "Yes, ma'am."

The Baron de Pontalba, or Joseph Xavier Delfau, as he was known before he returned to France to reclaim the family lands and title, had been merely another first cousin when he was a child.

Her interest piqued, Louise rose from her daybed.

"Go tell the baron that I shall be down in a few minutes."

Dour and austere, the Baron de Pontalba seemed less like a country noble and more like a priest or a cabinet minister in his plain, rather somber attire, an impression that was heightened by his long, thin face, solemn dark eyes, aquiline nose, and stern mouth. Stepping forward, he greeted Louise stiffly but gallantly when she appeared at the foot of the stairs in the flagstone patio, where a fountain splashed merrily and a brilliantly colored parrot hopped about in a cage that was suspended from the branch of a fig tree.

"Dear Cousin," he murmured, kissing her extended hand.

The baron was accompanied by his pallid, fluttery wife, Jeanne, who embraced Louise and greeted her in a thin, reedy voice. Jeanne de Pontalba, like her husband, had also been born in New Orleans and was a niece of the former governor, Miró.

"Congratulations, madame, on your husband's honor," the baron said.

Jeanne nodded. "I don't know when I've seen a more splendid investiture, certainly not in France. Nor in Spain, either."

"Yes, it was rather splendid," her husband agreed, although his tone lacked the enthusiasm expressed by his wife. "Three lackeys carrying the train of his great mantle, that immense crowd following him as he went in state from the cathedral to home. Extraordinary. Only Don Andrés could have carried it off with such ceremony."

Jeanne smiled. "You must be very proud, and Don Andrés must be very happy."

"Yes, I suppose so," Louise answered disinterestedly.

"Nonsense," the baron snapped, startling both women.

"What do you mean?" Louise demanded.

"I mean that Don Andrés will never be happy or satisfied."

"Really?" Louise said archly. "Perhaps you will be kind enough to explain yourself, dear Cousin."

"I hear that after the ceremony he was already wondering how he might achieve the title of brigadier," the baron replied. "It seems that that Spaniard's ambitions know no bounds."

While they were speaking, Jeanne's attention was suddenly captured by the sight of the enormous striped balloon rapidly inflating with hot air.

"Oh, I think it is so exciting," she squealed. "Imagine, Don Andrés going up in a balloon!"

Deliberately turning her back on the activity taking place in the dusty square opposite the house, Louise said, "Please, I prefer to ignore it. This stunt of my dear husband's greatly distresses me."

At that moment Flore came running down the stairs and across the patio, sobbing and flailing her arms in great agitation. "Oh, Miss Louise! Miss Louise!" she cried.

"What is it?" Louise demanded impatiently.

"Oh, Lordy, Miss Louise!" the slave wailed.

Alarmed, Louise grabbed her by the shoulders and shook her. "Stop that nonsense and tell me what's wrong," she ordered. The guests in the patio immediately fell silent.

"It's Miss Micaela," the woman said between sobs.

"What's happened to her?" Louise persisted.

"Oh, Lordy! Lordy!" Flore sobbed.

Coming to his cousin's aid, the baron intervened by slapping the slave. "Answer your mistress," he said sternly. "What's happened to Miss Micaela?"

Rubbing her stinging cheek, Flore sobbed louder.

"Answer me or I'll take a whip to your black hide," he threatened.

"Please don't let him beat me, Miss Louise," the slave pleaded. "It ain't my fault."

Fast losing her patience, Louise demanded, "Tell me this instant what's happened to Miss Micaela. Do you hear?"

Shaking with sobs, Flore raised her arm and pointed to the balloon, which was now completely inflated and pulling against the ropes that moored it to the ground. "There!"

Much to her horror, Louise spotted her little daughter racing through the shaggy sycamore trees toward the balloon, the hem of her nightdress lifted high above her ankles, her bright red hair flying loose behind her.

"Micaela! Micaela!" she cried, even though she knew that the child could not hear her.

At a signal from Don Andrés, Raymond, one of the husky Almonester slaves, raised his machete and began to slash the ropes holding the balloon. As each rope was cut, the air-filled vessel strained against its remaining anchors.

"Papa! Papa!" a small voice cried.

Don Andrés standing in a wicker basket attached to the balloon, was stunned to see his daughter a mere three feet beneath him.

"Take me with you! Take me!" she begged.

"No, no, Micaela," he said. "You must go home. Where is your mother? Where is Flore?" He gazed about and was shocked to realize that the child had made her way across the square alone.

"Take me, Papa!" she persisted.

Egged on by the crowd gathered around the balloon, Don Andrés gave in to Micaela's pleas. He picked her up, and lifted her into the basket. Once inside, the child clapped her hands with delight. "Up, Papa! Up!" she cried. "Let's go up!"

When all the ropes were cut, the yellow and maroon gas-filled bag rose slowly, gracefully, accompanied by the shouts and cheers of the assembled onlookers and by the pop of firecrackers set off by little boys.

In the gently swaying basket Don Andrés held Micaela tight, secretly pleased that she had decided to join him, and marveled at the child's fearlessness.

"You like this, don't you?" he asked.

"Oh, yes, Papa!" she answered gleefully. "I want to go higher. Make it go higher, Papa. Higher and higher!"

"Yes, higher." He clutched her against his chest.

"I want to go as high as the moon," she said in her high child's voice, pointing to the faint white sliver of a new moon rising over the horizon.

"We'll go as high as you want," he promised.

Once they were aloft, a gentle breeze from the north nudged the craft southward. Below them lay the city, crescent-shaped, on the shores of the gigantic Mississippi, and, farther ahead, the bayous and the marshes and eventually the Gulf.

"I love this, Papa," she squealed. "I don't ever want to go down. I want to go up forever!"

"We can't go up forever," he said, attempting to steady the swaying basket.

"Why? Does the sky end?"

"You don't want to leave Mama, do you? Or your sister, Andrea?"

"I want to go up," she insisted, ignoring his question. "Higher!"

"Look down, child," he directed. "You can see our house. At the corner of the square. Do you see it?"

She nodded. "Yes, Papa."

"And do you see the cathedral?"

"Yes."

"And do you see those buildings all along the plaza, next to our house?" Micaela nodded and Don Andrés continued. "Well, they belong to Papa. And the ones on the other side of the plaza as well. And that big plantation near Bayou St. John? That's Papa's, too. And beyond, those miles and miles of timber, do you see them? They look like green patches from up here. They are all Papa's. As far as your eye can see is Papa's timberland. There's his sawmill, too. And over there is his brickyard. Papa is responsible for nearly every building in the city, one way or another."

"Do you own everything, Papa?" she asked. "The whole city?"

Don Andrés chuckled. "No, not the whole city, child, but quite a bit of it. One day, when Papa is gone, it will all belong to you and Mama and Andrea. Almost everything you see beneath you will be yours."

The concept of property and ownership was beyond

the child's comprehension or interest, distracted as she was by the excitement of the ascension, but this didn't prevent Don Andrés from pursuing the subject. "Someday a goodly portion of New Orleans will be yours."

Micaela frowned. "Mine, Papa?"

"Yes, my pet," he assured her, gazing at the moon climbing higher over the distant horizon as the gaily striped vessel dipped and swayed with the passing air currents. "A goodly portion."

Part One

2

GIGGLING HAPPILY, HER long red curls bouncing and shining in the summer sun, Micaela rolled a hoop, which stood nearly as tall as she did, across the sweeping green lawns toward the twin rows of majestic oaks stretching from the great house down to the river. Binnie, her personal slave, and at ten the same age as her mistress, trailed behind.

"You know your mama don't like you runnin' like that, Miss Micaela," the skinny black girl scolded, forced to act as both companion and conscience. "Runnin's for boys and such. A lady ain't supposed to run, and you know that."

Ignoring Binnie's admonition, Micaela continued to run and followed the spinning hoop to the levee, urging it up the steep bank. At the top of the rise, she paused a moment and gazed apprehensively up the river toward the city. At breakfast she had overheard one of the slaves say that her mother was expected that afternoon, and she was disheartened by the prospect of ending what had been a carefree summer. Micaela loved Versailles, the magnificent Delaronde sugar plantation named after the residence of the French kings; she also loved the freedom she experienced there.

She spent most of her days, after a few obligatory lessons under the tutelage of her cousin Pierre, riding the superb mounts of the stable, swimming in the muddy Mississippi, or playing hide-and-seek with Binnie and the other slave children in the pecan grove at the rear of the main house, an imposing sixteen-room mansion owned by her uncle, Colonel Delaronde, and his wife, Eulalie. The Delaronde offspring numbered nine daughters and one son, and were affectionately referred to as Apollo and the Nine Muses. At present only Apollo, or Pierre, was still at home with his parents. His refusal to wed any of the local belles, coupled with his rumored infatuation with a beautiful slave on the plantation, caused his family great distress.

As Binnie struggled up the bank of the levee, Micaela sighed resignedly, realizing that eventually all good things had to come to an end. For more than a year Louise had talked about enrolling her in the convent school run by the Ursuline nuns, and any further postponement now seemed unlikely.

"Micaela is still too young for the rigors of such a school," Pierre had argued whenever Louise brought up the matter. The Ursuline school was known for its strict discipline and high academic standards.

"Nonsense," Louise had retorted. "There are girls as young as six at the school."

"But they're probably much stronger."

"There's nothing frail about Micaela."

"True, dear Aunt Louise," the dapper young planter had said, "but then—if you'll forgive me— you thought Andrea was strong, too."

Louise had flinched at the mention of her first child's name. Andrea's death caused by an attack of the bloody flux, had followed that of Don Andrés by only four months and left Louise badly shaken. Her only consolation was that Micaela had been spared the throes of cholera.

"Micaela needs the discipline of the Ursulines," she had replied. "She's been acting like a little wild animal lately. I do confess that it's partly my fault. I'm afraid I've neglected her rather badly the last couple of years and haven't given her the attention I should have, but it's not easy being a widow with burdensome responsibilities."

Throughout New Orleans and its environs it was common knowledge that at the time of his death Don

Andrés Almonester was one of the richest men in the region, if not the richest. Because the don had died intestate, his entire fortune, including those portions that would normally have gone to Micaela and Andrea, was assigned to Louise through the clever maneuvering of her attorneys, especially her cousin François LeBreton, one of the city's most brilliant young lawyers. Since that time it was generally acknowledged that, except for an occasional offering of astute advice from LeBreton, Louise had managed the estate on her own in a highly competent manner and increased its value considerably.

As soon as Binnie reached the top of the levee, Micaela deliberately rolled the hoop down the other side toward the river and raced after it.

"You come back here, Miss Micaela!" the slave girl shouted after her. "Don't you go fallin' in no water, hear? If you come back wet, both of us will get a lickin'."

When Micaela reached the water's edge, she headed for a clump of willows, quickly stripped off her clothes, and plunged naked into the muddy stream.

"Now you is gonna get us both in trouble," Binnie whined in her breathless, high-pitched voice. "Shame on you. Ain't you got no modesty? Oh, Lordy, if Aunt Sally finds out, she'll whip us both!"

When Micaela, mud-streaked, her wet hair clinging to her cheeks, and Binnie, trembling and frightened, returned to the main house, the first person they saw was Aunt Sally, the rotund black woman who ruled the house slaves at Versailles. She grabbed a switch off a peg on the hall wall and lashed at Binnie's legs for bringing Micaela home in such a state.

"Shame on you, you good-for-nothing pickaninny!" she berated the weeping Binnie.

Micaela attempted to inject herself between Binnie and the switch, knowing that Aunt Sally would not dare hit her. "Don't whip Binnie," she pleaded. "It was my fault. She tried to stop me from going in the water."

Aunt Sally straightened the red polka-dot kerchief around her head. "Shame on you, Miss Micaela," she said. "Comin' into this house lookin' the way you do. Your mama might arrive any minute."

Complaining that Binnie was too young and irresponsible to be trusted to look after Micaela, Aunt Sally led Micaela upstairs and proceeded to fill a copper tub with hot water, then brought it to Micaela's room, where she bathed and dressed her. When those chores were finished, she told Micaela that her cousin Pierre was waiting for her downstairs on the main gallery.

Micaela knew it was time for her lessons when she stepped onto the gallery and saw Pierre sitting at one of the oak tables lining the veranda. He had his glasses on. He was quite vain and wore them only when it was necessary for him to read.

"I want you to write down the following problems," he directed, pointing to the slate and piece of chalk lying on the table. A blue and white striped awning fluttered above him in the warm afternoon breeze, creating a rhythm of soft sounds that alternated with those made by the mockingbirds nesting in the nearby chinaberry trees.

Obediently, Micaela took a seat opposite him and waited for him to begin.

"Five plus seven," he dictated, trying to sound stern and businesslike, which was contrary to his normally carefree and urbane nature. "Twelve minus eight. Fourteen plus ten. Nine minus seven. Twenty plus eleven. Now, work out the problems, and when you have the answers, let me see them."

"Yes, Pierre." She nodded and immediately set about her task. Mathematics was easy for Micaela, and she dispatched the problems quickly.

Pierre checked her slate and pronounced all her answers correct. "I guess that takes care of mathematics for today," he said, removing his glasses and rubbing his long-lashed dark eyes.

A few moments later Roland, the butler, brought out a silver tray with a freshly baked cake exuding the aroma of ginger, and the usual glass of bourbon with ice for Pierre.

"What would Miss Micaela like to drink?" the black man asked.

"You have a choice of brown-sugar lemonade or sarsaparilla," Pierre offered, taking a healthy swallow of bourbon.

Micaela was aware that Pierre and his father, a blustery, white-haired former army officer, had frequent altercations about what the colonel termed his son's "excessive drinking." Pierre's mother, Eulalie, was a semi-invalid and much too feeble to involve herself in such matters.

"Sarsaparilla, please," she said.

From the seat of an adjacent white wicker chair Pierre picked up a familiar volume of classic French plays. He had a great love of the theater, in particular the plays of Molière, Racine, and Corneille, and often spent hours reading them aloud to Micaela, acting out all the parts in different voices and accents.

"You know what I've been thinking?" he asked.

"No; what?" she replied, eager to hear what he had to say. One thing she especially liked about Pierre was that he treated her more like an adult and less like a child, despite the difference in their ages of a dozen or so years.

"I've been thinking about building a little theater of our own right here at Versailles, perhaps back there near those chinaberries," he said, indicating the clump of trees filled with noisy mockingbirds some distance from the house. The birds greedily consumed the berries, a peculiar fruit that would eventually intoxicate them the same way that alcohol affected humans. "I would invite theater troupes down here to perform. I might even act in a few plays myself." He paused contemplatively and took another swig of bourbon. "You know what a ham I am," he added, swirling the chunk of precious and expensive ice around in the glass. "Perhaps you could act in the plays, too. You'd like that, wouldn't you?"

"Oh, yes!" she cried enthusiastically. "Yes, I'd love it!"

"Let's see, now," he mused. "Who would you like to play? Cinderella? Sleeping Beauty?"

Micaela had little patience with the foolish heroines of fairy tales and much preferred the strong ladies of the classics.

"I would like to play Phèdre. Or Chimène," she asserted, mentioning tragic heroines from the starkly dramatic plays that were her favorites.

Pierre threw his head back, shaking his wavy mane of rich brown hair, and roared with laughter. "Phèdre or Chimène!" he repeated.

"What's wrong with that?" she challenged.

"Nothing," he laughed, and reached over, hugged her, and planted a kiss on her cheek. Micaela loved Pierre for the attention and affection he lavished on her, both of which she had missed and yearned for since the death of her father.

The sudden clatter of a horse and carriage on the carriageway, which at Versailles was called the Chemin de Paris, or Parisian Way, interrupted their conversation. Looking up, Micaela saw the vehicle round the *garçonnière*—a bachelor's flat—on its way to the rear portico of the main house; she felt a catch in her throat when she recognized the familiar Almonester coat of arms on its door.

The moment Louise alighted from the carriage, she ordered Flore, who had accompanied her from the city, to pack Micaela's belongings. "I want her ready to leave with us today," she said.

Shaking her head, Flore muttered, "That child ain't gonna like that none."

"Whether or not she likes it is no concern of mine," Louise replied. "Now, do as I say and be quick about it."

"Yes, ma'am," Flore murmured, and trudged off toward the spiral staircase leading to Micaela's room on the second floor.

Louise proceeded into the house and stepped through the floor-to-ceiling windows of the parlor onto the gallery where Pierre and Micaela were seated, framed between two massive white Doric columns reaching to the eaves.

"Hello, Mama," Micaela said, rising and curtsying. She noticed that for the first time since the death of her father, her mother was not wearing her usual black mourning attire, but instead was outfitted in blue silk with a sprig of violets pinned at the throat. From both Louise's dress and her deportment it was obvious that a significant change had come over her during the summer. She seemed happier and more at peace with herself than when Micaela had left for Versailles.

Kissing Micaela's cheek, she murmured, "Hello, darling."

Pierre also rose to greet his aunt and received kisses on both cheeks.

"Nephew Pierre," she said. "Dashing as usual."

Pierre offered her a chair, for which Louise thanked him, joined them at the table, and removed her gloves.

"And what have you learned this summer?" she asked, turning to Micaela. "All the wrong things, I'll wager, if this rake of a cousin of yours had anything to do with it."

Micaela had rarely seen her usually dour mother in such a jovial mood.

"It depends on what one considers the 'right' and the 'wrong' things, Aunt Louise," Pierre answered for Micaela, signaling at the same time to Roland, who was hovering in the doorway, to bring Louise a cool drink and refill his own bourbon glass as well.

Reaching for a piece of Aunt Sally's freshly baked ginger cake, Louise said, "You know what I mean, Pierre."

"You're looking well," he observed. "Very well indeed."

Pleased by the compliment, Louise smiled. "Am I?"

"Yes. It's good to see you in blue."

"I decided that I have had enough of mourning."

"Just like that?" Pierre knew that such a decision for a serious-minded woman like Louise must have been made on more than mere impulse.

"Yes," she answered. "Just like that."

"I see." He nodded. "Have you had a pleasant summer?"

"A busy one."

"Profitable, I trust?"

"Quite, thank you," she replied coolly. Louise disliked discussing her business affairs with anyone, even someone she liked as well as her nephew. Changing the subject, she said, "I am pleased that my daughter is looking so well and that all of us have passed the summer season without coming down with that dread Bronze John." She referred to yellow fever by its local nickname. "I am grateful to my brother for allowing me to send Micaela away from the city for the summer, far from the pestilence that seems to dog us during the dreaded hot months. And I'm grateful to you, too, dear Nephew, all jesting aside," she continued, placing her hand over Pierre's, "for tutoring my daughter."

"Micaela's become quite proficient at mathematics," he said proudly.

"Oh, yes, Mama—"

"I do wish her penmanship would improve." Louise sighed. "It's so important for a young girl to have pleasing handwriting. In Micaela's case, I'm afraid it's rather hopeless."

"I'm trying to improve, Mama," Micaela said.

"I'm sure you are, dear," Louise replied, patting her cheek. "But sometimes trying isn't enough. If one is born without certain gifts . . ."

"Micaela has many gifts," Pierre asserted. "She rides well. She's good at sums. She's not a bad actress."

"If only her skills were the *right* ones," Louise lamented.

"What do you consider the 'right' ones?"

"I'm not sure. But whatever they are, I'm afraid Micaela lacks them."

After Micaela's belongings had been loaded onto the carriage, she bade a tearful farewell first to Aunt Sally and the house slaves, then to the colonel and

Aunt Eulalie, upstairs in her bed, and lastly to Pierre, from whom she was loath to part.

During the trip back to the city along the River Road, Micaela noted that her mother seemed preoccupied, as if she had something on her mind she wished to express but couldn't find the proper words. As always when they traveled by carriage, mother and daughter were accompanied by their respective personal slaves, Flore and Binnie. Binnie and Micaela amused themselves by making cat's cradles from leftover strands of yarn.

When they reached the Almonester townhouse opposite the weed-choked, muddy Place d'Armes, the coachman helped them out of the carriage.

"You still ain't told her yet, have you, Miss Louise?" Flore said as the two women climbed the short flight of stairs leading to the first floor of the house. Because of frequent flooding, the houses of New Orleans were built high off the ground. Micaela had lingered behind in the patio, visiting her parrot, Sancho Panza, a gift from her late father.

"I wish I knew how," Louise sighed.

"If you wait much longer, you won't have to tell her," Flore remarked. "That child will find out for herself."

"It's a coward's way, I know, but perhaps that might be best," Louise replied, removing her blue bonnet and patting her carefully coiffed hair before her bedroom mirror.

Later in the day Louise ordered Flore to see that Micaela was dressed in one of her better outfits for dinner that evening, explaining, "She'll dine with us."

As Flore began to lay out a flowered silk frock, Micaela suspected that something unusual was afoot. "Why do I have to wear that dress?" she asked.

"Because your mama done said so," the slave answered.

"But why?" Micaela persisted.

"Because you are a young lady and it's high time you was learnin' to fix yourself up nice and pretty."

"That's not the only reason," Micaela insisted.

"Well, it'll have to do for now."

Dressed in the flowered silk, Micaela fidgeted impatiently while Flore braided her long red hair, noting that all sorts of delicious aromas were emanating from the cookhouse in the rear of the patio. In addition, she could hear the voices and footsteps of the other house slaves as they scurried back and forth between cookhouse and dining room.

"Who is coming to dinner?" she asked.

"Somebody special," Flore answered cryptically.

"Who?"

"You'll find out soon enough."

When she was finally summoned to the dining room, Micaela was surprised to see the table arranged more elegantly than it had ever been before. There were three places, each set with gleaming silver, English bone china, Belgian crystal, and Irish linen. The fine dinner plates were not the customary black-bordered mourning variety, but a gay, flowered pattern.

Quizzically, Micaela regarded her mother, who looked ravishing in an exquisite gown of iridescent green silk that generously revealed the smooth fullness of her creamy breasts. "Mama, who is coming to dinner? Flore wouldn't tell me."

"To dinner?" Louise repeated rather distractedly as she poked a cologne-dipped handkerchief between the exposed cleavage. Although in her early forties, she was still remarkably attractive, having retained much of the youthful beauty for which she had been justly celebrated. "A most interesting person whom I'm sure you'll like very much."

Micaela observed that her mother's hands were trembling ever so slightly. Only on rare occasions was Louise Almonester nervous or unsure of herself, and this seemed to be one of them.

"Who, Mama?" she persisted, wondering why everyone was being so evasive.

"A distinguished gentleman," Louise finally said.

"What's his name?"

Fingering one of her cherry-sized ruby earrings, a wedding gift from Don Andrés, she replied, "Our guest's name is Monsieur Jean-Baptiste Castillon."

Puzzled, Micaela frowned. The name was unfamiliar to her. Monsieur Castillon was not a member of any of the local Creole families. "Who is he, Mama?"

"Monsieur Castillon is the French consul here in New Orleans," she explained.

Knowing she would be expected to speak proper French at the table and not the local patois, Micaela groaned.

"Monsieur Castillon is a most charming man," Louise went on, checking the hem of her skirt in the mirror beneath the mahogany sideboard to see if her petticoats were showing. It was obvious that her appearance was very important to her this evening. "I want you to be very nice to him."

"Yes, Mama," Micaela agreed unenthusiastically, convinced that dinner was going to be a very trying affair.

Shortly after eight Monsieur Castillon arrived, looking extraordinarily handsome and well turned out in his fashionable Paris clothes, cut in the latest style. He also looked very young, much closer in age to Pierre than to Louise, or so it appeared to Micaela, who was certain he was not more than twenty-five. In a most gallant fashion he greeted Louise, bending his blond head over her hand and keeping his lips pressed on her fingertips far longer than was customary. His green-eyed gaze seemed fixed on her, even when she introduced him to Micaela.

"What a pretty child," he said with a diplomat's practiced smile. "Like mother, like daughter."

"Nonsense," Louise scoffed coquettishly. "Micaela looks nothing like me. She is completely her father. His red hair, his eyes, his long face."

Dinner, the most lavish and delicious meal Micaela could recall, proved boring and uncomfortable. Both Louise and her guest seemed ill at ease and self-conscious in Micaela's presence, and their conversation, conducted in proper Parisian French, was stilted and overly polite.

"What a splendid man Napoleon must be," Louise said, raising her wineglass daintily to her lips.

"Yes, I can assure you he is most remarkable," the young consul replied to his hostess.

"Then you've met him, Jean-Baptiste?"

"Oh, yes, many times."

"Tell me," she began, "is it true he plans to proclaim himself emperor?"

"If Pope Pius the Seventh can be persuaded to go along with such a scheme," he said.

"Do you think his Holiness can be so persuaded?"

"Napoleon will find a way."

"And then Josephine will be crowned empress as well?"

"I believe that is Napoleon's plan."

"Imagine!" Louise sighed. "Empress of France. Is it true, Jean-Baptiste, that she is responsible for a trend in French fashion toward gowns that are cut very, very low? Almost indecently so?"

"Some say it is Madame Bonaparte's wish to shift attention from face to bosom," he replied. "You see, she has rather bad teeth."

"Well," Louise conceded, "a woman must capitalize on her assets. One can't blame her for that."

Castillon nodded.

"How unfair it was of Napoleon to sell us to this vulgar United States and deprive us of the opportunity to be part of the glorious French Empire," Louise said, pouting coyly.

"Unfortunately, madame, I'm not sure all your fellow Americans would agree with you."

"What do they know?" She accompanied this remark with an impatient wave of one diamond- and emerald-encrusted hand. Micaela had never seen her mother wear so much jewelry before. "Americans know nothing of the glory of France. Whereas I, from childhood, have worshipped that nation. From afar, naturally, but worshipped her nonetheless. And," she continued, turning her attention to her daughter for the first time since they had sat down to dinner, "I am trying to impart this same devotion to Micaela."

Castillon reached across the table and pinched Micaela's cheek. "And has your mother been successful?" he asked, looking at Louise instead of Micaela as he posed the question.

"I'm not at all sure," Louise replied.

"Nonsense. I am certain you are successful at anything you attempt, Louise," he said, calling her by her first name, which shocked Micaela. She could not recall anyone as young as Monsieur Castillon daring to address her mother in such a manner.

"Imagine France with an emperor!" Louise exclaimed, returning to the earlier subject.

"Yes, Napoleon the First. Exciting, isn't it?" The young consul placed his hand over hers and squeezed it as they exchanged smiles. "Shall we drink to the emperor?"

"Yes, let's," Louise agreed, raising her glass. "To Napoleon the First, emperor of France!"

Then, observing that Micaela had scarcely touched her meal, Louise diverted her attention from Castillon a moment. "If you're not hungry," she said to Micaela, "you may leave the table and go to your room."

After folding the heavy linen napkin and placing it beside her plate, Micaela rose and moved toward the door.

"Micaela, have you forgotten your manners?" Louise said. "You have not asked Monsieur Castillon to excuse you."

Turning to the consul, Micaela muttered, "Will you excuse me, monsieur?"

"Of course," he said, forcing a magnanimous smile. "Run along, child."

Later in the evening, when Louise and her guest had retired to the parlor, Micaela crept out of bed and down the stairs. Peeking through the crack in the closed parlor doors, she observed by the light of a single flickering candle that the handsome young Frenchman lay stretched out on the rose velvet settee, his head resting on Louise's breast, their fingers intertwined. Embarrassed to witness such intimacy, Micaela tiptoed back up to her room and hoped that Flore wouldn't catch her before she was in bed again.

When Flore came into Micaela's room an hour later to check on her mosquito netting, the child complained of a stomachache. The slave lighted the delicate china *veilleuse* beside the bed and prepared an herbal tea for her. "We'll fix you up right quick," she said.

Micaela drank the proffered tea and was dozing off when Louise swept into the room, looking radiantly happy although a bit disheveled with regard to her hair and clothing. Brushing the diaphanous netting aside, she sat on the edge of the bed, causing the mattress filled with Spanish moss to crackle loudly.

"Don't pretend you're asleep, Micaela," she said. "I know perfectly well you're not. Your eyelids are fluttering much too much to deceive me."

"But I was, Mama," Micaela protested indignantly, opening her eyes.

"Don't lie," she reprimanded. "I came here to tell you right now that Monsieur Castillon and I have decided to marry."

Micaela bolted upright in bed. "Marry?" she repeated with astonishment. Somehow the thought hadn't occurred to her that her mother might desire another husband.

"Yes," Louise said. "And very soon."

"What about Papa?"

"What about him?"

"You can't marry someone else," Micaela protested.

"I can and I shall," Louise asserted. "Papa has been dead for several years. I have been faithful to his memory longer than anyone has a right to expect. Now I must begin to think of myself once again. I've grown lonely lately and wish to have companionship. There's nothing wrong with that."

Tears filled Micaela's eyes. Somehow she felt that her mother was betraying the cherished memory of her father.

"You can't marry again," she said in a shrill, childish voice. "Not Monsieur Castillon."

"And what is wrong with Monsieur Castillon?"

"He's so young," she blurted. "Younger even than Cousin Pierre!"

"Jean-Baptiste happens to be four years older than Cousin Pierre, for your information, young lady," Louise replied. "But that is neither here nor there."

"I don't care. I don't want you to marry him," Micaela cried, and began pummeling the pillows with her fists in anger and frustration.

"I intend to marry Monsieur Castillon whether you or my family or my friends or the whole damned city likes it or not," she declared, her voice rising as if to emphasize her determination. "Stop this nonsense right now, or, so help me, I'll take you across my knee and warm your bottom."

"I don't care what you say," Micaela retorted. "I hate Monsieur Castillon. I don't want a stepfather. I only want my real father. I want Papa!"

"For God's sake, be reasonable. Your father is dead."

"I don't care," Micaela sniffed. "I still love him." With that she seized a pillow and impulsively struck Louise with it.

Stunned by such an act of defiance, Louise attempted to grab her, but Micaela slid across the sheets to the far corner of the bed, causing her mother to lose her balance momentarily and knock the china *veilleuse* off the night stand. A splatter of greasy whale oil cascaded down the front of her silk gown.

"You wretched child!" Louise cried. "Look what you made me do! You made me ruin this lovely gown!"

"I don't care," Micaela repeated, cowering against the bedpost beneath the ruffled yellow satin canopy.

"You'll care in the morning, young lady," Louise warned. Then she called for Flore to aid her in her attempts to wipe the oil from the folds of her dress. The perfumed handkerchief that had been tucked into Louise's bosom was proving to be woefully inadequate.

Watching her mother, Micaela felt her own defiance and resentment dissolve into helplessness. "Please don't marry Monsieur Castillon," she begged. "I don't want you to marry him. I don't want you to marry anybody."

Angry, and distressed by the failure of her efforts on the dark oil stains, Louise staunchly repeated, "I shall marry Monsieur Castillon whether you or anyone else likes it or not. And that is final."

3

A WELL-KNOWN member of New Orleans society like Louise Almonester would have found it impossible to keep her marriage plans a secret for long, even if she had wanted to. Aware that she risked possible ridicule because she was a rich and socially prominent widow in her early forties who was marrying a man nearly twenty years her junior, Louise was determined to keep the wedding as small and as private as possible.

News of the upcoming union began circulating quickly about the city and was greeted with amusement and wry speculation in certain quarters.

"So Monsieur Castillon has shaken the Almonester tree for one nearly shriveled peach, has he?" a Chartres Street merchant was known to have remarked to one of his customers.

Jean-Baptiste Castillon, originally of humble origins, displayed a rather disdainful attitude toward the local citizenry, which earned him the reputation of a snob who had little use for the city or its people. The fact that New Orleans had provided him with a civil-service post and the opportunity to make ambitious alliances, such as his forthcoming marriage, did not seem to carry any weight with him. As might be expected, he generated much resentment and animosity among the townspeople.

"Who does that Castillon fellow think he is, going around all the time with his haughty French nose in the air, acting as if our city had a bad smell?" a prominent planter remarked to an equally prominent banker over bourbon in one of the plush private gentlemen's clubs.

"And him pretending to be crazy about that widow with her foul disposition," the banker scoffed.

"You should know better than I, my friend," the planter said, tapping the banker on the chest, "that Madame Almonester is the richest woman in this city, perhaps the richest in the whole damned country."

"But still, for a young man to have to lie next to her every night . . ." the banker mused.

"I'm told that Monsieur Castillon gets a rise in his pants every time he thinks of the widow's money," the planter laughed, nudging his friend in the ribs.

Louise, of course, was aware of the cynical attitude shared by most of the populace, and she did her best to ignore the insults and slanderous remarks usually conveyed to her secondhand by Flore or one of the other slaves.

"There's lot of folks in this city you think is your friends, but they ain't, Miss Louise," Flore informed her mistress one day as she struggled with the laces of Louise's corset. "A lot of ladies around here got forked tongues, just like a bunch of cottonmouths."

"And the men are equally as bad, I'm sure," Louise replied with a weary sigh. She had an appointment with the dressmaker, who was preparing her trousseau, and she dreaded the long hours of standing while the woman fitted and pinned her various gowns. Micaela was to accompany her to be fitted for a dress of her own for the wedding, but she had complained of not feeling well and refused to leave her room.

When Louise was finally dressed in a mauve walking suit, she stood in front of the mirror and shifted the angle of her bonnet several times, attempting to arrange it in the most flattering position. She knew that a woman her age had to be much more careful with her appearance than someone younger, and this forced her to spend more time and effort on her clothes and her complexion.

"Is Micaela still sulking?" she asked. Turning from the mirror, she looked directly at Flore. "That's what she's doing, you know. I don't believe for an instant that she's really ill."

"That child just don't like the idea of your marryin' Monsieur Castillon," Flore said.

"She doesn't like the idea of my marrying anyone," Louise said.

Flore shook her head. "She sure is true to her daddy's memory."

"That's too bad," Louise snapped, annoyed at the maid's inference. Tying the purple satin ribbon of the bonnet beneath her chin, she added, "She'll just have to accept it. I'm tired of her being difficult. If she continues with this nonsense, I shall have to be really stern with her, and she's not going to like it." Appraising her reflection one final time, Louise said, "Go tell Freddie to bring the carriage around. I'm ready to go for my fitting."

When the Almonester house slaves were alone, they brushed gossip aside and expressed their concern about their mistress's future, since in many ways it directly governed their own. Some of them had come with her as part of her dowry when she married Don Andrés, and others had been acquired, often as gifts, by the don himself.

"That young French fellow can't wait to get his hands on Miss Louise's money," Raymond, Don Andrés's former manservant, declared. "And once he do, it won't be no time at all until there ain't nothin' left."

"Amen!" Cora, the cook, agreed as she, Raymond, and Flore sat around the warming kitchen munching slices of corn bread spread thick with bacon drippings, which they regarded as a special treat.

"Oh, I don't know," Flore responded. "Miss Louise is a whole lot smarter than y'all give her credit for. Ain't nobody gonna get their hands on her money but her."

"That's what you think, girl," Raymond scoffed.

"Once he starts whisperin' sweet things in her ear, that money is done gone!" Cora laughed.

"What you think?" Flore challenged. "That money of hers ain't in sacks under no mattress or in the safe at the bank. Miss Louise got her money all spent."

"How can she be so rich if she done spent all her

money?" Cora questioned, wiping bacon grease from her mouth with the back of her pudgy hand.

"Everybody say she's the richest woman in this here whole city," Raymond declared.

"Miss Louise done spent her money buyin' up property," Flore said.

"Don't she have enough with what Master Andrés done left her?" Raymond asked.

Cora shook her head. "Rich folks is never satisfied. They always got to have more."

"She just bought herself a new plantation out there on Bayou Road with over ninety slaves on it," Flore told them. "I went with her to Mr. LeBreton's office when she signed the papers."

"That means now she got two plantations," Raymond said.

"Two plantations and a whole lot more besides," Flore asserted. "She got stores and houses and property all over this city."

"I always knew Miss Louise was mighty smart when it come to her pocketbook," Raymond remarked, reaching for another piece of corn bread. "Master Andrés always said she was smarter than him when it come to money."

"She like a fox," Cora said approvingly. "If we stick with Miss Louise, we ain't got nothin' to worry 'bout. She gonna take good care of both us *and* her money."

"Amen!" Raymond agreed, but Flore was silent. Closer to Louise than the other slaves, she alone knew how strong Castillon's influence was on her mistress. The future was not at all certain. No one's future, in fact.

Eventually the day of the wedding arrived, and the brief but solemn ceremony took place. As soon as it was concluded, Louise and her husband returned to the Almonester townhouse in a closed carriage, closely followed by a second carriage bearing Micaela, Pierre, Flore and Binnie. Pierre was one of the few Delarondes to attend what most of the family privately considered an unsuitable match. The colonel had begged off, pleading the poor health of his wife. Pierre had agreed to attend the wedding as much for Micaela's sake as for Louise's, and now, glancing at his little cousin, who was obviously miserable, he was glad that he had come up from Versailles for the occasion. In his elegantly cut coat and fine nankeen trousers that were pulled tightly over his highly polished shoes by a strap looped around the instep, Pierre looked exceedingly handsome and sophisticated. He slipped a consoling arm around Micaela, and the gesture brought sudden tears to her luminous dark eyes.

Seeing this, Flore handed her a handkerchief and told her to dry her eyes, but Micaela, embarrassed, brushed her hand aside.

"What would your mama say if she saw you cryin'?" Flore asked.

"I don't care," Micaela sniffed, feeling adrift, and rejected by her mother's new state.

"You'll be all right," Pierre assured her. "Between Flore and me and little Binnie here, we'll look after you."

"Nobody has to look after me," Micaela said bravely, drawing herself up very straight against the back of the carriage seat. "I'll look after myself."

When they arrived at the townhouse, Louise and her handsome young groom proceeded to entertain the select group of guests at a simple reception on the flower-decked patio.

"Our desire today," Louise said to a circle of well-wishers while beaming at Jean-Baptiste, "was to keep things as quiet and dignified as possible. I think we've succeeded admirably, don't you?"

Although her question was directed at no one in particular, Pierre, already downing his third goblet of champagne, felt obliged to respond. "But the day isn't over yet, dear Aunt."

"What do you mean?" Louise asked anxiously.

"Oh, nothing," Pierre shrugged and moved away from the little group around the bride and groom.

When both family and friends had finally departed, Louise ordered Flore to put Micaela to bed. The child was still engrossed in a make-believe conversation with her parrot, Sancho Panza, when Louise and Jean-Baptiste retired to their bedroom on the second floor.

Before drawing the curtains of the nuptial chamber, Louise stepped out on the gallery and looked up and down the street with a worried frown, as if she were expecting something.

Noting her expression, Jean-Baptiste, in the act of removing his diamond cuff links, a wedding gift from Louise, asked her what was wrong.

"Nothing, dearest," she replied with a reassuring smile, clasping his face between her hands and giving his lips an affectionate peck.

Eagerly he took her in his arms, kissed her passionately several times, and urged her toward the bed. He began to undo the fastenings of her gown, all the while bestowing warm little nibbles on her throat, on her neck, and in the deep valley between her breasts. Louise giggled and protested halfheartedly, but in the sweep of her rising passion she completely forgot whatever preoccupations she might have had out on the gallery.

Once undressed and in bed, Castillion proved to be an ardent and energetic lover. Louise, lying beneath his agile, relentless body, moaned with a throbbing pleasure she had never experienced before and had begun to fear she never would.

Jean-Baptiste slowly began to cover Louise's taut body with feverish kisses, driving her to a frenzy when he reached the tender, moist area between her thighs. Then he raised himself up and entered her, moving gently at first, then with increasing urgency.

Louise's ecstasy mounted with his every thrust and transported her to a peak of pleasure so great, she became totally oblivious to all else beyond the immediate confines of the room.

"Oh, Jean-Baptiste," she whispered, her voice husky with erotic excitement, "I never knew it could be like this. It's so wonderful, so good. Oh, please, a little slower. A little slower, please. Let me catch my breath. Oh, you take my breath away, darling. I don't ever want it to be over. I want it to last forever. I want to savor every moment. Every magnificent moment. Ah, what a devil you are! What a delicious devil!"

Unknown to the newlyweds, a hushed crowd was quietly assembling in the street outside the house. In the space of only a few minutes the group swelled into a sizable throng that included not only those on foot but also horsemen, carriages, and carts, the hooves of the horses and the wheels of the vehicles padded with cloth to make them as silent as possible. All eventually gathered in eager anticipation beneath the window of the couple's bedroom. At a signal from their leader, the crowd suddenly burst forth with an ear-shattering explosion. Using cowbells, buckets, washboards, drums, horns, whistles, spoons, and firecrackers, they created every conceivable kind of noise and accompanied it with a raucous yelling and shouting of the most ribald remarks.

Startled nearly out of his skin, Jean-Baptiste leaped off Louise and out of bed in a desperate search for his nightshirt. Locating it under the bed, he slipped it hurriedly over his head, glanced down to see the extent of his erection, and headed for the gallery.

Raising her head from the pillow, Louise called after him, "No, Jean-Baptiste! You mustn't go out there. Stay away from the windows, too. If they see us, all is lost."

"But what in God's name is going on out there?" he asked, exasperated. "I have never heard such a racket."

"It's a charivari," Louise replied, clutching the bedcovers protectively to her chest. "I was afraid of something like this. I had a feeling they might attempt this sort of a carnival."

"What is a charivari?" he demanded. "Ah, you Creoles and your ridiculous customs! I shall never understand you."

"It's a kind of mock celebration to taunt a newly married couple," she explained, neglecting to mention that such celebrations were usually reserved for oddly matched couples. Seeing his agitation, she struggled to remain calm in the face of the terrible din rising from the street and invading the privacy of their bridal chamber.

On the floor above, the noise awakened and frightened Micaela. In the past she would have run to Louise for comfort, but tonight she knew that she would not be welcome in her mother's room. She huddled in one corner of her bed, hugging her pillow. Binnie, who normally slept on a chest at the foot of Micaela's bed, raised the lid of the hand-carved box and dived inside at the first firecracker blast, shrieking, "Oh, Lordy, save us!"

Below, Louise, trying to reassure her new husband, advised him to keep the curtains drawn and return to bed. "If we ignore them, they'll soon tire of this nonsense and go away," she said.

Shaking his head in dismay, he returned uneasily to his bride's side. "I hope you are right, dearest," he said dubiously as he slid beneath the covers.

Unfortunately, Louise was not right. The charivari, or "carnival of torment," as it was sometimes defined, continued throughout the night, all during the following day, and into the next night as well.

No official attempt was made to stop the noise or disperse the merrymakers, and to the haggard groom it seemed that all civil authority had been temporarily suspended.

"Where are the police?" he demanded when Raymond appeared at their bedroom door with a tray of food. The slaves had avidly been following the activities in the street without venturing outside.

"The police is all out there whoopin' and hollerin' with everybody else," Raymond chuckled.

"This is an uncivilized country full of savages!" Jean-Baptiste ranted.

"I seen lots of charivaris, but I ain't never seen a charivari like this here one in all my born days," Raymond said, shaking his head.

Rather than diminishing, the enthusiasm for the event grew, and as word spread, more and more people milled noisily about the beseiged house.

By the second night Jean-Baptiste was thoroughly

distraught, the slaves shaken, Micaela frightened, and Louise desperate.

"What do they want?" he demanded. "What can we do to make them stop and go away? What do we have to give them? I tell you, I can't stand much more of their awful racket. I'm about to lose my mind."

"They ain't never gonna go away until you and Miss Louise go out there and face them, Master Jean-Baptiste," Flore advised him.

Turning to an equally weary Louise, he asked, "Is that correct?"

"Yes," Louise sighed.

"Then what are we waiting for? Let's go out there!"

"Never," Louise declared. "I'll never give in to that rabble. That's just what they want."

"They ain't *all* rabble, Miss Louise," Flore said gently.

Louise knew the maid was right. Some of the most prominent citizens of New Orleans were part of the unruly mob, and she was certain she recognized several people in spite of their attempts to disguise themselves in outrageous costumes and masks.

"Forget your pride, Louise, dearest, and let's go out there," Jean-Baptiste pleaded.

"I have lived in this city all my life," she replied. "I know these people. I know exactly what they're like. They simply want a chance to humiliate me, and I'm not going to give it to them."

"But what alternative do we have?" he argued.

"There are other recourses."

"Then for God's sake, let's take one of them."

"All right," she agreed. Then, turning to Flore, Louise asked, "Where is Micaela?"

"In her room, Miss Louise," Flore answered. "Binnie is with her, but that child is scared half out of her wits. Both of them are."

"Go get her dressed," Louise ordered.

"What for?"

"Don't waste time asking questions," Louise snapped. "Do as I say."

Louise did have a plan, one that required a certain

daring, but under the circumstances everyone involved was willing to risk whatever was necessary to escape the nightmarish harassment. The first step of her escape plan was to dress Cora and Raymond as herself and Jean-Baptiste, dust their faces with rice powder, and send them out onto the upstairs gallery at the proper moment to distract the tormentors. While the crowd was riveted to the front of the house, Louise, Jean-Baptiste, Micaela, Flore, and Binnie would exit through the seldom used rear gate in the carriage driven by Freddie, the coachman.

All went according to schedule, and while Cora and Raymond trembled on the gallery before the throng, at the back of the house Louise gave the signal to Freddie. He brought the whip down on the skittish horse's back, and the carriage bolted through the rear gate and into the now deserted street. The mob had taken the bait, as Louise had hoped they would. Her escape plan appeared to be a success.

"Head for the levee," Louise called to the coachman. "And hurry!"

At the levee, much to their chagrin, they found their path blocked by merrymakers who had evidently seen through their strategy and dashed for the dike, hoping to intercept them. Louise ordered Freddie to turn the carriage around and head uptown, but eventually they encountered hastily erected barricades and hecklers in that direction as well, just as they did when they subsequently reversed their route.

Finally, their nerves worn to a frazzle, and badly fatigued, they realized that the possibility of an escape was futile. Louise, resigned to defeat, ordered Freddie to return to the house.

Oddly enough, when they arrived there, they were greeted by an unexpected quiet. In fact, only a single cart, dimly perceived at first in the darkness, stood in front of the gate through which they would have to pass. As the carriage drew closer, they observed that the cart was not empty, as they had first assumed, but contained an open black coffin with a wax figure shrouded in an ermine-trimmed scarlet cloak. On the side of the coffin the inscription "DON ANDRES,

KNIGHT OF CHARLES IV" was printed in huge letters.

On seeing the effigy, Flore's first reaction was to attempt to shield Micaela's eyes, but she was too late. The child had already recognized the wax corpse.

"Papa!" she gasped.

"Don't look!" Louise commanded, successfully clamping her hands over Micaela's eyes.

Squirming free, the girl pointed out the carriage window and cried, "It's Papa! It's Papa!"

"Don't look, I said," Louise repeated sternly, but at that moment she realized there was an additional figure, a live one, in the cart. Beside the coffin sat a grotesquely disguised man wearing a wig, false breasts, and flamboyant female attire. Around his neck was a sign identifying him as "LOUISE." As the carriage came alongside the cart, the man impersonating Louise stood up and emitted an earsplitting cackle, pointing an accusing finger in their direction.

At that, despite the bravery and stalwart defiance she had displayed during the past few days, Louise reached the limits of her endurance. With a shriek she collapsed into her shaken bridegroom's arms.

"Papa!" Micaela persisted, and sticking her thin arm through the carriage window, attempted to reach the wax effigy of Don Andrés, oblivious to her mother's distress. Her fingers strained to touch the scarlet cloak, and before Flore could restrain her, she had managed to seize a handful of the fluffy white ermine that bordered it.

"Shame on you!" the slave scolded.

"Papa," the girl murmured, staring at the soft fur clinging to her fingers. "Papa . . ."

4

ONLY WHEN LOUISE finally gave in and agreed to donate three thousand dollars to the poor, as well as to have her slaves distribute food and drink to the raucous crowd, did the uproar finally cease. For the first time since the wedding ceremony, Jean-Baptiste was able to relax and breathe a sigh of relief, but Louise still smoldered with anger and resentment, unable to view the episode philosophically or with any humor. Although peace was blissfully restored once again, Louise could not cease to pace the bedroom floor, hands on hips, skirts flouncing.

"So! They think they can disgrace and humiliate me and get away with it, do they? Well, I'll show them," she declared angrily. "I'll prove to them that I don't need this city or anyone in it. I can get along perfectly well without the whole lot of them." She paused a moment, and a sly, twisted smile brightened her taut face. "The question is, *can* they get along without *me?* After all, Don Andrés—don't take offense, Jean-Baptiste, darling, if I mention his name— gave this city every decent, humanitarian institution it has: the Charity Hospital of St. Charles, St. Louis Cathedral, the Ursuline chapel, just to name a few. His generosity knew no bounds. Since his death I have continued to support these charities, plus several of my own."

"Yes, my dearest, you do have a good and generous heart," her husband said, attempting to soothe her.

"In addition to my charitable and philanthropic

acts, I am sure I am not boasting when I say that I am
the single largest taxpayer in this city," she asserted.

Although her declaration that she was the leading
taxpayer came as somewhat of a surprise to him, he
knew his bride was certainly one of the wealthiest individuals in New Orleans. "I'm sure you are, my
treasure," he murmured.

"Well, I've made up my mind," she announced. "We
are getting out of here—leaving this city."

"Come, now," he laughed. "Where would we go?
Be serious, darling. I know you've been badly upset
by this experience. I have been, too, but—"

"We are moving to France," she interrupted. "To
Paris."

"But . . . my post?" he protested, thoroughly bewildered by her announcement.

"What about it?" she countered. "Surely you don't
mind leaving it, do you? It's nothing but a minor post,
anyway. Hardly worthy of you."

Miffed by her assessment, he said, "Well, I wouldn't
exactly say that."

"Listen, love," she went on, trying to smooth his
somewhat ruffled pride by caressing his cheek with the
tips of her fingers, "there is no need for you to work at
all. We can live quite nicely on my income. Besides, I
will need you to help me manage my affairs. That will
keep you busy enough."

Mollified by her words and by the promise of actually participating in the management of her valuable
and extensive holdings, Jean-Baptiste contemplated a
moment and then asked, "But if we go to Paris,
dearest, what about the child?"

"Micaela?" Louise said with a puzzled frown, unable to see that Micaela would present any special
sort of problem. "What about her?"

"What will you do with her? I mean, she won't be
coming to Paris with us, will she?"

Although well aware of the antipathy Jean-Baptiste
and her daughter shared for each other, Louise had
never considered that it might ever interfere with any
of her plans.

"Well, yes, I had thought that she would be coming

with us," she replied. "Don't worry, I won't allow her to be a bother. Flore and Binnie will accompany us. They'll look after her and keep her out of your way, darling."

Her husband did not seem satisfied with this answer. "For the last few weeks the girl's been outright hostile to me," he complained.

Pretending to be surprised by his words, although she knew there was some truth to them, she said, "Micaela is hostile to you?"

"Yes," he affirmed. "You know she hates me. Stop pretending you haven't noticed."

"I have noticed no such thing," she protested. "I will admit that she has been a bit rude on one or two occasions, but to call her hostile . . ."

"Rude? She's been downright hateful!"

"But she's only a child," Louise said quickly. "You must remember that she's experienced quite a lot for a girl of ten. She lost her father, whom she adored, when she was very young. And then, only a few months afterward she lost her sister."

"I can tell you, my dear, that in France I have known children who have also suffered, but they have never been as rude or spiteful to me as your daughter has been."

"Perhaps it's my fault. Perhaps I haven't spent enough time with her, as I know I should have," Louise admitted, genuine regret in her voice.

"Don't blame yourself, darling," he sympathized, taking her hand and pressing it tenderly to his lips. "If anything, you have indulged the girl too much. What she needs is less of you, not more."

"What do you mean, Jean-Baptiste?"

"I simply mean it will be good for her to be away from you for a while."

"I don't understand."

"She needs a good school with strict discipline," he explained patiently. "The Ursuline sisters have just such a school right here in New Orleans. It's one of the few decent institutions in this city."

"I know. I was planning to enroll her there myself. But strictly as a day student."

"Then you must go ahead and do it, dearest."

"Are you implying that I should go off to France and leave Micaela behind? Alone?" She was rather appalled by the suggestion.

"Don't be silly. She won't be alone. Your brother and his family are just down the river at their plantation. You know how fond your nephew Pierre is of the girl. As I said, it would do her good to be away from you for a while. Besides, there are many girls from far-off places boarding with the Ursulines. Girls from Boston, New York, Charleston, Savannah. Even from Mexico and Cuba."

Although she weighed his words carefully, Louise was uncertain of their merit. "Well, I don't know . . ."

"The nuns will take good care of her," he assured her. "After all, didn't your late husband build their convent for them? At least that's what you're always telling me."

"Yes, he did. And I have always been most generous in my support of the order as well."

Realizing he was beginning to convince her that his way of thinking was correct, Jean-Baptiste broke into a smile. "All the more reason why you should leave Micaela with the good sisters."

"But to be so far away from my only child . . . I would miss her very much."

"Believe me, dearest," he said, kissing the lobe of her ear as he gathered her in an embrace, "I will do my best to keep you from missing her. When we get to Paris, you will be so busy that you will have no time to miss anyone. There will be parties, balls, the opera, the ballet, the theater. All the wonderful things you love so much that are lacking in this dismal place. I shall introduce you to all the finest people, the crème de la crème. As a matter of fact, you will be so busy and so happy that even if Micaela were with us, she would be more neglected than ever. No, dearest, Micaela belongs here with the Ursulines. You owe it to the child and to yourself as well. She'll be in excellent hands, as you well know. After all, those devout nuns are noted for the fine education they impart to young girls."

"I suppose you do have a point," Louise conceded, her thoughts already dazzled by his hints of the gay and active life she might lead in Paris. "But still, the thought of my only child thousands of miles across the sea . . ."

"What's a few thousand miles today?" he scoffed. "It's nothing at all. Crossing the Atlantic now is merely a matter of a few weeks at most. She can visit us in the summer, and if necessary, you can return to see her quite easily, although I'll admit it will not be easy for me to part with you, dearest," he added planting a string of kisses along her neck. "Not even for a single moment."

"Oh, Jean-Baptiste," she sighed. "I do so much want to do what is right."

"It is right for you to leave Micaela with the Ursulines, I promise you."

"Still, I must think about it."

"What is there to think about? You must act now."

Gripping Micaela's hand, Louise strode through the gates of the convent, a large, rather imposing three-story building in the shape of a U, unadorned except for a clock topped with a crucifix in the center of the roof. Pulling a somewhat frayed cord by the door, she let the chimes ring for several moments, before a shy novitiate admitted them and asked how she could be of help.

"I am Madame Castillon, formerly Madame Almonester, and this is my daughter, Micaela," Louise replied. "We've come to see Mother Germaine."

Immediately recognizing Louise as an important patron of the order and its activities, the youthful novitiate ushered them into the office of the convent head.

Even in the presence of the somewhat formidable Mother Germaine, superior of the Ursuline Convent of New Orleans, nearly all of whose relatives had lost their heads to the guillotine during the French Revolution, Louise remained her imperious self.

"Good day, Reverend Mother," she said.

"Madame Almonester, how good to see you again," the patrician nun replied.

Louise smiled. "Thank you. Since our last encounter I have remarried. I am now Madame Jean-Baptiste Castillon."

"Forgive me, Madame Castillon." Turning to Micaela, the Mother Superior said, "And how are you, my child? What lovely red hair you have."

Since leaving Versailles, Micaela had known that sooner or later she would be a pupil at the Ursuline school, but she had expected to be a day student and not a boarder. The impending separation from her mother gave her a terrible feeling of anguish that was further intensified by this visit, to the point that she neglected to curtsy in response to the nun's greeting until Louise prompted her. Only then did she lift her skirt, bend her knee, and murmur, "How do you do, Mother."

"I have come today to enroll Micaela in school," Louise announced. "You see, Monsieur Castillon and I will be living abroad for a while."

"Then Micaela will be boarding with us?"

"That's correct."

"Wonderful." The pale, slender nun nodded and smiled at Micaela. "Welcome, my child. We're so happy you're going to join us. We have girls here from the finest families in the country. It will be a marvelous opportunity for you to avail yourself of a good, Christian education." Then, addressing herself to Louise once again, she continued. "As you know, madame, it is the belief of our order that women are the great moral force on which all decent society is founded."

"That is precisely why I have brought my daughter to you today," Louise said.

"Then you intend to enroll her at once?"

"Yes. I have all her things out in the carriage. I'll have Raymond carry her trunk in."

"You can be sure, Madame Almonester—"

"Castillon," Louise injected demurely.

"Castillon," Mother Germaine corrected herself, taking Micaela by the hand. "We shall take the best possible care of little Micaela."

"I'm certain of that," Louise replied. Responding to a sudden urge to leave before Micaela could erupt into tears, she started for the door.

Micaela shook her hand loose from the nun's grip, ran to the doorway, and clutched her mother's voluminous skirts.

"Please, Mama, don't leave me here," she begged. "I want to go home. I want to be home with you and Flore and Binnie and Cora and Raymond and Freddie. Don't leave me!"

"Let go of me," Louise commanded sternly, embarrassed by the scene her daughter was creating in front of the convent head.

"Please, Mama," Micaela pleaded, tears welling in her dark eyes. "Don't leave me. Take me to Paris with you. I'll be good, I promise. I won't be rude to Monsieur Castillon ever again."

Prying her hands loose, Louise said, "You are staying here, and that's final. Now, stop this nonsense or I'll be forced to punish you in front of the Reverend Mother."

"I'm certain that once you leave, Madame Castillon, Micaela will be fine," the nun assured her.

"Yes, of course she will," Louise replied with a forced smile, knowing that the nun's words were a gentle hint that she should depart quickly.

"Come, Micaela, dear," the Mother Superior said, taking her hand once more. "We must let your mother go on her way. I will take you to Sister Lucille so that she can measure you for your uniforms."

"I want to go home," Micaela insisted, straining to join her mother.

At the door Louise hesitated with her hand on the knob, as if she had some misgivings about her decision to leave her daughter at the convent and go off to France with her new husband.

Perceiving her indecision, the Reverend Mother waved her hand impatiently as a signal for her to leave. "Good day, Madame Castillon," she called, dragging Micaela down the hall and out of sight.

In contrast with the rather austere and forbidding
Reverend Mother, Sister Lucille, the nun who served
as head seamstress at the school, seemed warm and
benevolent. She had a round, jolly face and a good-
natured disposition, and she did her best to dispel
Micaela's feelings of abandonment and insecurity.
Bustling about the cluttered sewing room, chattering
through lips firmly clamped on a row of pins, she
busily jotted down the child's measurements and announced that she would have four uniforms, two for
summer and two for winter. During the course of the
fitting Sister Lucille explained that each girl was assigned a number that would be hers throughout her
years at the school. Tags bearing this identifying
number would be attached to all her clothing and other
belongings.

"You won't have to be measured for the veils, of
course. They're all the same size," she chuckled.
"Each girl has two, a black one for daily Mass and a
white one for special occasions." Smiling, she rose to
her feet and gave Micaela a reassuring pat on the
head. "You were a very patient young lady," she
said. "I've finished my part. Now it's time for Sister
Veronique to take you to your dormitory. She's in
charge of the younger ones."

Her hands dutifully tucked inside the full sleeves of
her habit, Sister Veronique, young and ascetic, with
thick spectacles perched on the end of her long, thin
nose, silently conducted Micaela to a huge long room
on the second floor that smelled of camphor, which
was thought to be an effective preventive of yellow
fever and other maladies. The room was lined with
about two dozen cots in opposing rows and was bare
of all other furnishings, except for a night stand beside
each bed containing a pitcher and a bowl. The only
decor in the Spartan dormitory was a huge crucifix at
the far end of the room. Each cot could be par-
titioned off by curtains, giving every girl some measure
of privacy.

"You will take the cot next to mine," Sister
Veronique directed. "All new girls are placed close to
the sister until they become accustomed to the school."

From the dormitory the slender nun conducted Micaela downstairs once again to the bathroom, a long corridor with rows of narrow cubicles on both sides, each containing a bathtub and a wooden stool. Sister Veronique pointed out the long cotton garments hanging on the back of each door.

"All girls are required to wear a gown while bathing," she informed Micaela. "At this school we place great emphasis on modesty. Everyone respects the other's privacy. We also have a very strict honor code. The Reverend Mother regards any infraction of the rules, all of which you will be expected to memorize, as serious, and as grounds for possible immediate expulsion."

The first time Micaela actually mingled with the other girls, if "mingled" was the proper word, was at dinner. Earlier, she had seen other students in the halls and elsewhere, and they had regarded her with curious stares. When introduced by Sister Veronique or Sister Lucille or Mother Germaine, they had unfailingly curtsied politely and murmured, "Pleased to meet you." Apart from these cursory, fleeting introductions, there had been no chance for any real exchange. Unfortunately, Micaela was to discover that meals afforded little opportunity for communication, either.

In the large dining hall, as cold and Spartan as the dormitory, the Reverend Mother shook a wooden clapper to command attention and announced that one of the girls, a senior honor student whose uniform was festooned with ribbons of various colors, would read Saint Ursula's story from *Lives of the Saints*. "So that our new scholar, Mademoiselle Almonester, might have the benefit of learning about the saint from whom our order has taken its name."

The girls were respectfully silent as the student, who wore a crown of real laurel leaves to denote her scholastic superiority, read the story, enunciating every syllable with great precision. Embarrassed at being singled out as the "new girl," Micaela tried to concentrate on the horrific tale of a group of eleven thousand virgins, led by Saint Ursula, who were attacked, raped, and eventually murdered by a pack of savage Huns on their way home from a pious pilgrimage to Rome. However, this story did not serve to ease her discomfort.

Several times during the meal Micaela glanced up from her plate and realized that the Reverend Mother was watching her closely. Her expression was one of disapproval, which caused Micaela to wonder what she might be doing wrong. Despite her uneasiness in this strange, new situation, Micaela felt she was displaying good table manners and behaving correctly, forcing herself to eat, although she scarcely had any appetite at all.

One of the six other girls who shared the table with her—each table seated seven girls and a nun—a blonde from Baton Rouge named Claire Villegrande, gave her a reassuring wink, and Micaela was certain they would be friends.

After dinner the girls filed outside for a quiet recreational period in the schoolyard. Micaela had hoped to join them, but Sister Veronique took her aside and informed her that the Reverend Mother wished to see her in the office.

Rising from behind her desk, Mother Germaine said, "During dinner I observed, regrettably, that you were holding your utensils in your left hand. Is that customary?"

"Yes, ma'am," Micaela replied, recalling how Louise had often expressed dismay at the same trait. "I've been left-handed since I was a baby."

The nun nodded. "So one would assume. It's nothing to be proud of."

"Yes, ma'am," Micaela answered automatically, wondering why everyone was always so upset by something that seemed perfectly natural to her.

"There is no place for left-handed people in this world," Mother Germaine said. "This is a right-handed world. Do you understand?"

"Yes, ma'am."

"Very well. You will report to Sister Lucille after Mass in the morning. She will remedy the situation. That's all. You may join the other girls outside."

Micaela was dismissed by a brusque wave of the hand.

After only a very short time at the school, Micaela realized that she was capable of being far more independent and self-reliant than she had ever imagined, and this discovery pleased her very much. In the past she had been so closely attended by her mother and a houseful of slaves that she never had the opportunity to find out how she might fare when left to her own devices.

In a matter of a few weeks she found herself falling into the routines and feeling reasonably adjusted, despite the detestable black bag sewn over her left hand to discourage her from using it. Much to her surprise, time passed quickly, and in the space of a few short months she was able to catch up with the girls who had already been at the school a year or more.

As planned, Louise and Castillon departed for France, designating Louise's brother, Colonel Delaronde, as Micaela's guardian in their absence, even though they realized that it would be Pierre who would take the most active interest in the child's welfare.

Regularly and dutifully, Louise wrote her daughter from Paris; her letters bore scarcely a hint of regret about the decision she had made. Micaela answered her mother's letters as she was expected to do, promptly and respectfully, submitting them to Mother Germaine, as required, for inspection before mailing. Except for occasional lapses, Micaela soon became accustomed to her mother's absence and accepted it, missing their association less and less as the months passed. In no time at all school replaced everything else and became the central focus of her life.

During holiday vacations Pierre would dutifully appear and escort Micaela to Versailles, where she would stay until school resumed. Often, as they rode down the badly rutted River Road, Pierre would confide his latest ideas for making the plantation the true showplace of which the Delarondes had always dreamed. Bursting with ideas and enthusiasm, he was continually hoping to add to its grandeur and prestige.

"I want Versailles to live up to its name," he laughed.

One day during the Christmas vacation Micaela asked, "What about the theater you were going to build where the chinaberry trees are?" She had just appeared as one of the wise men in the school's annual Nativity play and was fired with a sudden passion for the stage.

"I'll build it someday," he declared. "Just as soon as they get some architects with imagination in this city."

5

EVENTUALLY THE MONTHS at boarding school became years, and almost before Micaela was fully aware of it, she had been with the Ursuline nuns for over five years. Recently she had graduated to a section of the dormitory reserved for the older girls, two of which shared each room, and she and Claire Villegrande were now roommates. Sister Lucille had advised her to begin wearing corsets which she hated because of the stiff applewood stays that dug into her already developed breasts.

"Why must I be trussed up and harnessed like a carriage horse?" she complained.

"So that you develop good posture," the nun in charge of the girls' clothing replied.

"But my posture is all right without these awful contraptions," Micaela protested.

"Yes, but the applewood stays keep it from lapsing," Sister Lucille replied. "That's the whole purpose."

Tugging at the tightly laced top, Micaela said, "I feel I can never get enough breath. These corsets are so restricting."

The nun nodded. "They force you to behave as a young lady and not as a colt in the meadow."

In addition to the wearing of corsets, there were

other new restrictions placed on the school's post-pubescent girls: no running, no talking in a loud voice, no reaching for things above one's head, keeping one's hands folded in the lap while sitting, and so forth. Music and dancing were greatly encouraged, although art, considered a masculine preserve, was less revered. Each girl was expected to become proficient in a musical instrument, preferably the piano. Because dancing played a prominent role in the social life of the city, and because girls were judged by their grace and expertise on the dance floor, all older pupils were required to attend dancing classes. These classes were given by a special teacher named Mademoiselle La-Faye, who donned daringly short skirts so that the girls might observe the positions of her feet as she demonstrated the various steps. Music for the dancing sessions was supplied by an effete, pockmarked Italian fiddler called Signor Bruscantini, who all the girls swore wore corsets beneath his shabby, moth-eaten frock coat in order to achieve his wasplike waist. Signor Bruscantini had the nasty habit of switching the girls' legs with the bow of his violin whenever they failed to perform Mademoiselle LaFaye's steps to his satisfaction.

Since running and all other forms of strenuous exercise were strictly forbidden, the girls were taken for walks twice a day, rain or shine, in the interest of health. Because the Ursulines were a cloistered order, the nuns themselves rarely left the convent, usually assigning novitiates to escort the pupils on these daily jaunts.

During the welcome breaks in the daily routine the girls were well aware that they were objects of great interest to the adolescent boys who attended the surrounding schools. In no time at all the boys had learned the various routes the girls took, and managed to encounter them "by chance" from time to time. Although the girls could not display any reaction to these ambushes in the presence of their chaperones, they were secretly flattered and delighted by the attention of the youths. Occasionally a particularly courageous boy would try to slip a note to one of the girls, even though this form of communication was strictly forbidden. The girls, too, were frightened of receiving such clandestine notes, knowing that an infraction like this would be dealt with severely. However, on St. Valentine's Day an exception was made. The girls were allowed to receive cards from individuals who were not on the list approved by their respective families.

On the Valentine's Day following her sixteenth birthday, much to her delight and amazement, Micaela found that she had received more cards than any other girl in the school. Her impressive stack of lacy, beribboned hearts in red satin and velvet aroused much comment, some of which she found both disturbing and bewildering.

"It's that red hair of hers," Edith Gautier remarked, more than a little peevishly. "The boys can't help but notice her because of it." The majority of the girls at school, like most of the women in New Orleans at that time, were dark-eyed brunettes.

"No, it's not her red hair," Renée Houdaille disputed with poorly concealed resentment in her voice. Micaela was her principal rival in nearly all areas of school life, which resulted in frequent friction between them.

"Then what is it?" Claire Villegrande challenged. Of all the girls at school, the feisty blonde from Baton Rouge was not only Micaela's roommate but her closest friend as well.

"It's her money," Renée announced.

Flabbergasted, Edith repeated, "Her money?" Although nearly every student came from a relatively well-to-do family, it was considered a serious breach of etiquette to discuss such a topic. Talk of money was nearly as forbidden as talk of sex.

"Of course it's her money," Renée continued, undaunted by any consideration of ethics. "You all know who her father was. We walk practically on top of Don Andrés Almonester's tomb whenever we go to Mass. He built St. Louis Cathedral, for goodness' sake."

"But's it's unfair to talk about her money," Claire reproached. "Besides not being very nice."

"Well, it's certainly not her looks that attract so many boys," Renée argued. "Even if she does have all that red hair, she's still got that long face—just like a horse."

Edith covered her mouth with her hand and giggled.

"A lot of people think Micaela is pretty," Claire said indignantly.

"You're just saying that because she takes you down to her uncle's fancy plantation with her," Renée accused. "Besides, you're sweet on her cousin Pierre."

"Pierre Delaronde is so handsome!" Edith said in a near swoon. "No wonder they call him Apollo."

"That's not why they call him Apollo," Renée asserted. "They call him that because he's the only boy among nine sisters. Besides, some of the stories I've heard about Pierre Delaronde—" She broke off tantalizingly.

"What stories?" Edith asked anxiously.

"Oh, never mind," Renée said evasively.

Titillated by the hint of possible racy gossip, Edith begged, "Please tell us, Renée."

"All right," Renée agreed. "You might as well know. The rumor is that he has a colored mistress."

"Colored mistress?" Edith gasped.

"That's right," Renée replied. "He keeps her in the overseer's cottage down at Versailles, right under his family's nose. Some people say she's already borne him a pickaninny brat or two."

Talk of colored mistresses, let alone the knowledge that such practices were common among men from whom they would soon be expected to select a husband, was considered even more forbidden than either money or sex.

"You shouldn't say such things," Claire reproached Renée.

"Well, it's true," Renée said with an indifferent shrug, attempting to appear more sophisticated than her peers. "Just like it's true that practically every boy in New Orleans is after Micaela Almonester for her money. When I go home, that's all I hear my mother and my aunts and my cousins and their friends talking about. Every mother in this city would love her son to marry a girl with the kind of dowry Micaela will have."

Eventually Renée's remarks reached Micaela, but she chose to ignore them, convincing herself that the large number of valentines she had received had nothing to do with the fortune that she would eventually inherit. Still, as she sorted through the fancy cards once more and reread their romantic verses, they seemed to have lost some of their appeal.

Academically Micaela proved to be a competent student, with a keen aptitude for mathematics as well as a great interest in literature, especially the classic dramas of Shakespeare and the French playwrights.

"Not a bad combination of gifts," Pierre noted as Sister Veronique reported his cousin's progress to him toward the end of the school term. Over the years the Ursuline sisters had come to regard the dapper young sugar planter as Micaela's surrogate parent.

In addition to the regular academic subjects in the curriculum, other skills were encouraged as well. Every night after supper the girls gathered in the library and applied themselves to some kind of needle-work, such as knitting, crocheting, embroidery, or needlepoint, while one of them was assigned to read to the others. The most popular works were Rousseau's *Confessions* and Voltaire's *Candide,* although Mother Germaine usually favored readings from *Lives of the Saints* instead.

Unfortunately, Micaela disliked the various needle-crafts and had neither talent nor patience for such tedious endeavors. It was all she could do to accomplish the mandatory mending of her garments. Drawing alone seemed to be her talent. Although the school provided easels, paper, charcoal, and a studio with a northern exposure for the artistically inclined girls, they were permitted to draw only approved "feminine" subjects like flowers, birds, and trees.

"But I'm so tired of robins and blue jays and bowls of apples and pears," Micaela complained to Sister Veronique one day. The young nun was the most intellectual and understanding of those in the community.

"Well, what do you wish to do?" Sister Veronique inquired.

"Buildings," Micaela answered. For some unexplained reason, she had become increasingly fascinated with the various edifices about the city and longed to record them in a series of sketches.

"Very well, then," Sister Veronique sighed. "You may draw buildings. But don't tell the Reverend Mother it was I who gave you permission."

With the nun's reluctant approval, Micaela set about sketching New Orleans's most interesting and attractive structures.

"Drawing buildings doesn't seem a very suitable occupation for a young lady," Sister Veronique remarked as she flipped the pages of the sketchbook, "but if this is the talent the Lord has seen to fit to bestow on you, who am I to object?"

6

BECAUSE MICAELA AND Claire were now considered "older girls" by the nuns at the covent, they were permitted somewhat more freedom than the students in the lower grades. Many girls married at fifteen or sixteen, and it was therefore considered advisable to grant pupils in the upper grades some measures of leniency. A few nuns, such as Sister Veronique, who had a genuine desire to see the girls develop intellectually, were distressed when a student left school to marry and take on the responsibilities of a wife at such a young age.

"After all, it's mothers who really educate children," the slender nun was often heard to say. "If students are allowed to leave here uneducated, their children will be the ones who suffer."

Thoroughly bored with the prescribed strolls about the city with the younger students, Micaela and Claire, the most adventurous of the girls, persistently requested permission to pursue their own, more sophisticated interests outside the gates of the convent during these outings.

"Micaela wants to sketch and I wish to study aquatic life in its natural state," Claire explained to Sister Veronique.

Eyeing the pair suspiciously through her thick spectacles, the youthful nun said, "All right. You two girls may leave the group, but not for more than an hour or two. And you must remain together at all times—no going off on your own. Is that clear?"

"Yes, Sister," they answered in unison.

"With all those dreadful Americans descending on us from the North, a young girl isn't safe alone any more," the nun warned. "The streets are full of ruffians and cutthroats and worse. They say there is at least one murder a day down at the waterfront near Tchoupitoulas Street, where those riverboatmen tie up their craft."

"We'll stay together," Claire promised. "You can be sure of that, Sister."

Sister Veronique sighed, waved her hand, and with a look bordering on one of misgivings, dismissed them.

Claire's high spirits and adventurousness were tolerated by the nuns because her wealthy father, who ran a highly prosperous cotton plantation on the outskirts of Baton Rouge, kept the convent well supplied with hams and bacon throughout the year as well as with smoked turkeys at holiday times.

As they were going out the door, Sister Lucille, her yellow tape measure draped absentmindedly about her short, plump neck, spied Micaela with her sketch pad under her arm.

"I do so wish you'd draw that lovely, graceful palm tree in the cathedral garden," she said. "You know, Micaela, the one that marks the grave of the tiny baby whom Père Antoine loved so much."

Micaela, who had a reputation for being the most talented art student at the school, was about to reply that she had had her fill of drawing trees in art class when she received a sharp nudge from Claire.

"That's exactly what Micaela has in mind, Sister," Claire declared brightly as the two girls scurried out the door.

When they were outside, Micaela reproached her friend. "Why did you say that? Now we have to go to the cathedral garden. I want to sketch the new hotel that's going up above Canal Street, not trees and flowers."

"Listen, silly," Claire said, "it's a lot better for them to think we're going to cathedral garden than to know we're going to wander around other parts of town."

At the gates of the garden in the rear of the imposing St. Louis Cathedral, Claire and Micaela took their leave from the group and went inside while the other girls, marching obediently in pairs behind two novitiates, continued their afternoon stroll.

"Sit down and sketch that palm tree Sister Lucille wants as quickly as you can," Claire directed. "When that's done, we're free to do what we please."

With a sigh of resignation Micaela seated herself on a bench near the great white statue of Christ, its outstretched arms casting a shadow in the shape of a cross on the cathedral wall. After a few minutes of drawing, she said, "This tree is going to look awful." She felt guilty when she glanced at the statue and thought about the deception they had planned for the afternoon.

"Just so it looks feminine," Claire advised, snapping off a blade of grass from beneath her feet and sticking it between her teeth.

"Trees are neuter," Micaela said, her charcoal already flying over the paper with bold, slashing strokes. "Those nuns are so silly to consider my sketches of buildings unfeminine. I mean, what is so *masculine* about a building?"

"Well," Claire replied, after a moment's thought, "you do have to admit that men build buildings. After all, you never heard of a woman builder, did you?"

"There's no reason why there couldn't be one," Micaela countered.

"No, I suppose not," Claire agreed. "Although I'd rather fish myself."

When Micaela decided her drawing was finished, she closed her sketchbook and motioned to Claire, and the two of them left the garden and headed down Royal Street toward Canal. Because of unexpected heat during October, there were few people on the main shopping street, except for the little black boys sprinkling the dusty thoroughfares with water scooped from the deep gutters beside the banquettes. Micaela and Claire were especially relieved to note that the ladies in the traditional heavy green barège veils and gloves with whom they would have been obliged to exchange greetings were scarce. The less people to observe them running about the city on their own, the better.

Pausing before the window of a pet store, they admired the monkeys and birds inside. The sight of a parrot on his perch reminded Micaela of her own Sancho Panza, who had been sent with Binnie to her mother's Bayou Road plantation, and filled her with nostalgia and longing for the brightly colored bird. To intensify her sadness, they passed a Choctaw Indian woman in the adjacent doorway selling strings of grasshoppers. In the past Micaela had always bought one to feed Sancho with.

At the corner of Chartres and Canal they chuckled at the mechanical wax head in a dentist's window that automatically opened and closed its mouth, displaying two rows of gigantic false teeth. Right afterward they decided to stop at the nearby soda fountain and relieve their thirst with ginger syrup, dispensed for a picayune a glass.

When they emerged from the soda fountain, the two girls agreed to part and pursue their separate interests. Claire, who had secreted fishing tackle in her small handbag, opted for fishing in the deep ditch running down the center of Canal Street whose muddy bottom was reputed to be teeming with catfish. Micaela, on the other hand, planned to sketch the new hotel still under construction in the American part of the city above Canal. After making plans to meet again at the cathedral garden at an appointed hour, the two girls left each other with a cheerful wave.

Coming upon the hotel site, Micaela was undaunted by the rough, uneven ground and the huge mounds of dirt that had been excavated from the foundation of the building. She slowly circled the edifice, admiring its design and construction and determining the best angle from which to try to capture its essence.

As she stood back gazing at it, she was especially impressed by the great dome that capped the structure, aware that it could be seen from all parts of the city. Much controversy had surrounded this dome, she remembered. The Creoles had accused the Americans of ostentatiousness in topping the new hotel with such a conspicuous feature. But Micaela was fascinated not only by its smooth beauty but by the marvel of its construction as well.

Although construction had been under way for a long time, the hotel was still not completed, and piles of brick, gravel, and sand dotted the site. Frequently the local sawmills could not keep up with the demand for lumber in the booming city, and shortages often caused delays. As Micaela peeked in the doorway of the lobby, she noted that scaffolds were still in place.

After sketching outside for a while, Micaela was overcome with curiosity and decided to defy the "No Trespassing" signs. Inside, the place was quiet. Not a single workman was in evidence, except for a black watchman asleep behind a pile of slate. She stood in silent awe beneath the dome, gazing upward, and then proceeded to explore each of the three corridors that radiated from the lobby like spokes of a wheel. Peering into the rooms of the various wings, she inhaled the mingled odors of wet cement and pungent pine resins.

When she returned from the central corridor to the lobby, she was suddenly aware that she was no longer alone. Heavy masculine footsteps echoed hollowly in the empty vastness and seemed to be heading in her direction. Her first impulse was to turn and run back down the corridor, but instead, she drew her cape around her, clutched her sketchbook under her arm, and retreated into a dark doorway, where she hoped to conceal herself until the visitor left.

But the stranger did not depart. In the subdued, diffused light that filtered through a circle of tiny windows at the base of the dome, she observed that he was coming toward her. He was a tall man with broad shoulders, and his purposeful stride was marred by a slight limp that aroused Micaela's curiosity as she watched him from the shadows. He squinted as if straining to see better as he stared straight in Micaela's direction. His ruddy, sunburned skin and fair hair told her he was not a Creole, but probably a Yankee, one of that horde of newcomers who were streaming into the city from the valleys of the upper Mississippi ever since the Louisiana Territory had become part of the United States. His clothes, however, indicated that he was not a riverboatman, and he looked a little younger than Pierre, perhaps around twenty-five or twenty-six. Although he lacked the dark, smoldering looks of the men of French descent to whom she was accustomed, Micaela found him exceptionally attractive, so attractive, in fact, that her hands clutching her cape about her began to tremble as he drew nearer.

Micaela suddenly found herself wishing she had not disobeyed the signs and ventured inside the hotel. What a foolish and dangerous thing that had been. How she yearned for Claire to be with her at this moment, not because she actually feared this ruddy-complected, sandy-haired stranger, but because she was bewildered and a little frightened by her reaction to him. As the sound of his footsteps grew louder, a strange, new flush of excitement swept over her without warning.

"All right, you, out of there," he called sternly. "Don't try to hide. I see you."

As she shyly emerged from the doorway, he seemed startled by her appearance.

"What in blazes are you doing here?" he demanded. His words had an unusual musical lilt to them, were spoken with an accent she could not immediately identify.

"I, sir?" she replied meekly.

Looking around, he said, "Well, I don't see anyone else, do you?"

"No, sir."

"Then answer my question. What are you doing here? Come out where I can get a better look at you," he added.

Micaela obediently followed him into the lobby, where he appraised her in the soft light.

"What right do you have to disobey those 'No Trespassing' signs I have posted outside?" he asked.

"None at all, I suppose, sir. I was just sketching, and I got curious and wandered inside," she said. "I know I shouldn't have done it, and I do apologize."

"Sketching?" he repeated, intrigued by her answer. "That's a likely story. Who sent you around to spy on me and see whether I have any lumber you can steal? Come on, you little ragamuffin, out with it."

"I don't know what you're talking about, sir," she said, appalled that someone would refer to her in such a way.

"I can't get lumber any easier than anyone else in this city, and I'll not have anyone using a little red-haired street urchin as a scout so they can steal what little wood I did manage to get hold of today." He indicated some tarpaulin-covered stacks that Micaela hadn't noted previously. "My men haven't been able to work for weeks because I couldn't get them any wood until today, and I'm not going to let you spoil things for them any longer, miss. Tell your bosses they'd better train you before they send you out on another mission. You've left a clear trail from the door to over here."

Looking down at the floor, Micaela viewed her dusty footprints and realized what he was talking about. Naturally, there had been no reason for her to obliterate her tracks.

"Sir, I am not a thief or a scout for a gang of thieves," she protested indignantly. "And I resent your insinuations."

"Don't you be lying to me, either, you little wench," he said, suddenly lurching forward and grabbing her roughly by the scruff of the neck. "I'm personally going to throw you out of here, and if I ever see you anywhere around this site again, I'll turn you over to the police."

With that he dragged her across the lobby and tossed her unceremoniously out into the dirt.

As she landed, her cape flew open, revealing both her school uniform and the sketch pad. Standing in the doorframe, the stranger stared at her in surprise as he watched her scramble to her feet, attempt to dust herself off, and retrieve her notebook.

"Let me see that," he said, pointing to the sketchbook.

Reluctantly she relinquished it to him, hoping it might corroborate her story, and he flipped through the pages, studying each drawing she had done.

"They're all buildings, except for this lone palm tree," he commented.

"Yes, sir," she answered. "It's a project I'm doing for school. You see, I'm making a collection of the most impressive structures in New Orleans."

"For what school?" he asked, narrowing his pale blue eyes and appraising her as he spoke.

"The Ursuline Convent," she replied.

"And these are the buildings you consider 'most impressive'?"

"Yes, sir."

"Well, I'm glad to see you've included my hotel," he said, the hint of a smile playing on his lips.

"Oh, yes, sir. I could never omit it, not with that dome." Her gaze wandered almost reverently toward the half-globe structure.

His face broke into a sudden grin, displaying his white, even teeth. "So you like my dome, do you? Well, I can tell you, the city fathers don't. I had one devil of a time getting it approved. One of the so-called local experts swore that, according to my designs and specifications, it would collapse the moment the supports were removed. As you can see, the expert was wrong, as experts frequently are, and I was right. I carefully considered every aspect of the construction and designed the dome on basic principles laid down by Tredgold. I don't suppose you know who he was, do you?"

"No, sir," Micaela replied, shaking her head, grateful that he seemed to be taking an entirely new attitude toward her.

"Mr. Tredgold happens to be one of the world's finest architects," he informed her.

"If I may ask, sir, are you an architect as well?"

The stranger smiled again. "Permit me to introduce myself. I am Mr. Patrick Lynch, born in Ireland, recently of London and New York. Yes, I am an architect. And who might you be? I feel I have a right to ask since I caught you snooping about my hotel."

The nuns had repeatedly cautioned the girls about talking to strangers and revealing their names, but Micaela somehow felt that she could trust the Irish Mr. Lynch.

"My name is Micaela Almonester," she replied.

"I am pleased to make your acquaintance, Miss Almonester," he said with an exaggerated bow from the waist. "And does your family reside in this city?"

For a moment Micaela was surprised that he didn't recognize the name at once. She was tempted to inform him that her father, Don Andrés, had been one of New Orleans's most illustrious citizens, but she checked the impulse and merely answered, "My mother lives in Paris."

"Then you're French?"

"My mother is of French descent. My father was Spanish, from Andalusia."

"I thought for a moment, with that red hair of yours, you might be an Irish lass."

"No, sir."

"You may stop calling me sir," he said. "Call me Mr. Lynch. Or, better yet, call me Patrick."

Micaela was horrified. It was unthinkable to refer to an older man by his first name unless, of course, he was a relative or a slave.

"Oh, I couldn't do that, sir," she protested.

"Certainly you could," he insisted. "You can do anything you set your mind to. Now, call me Patrick. Go on, let me hear you."

"Yes . . . Patrick," she murmured, pronouncing the name with difficulty.

"That's better." He nodded. "Now that you've learned to call me by my first name and have convinced me you're not out to steal my lumber, would you care to come back inside and let me show you around?"

"Oh, yes, sir," she replied enthusiastically.

Cocking one eye, he said, "What?"

"Yes, Patrick," she corrected herself.

Together they strolled the length and breadth of the new hotel, which, she learned, was to be called the New Hibernia, and Patrick explained with great enthusiasm the intricacies of its design and construction in far greater detail than Micaela could comprehend. She was flattered by the way he treated her, not as an adolescent child, but as an equal, something even Pierre did not do.

"I can tell you frankly, it's not easy for an Irishman to establish himself in this city," he said. "What little work I've had since my arrival I owe to my fellow Irish. As you may have guessed from the name of this hotel, a group of Irish merchants are responsible for it. The Creoles are too clannish to give work to anyone who's not one of them—if you'll forgive me for saying so."

"What else have you built?" she asked eagerly.

"Nothing much to speak of," he replied. "Mostly alterations to a few of the better private homes, all Irish, of course. I've done a chimney here, a bridge there, even a jail. Mostly smaller things the local architects either don't want to bother with or don't know how to build. You see, I've had lots of practical experience that your local architects haven't had. I know all phases of construction. I started out as a laborer carrying bricks for my father, God rest his soul, who had a bit of talent for building himself. I'm grateful for that experience, because most architects I've met lack a knowledge of the various crafts involved in construction. Together my father and I designed and built the mansion of a squire who owned the local linen mills near where I was born. It was my dear mother, however, who insisted I go to Dublin and study formally. Even when I was in school, I continued to work as a builder whenever I could. Dublin is where I got my first real training in drawing. From there I went to England to seek my fortune, like many a naive Irish lad, but I soon learned that England is no place for a poor Irishman without connections to get his start, so I came to America—New York, to be exact. In New York, I heard about the fine opportunities in the South, especially in New Orleans, so I came here. And here I am making a fool of myself by telling my whole life's story to a schoolgirl who couldn't care less!"

"Oh, but I do care!" Micaela protested. "I find your story very interesting. Really I do."

"Thank you, lass," he said, laying his large hand gently on her shoulder. "That's the first time I've talked so intimately with anyone since I arrived in this town. I don't know what it is. Perhaps it's that red hair of yours."

As he finished the tour, Micaela found herself feeling increasingly reluctant to leave the fascinating Irishman, but she knew she had to meet Claire as planned. She desperately began to hope that she might have the opportunity to see this Patrick Lynch again, but feared he would have no desire to spend more time with a girl who had little to offer a man of his maturity except, perhaps, a sympathetic ear.

"Thank you for the tour, Patrick," she said, still speaking his name with difficulty. "It's been most enjoyable, but I must be going now."

"Surely you're not going to run off without seeing my proudest accomplishment?" he declared. "It's the dome I'm talking about."

"But I *have* seen it."

"Not up close you haven't." He took her hand in his. "Come on, let's climb the scaffold to the top. Then you can see how it's all put together."

With her pulse racing, partly at the prospect of climbing the scaffold all the way to the roof and partly because he seemed as reluctant to allow her to leave as she was to go, she said, "Oh, I couldn't do that."

"Why not? Are you afraid?"

Never ready to admit fear or trepidation, she replied, "Of course not."

"Come on, then," he urged, placing his hands about her slim waist and hoisting her onto the rough planks that formed the first level of the scaffolding. In seconds, despite his limp, he had swung himself up beside her with the ease of an athlete. Chuckling at her timidity, he nudged her up the gently inclined platforms hugging the lobby walls until they stood directly beneath the awesome half globe.

For a split second Micaela glanced down at the lobby two stories below and felt faint. Apparently observing her reaction, Patrick reached out and pulled her against him. She could feel the warmth and firmness of his muscular body through the fabric of her cape.

"Don't worry, I've got hold of you," he assured her. "I won't let anything happen to you."

7

FINALLY MANAGING TO tear herself away from the intriguing architect, Micaela hurried toward the cathedral garden, where she and Claire had arranged to meet. Oblivious to the dangers a young, unescorted girl might encounter, Micaela could think of nothing except her afternoon escapade. Patrick's voice with its Irish lilt, his words, his pale blue eyes beneath their light lashes, swirled inside her head and made it impossible for her to focus her attention on anything else, even the flock of gobbling turkeys being herded toward her en route to the French Market.

When she finally reached the garden, she faced two angry novitiates who had been frantically searching for her.

"Where have you been?" one of them cried. "How dare you disobey Mother Germaine and go off by yourself? Do you have any idea the anguish you have caused? You are a selfish, thoughtless girl, Micaela

Almonester, and you deserve whatever punishment
the Reverend Mother gives you."

At the convent, Mother Germaine was more controlled in her anger than the novitiates. She had experienced too much of the world to become overly
ruffled by the transgressions of a single student. After
more than twenty years the bloodcurdling thud of the
guillotine still echoed in her ears.

"Are you prepared to accept your punishment,
Micaela?" she inquired, a note of weariness in her
carefully modulated voice. "As you know, your offense was quite serious."

"Yes, Reverend Mother," Micaela answered, her
head lowered contritely.

"Your mother has entrusted you to my care in her
absence," the austere nun continued. "I am responsible
for your safety. If something had happened to you today, I would have suffered greatly in relaying such
news to your mother."

"I realize that, Reverend Mother."

"Very well. I shall turn you over to Sister Veronique
so that she may administer my orders."

Mother Germaine's orders were that Micaela was
to kneel in the corner of the classroom on a mixture of
brick dust and tacks and recite her lessons aloud. In
addition, she was to be confined to the dormitory for
the remainder of the term and was permitted no visitors. The prohibition of visitors was more difficult to
accept than the rough pieces of brick and sharp tacks
that dug into her bony knees.

When the news of her sentence reached Pierre, he
appeared at the school, demanding to see the Mother
Superior. Basically bored with his bucolic existence at
the sugar plantation, his only diversions being his black
mistress, billiards, and visits from his young cousin, he
welcomed this chance to involve himself in something
apart from the usual routine.

"This punishment seems excessive, Reverend
Mother," he protested to Mother Germaine, who sat
calmly at her desk beneath an enormous crucifix and
met his angry gaze with a serene smile. "You cannot
put such severe restrictions on a young girl, especially

one who is virtually without any family except myself."

"May I remind you, Monsieur Delaronde, that I have the explicit written permission of Madame Castillon to deal with Micaela in whatever way I see fit. I don't have to tell you about the seriousness of her infraction. Micaela placed herself in grave danger by wandering off alone the way she did, especially in the American section of the city. If any harm had come to her, I would have been the one responsible. Madame Castillon has entrusted her to my care. As you know, this city is a dangerous place for a young girl, but Micaela apparently doesn't realize it despite my repeated warnings. It is my hope that the punishment will make that fact clear to her once and for all."

Frustrated, but knowing that Mother Germaine was basically correct, Pierre rose, excused himself, and left the convent in a huff, ordering his coachman to take him to a notorious brothel-saloon in a voice loud enough to penetrate the wooden jalousies of the Mother Superior's office.

After a short time Micaela realized that the worst aspect of the punishment was not that she was forbidden visitors or excursions to Versailles, but that her confinement would make it impossible to see Patrick Lynch again. When they had reluctantly parted in front of the new hotel, he had told her that he hoped they would meet again, and she had replied that she was often in the general area.

He had smiled. "Good. Then we'll undoubtedly encounter each other in the future. I shall look forward to that."

The meeting with Patrick, brief as it was, had affected her profoundly. She was unable to concentrate on Latin or algebra for more than a few minutes before she was stirred by the memory of his deep, lilting voice or his pale blue eyes.

What's wrong with me? she asked herself. How can I be so silly about a man who's probably ten years older than I?

Try as she might, Micaela could not get Patrick Lynch out of her mind.

One night as she and Claire were secretly sharing

thimble-sized glasses of brandy that Claire had smuggled back from her family's plantation, Micaela realized that her preoccupation with the Irish architect had not escaped her roommate's attention.

"Whom are you mooning over?" Claire asked as the two girls faced each other from their respective beds.

Looking surprised, Micaela repeated, "Mooning over?"

"Don't try to deny it," Claire said. "It's that architect you told me about, isn't it? What's his name?"

"His name is Patrick Lynch," Micaela answered, "but I'm certainly not mooning over him. I'm not mooning over anyone."

"Don't lie to me, Micaela Almonester. After all, I *am* your best friend."

"Well, I admit I have been thinking of Patrick—I mean Mr. Lynch—occasionally," Micaela conceded, "but that's hardly mooning."

"It's just as well," Claire told her. "He doesn't sound right for you, anyway."

Indignant, Micaela challenged, "How do you know?"

"From his name," Claire answered. "He's not French."

"Mr. Lynch happens to be Irish."

"See? I told you he's not for you," Claire said, delicately licking the brandy on her lips. "Your mother would never permit you to marry anyone who wasn't one of us."

"For goodness' sake, Claire, who said anything about marrying Mr. Lynch?"

"How old did you say he was?"

"At least twenty-five."

"That's too old."

"Claire, why are you going on this way?" Micaela asked.

"I suppose it is a bit foolish," her friend admitted. "Our families will simply arrange our marriages, and we won't have a single thing to say about it."

"I will," Micaela declared staunchly.

"No, you won't, and neither will I," Claire insisted, refilling both brandy glasses from the flask she kept hidden under her mattress. "The only thing I can tell you for sure is that when your mother does select someone for you, it won't be an Irishman. You can count on that."

"My mother's not going to select anybody for me, and neither is anyone else," Micaela asserted. "Besides, my mother's in France."

"There are eligible young men in France, too, you know," Claire pointed out. "In fact, I wouldn't be a bit surprised if your mother is going around to all the salons and parties and balls with her eye out for a husband for you right now."

"My mother still thinks I'm a child. You should see the way her letters are written. I'm sure she thinks I'm much too young for marriage."

"You'll suddenly grow up very fast when she finds an eligible man," Claire said, adding, "Hurry up and finish your brandy if you want some more."

Shortly before the other girls left to go home for the Christmas vacation, a recess that came early in the season because some of the girls were needed at home during the sugar-making period, Mother Germaine called Micaela into her office and informed her that she would not be required to remain at school but would be permitted to go to Versailles for the holidays.

As soon as he was notified of Micaela's release, Pierre called for his young cousin in the Delaronde carriage.

"So the old ogre finally let you out, did she?" he remarked. "Sometimes I think it's too bad Robespierre missed her when he guillotined the rest of her family."

"Shame on you, Pierre," Micaela scolded, suppressing her glee at his words.

Because it was the Christmas season, Micaela requested that before heading down the River Road to the plantation, they drive through the city so that she might see the decorations and gifts displayed in the various shop windows. Pierre agreed, and Micaela felt a twinge of excitement as the carriage traveled up and down the streets until it eventually passed the domed New Hibernia Hotel. Although a virtual army of workmen was busily engaged, Patrick Lynch could not be seen anywhere about. Disappointed, Micaela sank back into the upholstery of the seat, oblivious to the applewood stays of her corset that jabbed her swelling breasts.

The ride along the levee was dismal. The sky and the river blended into a uniform shade of gray, and most of the cane fields were bare, dotted only by rows of stumps, remnants of the waving green stalks that had been harvested by slaves and their gleaming machetes. The bleakness of the scene communicated itself to Micaela, and she fell silent.

"You're not saying much," Pierre eventually remarked. On these rides he usually depended on her to entertain him with tales of pranks and intrigues at the convent school.

"I suppose I just feel like being quiet," she replied, still nursing her chagrin at not catching so much as a glimpse of Patrick before leaving the city. "Please forgive me, Pierre."

When they arrived at Versailles, Pierre brought Micaela into his study and read her a letter from Louise in which she requested that he arrange a series of parties and balls during the Christmas holidays for his young cousin.

I feel that this season Micaela should be presented to society. It is my deepest wish that among the finer Creole families she will eventually meet the proper mate. As you know, for the past year or so my dear husband has been seriously ill, and I have had to attend him constantly. I regret to say that his condition is no better. In fact, I fear that it has worsened somewhat. As a result, I have rather shamefully neglected my daughter, a consequence I hope to make up to her as soon as I am able. I pray she understands the difficulties I have faced since my move to France. Dear Nephew, I shall naturally appreciate any efforts you may expend in behalf of Micaela.

Pierre laid the letter down and said nothing more, feeling that it spoke for itself.

One sunny day in mid-December, when Micaela was in the pecan grove gathering nuts with the slave children for Aunt Sally's legendary cakes, Pierre came by and invited her to the stables to inspect a new horse, a jumper he had recently purchased. As they wandered through the clump of chinaberry trees he casually remarked, "You know what I'd like to do? I'd like to chop down these trees and finally build that little theater I'm always talking about. As you know, I've always wanted a private theater here at Versailles —like Marie Antoinette had at the original Versailles."

"You know what happened to her," Micaela teased.

"It might be worth losing my head over," Pierre replied. "But seriously, we could have troupes come down here from the city to perform. Even Pelagie could attend. She loves playacting, you know," he said. Micaela was one of the few family members to whom he could speak openly about his mistress, a relationship that was considered scandalous. Most men who had black mistresses were far more discreet, keeping them sequestered in neat little cottages on Rampart Street in the city.

"They're not discreet, they're hypocritical," Pierre had often protested to his father or mother whenever they reproached him for his boldness with Pelagie. Although the beautiful slave woman avoided as much contact as possible with any of Pierre's family, Micaela found her exceedingly intelligent and charming, radiating a dignity and warmth of which few white women she had encountered seemed capable.

"The cane crop has been exceedingly bountiful this season," Pierre continued as they approached the stables. "The profits are bound to be good."

Ever since Micaela had arrived at Versailles, the grinding mills had been operating night and day, filling the sky with clouds of thick black smoke from the burning leaves and pressed-out stalks. The peculiar sweet-sour odor of boiling cane syrup permeated every inch of the air, or so it seemed, and at times the rumble of machinery and the clatter of cane wagons grew so loud that Micaela found it difficult to think.

"It would be nice to have a theater here," she said. She still shared her cousin's passion for the stage.

"The big problem is to find an architect with some imagination."

"I know one," she volunteered after a moment's hesitation.

Pierre looked at her in surprise. "You do?"

"Yes. A Mr. Patrick Lynch."

"Oh? The father of one of your school chums?"

"No." She shook her head.

"Then how on earth would you meet an architect? And an apparently Irish one at that?"

"Quite by accident."

"I see." Pierre accepted her explanation with a nod. "And how can I be sure he is competent?"

"Oh, I'm sure he is."

"How would you know, my dear?"

"I saw his building, the New Hibernia Hotel."

"The one with the dome?"

She nodded.

"I've seen it, too," he remarked. One could scarcely miss it. You can spot that dome from way down the river. But I like it. I especially like the fact that the dome hasn't come crashing down, as all the city fathers predicted it would."

"Are you going to contact Mr. Lynch?" she asked.

"You mean for the theater? I don't suppose there could be any harm in it, do you?" He gave her a broad smile as they entered the stables.

8

A SECOND LETTER from Louise in Paris was more specific and requested that Micaela be presented to New Orleans society at a ball during the current season, preferably New Year's Eve. She went so far as to outline her wishes about the decor, the music, the floral arrangements, the refreshments, and, most importantly, the guest list.

I want my only daughter's coming-out to be an occasion all New Orleans will talk about for a long time to come. After all, I am quite sure there is no other girl in the Louisiana Territory who has Micaela's qualifications: beauty, intelligence, refinement, and wealth. What more could anyone ask? I am aware, however, from the letters I have been receiving from Mother Germaine, that Micaela is rapidly growing into a high-spirited, headstrong, and adventurous young lady, and I am somewhat concerned about certain incidents that have recently occurred. Therefore, I have decided that it would be desirable for her to marry as soon as a suitable young man can be found. If we delay, we may run certain risks. We both know, dear Nephew, that there are those in the city who would relish nothing more than a scandal involving my daughter. Because of our fortunate economic circumstances, you must be aware of the enormous jealousy that abounds in some quarters. If you think I exaggerate, I beg you to recall the nightmarish events surrounding my own marriage to Monsieur Castillon, who at this moment still lies seriously ill, the state of his health due, perhaps to those very events of which I speak.

With the letter Louise included a list of suggested guests, which Pierre passed to Micaela. Looking it over, she decided that her mother had assembled the biggest group of bores and dullards imaginable, and when Micaela confided this opinion to Pierre, he agreed.

"It seems as if her intention is to bury you rather than to get you married," he remarked.

"I don't intend to submit to either," she said defiantly.

He grinned. "Good for you."

Many of the young men on her mother's list were the brothers or cousins of the girls at school whom she had had ample opportunity to meet when they came to the convent for Sunday visits or to attend special functions. Among them were clumsy, boastful, and pimply Alexandre Mouton, Octave Blanchard, interested only in horses and causing fights, and Jacques DuPré, at eighteen already as stuffy and conventional as his banker father.

Disheartened by the prospect of a ball with such unexciting dancing partners, Micaela was temporarily cheered by the unexpected arrival at Versailles of Claire Villegrande.

"Papa had some business in New Orleans, so he permitted me to accompany him from Baton Rouge so that I could spend a few days with you," she said. "Honestly, Micaela, Baton Rouge is so boring. There's nothing to do and no one interesting."

"I'm so glad you've come. Pierre is giving a ball for me on New Year's Eve," Micaela announced. "Now that you're here, you must stay until then, at least. After all, you are my very best friend."

"Are there any interesting boys coming?" was Claire's first question.

"I'm afraid not," Micaela replied. "You know, all the usual ones that are at every party: Alexandre Mouton, Octave Blanchard, Jacques DuPré—"

"You needn't go on," Claire interrupted, adding with a teasing glint in her eye, "What about your Irish architect? I thought he'd certainly be coming."

"I wouldn't mind inviting him, if it were possible," Micaela admitted. "At least he has some maturity and doesn't behave like a silly child."

"At his age I should hope not."

The two girls wandered into Pierre's deserted study, and Claire began uncorking the various liquor bottles and sniffing each one.

"You don't understand, Claire," Micaela continued. "He spoke to me as if I were a person of some intelligence, an equal, not some silly schoolgirl."

"You probably kept your uniform hidden by your cape," Claire guessed correctly. "Like you always do whenever we go out."

"He didn't patronize me just because I was younger than he is."

"By close to ten years," Claire reminded her, putting the last bottle aside and eyeing the brown leather humidor on Pierre's desk. "Have you spoken to Pierre about him?"

"I did mention his name."

Claire opened the humidor and smelled the cigars. "You did?"

"For a long time Pierre has wanted to build a theater here at Versailles," Micaela told her. "I suggested Mr. Lynch as a possible architect."

Putting the humidor back on the desk and wandering to the billiard table, Claire asked, "Is that *all* you said about him?"

"What else could I say?"

Claire selected a cue from the rack and a ball from the tray beneath the felt-covered table. "That you're sweet on him," she said, placing the ball on the green felt.

"Oh, Claire, that's not true," Micaela protested, but a deepening blush betrayed her real feelings.

"Isn't it?" Claire laughed, then smacked the ball with the cue and knocked it into a side pocket.

When the plans for the ball were completed and the final guest list drawn up, Roland, the butler, was dispatched to the city so that the invitations might be written by a popular scribe noted for his particularly florid hand. When the scribe had finished the invitations, Roland, wearing his finest livery, would carry them about the city in a ribbon-festooned basket and properly hand-deliver each to the appropriate guest.

On December thirty-first, the day of the ball, Micaela was confined to her room, while Claire, who had been allowed by her family to remain for the occasion, was permitted to go riding with Pierre.

"A day of rest is absolutely necessary," Eulalie decreed from her sickbed, "if you are to look your best. After all, this ball is in your honor. Everyone will be looking at you. Let Claire go riding if she wishes. No one will be looking at her. It's your debut, not hers."

Early in the afternoon Aunt Sally appeared in Micaela's room with a bowl of foul-smelling buttermilk and some linen cloths. Assuming she was expected to consume the buttermilk, Micaela shook her head. "I'm not hungry," she said.

"This ain't for you to drink," Aunt Sally chuckled, placing the bowl on the oak night stand next to the high-canopied bed. "This here buttermilk is to put on your face to make your complexion all nice."

The rotund slave dipped one of the cloths into the bowl, soaked it in the thick, lumpy substance, and prepared to place it across Micaela's face.

Bolting upright in bed, Micaela waved her arms in protest. "How dare you try to put that awful, smelly stuff on my face?" she cried.

"If a girl's been gettin' herself too much sun, like you been doin', ridin' horses all day with Miss Claire and Master Pierre, buttermilk makes her skin all soft and white again, the way it's supposed to be. Buttermilk's the best thing there is for a lady's complexion. Now, you come on and lie back there, Miss Micaela, and let me lay this cloth over your face."

"Take it away. It smells hideous!"

"All right, then," Aunt Sally said. "I'll have to go and tell your Aunt Eulalie you refused, and you know she ain't gonna like that none. This buttermilk was her idea. You know she ain't well, and if you go and upset her too much, she could take a bad turn. Why don't you come on and let me put it on you for a little while? It won't hurt nothin', and it might make you look real pretty for tonight."

"There's nobody coming that I care to look pretty for," Micaela pouted.

"You never can tell. You might just be surprised," the maid said. "Now, come on and let me do it."

Micaela sighed. There was a chance that Aunt Sally could be right. "All right. Go ahead." The maid plopped the buttermilk-soaked cloth over her face, nearly smothering her with its sour ooze.

As Micaela lay on the bed, inwardly fuming about the foul-smelling facial imposed on her against her will, she heard the sound of a horse's hooves below in the carriageway. Curious to see who the rider was, she tore off the cloth, her face still coated with curds of the lumpy white buttermilk, and flew toward the French windows and out onto the gallery. Peering through the tangled winter-bare branches of the trees, she observed a lone man, atop what was obviously a poor-quality, livery-stable horse, approaching the porte-cochere at the rear of the house. Scarcely able to believe her eyes, she gasped and felt her pulse begin to race. Could it really be he? The fair-haired rider looked like Patrick Lynch!

Almost as if he sensed her presence at the same moment, the rider glanced up at the second-floor gallery. Suddenly remembering the horrid buttermilk covering her face, Micaela darted back into the house, not wishing him to see her with her face all smeared.

"Aunt Sally!" she cried, leaning over the hall banister. "Come here. Quick!"

Eventually the elderly slave lumbered into her room. Micaela ordered her to help her wash and dress at once.

"The way you is actin', Miss Micaela, you'd think the ball was this afternoon instead of tonight. What's all the excitement about?"

"Don't ask questions," Micaela directed. "Just get me some soap and a basin of hot water. And hurry!"

Aunt Sally put her hands on her wide hips and said, "You think I ain't got nothin' to do all day 'cept wait on you?"

"Please, Aunt Sally," Micaela pleaded in a far less imperious tone. "Just do as I say, please, and don't argue."

"I never saw buttermilk affect a girl like this before," the servant said, shaking her kerchiefed head. "What's come over you, child?"

"Hurry, please," Micaela repeated, gently urging the black woman toward the door.

Later when Micaela "chanced" to saunter by, Pierre was engaged in a serious discussion with Patrick Lynch near the grove of chinaberry trees. Before leaving the house, Micaela had made sure that Claire was forced by Eulalie to rest, and silently she gave thanks that her friend was not aware of the architect's unexpected arrival at the plantation. She had no desire for either teasing or competition from Claire.

"There was a strange horse in the stable when we got back from our ride," Claire had remarked.

"Probably just an overseer from one of the neighboring plantations," Micaela had replied, attempting to sound as disinterested as possible.

Despite Aunt Sally's exhortations, Micaela refused to cover her head with a bonnet or a scarf, knowing how much Patrick admired her red hair. Besides, she preferred to have it loose and free, swirling about her shoulders in the chilly wind that blew down river.

So engrossed was Patrick in his discussion with Pierre that he didn't see Micaela at first, and she feared that he had failed to recognize her. After all, she reasoned, trying to console herself, it wasn't surprising that he didn't immediately connect a schoolgirl he had met at the hotel site with a young lady on a downriver plantation. However, a look of pleasant surprise crossed his ruddy face as she drew closer, and she knew instantly that her misgivings had been foolish. It was obvious from his expression that he hadn't forgotten her.

"Miss Almonester, is it not?" he said with a wide smile. The pale winter sun imbued his sandy hair with highlights of burnished brass. There had been times since their first meeting when Micaela had wondered whether she imagined him to be more attractive and appealing than he really was, but seeing him again face to face convinced her that he was even more ruggedly good-looking than he had been in her daydreams.

"Good day, Mr. Lynch," she replied politely, her knees trembling beneath her voluminous skirts.

"Your cousin tells me that it is you to whom I must be grateful for this opportunity," he said.

"Opportunity, sir?"

He nodded. "To meet and talk with him."

"Really, Mr. Lynch?" she responded, feigning surprise. "Grateful to me?"

"Yes," Patrick replied. "He tells me you are the one who suggested my name."

"That's quite true," she confirmed. "I did mention your name when I said how much I admired the New Hibernia Hotel."

"Thank you. That was very kind of you." Then, turning to Pierre, who was listening to their rather stilted interchange with a bemused expression, Patrick said, "You have no idea, sir, how pleased I am that you wished to discuss your theater project with me. This is the first time I have had the privilege of meeting with someone in New Orleans who isn't Irish like myself. It's a pleasant feeling to know that one's work counts as much as one's nationality."

"As well it should," Pierre agreed. "And I am anxious to view your preliminary sketches for my little theater whenever they are completed."

"I can assure you, sir, I shall get to work on them right away."

"I'm certain that once you see Mr. Lynch's plans, you will fall in love with them," Micaela said, blushing as soon as the words had left her lips; she feared she had been too impulsive in her display of enthusiasm.

While Patrick Lynch sipped cognac in Pierre's study from the same bottle out of which she and Claire had been taking nightly nips, Micaela summoned Pierre away for a few moments to ask him if the architect might be invited to stay for the ball that evening.

"I'm afraid not," Pierre said.

"Oh, please, Pierre," she begged.

"He's a sly devil beneath all that Irish charm of his." Pierre grimaced. "Cunning and ambitious. Do you know how he wants to arrange for his fee to build the theater? He is demanding ten percent of the cost instead of a flat fee, which is customary. But if he is really as good as I have a hunch he is, I won't mind paying him what he's worth."

Micaela had no wish to hear any talk of business. "What has that to do with the ball tonight?" she asked impatiently.

"Nothing, I suppose," Pierre admitted. "You know, I really don't think your mother would approve of his presence. There wasn't a single Irishman on her guest list."

"She won't even know. She's in Paris."

"Ah, but your aunt Eulalie will write and tell her, my pet."

"Your mother will be upstairs in bed."

Pierre shook his head. "I'm afraid not. She's insisting that Roland carry her downstairs, at least for a little while. Having an Irishman at a ball in this house would not sit well with either her or my father. It would be almost as bad as inviting Pelagie, although, God knows, I've thought of doing that on more than one occasion."

"What possible objection could they have?" she wondered. "Mr. Lynch has fine manners. You saw that yourself."

"*I* have no objection to him," Pierre assured her. "It's just that he wouldn't be considered one of us. He wouldn't fit in. You know what everyone thinks of the Irish in this city. They're the cabdrivers, the bellboys, the kitchen help at the hotels. The Creoles—and even some of the Americans—regard them as a lowly race. Only the color of their skins places them above the Negroes in some minds."

Undaunted by her cousin's reasons why Patrick Lynch should not be invited to the ball, Micaela proposed, "If he should arrive—let's say quite by chance—Aunt Eulalie or my uncle would not be rude enough to ask him to leave, would they?"

"Of course not," Pierre said.

"Then I shall invite him myself," she declared, and headed for the study.

9

EULALIE DELARONDE SAT up in bed and gazed sadly out the window, watching the flurries of snow drifting downward in the chilly late-afternoon air.

"If this snow keeps up, no one will come to the

ball," she fretted to Aunt Sally, who was in the act of preparing the semi-invalid mistress of Versailles for the occasion. For days the elderly woman had been eagerly anticipating the event, even if it meant her sitting before the fire in an easy chair, swaddled in blankets and afghans, while everyone else was dancing.

"Don't you be silly, now, hear?" Aunt Sally scolded as she picked up a tortoise-shell hairbrush from the dressing table and teased the sparse wisps of silvery hair on her mistress's head. "Of course they'll come. Folks always come out for parties at Versailles. Besides, it's New Year's Eve."

Eulalie smiled a weak smile. "In the old days, when the girls were still here, we had so many parties. Wonderful parties, remember? The house would be full of attractive young people, everybody laughing and dancing and having a grand time. Now there's no one left except Pierre. And my niece, of course. But it's not like it was."

"Nothin' is like it was, Miss Eulalie," the maid agreed. "Nothin' at all. Everythin's changed."

"You know how it is with the people of New Orleans," her mistress continued. "It snows so seldom that the moment they see a few flakes in the air, they think it's a blizzard and become alarmed."

"I'll bet every single person on that guest list will be here," Aunt Sally assured her, "even if there *is* a blizzard."

"I hope so," Eulalie murmured wistfully. "For Micaela's sake."

"Nobody's gonna miss this ball for Miss Micaela," Aunt Sally said as she stepped back to inspect her handiwork. "She's so pretty and nice and growin' up real fast."

"*Sometimes* she's nice," Eulalie amended. "But not always. That girl is headstrong and willful, like her father. She must have her own way all the time. She doesn't get *that* from the Delaronde side of the family. There'll be a rude awakening one of these days. Of course, part of the trouble with her is Pierre's fault. He adores her and spoils her outrageously, catering to her every whim."

"Miss Micaela don't have to worry 'bout nothin'," Aunt Sally said firmly as she clipped a silver barrette studded with diamonds in the elderly woman's hair. "Folks say she's gonna be the richest girl round these parts someday."

"That's probably true," Eulalie sighed, reaching for a mirror so that she could inspect her maid's work. "And that makes me feel sorry for her. Wealth can be a terrible burden."

Shortly before eight o'clock the first boat docked at the Versailles batture, a rickety wooden pier jutting out over the water from the riverbank at the end of the long alley of oaks leading to the main house. House slaves carrying flaming torches were stationed along the alley to light the way for the guests while field hands toted their bundles and luggage. Because of the distances between plantations and the difficulties encountered in traveling from one place to another, it was not unusual for party guests to remain at the host's home overnight or even for several days.

Giggling, the female guests sloshed cheerfully through the winter mud, hiking their voluminous skirts high and holding their delicate satin or velvet dancing slippers in one hand and their silk stockings in the other. Some of the younger girls were carried piggyback by their escorts, who, on reaching the main gallery gave their mud-caked boots to the slave boys to clean while they retired to Pierre's study and changed into their patent leather dancing shoes. Despite the inclement weather, spirits ran high, and it was obvious that everyone was anticipating a good time.

Those who did not choose to arrive by boat came by carriage along the River Road, braving the ruts and the axle-deep mud. River travel was considered risky in wintertime because of the huge chunks of ice bobbing about in the cold gray waters. The amazing thing was that nearly everyone on the guest list showed up—planters and their wives, city folk, schoolmates of Micaela's, elderly friends of the colonel and Eulalie's. Some families were represented by three generations.

Music for the ball was furnished by the slave orchestra of Versailles, which enjoyed a reputation for being the finest in the area. It was rumored that Pierre often purchased a slave for his musical talent alone.

Although Micaela had initially objected to including Renée Houdaille, the colonel had persuaded her to invite the girl, pointing out that her father was a leading client of the Versailles sugar mill. When Renée arrived, accompanied by her parents, she was wearing one of the most obviously expensive gowns Micaela had ever seen, a bright red silk lavishly embroidered with seed pearls and tiny diamonds. It far outshone her own many-layered pale pink organdy whose silver-threaded dark pink shawl was draped across her exposed shoulders.

"My, what a pretty gown, Renée," Micaela found herself forced to say. Because Colonel Delaronde was standing next to her in the receiving line, she knew she could not be rude to the daughter of one of his closest associates.

"Why, thank you, Micaela. Coming from you, I regard that as a real compliment. I know you wouldn't say anything that wasn't sincere," Renée replied with a sweetly exaggerated smile. "Mama had it made for me last summer during our trip to Paris."

As Renée went upstairs to freshen up after the long trip from her family's plantation, Micaela had to admit to herself that although she had an abrasive personality, her classmate was rapidly becoming one of the real beauties of her set.

Because of the poor weather and the icy drafts from the continuous opening and closing of the front door, Pierre decided to abandon the formal receiving line, informing Micaela that she could casually greet her guests during the course of the evening. The gathering was not so large that she would run the risk of slighting anyone.

Upstairs, in one of the bedrooms where slaves were helping their mistresses with last-minute touches to hair, makeup, and clothing, Renée encountered Claire, dressed in an ice-blue taffeta gown trimmed with white lace at the throat and ankles.

"I hope there's going to be some excitement tonight," Renée said. "All the parties and balls this season have been exceedingly dull."

"If this one's not lively enough for you, perhaps you can do something about it," Claire replied.

Renée smiled. "Yes. I just may."

Of all the gorgeously gowned women and elegantly attired gentlemen, the guest who caused the greatest stir that evening was Patrick Lynch. Most Creoles knew one another so well that a new face, any new face, in their midst commanded instant attention, and Lynch's magnetic presence dominated the vast ballroom.

After Micaela had invited Patrick to the ball, Pierre, at her urging, had conducted the architect to the *garçonnière,* sent Roland to him with some hot water, soap, and a sharp razor so that he could bathe and shave, and loaned him some of his own clothing for the evening. Even in Pierre's ill-fitting navy velvet coat and trousers, the sandy-haired, light-eyed Irishman looked dashing and provided a striking contrast to the darker Creoles.

Micaela was at the punchbowl pouring refreshments when she first saw him; she overfilled the outstretched cups before her and spilled punch on the linen tablecloth.

"Relax," Pierre chided gently as he took the ladle out of her hand.

When the dancing began in earnest, couples whirled about the polished floor of the ballroom to the strains of a waltz played by the black musicians. Because the ball was in Micaela's honor, all the young men present were expected to dance at least once with her, an obligation they discharged with apparent relish. At one point the competition for a dance with her became so intense that Octave Blanchard, notorious for his quick temper and love of a good brawl, attempted to start a fistfight with a rival, forcing Patrick, who was standing nearby, to intercede.

"Here, here, lads, what is this business? Shame on you, fighting on New Year's Eve when we're all supposed to be friends," he said as he tactfully, and carefully, separated the two young opponents.

"It's my dance with Micaela," Octave insisted.

"No, it's mine," his rival argued.

Seeing the two about to come to blows again, Patrick settled the matter by saying, "In that case, I shall dance with the young lady myself, if she'll agree."

Turning to Micaela, he bowed and asked her to join him on the floor.

"With pleasure, sir," she replied, accepting his proffered arm.

After so many dances with boys who held her awkwardly, had no sense of rhythm, tread on her toes, or reeked of whiskey, Micaela was suddenly aware how good it felt to be dancing with a man who knew what he was doing. He held her with such assurance that she was prepared to abandon herself to him and willingly follow wherever he led. Whether at a construction site or on the dance floor, it was obvious that Patrick Lynch was a man who took charge of things.

"You dance very well, Mr. Lynch," she said.

"I thought we agreed you would call me Patrick."

"Very well, Patrick."

"This is only a waltz," he said, pulling her closer. "You should see me do a jig on Saint Paddy's day."

When the waltz was concluded, they danced another and still another, and would have continued if Eulalie hadn't summoned Micaela and insisted that she dance with Alexandre Mouton. Patrick, across the room, smiled, nodded his amused approval, and retreated into Pierre's study for a smoke and a probable game of billiards with some of the men.

Much to Micaela's chagrin, Patrick remained in the study as the evening wore on, playing game after game of billiards, downing bourbon, and puffing on Pierre's fine perique cigars. Leaning on his cue while his opponents considered their next shots, he chatted with the various planters, merchants, and businessmen who wandered into that all-masculine preserve. He was ignoring Micaela, and her unhappiness over such treatment was obvious despite her best efforts to hide it.

"Well, it looks like you've lost your favorite partner to the billiard table," Renée Houdaille remarked.

"What are you talking about, Renée?" she countered, feigning ignorance.

"The fair-haired gentleman nobody seems to know. I was watching the two of you on the dance floor. You looked absolutely transported! Quite a contrast to your expression when you were dancing with Octave Blanchard or Alexandre Mouton."

"How you do exaggerate, Renée," Micaela murmured.

"I admit he is rather attractive," her schoolmate conceded. "But at the moment, I think he is more interested in business than he is in you."

"Really?" Micaela replied, attempting to sound disinterested, and walked off toward her aunt.

Eulalie Delaronde, propped against a mound of goose-down pillows in a fine horsehair fauteuil, was thoroughly enjoying her excursion away from her sickbed. Taking Micaela's hand in hers, she said, "Who, may I ask, was that strange gentleman you were dancing with earlier? You seemed to be having a lovely time, and I hated to tear you away, but really, dear, don't you think you danced with him a bit too much? I didn't observe whom he came with, but the poor girl must have been quite upset by all the attention he paid you this evening."

"He came alone," Micaela replied.

Eulalie was surprised by her answer. "Alone?" she repeated. "Who on earth invited him? I don't know him. Is he a friend of Pierre's?"

"Yes. His name is Patrick Lynch."

"Patrick Lynch?" A puzzled frown creased Eulalie's forehead. "I know all of Pierre's friends and I don't recognize that name. I don't think I've ever heard Pierre mention him."

"They've met only recently."

"Well, who is he?" the elderly woman insisted impatiently. "Surely you must know, child. You were dancing with him."

"Mr. Lynch is an architect."

"Is he Irish?"

"Yes, Auntie, he is."

"Oh, dear, what have we come to—inviting an

Irishman to Versailles?" Eulalie bemoaned. "I'm so glad I'm old and won't live much longer. All these changes are too difficult for me."

Shortly before midnight Micaela was relieved to see Patrick emerge from the study. He was flanked by a group of men who seemed to be either paying off bets to him or congratulating him on his skill at billiards. Maneuvering her way toward him, she managed to attract his attention at an opportune moment.

"May I have the pleasure of this dance?" he asked, bowing from the waist.

"You may," she replied happily. She knew that in a few minutes the clock would strike midnight and there would be a great deal of kissing. At that moment she wanted very much to be with someone whom she dearly wanted to kiss her.

"Are you glad you stayed at Versailles for the ball?" she asked.

He responded with a question of his own. "Are you glad I stayed?"

"Of course." She smiled, gazing into his light blue eyes.

"Good," he said, pulling her close to him once again.

At twelve o'clock the slaves rang every bell on the plantation and then circled the house, banging on pots and pans and singing lively ditties. In the great house everyone hugged and kissed, toasted goblets of bourbon and champagne to the new year, and sang nostalgic songs while tossing confetti and multicolored streamers at one another and blowing noisy snakes and toy horns.

"Happy New Year," Patrick whispered, pressing his lips to Micaela's.

When he lifted his mouth from hers, she replied, "Happy New Year, Patrick," and kept her face tilted upward, her eyes closed, hoping he would repeat the midnight kiss. She was not disappointed. Once again his mouth found hers, this time open and demanding. Her pulse pounded as his tongue probed deeply, and she responded to his searching kiss with equal intensity.

"Happy New Year!" a chorus of voices screamed.

Patrick and Micaela were pelted with streams of confetti, but Micaela was aware of nothing beyond the warmth of Patrick's hard, muscular body against hers as they melted into each other's embrace.

10

WRINGING HER HANDS in her red calico apron, Aunt Sally wept as she watched the slaves march to the chinaberry groves with axes slung over their shoulders.

"Stop that sniveling, you silly goose," Pierre ordered. "Those trees aren't worth crying over. They're messy, the wood is brittle, and they can't stand up to high wind or ice."

"I don't care," the rotund black woman sniffed. "I used to love to watch the mockin'birds gettin' themselves drunk on the berries."

Putting his arm around her, Pierre chided, "You're a sentimental old fool, Aunt Sally."

"Don't you go callin' me no names, Master Pierre," she reproached him. "Don't forget, I done suckled you at my titties just like you was my own, when you was a little sucker."

"I know, and I'm eternally grateful," the Delarondes' only son chuckled. "You'll forget all about those trees when my new theater goes up."

"I don't care nothin' 'bout no theater," Aunt Sally declared.

Patrick, standing by and listening to the banter between master and slave, was amused by the casual use of words like "suckled" and "titties," which would have been excluded from polite conversation in the places where he had lived before. There was no doubt in his mind that the American South was truly unique, but there was also much that he would have to accept or overlook if he planned to establish a successful career there. He sincerely hoped that this commission for building the theater, even if it turned out to be a project catering only to the vanity and grandiose ideas of Pierre Delaronde, would open some doors for him within the tightly knit Creole community. The ball had been his first entree into the local society, and he had taken advantage of the occasion to make the acquaintance of several influential men. He hoped the theater would be his second foot in the door. He had Micaela to thank for both and could scarcely forget how helpful she had been. In fact, she was on his mind so much lately, he was beginning to feel slightly uneasy about it.

"When do you propose to begin work, Mr. Lynch?" Pierre inquired.

"My men can probably begin digging the foundation tomorrow if we get all the trees cleared from the site. I assume that tomorrow is satisfactory to you?"

"Your men?" Pierre said with a puzzled frown.

Lynch nodded. "Yes. I've hired some laborers from the city."

"I'm afraid I have no need of your men, Mr. Lynch," the young Creole planter said. "We have plenty of slaves to do the digging. In fact, here at Versailles we have some highly skilled slaves who are first-class carpenters, bricklayers, and stonemasons. They are all at your disposal. At this time of year there's very little for the lazy louts to do except to mend fences and make repairs on the mill and the other buildings around the plantation. Most of the sugar cane has already been ground. If Negroes aren't kept busy, they get restless, and restless slaves can mean trouble."

"The condition of slavery, Mr. Delaronde, means trouble wherever human beings are concerned," Patrick declared.

"Good Lord, man, you sound like one of those Yankee abolitionists." Pierre shook his head. "For an Irishman that's mighty peculiar."

"I'm afraid I've been deeply influenced by the conditions in Ireland when we were forced to live under the British yoke," Patrick replied. "Freedom is a very precious thing. Only when it's taken away does one really begin to appreciate it."

"I hardly expected such talk from you," Pierre said,

obviously annoyed, but forcing his tone to remain genial.

"I'm sorry if I offend you, but my beliefs are very strong."

"Indeed they are."

As much as he hated risking the loss of the commission by displeasing his new client, Patrick felt obliged to say, "If you regret having engaged my services, Mr. Delaronde . . ."

"No, no," Pierre hastened to assure him. "I like your ideas—that is, your architectural ideas—very much. The sketches you showed me were excellent. The best I've seen. You have more vision and imagination than any other architect in this city and are obviously well grounded in your profession. It is your political outlook about which I have reservations. Nevertheless, I expect you to proceed with the theater as agreed."

"Good." Patrick smiled. "But as to the workmen, I prefer to work with those with whom I am familiar. At this time I have at my disposal some of the finest craftsmen in the city. I attract good men because I pay them well and treat them fairly. I require that they put in only a ten-hour day instead of the usual sunup to sundown. I also pay them every two weeks instead of monthly."

"You are a most generous employer, sir," Pierre remarked.

"I try to be fair, Mr. Delaronde."

Because of the chilliness of the day, Pierre invited the architect into the house for coffee. After Roland had brought the requested coffee service into the study, Pierre offered his guest brandy and a cigar.

"Ah, yes, I remember these fine cigars when I was here at New Year's," Patrick said. "It was most kind of you to ask me to stay on for the ball. I quite enjoyed it."

"So it appeared," Pierre laughed. "But you must thank my young cousin. It was she who first suggested your staying."

"I do indeed. A lovely girl. She must be breaking the hearts of all the local swains."

Exhaling the pungent smoke of the perique tobacco,

Pierre said, "Frankly, I don't think she cares a damn for any of them."

"Really?" Lynch replied, raising his eyebrows slightly.

Pierre took a sip of the brandy-laced coffee and replaced the cup on its fine white china saucer. "You must understand my cousin. Micaela lost her father when she was very young. Despite that, she still has vivid memories of Don Andrés. He had a very lively personality and made a strong impression on everyone —not the least of which on his daughter. Somehow I think Micaela is still looking for him—or someone like him. It's a need she's trying to fill, but I don't know if she ever will."

"Really," Patrick said again.

"Yes," Pierre affirmed. "The reason I'm telling you this, Lynch, is because I think the girl is developing an infatuation for you, and I'm asking you to be careful. Do not toy with her affections."

Somewhat surprised by such a warning, Patrick said, "Well, sir, I have no intention—"

"Just a word to the wise," Pierre interrupted.

"Let me tell you, sir, that I regard your young cousin as just that, although I must admit that she does display amazing maturity at times. She's also lovely, and frankly, I'm afraid the Lord has not made me immune to the charms of such an attractive young lady. Still, I can assure you there's nothing more."

"Good," Pierre said, and rang for Roland to bring more coffee. "Feel like a game of billiards?"

"Why not?"

"Excellent." Pierre rose and grabbed his favorite cue. "Maybe I'll have a chance to win back what I lost to you on New Year's Eve!"

As winter merged into spring and better weather, Patrick and his men made rapid progress on the little plantation theater. The roof was now on and shingled, and much of the rough interior completed. Everyone agreed that if the theater were finished according to Patrick's original sketches, it would be a true gem. Planned for a capacity of about one hundred people, it was designed to have no fixed seats as such, but freely movable upholstered chairs. The stage, though small by the standards of public theaters, was well fitted with the latest equipment, including a system of ropes, pulleys, and weights, all designed and executed by Patrick, so that scenic flats might be easily raised and lowered.

For Micaela school had resumed, but since her restrictions had been lifted for the Christmas vacation, she was permitted to spend weekends at the plantation. While there, she became thoroughly engrossed with the progress of the theater, seeking every excuse she could dream up to spend time with Patrick and his crew. It fascinated her to study the intricacies of construction, watching a building grow from nothing—a mere muddy pit—to a beautiful well-designed structure. In spite of her enthusiasm for the project and her eagerness to see it finished, she was filled at the same time with a feeling of sadness. When the day of completion arrived, she knew Patrick Lynch would leave Versailles and that they would probably never see each other again—not that he paid much attention to her, anyway. In fact, since the construction started, he had kept a discreet distance between them, treating her with courtesy and friendliness and yet maintaining a certain reserve. This coolness on his part left her baffled and disappointed; she believed he was silently telling her to forget his ardent kisses at the New Year's Eve ball.

The only person at Versailles to whom she could confide such matters was Aunt Sally, who assured her, "Sometimes men act the coldest outside when they feel the hottest inside. I think Mr. Lynch treats you the way he does, not 'cause he don't like you, Miss Micaela, but 'cause he likes you too much."

"That doesn't make sense," Micaela said.

"It does if you is a man and sweet on a girl you think is too young for you. Or if you think her family don't approve. I think Master Pierre has done had a talk with Mr. Lynch 'bout you."

"Why would he do that?"

"Because he done give your mama his word that he

would look out for you." The black woman sighed
deeply. "You know your mama wouldn't approve of
Mr. Lynch. I done know your mama for a long time,
and he ain't what she's got in her head for you."

Despite Patrick's lack of attention, Micaela could
not force herself to stay away from him. There was
something vital, irresistible, about his presence, and
she even went so far as to decline invitations from
other young men to parties, balls, oyster suppers, and
barbecues if she thought there was a possibility of a
few moments alone with him. Eulalie herself was aware
of Micaela's penchant for spending time around the
architect and his workmen and refusing the company
of eligibles like Octave Blanchard; she considered the
matter most unusual and Micaela's behavior extremely
unladylike.

Although the relationship between Pierre and the
Irish architect was primarily a business one, the two
men shared a certain mutual liking and respect, and
frequently got together on warm spring afternoons to
discuss the progress of the theater, to play checkers or
billiards, or to share cool drinks in the shade of the
awning over the main gallery. Unlike his client and
host, who fancied exotic local drinks such as a Ramos
Gin Fizz or a Sazerac, Patrick preferred his bourbon
unadulterated.

"I can't get over the way you Creoles make everything a concoction—your food, your liquor . . . " he
remarked.

"Our women as well," Pierre added with a sly grin
as he gazed across the spring-green lawn at his black
mistress, Pelagie, who was strolling hand in hand with
one of their mulatto children. "We have an apprecia-
tion for the mingling of many fine ingredients."

"I'm afraid we Irish go for plainer things," Patrick
said.

"Too bad," Pierre sighed, leaning back into the blue
and white striped cushion of the white wicker settee.
"You know, Mr. Lynch, one thing I don't want 'plain'
is my theater. I want it to be the fanciest damned
thing around, a veritable jewel box, if you will. I want
it filled with exquisite detail—in the moldings, the

cornices, the friezes, the centerpieces, the lighting fixtures, the mirrors—in everything. I want my guests to enjoy chandeliers with the clearest crystal prisms— prisms that capture light and then fling it about the room. I want mantels of the finest white Alabama marble, wainscots of the best mahogany, hardware of the highest-quality bronze. I want no expense spared to make my theater the finest anywhere."

"As an architect, I am obliged to carry out my client's wishes," Patrick replied. "You may be sure that I will try my best to satisfy you, but you must remember that many of the items and materials you are requesting are scarce on this side of the Atlantic. If we were in Europe, it would be quite another matter."

"One can acquire anything in Louisiana that is found in Europe," Pierre assured him. "It's just a matter of knowing where to look."

"I'm afraid I must plead ignorant, Mr. Delaronde. I have not yet acquainted myself with all the dealers."

Pierre leaned forward and spoke in a confidential tone. "The man you must meet is Jean Lafitte. He has anything you want. Anything."

Patrick frowned. "You mean Jean Lafitte, the pirate?"

"Call him what you will," the Creole said with a casual wave of his hand. "In the labyrinths of Bayou Barataria Lafitte has hidden ships loaded with every luxury known to man. Deep in the bayou is a spot popularly called the Temple, where Lafitte runs a kind of market for the wealthy and privileged of this city. They go there secretly at night in excursion boats, seeking the rare luxuries they crave. Naturally, Lafitte's market is illegal, but the shopping is duty-free, and the merchandise staggers the imagination."

Astonished, Patrick asked, "Are you suggesting that I purchase the materials with which to finish the theater from this pirate? This brigand Lafitte?"

Pierre shrugged. "I'm not suggesting anything. I am merely pointing out that you have an obligation to fulfill your contract, Mr. Lynch. Where or how you do it is really none of my business."

When the theater was completed, except for the decorative trim of the interior, Micaela wandered inside, thinking no one was about—just as she had done at the New Hibernia Hotel. She hopped up on the stage and, to test the acoustics, began declaiming a dramatic monologue from Racine's *Phèdre* that she had memorized for literature class. As she approached a particularly emotional moment in Phèdre's speech, she stopped short, startled by the sound of footsteps in the foyer.

"Who's there?" she called out, assuming it was Pierre or one of the slaves cleaning up after the workmen who had gone for the day.

"Bravo!" a familiar voice exclaimed, and Patrick emerged from the shadows of the entranceway. "You have a real flair for the stage, my girl."

"You're making fun of me," she said.

"No, I'm quite serious."

She walked to the edge of the stage and prepared to hop down, but he blocked her way. With his arms outstretched toward her, he offered to assist her. Micaela hesitated a moment before allowing him to grasp her about the waist and swing her to the floor.

"There!" He did not release her immediately. Looking directly into her eyes, he said, "I would never make sport of you, lass."

Trembling, she attempted to disengage his hands from around her narrow waist, but he resisted. "Please Mr. Lynch . . ."

"What did you call me?"

"Please, Patrick . . ."

"That's better," he said, releasing her.

"From now on, you must call me by my Christian name as well," she suggested.

"Very good, Micaela," he agreed, adding, "That's a lovely name."

Strolling about the empty auditorium, he gazed at his work crew's accomplishments. "They've done a good job, if I have to say so myself," he said. "Of course, now your cousin has given me a very difficult task. He wants trimmings for his theater that can be obtained only from a pirate who hides himself in one of your bayous."

"Yes, that would be Jean Lafitte. Excursion boats go to Bayou Barataria all the time. All the best people in New Orleans buy his plundered goods."

"I'm shocked that a young lady like yourself would know about such things and would speak so openly about pirates and their loot," he said half jokingly.

"All the finest ladies in the city patronize the Temple."

"I'd hate to have to go there in the company of a pack of ladies bent on shopping," he mused.

"You don't have to," she told him. "Lafitte has agents in town. You can arrange purchases with them."

"And how does one locate these agents?"

"They can usually be found hanging around his blacksmith's shop on St. Philip Street."

"You know, Micaela, for a convent-bred girl, you're rather well informed about pirates and their trade," he remarked.

"All the girls at school know about Jean Lafitte. He's considered quite romantic. He's said to be a very polite, well-spoken gentleman and is welcomed in the finest homes in New Orleans."

Amused by this unexpected store of information, and captivated by the earnestness in Micaela's dark eyes, Lynch reached out and pulled her into his arms.

"You're quite a young lady," he said, his voice strangely hoarse as he brought his face down so close to hers that she could feel the warmth of his breath.

"Please, Mr. Lynch . . ." she started to protest.

"Patrick, damn you!" he snapped sharply. Without warning he placed his half-open mouth over hers. Micaela's first impulse was to resist, but she was unable to, admitting to herself that she had been hoping for this moment since New Year's Eve. The pressure of his mouth was almost painful, yet she yearned for more, awed and intrigued by the strange sensations flowing through her ripening body.

Just as suddenly as he had swept her into an embrace, he released her, shaking his head and saying, "What am I doing? I must be mad."

"No, Patrick," she whispered breathlessly, her heart still pounding, her breasts rapidly rising and falling, mystified by the sudden change in him. "It's all right."

"All right, is it?" he echoed. "What the hell do you know about it?" With that he turned and walked away, the footsteps of his boots reverberating through the empty theater.

11

ACCORDING TO THE strict policy at the Ursuline Convent school, a pupil was not permitted to purchase new articles of clothing without first demonstrating that she had outgrown the current ones or that they were beyond repair, so when Micaela went to Sister Lucille and requested permission to buy a new pair of shoes, she fully expected the nun to insist on inspecting her current footwear. Each girl had two pairs of shoes, one for every day and one for Sundays and special holy days. Micaela dutifully presented the nun in charge of clothing with a pair beyond salvation.

Reacting with surprise, the sweet-faced sister said, "I cannot believe that these are yours, Micaela."

"Oh, yes, Sister, they are," Micaela assured her with a straight face, knowing perfectly well that they were an old, castoff pair she had taken from one of the house slaves at Versailles.

"You're always so fussy about your clothing," Sister Lucille said. "I cannot believe a girl with your pride—to say nothing of your mother's means—would allow herself to wear shoes in such disgraceful condition. I have no choice except to allow you to buy a new pair."

Micaela secretly breathed a sigh of relief. "May I purchase them today? My cousin Pierre is coming to town. He could take me to the shoemaker."

Sister Lucille shook her head. "Ah, Micaela, you're such an impatient one. But go on. Go on. Get your shoes."

Later, when she and Pierre were having coffee in

the French Market, Micaela casually asked him if she could stop at the shoemaker's and order a new pair of shoes, adding, "He might have to make new lasts for me. I think my feet have grown since last year."

"Good Lord, you mean I must sit in a hot carriage and wait until the shoemaker prepares new lasts?"

"It shouldn't take long," she replied. "Not more than an hour."

"An hour!" he exclaimed. "Do you realize what you're asking?"

"Well, if you don't want to wait in the carriage, you could go to your club and then come back for me," she suggested slyly, knowing how fond Pierre was of a quick game of trente-et-quarante.

His frown of annoyance was immediately transformed into a smile, indicating that as she had hoped, he had taken the bait.

Knowing perfectly well that her feet had *not* grown since her last purchase of shoes, Micaela had no intention of ordering a new pair, but nevertheless, she entered the shoemaker's shop and waited until Pierre's carriage was out of sight. Then she dashed out, after mumbling an incoherent excuse to the baffled shoemaker, and made her way to the address printed on the card she had taken from Pierre's study during her last visit to the plantation.

The address turned out to be a rather shabby building on a side street off Canal. Entering it, she climbed a narrow, rickety, winding stairway to the top floor. On the door facing her was a sign, attractively lettered in gold, marked "Patrick Lynch, Architect." As she waited for some response to her knock, her heart pounded, and Micaela wasn't sure whether it was from racing up the three flights of steps or in anticipation of seeing Patrick again. How impulsive she had been to place herself in this daring situation. After all, girls from good families simply did not run around New Orleans seeking gentlemen in their offices. She gave a slight gasp as she heard someone approaching the door. She was certain it was Patrick because his slight limp gave his footsteps a distinctive rhythm, which she had quickly learned to recognize.

Patrick, in his shirt sleeves and suspenders, opened the door and was obviously surprised to see her.

"Micaela! What on earth are you doing here?" Looking down the stairwell and seeing no one else, he asked, "Good Lord, have you come alone?"

"Yes," she replied. "May I come in? I hope I'm not disturbing you."

"No, not at all." He opened the door wider and motioned her inside. His collar was unbuttoned and his sleeves were rolled up, revealing sinewy forearms thick with sandy hair. Attempting to make himself more presentable, he rolled his sleeves down and fastened the cuffs.

The large office-drafting room occupied the entire top floor of the building and could best be described as a loft. Because the room was bare except for a desk and a drawing board, the space appeared much larger than it actually was. There was no ceiling as such, just a sharply slanting roof and exposed beams, beneath which pans and buckets were strategically placed, indicating that the roof often leaked. Two long rows of windows spanned opposite walls, admitting light of excellent quality; one row faced the river and the other looked out over the roofs of the city. Stains on the walls and cracks in the plaster were cleverly concealed by attractive drawings pinned over them. A faint odor of ammonia and India ink permeated the air.

"I suppose you're wondering why I'm here?" she asked.

He nodded. "Yes, I am. I'm also curious how you were able to leave the convent unescorted."

She smiled. "I didn't. I left with Pierre. He took me to the shoemaker. I finished my business there quickly and had a few minutes to spare before Pierre returned from his club, so I decided to come around and say hello to you. I hope I'm not intruding. You don't mind, do you?"

"No, of course not. I was just working on sketches for a new Masonic temple. I thought I might bid on the job." He indicated some preliminary drawings tacked to the drawing board.

"I was just wondering whether you had gotten up enough courage to seek out Monsieur Lafitte," she said.

"Yes, as a matter of fact, I have," he replied, adding, "Although I wouldn't like it generally known that I'm dealing with pirates."

"Is he going to supply you with the materials you need to finish my cousin's theater?" she asked anxiously. "I am so eager for it to be completed."

"I was invited by one of Monsieur Lafitte's lieutenants, a gentleman by the name of Dominic You, I believe, to come to Grande Terre and look over the merchandise. Mr. You was kind enough to offer to supply me with a boat and a map for the trip. He also offered an Indian guide, but I told him if I had a decent map to assist me through the intricacies of the bayou, a guide wouldn't be necessary."

"I'd love to go with you," Micaela exclaimed, her eyes bright with enthusiasm. "It would be so exciting! I've always wanted to go there."

"It's no place for a young girl among all those pirates and cutthroats and smugglers," he cautioned. "What would the good sisters at the convent say if they could hear you now?"

"I am fascinated whenever we pass Lafitte's blacksmith's shop on our walks," she continued. "The men around there always look so sinister."

"That's because they are. You know, of course, that it's not a *real* smithy, don't you? It's merely a facade for Lafitte's more unsavory activities. And you must be aware—since you seem so interested in Monsieur Lafitte and his activities—that the man's engaged in illegal slave trade. Because it's no longer legal to import Negroes from Africa, he conducts a lively smuggling operation, and uses the blacksmith's shop as a place to break in and train the heathen savages from the Dark Continent before he puts them on the auction block."

"When will you go to Grande Terre?" she asked eagerly.

"Wait a minute, lass. I haven't said I'm going yet."

"But you will, won't you?"

"Yes," he admitted. "Dominic You suggested I begin my journey tomorrow night."

"Tomorrow night?" she echoed.

He nodded. "I'm told one must travel at night to avoid the authorities. I have to meet a Choctaw named Queequahik, who wears a silver pin through his nose, at midnight on the dock at the foot of Tchoupitoulas Street. Dominic You has arranged for him to supply me with a canoe and a map."

"Men are so lucky," Micaela sighed.

"What is so lucky about meeting an Indian with a pin through his nose at midnight down by the waterfront? Good God, lass, I could lose my scalp!" He shuddered. "Or worse!"

"You men can do anything you please, go anywhere you want, whenever you want."

"Sure we're lucky," he said, his voice full of irony. "We can fight wars, dig coal out of the mines in the bowels of the earth, be fishermen and end up on the bottom of the sea." Placing his large hands on her shoulders, he advised, "Be glad you're a woman, lass. You're far too pretty to be a boy, anyway."

Realizing that she should return to the shoemaker's shop before Pierre arrived there, she slowly backed away from Patrick. "I'd better be going," she said, not really knowing why she had come in the first place, except that she had desperately longed to see him again.

"And I'd better get back to my sketches," he replied. "Still, I'm glad you dropped around. A man gets tired of nothing but work." He flashed her a smile that shook her to the core.

The next day, while the nuns were busy outside in the schoolyard supervising the younger girls at recess, Micaela and Claire rummaged through an old trunk that was kept beneath the stage of the auditorium to store costumes for the school plays. In these plays girls assumed both male and female roles, so the trunk contained an assortment of men's clothing in addition to women's. Together the two girls eventually assembled a complete men's outfit: breeches, waistcoat, shirt, frockcoat, and a cape, all of which fitted Micaela reasonably well. Rolling the clothes into a tight bundle, they smuggled it into their room and hid it under Micaela's bed.

Later that night Micaela waited for what seemed like hours until Sister Veronique stopped pacing the halls while reciting the Rosary, which she did every night, and finally went to bed. When all was quiet, Micaela crawled out of her cot, dressed in the pilfered men's clothes, and started for the door.

"Wait until I'm downstairs," she whispered to Claire.

"All right," her roommate replied. "Good luck!"

After a few moments had passed, Claire, as arranged in their carefully formulated plan, emitted a bloodcurdling shriek and ran from the room, crying that a bat was after her and trying to entangle itself in her hair. Her frenzied screams awakened the other girls, creating instant pandemonium, for they immediately imagined that bats were after them as well and joined in her shrieking. The hysterical uproar roused all the nuns, including Mother Germaine, who appeared at once in the second-floor dormitory, a whale-oil lamp in her hand.

Downstairs, Micaela took advantage of the bedlam overhead to climb out a window in the bathing wing, landing in a clump of oleander. Brushing herself off, she got to her feet, looked about for the watchman, and, satisfied he was nowhere in sight, dashed across the lawn to the fence. She grabbed hold of a pair of spiked pickets, hoisted herself to the top, and prepared to jump down to the street. During her flight the long black cape she was wearing caught on one of the pickets and might have hanged her if the fence had been a few feet higher. Her feet once again solidly on the ground, Micaela breathed a sigh of relief. From the convent she could still hear the cries of the frightened girls and chuckled softly to herself. So far, her escape had been a success.

With her hair tucked under her jaunty boy's cap and the voluminous cape concealing her womanly curves, she strode down the dark street, imitating a loping masculine gait as best she could. As she headed down various streets and alleys, muddy from recent rains, on her way to the river, she began to have some misgivings about this escapade, realizing suddenly that she had been reckless to venture out alone at such an hour. The area around the waterfront was dangerous enough for a girl by herself in broad daylight, let alone at this time of night. Stories of the terrible things that had happened to women who had dared to walk around New Orleans unescorted swirled about in her mind, causing her pulse to race, her mouth to go dry, and a thin layer of perspiration to break out at the nape of her neck.

For a moment she thought she heard footsteps behind her, but pausing to listen, she realized it was only the water flowing along the deep gutters at the edge of the wooden banquette. She admitted to herself that her imagination could get the better of her if she allowed it free rein.

The waterfront at the foot of Tchoupitoulas Street boasted an evil reputation as the center of crime and vice. It was here that the flatboats, keelboats, and barges bringing hides and produce from the rich upper Mississippi Valley tied up, and their crews, if they were innocent, fell prey to every manner of thief and cutthroat. It was also in this area that rowdy, dangerous saloons, gambling dens, and brothels flourished. At certain times there were so many crude, small craft moored to the stout posts driven into the mud in this shallow part of the river that there was scarcely any room between them. Farther downriver, by the French Quarter, the channel was deeper and therefore dominated by the larger vessels that plied the oceans. Most of the boatmen from upriver were rough-and-ready types, able to defend themselves and their precious cargoes from those who tried to assault them. Their reputation for toughness, however, failed to discourage cutthroats and thieves from prowling the waterfront area around Tchoupitoulas. This was a part of the city the nuns carefully avoided when they took their charges on their daily strolls.

With the waterfront in view, Micaela uttered a

silent prayer for protection, swallowed hard, and proceeded forward, after a couple of minor urges to return to the convent. Her determination to accompany Patrick to Grande Terre was stronger than her trepidation.

Thanks to her prayers, perhaps, the only people she encountered before reaching the docks were a besotted Kentuckian in a fringed buckskin and fur hat and a mulatto prostitute, both of whom she managed to avoid without difficulty. Her main task, she realized as she glanced at the silent, softly creaking boats, would be to locate either Patrick or the Choctaw with the silver pin in his nose. She hoped she would see Patrick first.

Moving briskly along the water's edge, she observed that there seemed to be fewer boats than usual anchored in the harbor. Most were guarded by either the owner—usually with a shotgun across his lap—a crew member, or a hired free black man.

In the distance the cathedral bells began to chime midnight, the hour of Patrick's planned departure. For the first time the thought occurred to her that he might have changed his plans for one reason or another. Perhaps he had decided on another date or canceled the trip altogether. What an impulsive, impetuous thing this was for her to have done! God only knew what would happen when—and if—she got back to school. She did not even allow herself to think about facing the Mother Superior after such an escapade. Still, the excitement of the adventure and the joy of being with Patrick Lynch again would make whatever happened afterward seem worthwhile, regardless of the consequences. Listening to the distant cathedral bells brought back memories of her father and made her wonder what Don Andrés would think of his daughter now if he were alive. Closing her eyes, she saw the two of them in the gently rocking striped balloon, sailing over the city, and concluded that her father had been a bit of an adventurer himself. Whatever leanings she had in that direction she had come by honestly.

Aboard one of the barges a few yards distant a young black boy was perched atop a barrel of lard, and Micaela decided to ask him whether he had seen an Irishman named Patrick Lynch or a Choctaw with a silver pin in his nose. As she headed toward the barge, she suddenly heard footsteps behind her and attempted to duck around a pile of orange crates. Before she could escape, a hand reached out and grabbed her cape. Terrified, she opened her mouth to scream, but a strong arm clamped itself around her neck in a viselike grip, choking off her cry. At the same moment she felt the sharp point of a knife brush against her ribs, and an evil-sounding voice threatened, "Give us all your gold, lad, if you want to live."

"I haven't got any," she gasped.

"Don't lie," the voice warned menacingly as the arm around her neck squeezed tighter. Spots began to dance like bright lights before her eyes, and Micaela struggled to keep from losing consciousness. Just as she felt her knees about to buckle beneath her, she heard, fuzzily, somewhere in the distance, the sound of an approaching horse. Summoning all the strength within her, she managed in one desperate move to upset a crate of oranges, scattering the fruit in the path of the oncoming rider.

Shouting, "Whoa!" the man on horseback brought his mount to an immediate halt. Suspecting foul play, he dismounted and advanced cautiously, shotgun in hand, ready for action.

Almost at once Micaela's attacker released her, throwing her roughly to the ground, and fled down a nearby alley. The rider saw him and gave chase.

Picking herself up out of the mud, Micaela brushed off her clothes and rubbed her aching neck while searching about for her cap, which had been knocked off in the struggle. She knew it was imperative to conceal her long red hair again.

In a few minutes the stranger returned, shaking his head, obviously dismayed that the assailant had escaped. Startled to see long red locks cascading down the back of someone he assumed to be a young man, the man was stunned.

"Micaela?" he murmured. "Is that really you?"

Instantly recognizing the voice as Patrick's, she

realized that his appearance on the scene had not only saved her life but ended her search as well.

"Patrick . . ." she said softly.

Adjusting his knitted blue tam-o'-shanter, he shook his head. "What in God's name are you doing here? Have you gone and lost your mind, lass? If I hadn't come along just now, you'd be dead and your body lying in the mud at the bottom of that river."

"Yes," she managed to utter, still shocked and stunned by what had transpired only moments earlier. "Thank you."

"Is that all you have to say for yourself?" he reproached. "What are you doing here alone at such an ungodly hour? I could scarcely believe my eyes when I saw that red hair!"

"Patrick, I want to go to Grande Terre with you," she blurted out.

"Impossible. You can't go there. It's much too dangerous. I thought you were joking when you said that at my office. I never dreamed you might be serious."

"Please take me with you," she begged.

"Are you mad, girl? I'm taking you back to the convent."

"I can't go back to the convent now. It's locked up tight for the night. Besides, if I did get in, the Reverend Mother would punish me severely—most likely expel me. Oh, please, Patrick, take me with you," she pleaded desperately.

"I'll do no such thing. It'll do you good to be punished for such a rash act."

"If I am expelled from school, my mother will make me go to France to live," she continued. "I don't want to leave New Orleans. I would just die if I were forced to go to France."

Hesitating for a moment, he realized that if she were expelled and sent to France, he might never see her again. "When you put it that way, I have very little choice," he replied, and slipped his arm around her.

At a prearranged spot Patrick located the Indian with the silver pin through his nose. With scarcely a glance at Micaela, the guide led them to a canoe fashioned from a hollowed log and called a pirogue. The Choctaw's expression was impassive, and Patrick's questions were answered only by grunts or snorts. Black, stringy hair reeking of rancid animal fat fell limply about his shoulders, framing his gaunt, narrow face with its prominent cheekbones. Apart from his tattooed brow, his most memorable feature was undoubtedly the celebrated long silver plug that pierced the septum of his nose and extended from each nostril. Micaela was trying her best to appear boyish, her cap once again concealing her long red hair, and apparently she had succeeded in fooling the Choctaw.

"Here map," the Indian said, handing Patrick a piece of deerskin on which some markings had been made in India ink. In return for the map, and presumably the pirogue, Patrick slipped him some coins, and he departed silently.

Patrick helped Micaela into the wobbly canoe, which she feared might overturn at any moment, and then climbed in after her.

"I still think I should paddle you right back to school," he said as they glided down the river.

Eventually, after consulting the deerskin map, Patrick veered the craft into a tributary somewhere below the approximate location of Versailles and followed the stream until it grew increasingly narrow, barely wide enough for a boat as slender as the canoe.

"In case you're wondering why I'm doing so well, I've been practicing," Patrick said with a sly wink. Micaela wasn't sure if he was serious, but she knew he was handling the canoe with considerable skill.

Several hours later dense clouds drifted northward from the Gulf and began to cover the moon, only intermittently allowing its pale light to filter through so that Micaela could observe the banks on either side of them crowded with willows, elephant ears, sycamores, and an occasional cypress. At times the channel itself became so clogged with bulbous water hyacinths that Patrick had to hack a path through them with his hunting knife.

Despite his urgings, Micaela was so intrigued by the

journey through the silent bayou that she was unable to sleep, her eyes constantly surveying their surroundings. Bayou Barataria, a dense marsh, teemed with wildlife of all kinds, and she was thoroughly fascinated. From time to time her steady surveillance was rewarded by the curious stares of mountain lions, bears, deer, and racoons, who monitored the progress of these intruders along the labyrinthine waterways.

By dawn Micaela was resting wearily against Patrick as they sat back to back, both still wide awake. Just as the sun edged over the horizon, he proceeded to head the boat toward a kind of bayou island called a *chenière* by the natives. A *chenière* was a high mound of shells topped by a layer of earth on which live oak trees frequently grew. These islands had been created by Indians who had once roamed the area and lived primarily on shellfish.

After pulling the canoe up on the ground Patrick picked up his shotgun and announced that he was going after some game. Taking a pile of deerhides from the bottom of the pirogue, he spread them on the ground and advised Micaela to sleep until he came back. A few moments later he disappeared into the dense undergrowth along the bayou.

Utterly exhausted, Micaela lay down on the deerskins and fell asleep almost at once, awakening sometime later to the aroma of roasting meat. Apparently Patrick had been successful on his hunt and had returned while she slept. Raising her head, she stretched and glanced at him as he turned a spit above the fire.

Realizing she was awake, he left the nearly cooked meat and came over to her.

"Hungry?" he asked with a smile.

She nodded.

"You little minx," he chuckled. "I still can't believe you've tagged along like this. It's utter madness, that's what it is."

"Are you sorry?"

"No," he answered thoughtfully. "In fact, I'm rather pleased—but God only knows what the consequences of this foolishness will be for both of us. They might haul me off to jail. Or string me up."

Before she could say a word to soothe his concern, Patrick had slid down beside her on the deerskins. Almost at once he began to caress her slowly and gently. She felt that she should protest, but the smooth stroking of his hands along her throat and arms caused her breath to quicken and a pleasant warmth to flow through her, stirring memories of their kisses on New Year's Eve and again in the half-completed little theater. Bringing his face close, he pressed his mouth hungrily over hers, his tongue stealthily shoving its way between her parted lips. His fingers tugged at the man's shirt she was wearing, gradually releasing it from the breeches; then his searching hand inched up to her breasts and began to caress her nipples until they hardened and were sweetly aching.

Frightened as much by her own confused feelings as by his advances, she tried to resist and shrank away from him, but Patrick pressed his lips to her ear and murmured soothing, tender reassurances. Surrendering to her impulses, she slowly encircled his powerful body with her arms and felt the smooth muscles of his wiry back rippling beneath her touch. A floodgate of tingling sensations broke over her in waves, creating an ever-increasing, undeniable desire for him deep within her, stripping away all fears and apprehensions.

When he could contain his passion no longer, he undressed her completely and gazed in awe at her smooth, pale body with its full, creamy breasts and gently rounded hips bathed in the soft morning light. Her beauty stirred him immensely.

Sighing deeply, he said, "This is wrong, Micaela, but I can't help myself."

"I know," she replied, surprised by the huskiness of her own voice.

"It's you who must stop me now."

"I can't, Patrick." She pulled him close to her. "I can't."

His hands fondled the smooth, silky skin of her inner thighs, slowly moving higher and higher, until they reached her sex. Now her desire seemed boundless; she writhed and moaned, her lips parted, her breath coming in rapid little gasps.

All at once the caresses stopped, and she felt curiously abandoned in a moment of great longing. Opening her half-closed eyes, she saw that he was removing his own clothes.

When he was naked, modestly attempting to conceal his jutting manhood, he murmured, "Try to relax. I don't want to hurt you."

Then he knelt between her legs and spread her knees apart with his own. Ever so slowly he began probing her with his organ, entering her gently, aided by the unexpected wetness of her unrestrained excitement. For a single instant she experienced a sharp stab of pain and cried out. Patrick halted his forward movements, withdrew a little, and when she had relaxed, entered her again. This time the pain transformed itself into a far more pleasant sensation. As though to assuage any discomfort he might have caused her, he slipped his hand under her neck, raised her head, and nearly smothered her with kisses. A strange tingling—frightening and at the same time pleasurable—was rapidly building up and spreading throughout her entire body, removing it from her conscious control, making her want to rise and meet each of his deep hard thrusts.

His strokes accelerating, he drove faster and faster, taking her very breath away and making her feel as if she might faint, or even die. His face was growing red and contorted, as if he, too, were in the grip of an all-consuming, overpowering force. Uttering a hoarse cry from somewhere deep in his throat, he suddenly went rigid and then, after a series of spasms, relaxed, becoming heavy on top of her.

When he moved off her to lie on his side, she slid her fingers slowly down along her smooth belly to the little mound of bright red hair. Peering curiously at her fingertips, she gasped. They were covered with blood —her blood.

He, too, saw the blood and muttered in anguish, "Oh, my God! What have I done? I've taken your virginity!"

"Please, Patrick, it's all right," she whispered comfortingly, attempting to reassure and soothe him. What was done was done. At the moment, she had few regrets. "It's all right."

Cradling her in his arms, he held her close and covered her face with kisses. The two of them lay together in a tight embrace for a long time, listening to the shrill cry of the gulls circling overhead, heralding their nearness to the sea, to eternity.

12

WHEN MICAELA AND Patrick awoke, neither knew how long they had slept, although they assumed it had been several hours because the sun was now high in the sky.

"We'd better get going," he said, giving her a gentle nudge with his elbow.

Reluctantly Micaela rose and dressed once more in her men's attire, sorry to have to dispel the romantic haze surrounding the morning. She was feeling intensely feminine, and the act of pulling on a pair of men's breeches seemed out of place.

When she was dressed, Patrick helped her into the pirogue, and they continued the journey to Grande Terre.

As they drew near to their destination, they began to pass an occasional ship or two anchored in the concealed waterways, all undoubtedly loaded with every kind of precious booty.

"The rumor is that Lafitte has a private navy of more than fifty ships, all of them captured or stolen," Patrick said. "And five thousand men in his command as well."

When at last they caught sight of Grande Terre, one of two small islands that separated Barataria Bay from the Gulf, Patrick advised Micaela to continue the masquerade while they were there. "Grande Terre is a dangerous place, at least from what I've heard. The only law there is Lafitte's own pirate code. Let's see, now, we'll have to give you a name. I'll say you're my assistant—Michael. That's a good Irish name. I'll have to remember to keep my hands off you, of course, and I admit that that's going to be difficult."

As the little pirogue glided into the harbor at Grande Terre, Micaela was surprised to discover that the pirate stronghold was a large and complex settlement, a small town, in essence. Although Grande Terre was a sandy sea island, it was not bare of vegetation. On the contrary, its rolling dunes were covered with groves of orange trees, oleanders, and dwarf oaks, as well as huge Indian shell mounds, all of which nicely concealed the pirates' storehouses and hideaways.

Perched on the highest point of the island, a fort guarded the harbor, its high, thick walls punctuated at regular intervals with powerful cannons. Below the fort was a scattering of palmetto-thatched houses, homes of the lesser smugglers and privateers, as well as huge warehouses for confiscated goods. The most conspicuous structures, however, were the barracoons, the compounds in which contraband slaves were imprisoned until they could be sold on the auction block.

Situated near the slave enclosures, in the heart of the colony, was a large mansion of brick and stone that stood out boldly from the humble dwellings surrounding it. Its windows were barred with stout but attractive iron grilles, and it was fronted by a wide veranda that overlooked the azure Gulf.

"I'd venture to guess that that's Mr. Lafitte's home," Patrick said as he headed the pirogue toward a small dock projecting from the shore.

As they pulled up beside the pier, they were met by a group of sinister-looking men, each armed with pistols, and knives, who eyed them suspiciously. The leader was a man whose face was horribly scarred and disfigured, undoubtedly the result of past battles. His most outstanding feature was the false nose he wore in the center of his face, held in place by a leather thong tied in back of his head. Stepping forward, he introduced himself by the nickname Nez-

Perdu and questioned Patrick about his reasons for coming to Grande Terre.

"I've been sent by Mr. Dominic You," Patrick replied, seemingly unruffled by his pirate hosts. "My name is Patrick Lynch, and this is my young assistant, Michael. I'm an architect by profession, and I have come here to look over certain building materials that I understand Mr. Lafitte has for sale."

When the pirates were finally convinced that Patrick and Micaela were not there to cause trouble, Nez-Perdu permitted them to come ashore.

"Follow me," he directed, leading them toward the imposing mansion.

The strange pair of newcomers, an Irishman who handled a pirogue with the skill of an Indian and a smooth-cheeked boy with wisps of bright red hair poking out from under his cap, evoked curious stares as they proceeded up the trail from the dock.

Among the pirates and other ruffians, Micaela noted with surprise, there were several women. Although scruffy and inelegant for the most part, a few of them were wearing fine gowns. Only when she saw the bloodstains on the expensive fabrics did she realize that these dresses had most likely been ripped off their owners, who were undoubtedly no longer alive. Such a thought made her shudder, and she hoped that no one had noticed.

Leaving the other pirates behind, Nez-Perdu led them to the front door of Lafitte's home, where they were met by a liveried butler with impeccable manners who greeted the visitors cordially and invited them inside.

The interior of the mansion was luxurious, filled with the finest furniture, carpets, and appointments, most of which had doubtless been plundered from the ships plying the Spanish Main. In addition to the butler, many other well-trained African slaves moved quietly and efficiently through the house.

"Monsieur Lafitte is in the garden," the butler announced, and conducted the trio through a rear portico to an enclosed garden fragrant with the scent of jasmine and orange blossoms. Amid the bright blooms, lounging in a red hammock suspended between two oaks, was the notorious Jean Lafitte. He did not rise at once to greet them, as Micaela had expected, since she had always heard that Lafitte had impeccable manners and was exceedingly gallant in the presence of ladies. Only when she remembered that she was disguised as a boy did she comprehend the pirate's apparent lack of courtesy.

"Monsieur Lafitte, may I present Mr. Patrick Lynch of New Orleans and his assistant, Michael," Nez-Perdu said.

With that introduction, Lafitte casually swung his legs over the edge of the hammock and rose, extending his hand first to Patrick and then to Micaela. "Welcome to Grande Terre," he said.

Micaela thought the famed pirate chieftain an extraordinarily handsome man, with his gleaming black hair, hazel eyes, and neatly trimmed mustache. She noticed that he had a habit of keeping his left eye closed as he spoke.

"Your assistant, Michael, looks very young," Lafitte remarked.

"He's got a mighty smooth face," Nez-Perdu commented.

"Don't let his youth fool you," Patrick said. "Michael's extremely capable."

"Nothing fools me, monsieur." Lafitte smiled. "I understand that you are here to look over my merchandise. Is that not correct, Mr. Lynch?"

"Correct, sir," Patrick affirmed.

"Well, then, let me invite you to tour my various warehouses. I am sure you will be able to find whatever you are looking for."

"Much obliged."

"The trip here by canoe is long and tiring," the pirate continued. "I expect you and the boy to be my houseguests while you are here."

"Thank you, sir," Patrick said.

In a few minutes the butler returned with a tray of iced drinks, which he passed to the guests. As she accepted a frosty glass, Micaela gave silent thanks to Claire for having introduced her to liquor; otherwise she would have been alarmed at the prospect of having to drink now.

For a while the four of them sat and conversed politely in the cool garden, until Lafitte eventually indicated by a subtle signal to Nez-Perdu that it was time to conduct the visitors to the warehouses. He bid them a polite goodbye, and as they departed in the care of the sinister lieutenant, Lafitte returned to his hammock, closed his eyes, and continued his siesta.

As Micaela and Lynch followed Nez-Perdu up and down the narrow aisles crammed with piles of rare Italian marble, rosewood, teak, mahogany and other fine woods, high-quality glass and mirrors, exquisite Oriental rugs, and bolts of barège silk, gleaming satin, and French calico, they were overwhelmed by the contents of Lafitte's warehouses. From his pocket Patrick extracted a folded piece of paper containing a list of what was needed to complete the decor of the theater at Versailles. With Micaela's help he began inspecting and measuring pieces of mahogany for moldings and wainscots, slabs of Carrara marble for mantlepieces, and checking gilt-edged mirrors for imperfections in the glass.

Lifting the tops of lacquer pots and paint jars, he sniffed their contents for freshness and said, "This place is an architect's dream."

While he was absorbed in the merchandise Lafitte had to offer, Micaela noted that Nez-Perdu scarcely took his eyes from her. His steady gaze made her feel uneasy and apprehensive. Certain that he suspected she was not the boy she pretended to be, she worried that he might try to penetrate her disguise the moment Patrick's back was turned. The deception was particularly difficult for her to maintain because of the great stress placed on femininity by the Ursuline nuns.

During their tour of Grande Terre, they could scarcely avoid the barracoons in which the slaves were penned. Cries and moans of the miserable, fettered blacks emanated from behind their walls. Because the Congress of the United States had recently passed laws forbidding the further import of slaves from Africa, they had to be obtained illegally and smuggled into the country, thereby making them the most valuable merchandise Lafitte had to offer. Since the embargo on their importation, the price of slaves had escalated rapidly. Periodically the pirate king held secret auctions attended by some of the most powerful and distinguished planters in the South. Micaela wouldn't have been surprised to learn that Pierre or her uncle had witnessed such auctions.

"Grande Terre is the perfect place to tame those savages," Nez-Perdu remarked, fingering the shiny leather whip attached to his belt. "Once we have broken their spirits, we take them to the blacksmith's shop in the city and put them to work until they're ready to go on the block."

"Poor devils," Patrick said sadly, shaking his head at the sight of the shackled Africans, many of them bearing the scars of severe beatings.

As long as Micaela could remember, slavery had been a part of her existence and seemed perfectly natural, but now, seeing this cruel and disturbing aspect of the trade, she began to share Patrick's disapproving attitude.

"What do you mean, poor devils?" Nez-Perdu challenged. "They're not fit for anything else. You talk about these blacks as if they were human."

"They are human," Patrick returned. "As human as you and I."

"Yes," Micaela staunchly agreed, visualizing the slaves she loved—Flore, Aunt Sally, Binnie, and Raymond—treated in such a cruel and heartless fashion.

"I see your assistant has inherited your tender heart, Monsieur Lynch," Nez-Perdu commented, eyeing Micaela slyly as he adjusted his prosthetic nose.

With the exception of Lafitte's beautiful mulatto mistress, Micaela was the only female at supper that evening. Of course, she was forced to continue her male masquerade and therefore did not count as a female at all. Knowing that she would have to remove her hat at Lafitte's very formal table, she had gathered her hair together and tied it with a leather cord, then tucked it into the collar of her shirt to conceal its length. She prayed that the suspicious Nez-Perdu wouldn't join them at the table, but, as luck would have it, he was seated directly opposite her.

"Before I took over Grande Terre," Lafitte was saying as he spooned the fragrant crab gumbo before him, "ordinary people like yourself, Mr. Lynch, were afraid to come here. I brought order and civilization to this island. Now the finest people in New Orleans visit Grande Terre and clamor for my merchandise. Even ladies venture down Bayou Barataria to shop for bargains at the Temple."

Observing Micaela, Lafitte's mistress turned to Patrick and remarked, "What lovely table manners your assistant has."

"Yes, Michael does have nice table manners, doesn't he?" Patrick agreed.

"Have you trained him as well in all things?" she continued. Her voice indicated great charm and refinement, and she was the loveliest black woman Micaela had seen since Pelagie.

"I'm afraid I'm not responsible for young Michael's training," the architect replied, looking a little uncomfortable with the present trend of the conversation.

"Then who is?" the mulatto mistress persisted.

"Don't tell us your assistant has been educated by nuns," Nez-Perdu joked with a note of suspicion in his voice.

"Hardly." Patrick dabbed nervously at the corners of his mouth with a white napkin of the finest linen.

"The trouble with you, Nez-Perdu," Lafitte said, turning to his lieutenant, "is that you have always associated with scoundrels and ruffians. Do not cast aspersions on young Michael here just because he happens to have agreeable table manners. Manners has nothing to do with masculinity. I'll wager that Michael is every inch as manly as any of us at the table," the pirate chief declared; then, turning to his lovely mistress and squeezing her hand, he added, "With one exception, of course."

After dinner the men retired to a smoking room.

Micaela tried desperately—and unsuccessfully—not to choke on the cigar given her, and her spasms of coughing provoked great merriment between Lafitte and his lieutenant.

"Michael comes from a very strict family," Patrick said, coming to her rescue with an explanation. "His mother is highly religious and has always tried to shield him from the evils of tobacco."

"It seems as if Michael's mother has shielded him from a great many things," Nez-Perdu observed.

When it was time to retire, Micaela and Patrick were given adjoining but unconnected rooms. She felt disappointed that they couldn't spend the night in each other's arms between fine, fresh linens, and she confided her feelings to him when they were alone.

"Leave your door open," he told her. "I'll see if I can't sneak into your room during the night. It might be a little tricky, but it's worth taking the chance."

Micaela agreed, although she was apprehensive about sleeping alone in a strange house in such a wild, remote location, especially with her bedroom door unlocked, but she did as Patrick had requested in the hope that they might spend at least part of the night together.

For a long time she lay awake in the darkness, a single small candle flickering on the night stand, listening to the wails and sobbing of the slaves imprisoned in the barracoons, but eventually fatigue overcame her uneasiness and she drifted off into a sleep so sound that she heard neither the door opening softly nor the footsteps stealthily crossing the room to where she lay. In fact, the first thing of which she was aware was the drawing aside of the mosquito netting around her bed by unseen hands.

"Patrick!" she murmured sleepily.

When a reassuring reply was not forthcoming, she drew herself up against the pillows, her hair falling in soft curls about her creamy shoulders and gently swelling breasts.

"Patrick, is that you?" she whispered, instinctively holding the bedclothes to her bosom.

As her eyes penetrated the darkness, she was able

to discern the figure of a man. She was about to repeat Patrick's name for the third time when the man reached out, seized her, and yanked her toward him.

"I knew you were no boy." The man reeked of sour wine. Micaela immediately recognized the gruff voice as that of Nez-Perdu. "Not with those smooth, rosy cheeks and that fine red hair. The first time I set eyes on you, I knew that if you were truly a boy, then I was a pederast. Even during the most desperate times at sea that's something I've never wanted any part of." As he spoke, his hands clutched roughly at her breasts and hair.

Fearing the consequences for both Patrick and herself if their deception should be discovered, Micaela fought the urge to scream.

"Please, sir, go away and let me alone," she pleaded.

"Not until I've gotten what I've come after," he growled. Jerking her carelessly by the arm, he dragged her out of bed and pulled her against him, cupping his hungry mouth over hers so hard that she whimpered in pain and tried to pummel him with her fists. With one huge, powerful arm he held her immobile and used his free hand to paw at her body, attempting to strip her of the loose-fitting man's shirt she wore as a nightgown.

"Please, let me go," she begged, squirming against his mighty grip.

From his wide leather belt Nez-Perdu drew a dagger and flicked the sharp point against her neck.

"One more sound out of you and I'll slit your throat from ear to ear," he threatened. "I've no hesitation about it. It wouldn't be the first pretty young throat I've sliced."

"No, please, sir, I beg of you . . ."

Ignoring her pleas, he threw her onto the bed and jumped on top of her, knocking the wind out of her. She cringed under his touch as his roughened hands stroked her body. As he hurriedly struggled out of his clothes, he warned, "One false move and you're dead."

When his trousers were around his ankles, Micaela decided that if she were ever to try to escape, it had to be now. Wiggling out from beneath him, she slid across the bed and headed for the door. Quickly kicking off his pants, Nez-Perdu pursued her, leaping at her as she turned the doorknob. Seizing her by the hair, he dragged her across the tiled floor, overturning a chair and the prie-dieu. Tossing her onto the bed once more, he tried to pin her down with the weight of his body, but Micaela fought him desperately. Her resistance seemed to excite him and goad him on, making him more determined than ever to possess her. Over and over they rolled, and at one point she grabbed his false nose and ripped it off, recoiling in horror at the two great black gaping holes she had exposed in the center of his face.

Eventually overpowered by his sheer strength and endurance, she could no longer battle him. Lying limply beneath his body, she allowed him to spread her legs wide as he prepared to shove his rigid manhood into her.

Grinning, he said, "Once I've dipped my wick in your tallow box, you'll never want that Irishman again."

"Please, let me go," she begged in desperation, her eyes brimming with tears.

Unexpectedly the door was flung open and Patrick appeared with a lighted candle. "Micaela?" he said.

Before she could call out to him, Nez-Perdu had grabbed his knife and pressed it so hard against her throat that it broke the skin. She could feel a trickle of blood dripping down her neck.

"One word from you and you're dead," he hissed in her ear.

Going directly to the bed, Patrick was shaken to find Micaela pinned beneath Nez-Perdu. In seconds the noseless pirate leaped at him with the knife, but Patrick brought up his arm with such force that he knocked the dagger out of his assailant's hand. The candle he had been holding slipped from his grasp and was extinguished. The two men scuffled violently and fell to the floor, tumbling back and forth across the room, overturning more pieces of furniture. Mi-

caela, still stunned by the attack on her, attempted
to rouse herself and come to Patrick's aid.

Still locked together, the two men rolled toward the
door, Patrick struggling to keep Nez-Perdu's hand as
far as possible from the dagger, which lay on a nearby
tile.

Covering her nakedness with a sheet, Micaela
searched desperately for something that could serve
as a weapon. This room in the house of a pirate was
remarkably devoid of any weapons, or even potential
weapons.

During their tussle neither man succeeded in gaining
the upper hand for long, but through a clever, deceitful
maneuver Nez-Perdu managed to pin Patrick beneath
him, just as he had done earlier with Micaela, and
keep him there. Reaching out and touching the dagger
with the tips of his fingers, he teased it toward him,
eventually closing his hand around its handle. Just as
he raised the knife to strike a fatal blow, an ear-
shattering blast obliterated the silence of the night.
Nez-Perdu uttered a strangled, animal-like cry and
sprawled lifeless next to Patrick, blood spouting from a
huge gaping wound in his chest and flowing over the
glazed tiles.

Stunned, both Micaela and Patrick whirled around
and stared in the direction from which the gunshot
had come. Lafitte himself stood coolly in the doorway,
a smoking pistol in hand.

"I regret that my hospitality has been violated," he
apologized calmly. "And by one of my own men. You
see how highly I prize the safety and comfort of my
guests."

13

THE FULL IMPACT of the excursion to La-
fitte's hideout was not apparent to Micaela until they
had returned to the city and she realized that she had
to go back to the convent and face Mother Germaine

and the sisters. She was terrified of the consequences of such a confrontation. There was no possibility that her absence had been overlooked, not for the several days she had been away, and she dreaded having to account to the stern Mother Superior for her activities. She had no idea what responses she would give to the inevitable questions. As carefully as she had planned her escape, she had foolishly given little thought to her reappearance. At the time, it hadn't seemed as important as seeing Patrick again and going with him to Grande Terre.

Originally she had thought of the escapade as nothing more than an adventurous lark—or so she had convinced herself at the beginning—but now it appeared far more serious than that. She had left New Orleans a silly, innocent girl and returned a woman, or at least more like a woman, a transformation she had never expected to occur with such suddenness. Not only had she lost her virginity and recklessly made love with Patrick Lynch, a man about whom she really knew very little, but she had been nearly ravaged by a half-crazed buccaneer whose lust had brought about his own death. Perhaps because of the intimacy and the adventure she had shared with Patrick, her feelings for the blue-eyed Irishman had grown more intense. She now discovered that he was fast assuming great importance in her emotional life, becoming much more than the object of an innocent girlish crush. On the return trip she had wondered, gazing at him expertly whether he felt as strongly about her. Certainly the ardent way he had made love to her and the passionate declarations he had whispered in her ear seemed to indicate that he shared her feelings. At Lafitte's, once she had dropped her disguise and assumed her true gender, he had made no attempt to conceal his affection for her. Strangely, the pirate chief had seemed curiously unmoved by her sudden change of sex. After the attempted rape and the killing of Nez-Perdu, it would have been both pointless and ridiculous for Micaela to have continued the masquerade.

Just before they left, Lafitte had said, "I knew you were no boy, my dear." Fortunately, he had been much too gallant to delve into her true identity, although she was certain he knew that she came from one of New Orleans's better families. She was relieved that he had discreetly asked no questions, because, knowing the social circles in which he moved within the city, she could have become the subject of ruinous gossip if he had chosen to discuss the incident.

Arriving in New Orleans under the cover of darkness—the same way they had departed—Patrick maneuvered the pirogue into the harbor, gliding smoothly between the anchored keelboats and broadhorns, and pulled up to a wooden dock at which the Choctaw with the silver nose plug was waiting. Wordlessly he exchanged Patrick's horse for the map and canoe. Micaela wondered how long he had been there anticipating their arrival.

"Now we must get you back to the convent," Patrick said, boosting her into the saddle. "I hope you have a suitable alibi prepared for the Reverend Mother. God knows, I would never know what to tell her."

"No, I don't have an excuse," she replied. "But you can be sure that whatever explanation I give for my absence, I shall leave you out of it."

"That's very considerate of you. I could be in a lot of trouble."

"I know. That's why I promise not to mention your name."

"Still, if difficulties arise, I want you to know that I'm willing to help. All you have to do is call on me," he offered. "I have to admit that I'm a bit worried about you, and I do feel somewhat responsible."

"No, you're not responsible for me, Patrick," she told him solemnly. "I'm responsible for myself. You didn't ask me to go. I insisted on tagging along. Whatever I did was of my own free will. I have no regrets."

Taking hold of her chin, he raised her face toward his. "None?"

"None at all," she answered with a smile.

"Good," he said, and kissed her tenderly.

He decided that the levee road was probably the safest route back to the French Quarter, and headed the horse in that direction. He also decided that it might be advisable for Micaela to continue her male disguise. "It's safer in case of trouble," he said, and she complied by tucking her red locks beneath her cap once again. "There's no telling who's about at this hour," he added, cautiously surveying the shadowy waterfront before them.

They had not ridden far before they were hailed and stopped by an officer of the Civil Guard, a rather ineffective group of Spanish ex-soldiers who attempted to bring some measure of law and order to the unruly city. The guard called out to them, "Your papers, please, sir."

"Certainly, Officer." Patrick passed a packet of documents to him.

The guard looked them over and handed them back with a nod. Staring suspiciously at Micaela, he said, "The boy's papers also, please."

"This is my assistant," Patrick shot Micaela a warning glance. "He has no papers. I am responsible for him."

"Where are you and your assistant heading at such an hour, Mr. Lynch?" the officer inquired. It was well after midnight.

"There was some merchandise aboard a ship that I wished to inspect," Patrick replied. "The captain offered us some rum, and—well, Officer, I'm afraid we drank too much and lingered a little too long as well. We're on our way home now."

"And the boy resides with you?"

"Yes, sir, he does."

"Very well," the guard said, apparently satisfied with Patrick's explanation. "Be on your way, but be careful. These wharves are full of bandits and thieves, all that trash pouring into our city from the north. A couple of days ago we were advised about a girl who's missing from the Ursuline Convent, and we've been instructed to question all passersby. You haven't seen a girl wandering around, have you? She's seventeen and red-haired. So far, there's been no sign of her. If you want my opinion, I think it's all a waste of time. If she's wandered into these parts, she's probably lying in the mud at the bottom of the river by now." With that the guard tipped his cap and continued on his way. Micaela and Patrick breathed a sigh of relief.

When they reached the convent, Micaela cautioned Patrick to wait before helping her over the fence until the watchman who patrolled the grounds at night with his lantern had disappeared around the corner of the building. The watchman, an elderly free black in the employ of the sisters, moved very slowly and always followed the same route on his rounds. Their encounter with the guard had shaken them badly and made them doubly cautious now that they knew her absence had been officially reported to the authorities.

"Oh, Patrick, I'm so scared," she said, her arms locked tightly around his neck as he helped her to dismount. "What shall I say? What story can I tell them?"

"I'm afraid you're asking a man who's not a very accomplished liar," he replied. "But one thing's certain, lass. You'd better not tell the truth."

Thoughtfully biting her lip, Micaela agreed that he was probably right, but again promised not to implicate him, no matter how grueling her interrogation. "I would never betray my promise to you," she vowed, and then asked him to give her an assist over the fence.

"With pleasure." He crouched down and directed her to climb onto his shoulders.

"Patrick . . . ?" she began hesitantly.

"What?"

"Will we see each other soon?" she blurted out. "I hope we will."

"I hope so, too."

"It will be difficult."

"We'll find a way," he assured her.

"Promise me we'll be together again," she persisted, her eyes pleading with him.

"Of course we will. Now, put your feet on my shoulders . . ."

Her feet planted on his shoulders as he directed, she tightly gripped his hands as he sprang to his full height, lifting her high in the air and catapulting her over the fence onto the soft, damp grass on the other side.

"Goodbye, lass," he called out in a loud whisper.

"Goodbye, Patrick," she called back, and heard him disappear into the night.

Micaela sped across the lawn to the bathing wing of the convent, and finding a window unlatched, climbed through. Getting out, she concluded, had been far easier than getting back in. Once inside the narrow bathing stall, she doffed her man's attire, rolled it into a ball, and stuffed it under the high, cast-iron bathtub. Later, she would return the clothing to the trunk at her leisure. Naked, she was about to reach for the muslin nightgown hanging on the back of the door when it was suddenly flung open and a smoking whale-oil lamp was shoved in her face. Micaela squealed and attempted to cover her nakedness with her hands.

"So it's you, is it?" the stern voice of the Mother Superior intoned. "Cover your body at once and follow me to my office."

Micaela did as she was told and meekly entered the cold, forbidding room. The austere head nun ordered her to kneel on the floor in front of the enormous crucifix.

"Keep your eyes on our Saviour," she directed. "It is He who will ultimately judge you for your actions."

Pacing back and forth, her slender, aristocratic hands tucked inside the sleeves of her habit, Mother Germaine struggled to remain calm and in control of her anger. "I needn't tell you the great distress you have caused me and the sisters of this convent. The concern and anguish we have suffered over your whereabouts and your safety have been enormous. I was forced to notify your cousin, Monsieur Delaronde, as well as the authorities. You've always been a difficult girl, with little respect for rules or authority, and I have been willing to overlook many things, but this 'disappearance,' I assure you, will not be ignored. In all the years of this school nothing like this has ever happened before. Girls of your background simply do not 'run away.' It's unheard of."

"I'm truly sorry, Reverend Mother," Micaela said, trying to sound genuinely contrite.

"I hope you are sincere in that, not just for my sake or the sake of the sisters here, but for your own sake as well. Do you wish to begin by telling me exactly where you have been? We expected to find your body in the Mississippi or cut up in pieces in some muddy alley. You're lucky you're alive, young lady."

"I was nowhere in particular," Micaela replied, feeling instantly foolish at having engaged in such blatant evasiveness.

"Do you expect me to believe that you ran away from this convent in the middle of the night to go 'nowhere in particular'?" Mother Germaine struggled to restrain her outrage at such an answer. "I want to know specifically where you went."

"I went down the river," Micaela offered feebly. "On a boat."

"Whom were you with?"

"A friend."

"What friend?"

"Just a friend, Reverend Mother."

"A male friend?"

Micaela hesitated before sheepishly replying, "Yes, Reverend Mother."

Mother Germaine raised her eyebrows. "Who was this male friend?"

"I prefer not to say."

"Let me give you a choice. Either you inform me who your male companion was so that I may take appropriate action where he is concerned, or you will be expelled from school. Is that clear?"

"Yes, Reverend Mother," Micaela acknowledged, adding, "But I cannot tell you. I have given my word."

"To this man?"

"Yes, Reverend Mother."

Mother Germaine folded her arms. "Then I assume you are prepared to take the consequences?"

Micaela nodded, tears beginning to glaze her eyes. As much as she feared expulsion from school, she could not bring herself to break her promise to Patrick.

Pierre, frantic when he had received the notification from Mother Germaine of his cousin's disappearance, lost no time in arriving at the school after learning of her safe return.

Although always lenient and easygoing with Micaela in the past, he was incensed by her recent escapade, more because of the anguish he had suffered over her welfare than anything else.

Before leaving the convent with Micaela in tow, he promised the head nun that he would continue to question Micaela at Versailles until the whole story was disclosed and the culprit responsible for leading his cousin astray was punished.

"Her mother and I are anxious that she complete her studies at the school," he said, requesting that Mother Germaine leave the matter to him and not inform Micaela's mother.

"But, Monsieur Delaronde, I have already dispatched a letter to Madame Castillon in Paris," the Mother Superior told him. "It was my duty to notify her at once. A parent must know of these things, distressing as they may be. I wanted to prepare her in case—"

"You should have asked me first," he snapped, and taking Micaela by the hand, left the convent.

When they reached Versailles, Micaela observed that a barge, heavy with marble, rare woods, glass, and other materials that Patrick had purchased from Lafitte at Grande Terre, was docked at the plantation batture and was being unloaded by the Delaronde slaves.

"You, of course, went to Grande Terre with Lynch, didn't you?" Pierre guessed correctly. "Don't lie and try to deceive me. I am too much of a liar myself not to know whether somebody is telling the truth or not."

"Yes, Pierre," she confessed with her eyes lowered. She felt safe telling him, believing it would go no further.

"Damn!" He banged his fist against the side of the carriage. "It's my fault for allowing you to hang around him so much. I should never have permitted it."

"I'm sorry," she murmured, confident that she could eventually smooth things over with her cousin.

"The best thing that can happen now is for your mother to arrange a quick wedding," he declared.

"What?" Micaela was aghast.

"It's the only way a major scandal can be avoided."

The idea of marrying Patrick Lynch was most appealing to her, and Micaela broke into a wide smile. "Is that to be my punishment?" she asked.

"It'll be a punishment, all right," he assured her.

"I don't think it would be so unpleasant to be married to Mr. Lynch," she mused. "He's a rather nice gentleman."

"It isn't Mr. Lynch you'll be marrying," Pierre informed her.

"Why? Just because he isn't a Creole?"

Pierre gave an ironic laugh. "Just because he isn't a Creole?" he repeated incredulously. "My God, girl, you go running off with the man and you don't even know?"

"Know what?" she said, mystified.

"Mr. Lynch happens to be a married man. He has a wife and a child in New York."

14

IN REPLY TO Mother Germaine's letter informing Louise of Micaela's unexplained disappearance and that the probable consequence of her obstinate refusal to divulge the details of her absence would be expulsion from school, Louise wrote:

I shall prepare to leave at once for America, even though my husband, who has been ill for some time, has recently taken a turn for the worse. When I arrive I shall take matters into my own hands, but until I do, it is my wish that my daughter be entrusted to my nephew, Pierre Delaronde's, care. She will be confined to her room at Versailles and allowed to see no one. I will have to assess what harm has been done by this unfortunate incident and will then decide how best to remedy the situation. Naturally, I apologize for the anguish my daughter's shocking behavior has undoubtedly caused, and I am certain that it is of little comfort for me to say that whatever distress you have suffered has been very small in relation to my own.

One morning as Pierre and Pelagie were lying in bed, he brought up the matter with her. Earlier, the slave had entered the main house and gone up to his room by the little-used back stairs, as she had been compelled to do since becoming the young planter's mistress.

"It seems like Miss Louise is makin' a lot out of this," Pelagie mused as she traced circles with her forefinger on Pierre's bare chest.

"You don't understand," he said impatiently. "It's very serious."

"What don't I understand?" she challenged. "Of course I do. Miss Louise is worried that Miss Micaela has gone and ruined the chances of gettin' herself married good because she ran off for a few days with that architect fellow who was hangin' around here."

"There's more to it than that."

"When Miss Louise dies, Miss Micaela is gonna inherit all her money, ain't she?"

"Yes, but what has that got to do with it?"

"Well, that is gonna make her a mighty rich lady. I think plenty of men are willin' to overlook whatever she done if she's as rich as everybody says she's gonna be. I've yet to see a stain so bad that enough money couldn't rub it out."

Reaching for a cigar from the humidor beside the bed, Pierre bit off the tip and indicated to Pelagie that he wanted her to light it. She got out of bed and searched for some matches.

"I'll tell you one thing," Pierre said. "Lynch is through around here. I intend to dismiss him as soon as he shows his face."

"What are you gonna go and do that for?" she asked. "Especially since you already told me over and over how much you like what he's doin' on that theater of yours."

"He ought to be ashamed of himself," the Creole planter fumed. "A man his age—and a married man with a family—seducing a young, innocent girl like Micaela. He ought to be arrested, placed in the pillories in the main square, and horsewhipped. If Aunt Louise hadn't forbade me, by God, I'd challenge him to a duel myself."

Pelagie looked at him skeptically and struck a match on the sole of her bare, calloused foot. Touching the flame to the end of his cigar, she said, "I suppose you ain't never done nothin' to be ashamed of?"

"Not like that," he snapped.

At that moment they were both startled by the sound of a horse and rider in the carriageway below. Pelagie went to the window, and peeked through the white gauze curtains.

"Speakin' of the devil," she announced. "It looks like your man's here right now."

Pierre puffed rapidly on the cigar. "He's got a lot of damned nerve showing his face around here."

"He has work to complete," she reminded him.

"I don't care about the theater any more."

"I think you're actin' mighty silly about all this."

"If I want your opinion, I'll ask for it. Otherwise keep your mouth shut."

"Yes, sir, marse boss man," she replied, mocking the obsequiousness of a field hand.

"Get me my clothes," he demanded. "I want to go out there and have a talk with him right now. He'll do nothing more on my theater. As far as I'm concerned, a man's principles are reflected in his work, and his are plainly shoddy."

"I sure am glad I ain't white," Pelagie sighed, tossing Pierre his shirt and a pair of trousers. "All you white folks are such damned hypocrites. There ain't nothin' Mr. Lynch has done that you ain't done yourself. And more than once, too!"

Patrick stood in the center of the unique little theater, admiring his design and contemplating how it would look when he installed the fine fixtures he had purchased from Jean Lafitte, which now lay all about him in packing cases. This theater would be a lavish showplace to which the Delarondes could summon that excellent company of French actors, refugees from the uprising in Santo Domingo, who performed regularly in the theater on St. Peter Street. Many of the guests whom the Delarondes would entertain had traveled to Europe many times and been exposed to the excellent theaters there. Patrick was confident that his structure would rank with the finest the continent had to offer. When the guests attended performances in it, they would undoubtedly pass on their compliments to Pierre and perhaps, hopefully, inquire about the name of the architect. Because of this elegant little edifice, Patrick prayed that he would become firmly established within both the Creole and the American communities and that he would no longer be considered an interloper but a respected professional.

As he paced about the empty auditorium he thought about Micaela and the day that he had lifted her off the stage when she was declaiming Phèdre's dramatic speech. How he longed to hold her again. Since their return from Grande Terre, he had had no word from her and had begun to be concerned. If she had met with difficulties, he would have no way of knowing it. He was filled with yearning as he recalled her musical voice, the fresh scent of her creamy skin and long, silky red hair, her innocent, yet wildly passionate lovemaking. When he closed his eyes, he could feel her eager fingers digging into his back; could hear soft moans in his ear. How he wanted to see her again, but he knew that was impossible as long as she was behind the walls of the convent. While they were apart, he consoled himself with the thought that his work at Versailles would require several more weeks to complete, and he felt confident he would see her again during that time.

His musings were interrupted by the approach of Pierre, who looked rather agitated and he rhythmically slapped the open palm of his hand with his riding crop.

"Good morning, sir," Patrick said affably.

"I'm afraid I have some rather unpleasant news for you this morning, Lynch," Pierre informed him.

"Unpleasant?" Patrick repeated with a puzzled frown.

Deciding to come right to the point, Pierre said, "I am forced to dismiss you from this project."

Patrick was stunned. "What?" he exclaimed. "Dismiss me *now?*"

"You will be paid in full according to our contract, but I am terminating your professional services immediately."

Dumbfounded, the architect asked, "May I know your reasons, sir?"

"Of course. I was going to get to that in a minute, anyway. I refuse to tolerate the presence of a man who is the seducer of my young cousin."

Incredulous at what he was hearing, Patrick repeated, "The seducer . . . ?"

"You needn't affirm or deny it. To discuss it further would aggravate me even more. Believe me, Lynch, I am being more than lenient with you. If my aunt hadn't forbidden it, I'd avenge her honor in a more satisfying fashion."

"I am hardly a seducer, sir," Patrick protested, dismayed that Micaela had betrayed her promise and apparently incriminated him, even though he had tried to prevent her from tagging along.

"I said that we will talk no more about it," Pierre grunted. "Understand, Lynch, this is no reflection on your work, which has been excellent. I am greatly disappointed. No one was looking forward to the completion of this theater more than I. Now it will have to be either abandoned or turned over to someone else to complete."

"Abandoned? Turned over to someone else?" To abandon work on the theater, a project he had grown to love, was, for Patrick, like asking a father to give up his child. Sadly he glanced around at the various crates containing the articles of trim he had been looking forward to installing. "I can't do that, Mr. Delaronde," he said.

"You can and you will," Pierre declared. "I will give you fifteen minutes to climb on your horse and get out of here."

"May I ask where Micaela is and what has happened to her?" Patrick felt that if perhaps he could see her, could hear her story, the devastating situation might somehow be remedied and their relationship and the theater project saved.

"On the orders of her mother, my cousin is confined to her room here and will remain so until my aunt arrives from France," the Creole planter informed him.

"May I be permitted to speak to her for a moment?"

"How dare you ask such a thing?" Pierre snapped, his dark eyes flashing with anger. "Besides, Micaela no longer wishes to see you. I repeat, Lynch, you are a very lucky man. I have every justification for killing you. The only thing that restrains me is my aunt's express insistence against a duel."

"And I assume you have no wish to hear my side of the story?"

"Do you deny that you were with my cousin?"

"No, I don't."

"Do you deny that you failed to return her to the convent the moment you learned that she had run away?"

"There was no changing her mind. Micaela is a very strong-willed, determined girl. She begged me, and I admit that I was weak." Patrick sighed heavily.

"That's no excuse," Pierre countered. "You are a man, and one who's nearly ten years her senior. It's your will that should have won out."

"True, sir, but—"

"Enough, Lynch!" Pierre bellowed. "Get out of here as fast as you can if you know what's good for you! I just might lose my temper yet and forget about my aunt's edict!" With that he slapped the wall angrily with the riding crop and stomped out of the theater, leaving Patrick feeling utterly bewildered and dismayed.

From the window of her second-floor room Micaela had seen Patrick arrive and enter the theater, to be followed a short while later by Pierre. The two men had apparently exchanged angry words, because Pierre emerged looking furious and went straight to the stables. A few moments later he galloped across the cane fields at breakneck speed. As far as she could tell, Patrick was still in the theater and probably alone.

I must see him. I must talk to him, she said to herself as she searched about the locked room for some means of escape. For days she had agonized over Pierre's disclosure of Patrick's supposed married state; she had to learn directly from him if it was true. She also wanted him to know that she had not betrayed him to Pierre. Taking a buttonhook from the dresser, she pried it into the keyhole and wiggled it around until she felt something give. Turning the knob, she was astonished and gratified to hear the latch click and see the door open.

Afraid that if she dashed down the stairs and through the house she might be apprehended by the colonel or one of the slaves, she chose to go out the gallery through the adjoining room, whereupon she climbed over the railing, seized the branches of a wisteria tree, and dropped to the ground, landing on her bottom in a flower bed. Jumping up and dusting herself off, she raced toward the theater.

Entering the foyer, she was surprised to hear what sounded like someone chopping wood.

What on earth can be going on? she wondered.

As she went into the main auditorium she saw Patrick with an ax in his hand, his face flushed, his fair hair flying about his face, and was shocked to realize in his fury tht he was attacking the very building itself. This perception made her totally forget that she had come to question him about his alleged wife and child.

"Patrick!" she cried. "What are you doing?"

Barely breaking the rhythm with which he swung the ax, he replied, "What in the hell does it look like?"

"Stop! You mustn't," she pleaded.

"Get out of here and let me alone," he snapped,

and continued the frenzied task of destroying the theater.

"I know Pierre is angry and may have dismissed you, but it's not my fault. Honestly. I had nothing to do with it. You must understand that. I told Pierre nothing. He guessed it all." She choked on her words as tears began streaming down her cheeks.

"And you were kind enough to tell him he was right?" Patrick paused long enough to wipe the sweat from his forehead.

"I told him nothing. He was able to surmise everything." She was nearly overcome with anguish and desperation. How could she possibly make him believe she had nothing to do with Pierre's action, that she had not betrayed her promise to him?

"Get out before I lose all control," he warned.

"Let me talk to Pierre," she begged. "Perhaps I can change his mind."

Glaring at her, he said, "Haven't you done enough already?"

"I'm sorry, Patrick. Honestly I am. Please believe me."

"You and your silly little schoolgirl caprices have ruined me, ruined everything I've strived for!"

"I'm sorry—"

"Sorry, are you?" he cut her off. "A fine lot of good that does. What do you know? What do you care? You're nothing but a pampered, spoiled, rich brat with a head full of nothing but your own desires. What do you care about me? What do you care about anyone or anything?"

Attempting to approach him, she cried, "But I do care about you, Patrick. I do. I swear I do!"

Starting to swing the ax once more, he retorted, "The hell you do. Now go on and get out of here before you get hurt."

"Please, Patrick, listen to me. I beg you—"

"I've listened to you for the last time," he declared, and brought the ax down with a splintering crash against an important supporting column. The roof began to creak and groan, as if it might collapse at any moment.

"Stop, Patrick!" she screamed, glancing fearfully at the ceiling. "You must stop this destruction!"

"If I can't finish this theater, I'm going to see that nobody else does, by God," he vowed.

Spotting a crated French mirror, he raised the ax once more and smashed it against the box, shattering the glass and sending a hail of silver slivers, like a shower of meteors, throughout the once-beautiful theater.

15

FOLLOWING PATRICK LYNCH'S ax attack on the theater, the next event to cause havoc at Versailles was the arrival of Louise from Paris.

In the room where she was confined, Micaela awaited the face-to-face meeting with her mother with great anxiety, not knowing what Louise had in store for her. Thus, when she heard the clatter of a horse and carriage in the carriageway, she knew that the moment she had been dreading had finally arrived. Almost at once, Micaela's stomach began to churn and a great lump rose in her throat, choking off her breath. She was suddenly aware that facing Louise could easily be worse than facing the Reverend Mother had been. She could only hope for the best.

Pierre was the first of the Delarondes to greet Louise as she swept up the stairs to the gallery, trailed by Flore.

"Dearest Aunt," he said, taking her hands in his and kissing both her cheeks. "Please sit down." He indicated the white wicker settee beneath the striped awning. "You must be hot and tired after your trip. Let me have Roland bring you a cool drink."

"Thank you, Pierre," Louise murmured, dabbing at her temples with a cologne-soaked handkerchief. "That would be very nice."

Over iced drinks, nephew and aunt made the usual

polite small talk. He inquired about the health of Castillon, and she, about his mother and her brother.

"The colonel is fine, his usual old blustery self," Pierre chuckled. "And Mother is no worse than usual."

"I wish I could say that Castillon is well, but, alas, such is not the case." Louise was anxious to get to the real purpose of her hasty transatlantic journey, so she dispensed with the casual conversation and came right to the point. "And Micaela? Where is she?"

"Upstairs in her room," he replied. "Awaiting you. Please, Aunt Louise, for my sake, try not to be too harsh with the girl. She's already suffered considerably for her transgressions, which I now believe was not entirely her fault. Being expelled from school and separated from her friends has not been easy for her."

Seemingly unmoved by his plea for leniency, Louise rose and headed toward the front door. "We shall see what we shall see."

Following her inside, Pierre continued, "There are some factors of which you may not be aware."

"I believe that Mother Germaine's letter was quite comprehensive," she said. "I feel she has informed me of all that I need to know. Micaela has been expelled from school for disciplinary reasons. What more is there to know? I think that's quite sufficient."

"I suppose you'll be taking her back to France with you?" he asked.

"Simply coming here and taking Micaela away to France is not the answer. That would merely be running away and could aggravate the situation. The distressing incident occurred here, and it is here that it must be remedied," Louise declared. "One way or another."

"May I be bold enough to ask what you have in mind? You see, since I have been more or less looking after Micaela in your absence, dear Aunt, I have developed not only a strong attachment for the girl but also an interest in her welfare."

"Let's just say, dear Nephew, that I have made some plans for her future that as yet are neither definite nor implemented," Louise replied, starting up the wide staircase. "Therefore, I have no wish to disclose the details at this time."

It was necessary for Aunt Sally to unlock the door so that Louise might enter her daughter's room. As they stood facing each other, Micaela was surprised to see that her mother still retained much of her beauty, despite her evident weariness from the trip.

"Don't stand there staring at me as if I were a ghost," Louise admonished. "Come and kiss me. I'm still your mother, even if it has been nearly seven years since we've seen each other."

Micaela crossed the room and embraced Louise. Her mother was still her mother, and Micaela realized she loved her in spite of the resentment she harbored at having been abandoned when Louise went off to live in France with Castillon.

"Mama . . ." she said, on the verge of tears.

"Micaela, dearest," Louise murmured. "Come, now, you mustn't cry. There's nothing to cry about. Nothing at all. Nothing that can't be remedied."

She handed her daughter a delicate lace handkerchief impregnated with expensive French cologne and urged her to dry her eyes.

"How is Monsieur Castillon?" Micaela asked politely.

"Not well." Louise shook her head. "It's been a difficult chore caring for him. I hated leaving him behind, but it was not possible for him to make the voyage."

"I'm sorry . . ."

With an impatient wave of her hand, Louise put an end to the small talk. "We'd best come to the point at once. As you know, I made this journey because of serious matters of which I was informed by Mother Germaine. I assume you are aware of what I'm talking about, are you not?"

"I think so, Mama."

"She wrote me that you fled the school one night and mysteriously disappeared for a number of days with a man whose identity you refused to disclose. You also refused to admit your whereabouts during that time, except to say that you had been on a river trip. As a result of your obstinacy in refusing to cooperate, the Reverend Mother has found it necessary to expel you from school. Is that correct?"

Micaela nodded.

"From this point on, I suppose it's a matter of repairing things as best we can. During the crossing I had considerable time to think about this matter and formulate a plan of action. Since you are already seventeen and obviously not very serious about your education, I think it is time you married," Louise said flatly.

"Married?" Micaela repeated with a gasp. The possibility had occurred to her, but she had stubbornly refused to consider it.

"Yes. I would like to announce your engagement as soon as possible. The faster we go about our business, the less chance our enemies will have to indulge in slander and vicious gossip. In other words, the quicker you are married, the easier any possible scandal can be averted," she explained.

Baffled and confused, Micaela asked, "But whom am I to marry?"

"That will still have to be decided," Louise answered. "At the moment, there is a wonderful young man whom I would like very much for you. He is the son of my first cousin Joseph Delfau, the Baron de Pontalba. The boy was born in Louisiana but raised in France. You've never met him, but his parents remember you when you were very young. The baron and his wife, Jeanne, were at your father's investiture as a Knight of the Order of Charles the Fourth."

"You want me to marry a man I've never met?" Micaela was stunned.

"Many girls never know their husbands prior to marriage. They rely solely on the judgment of their parents. In this case, you must put your trust in me and bear in mind that whatever I do is for your own good. This young Pontalba, a foreigner, seems ideal."

"Why a foreigner, Mama?"

"Because I doubt if the young swains from the better families here will be avidly seeking your hand once the scandal of your expulsion from school gets around."

"It's not a scandal, Mama," Micaela protested. "At least not yet. All anyone knows is that I've been dismissed from school."

"That fact is scandal enough. I am sure that the gossips of this city are circulating at least a dozen different explanations right now, each worse than the other." Louise's tone grew hard. "Naturally, I am aware that there are undoubtedly many fortune hunters and social climbers who would be quite happy to overlook any scandal at all and marry you, but that's not what I want. As I see it, dear, the most logical choice at this point for a husband is an outsider, one apart from the social world of this city. That's why I feel Celestin is perfect."

"Who on earth is Celestin?" Micaela asked.

"He's the baron's son, of course, and I can assure you he has all the correct qualifications. He's twenty, and thus, three years older than you—a proper age difference, not that it matters so much. Already he has distinguished himself in the service of Emperor Napoleon. I'm told by the best authorities that he is intelligent, sensitive, gentlemanly, and well educated." From her purse Louise extracted a delicate porcelain miniature and passed it to Micaela. "And as you can see from this portrait, he's also quite handsome."

Micaela dutifully inspected the face in the miniature and observed that her mother was correct. The young man's portrait indicated that, with his dark eyes, pale skin, rosy cheeks, and mass of jet black curls framing his fine features, he was indeed very good-looking. How different this delicate face was, she thought, from Patrick's with its crooked nose, pale blue, squinting eyes, and freckled, ruddy skin coarsened by the sun and the elements.

"He looks very nice," Micaela remarked indifferently, and handed the miniature back to her mother. She wondered if Louise really intended for her to marry this French youth on whom she had never laid eyes. Granted, he did have a pleasant, sensitive face, but that was scarcely sufficient grounds for marriage. Besides, she was in love with Patrick Lynch—married or not—and her present emotional state would not allow her to consider anyone else. Suddenly realizing that her mother was serious about her marrying, Micaela decided she would have preferred Louise's anger instead.

"Is that all you can say?" Louise chided.

"Do you mean about this Celestin?"

"Let me tell you a few things about him, young lady," Louise continued, as if she hadn't noticed Micaela's obvious lack of interest. "First of all, he's the only child of the baron and will therefore inherit the title and all that goes with it. If you marry him, you will, of course, be the Baroness de Pontalba someday." Louise's eyes were bright in eager anticipation of the respectability that an aristocratic title would bestow on the Almonester wealth. "Think of it! You will be a noblewoman with a lovely château in the Oise district of France, a fortunate young lady indeed. No more will we be looked upon as merely rich, vulgar Americans. We will enjoy an ancient title and be members of the finest European aristocracy. That is, if the baron will consent to this match for his son."

"If Celestin is as eligible as you say, Mama, then surely every young woman in France must be pursuing him."

"I suppose many are."

"Then why should he want to marry me?"

"And why not? You are quite pretty, although you have unfortunately inherited your father's rather long face. It's a pity you couldn't favor the Delarondes more in looks, but no matter. You are intelligent and well bred. You have a gift for drawing, according to the nuns, although little for music or needlework, I'm afraid," Louise sighed.

"Many girls have such qualifications," Micaela said reasonably.

Louise sighed again, and continued in an entirely different, more serious tone. "Few girls anywhere will be as rich as you, my dear. You might as well know that now. My dear cousin Joseph Delfau has a hunger for wealth and the prestige it affords in this new, more materialistic world in which we live, which knows no bounds. He is literally obsessed. He cannot possess enough. Curiously, it is the possession of wealth, not the enjoyment of it, that is his obsession."

Micaela had never heard her mother speak with such candidness before. In the past she had always been most reticent to discuss the family's wealth or the shortcomings of relatives.

"Are you saying that Celestin's father, the baron, is greedy, Mama?"

"Since childhood, Cousin Joseph, as I call him, although he much prefers the title of baron, has always had to possess more than anyone else—more toy soldiers, more stuffed animals, more building blocks. He can never be truly satisfied. Because he lived here in Louisiana for many years, he acquired some holdings, but nothing in comparison to your late father's estate, however, a fact of which he is well aware. In France, where he has resided for years, he has land, jewels, and, of course, his château, Mont L'Eveque. One would think he has enough to satisfy any normal man, but he always lusts for more."

Frowning, Micaela asked, "Just how do I figure in his lust for wealth, Mama?"

"Cousin Joseph is aware of the vast fortune I now control. He knows Louisiana well enough to realize that Don Andrés made some excellent investments. Your father, God rest his soul, had an uncanny instinct for recognizing a profitable thing when he saw it. The baron knows how enormously these holdings of your father's have appreciated. He is also cognizant that, since moving to Paris with Jean-Baptiste, I have made additional investments in Parisian real estate, which have been most excellent as well. In short, my dear cousin respects me not only for my fortune but also for my ability to increase it, an ability I acquired from your father.

"Although the baron has minor holdings in America," Louise went on, "the majority of his property is in France. Very soon, whether we like it or not, Louisiana will become a state in the United States, America is not threatened by class strife and discontent, which could once again rip apart the very fabric of French society. Despite the appearance of the apparent stability that Napoleon has brought to France, discontent still rages beneath the surface, unsatisfied by the bloodshed and chaos of the Revolution. When Napoleon is gone, who knows what will happen to France?

"But getting back to the baron, he realizes that should another revolution occur, he could well lose his holdings in France."

Micaela nodded. "What you are saying, Mama, is that with my American wealth I will bring safety and stability to the baron's fortunes. Is that correct?"

"What a quick mind you have," Louise said with a smile. "Just like your father."

"In other words, if I should marry this Celestin, I am exchanging my wealth for the Pontalba title and prestige."

"And rescuing your good name as well," Louise reminded her. "Don't overlook that. It's no small matter, you know. After all, you brought this on yourself with your recklessness."

"You're *buying* me a husband, aren't you, Mama?"

"Yes—if you choose to look at it that way," Louise conceded. "But a lovely, titled husband."

Micaela shook her head in bewilderment. "I can't believe you are doing such a thing, Mama."

"All I am merely trying to do is to insure your future happiness," Louise insisted. "That's the most any parent can offer a child."

During the subsequent weeks of her stay at Versailles, Louise actively pursued various business matters and spent much of her time with her lawyer and trusted adviser, François LeBreton. Because of her involvement with LeBreton and with several other lawyers and agents, she had little time for Micaela, and since she had released her from her confinement to the house, the girl was more or less free to come and go as she pleased.

One afternoon, however, Louise did not go to the city as usual but remained instead in her room, working on a letter to the Baron de Pontalba. When she felt she had completed a satisfactory draft, she summoned Micaela and asked her to read it.

Dearest Cousin,
I have shown my daughter, Micaela, the portrait of your Celestin, and she is quite taken with him. She has asked me to beg you to send him to us as soon as possible. What a fine match that would be, my Micaela and your Celestin. They seem truly made for one another.

I must, however, warn you that I am afraid some people, prompted by selfish and jealous motives, might try to prevent this union. Be on your guard against such individuals and discount any letters you might receive conveying untrue and malicious gossip about my daughter. Our wealth and status make many people envious and anxious to harm us.

Give my regards to dearest Jeanne and to her aunt, Madame Miró, as well. I have not forgotten them.

My daughter assures you of her respectful love.
Sincerely,
Louise

"Well, what do you think?" Louise asked anxiously when Micaela had finished reading the letter.

"I think that you have presumed quite a lot, Mama," she replied indignantly.

Louise snatched the letter out of her hand. "Nevertheless, I shall send it."

"I can't stop you," Micaela admitted resignedly.

"No, you can't," Louise said angrily. Folding the sheet of paper, she slipped it into an envelope, and tilting the candle, sealed the flap with wax.

With that gesture Micaela felt as if the fate of her future had been sealed as well.

16

IN A RETURN letter the Baron de Pontalba enthusiastically agreed to a meeting of the young people, just as Louise had predicted he would, and promised to send Celestin to New Orleans as soon as possible.

Panicked by the imminent arrival of the young Pontalba, Micaela racked her brain to think of some way to extricate herself from the present dilemma. She had no wish to be forced into a hasty wedding just to save her reputation.

In a letter from Baton Rouge, where she was spending the summer under watchful eyes at her father's plantation, Claire Villegrande wrote that the news of Micaela's expulsion from school had filtered outside the convent walls and circulated through New Orleans society. "Naturally everyone is shocked," Claire wrote, "and saying you were expelled from school for running off with an older man who was not a Creole. How do they ever learn these things? How tongues do wag!"

Pacing back and forth across her room, Micaela wondered how she could avoid marrying this future French baron. Whatever plan she decided on would have to be carried out quickly. Once he arrived, it would be too late, unless, of course, he refused to marry her, which was unlikely because, according to Louise, young Celestin was under his father's thumb and quite willing to carry out his wishes.

Since the Baron de Pontalba himself seemed so eager for the proposed match, Louise's spirits soared, despite her concern for Micaela's reputation and for her ill husband in Paris, and she busily set out to prepare for such an eventuality. Rather than the usual gowns, flowers, refreshments, and guest lists, Louise's preparations were centered about such matters as dowries and prenuptial financial arrangements.

Despite the fact that Micaela found herself free from the restrictions that had been placed on her,

Louise had Binnie brought from the Bayou Road plantation, where she had been assigned to the cookhouse, and installed her once again as her daughter's personal maid, instructing her to keep a good eye on Micaela.

"I'll try, Miss Louise, but it ain't gonna be easy," the young black girl said.

"Monsieur LeBreton is arranging for Binnie to become part of your dowry," Louise informed Micaela.

Because of her low spirits, Micaela had little inclination to take advantage of her restored liberty, until she had formulated a scheme, one that was a long shot but might serve to rescue her.

"Mama, if Celestin is to arrive soon, I think I should have some new frocks made, don't you?" she asked Louise one day.

Her mother, surprised by this sudden display of interest in the upcoming visit of her prospective suitor, was only too happy to comply.

"Nothing would please me more, dear, than to have you be the most fashionable and attractive girl upon whom the future baron will cast his eyes," she said. "Cost is no object. You may order whatever you desire. I shall impose no limits on you." These were indeed extravagant words from the usually frugal Louise.

Micaela rode to the city in her mother's own carriage, driven by their former coachman, Freddie, who, like Binnie, had been transferred to Versailles from Louise's plantation. With Binnie in tow, she went through the ordeal of measurements and fittings at the dressmaker's, milliner's, and glovemaker's. The two young women, slave and mistress, were almost instantly as close as they had been as children, despite the fact that they had been separated for seven years, and Binnie was glad to be a lady's maid again, freed from plantation cookhouse duties. The day was extremely hot, even for summer, and Micaela was most uncomfortable in the thick green barège veil and gloves her mother and Aunt Eulalie had insisted she wear.

"Only married women wear veils and gloves to town," Micaela had protested.

"Well, now is a good time to get used to them," Louise had responded. "After all, you may be a married woman very soon."

On the pretense that she had forgotten her gloves in one of the shops, Micaela sent Binnie back to look for them. The moment the slave was out of sight, she headed straight for Patrick's office.

Racing up the steps two at a time, smiling inwardly when she thought of how horrified the nuns would have been to know what she was doing, Micaela knocked at the door at the top of the landing and waited breathlessly for a response from within. She had no idea how Patrick would receive her or if he was in.

Eventually he opened the door, and seeing her standing there, looked quite startled.

"Micaela . . ." he said quietly.

"May I come in?" She hoped her tremulous voice did not betray her uneasiness at their meeting. She was considerably apprehensive about seeing him again, recalling the angry, violent scene in the now destroyed little theater.

"Of course." He opened the door wider. "How did you get here? I thought they would have you under lock and key at Versailles again."

"They did," she replied. "But my mother arrived and let me out."

Patrick smiled ironically. "I had no doubt your mother would come when she got wind of your little escapade."

"She's trying to arrange a marriage for me," Micaela informed him, and watched carefully for his reaction.

He did not seem surprised. "An advantageous one, I hope? That way at least one of us will make out well from our little bayou excursion. As for me, I would say I'm pretty well finished, at least as far as the Creole community is concerned. Your cousin Pierre saw to that. There's not a Creole in town who would give me a commission now, not even if I were the last architect in New Orleans. By the way, he's also suing me for the damage I inflicted to his theater," he added, patting a stack of official-looking legal papers on his desk.

"So what am I left with?" he went on. "A few crumbs the loyal Irish in town manage to throw me now and again—the ones who aren't starving as cabmen and bellboys, that is. They come to me with such challenging and stimulating jobs as room additions, chimneys, stairways, and the like. That's what I've gotten out of it. At least you'll get a husband. And that's not bad. Maybe that's just what you need, lass."

Dismayed and hurt by his attitude, Micaela asked, "Is that all you're going to say about it?"

"Did I forget something?" He narrowed his eyes at her. "Oh, yes, I did . . . Congratulations."

"You don't understand, Patrick. I don't want to marry."

He shrugged indifferently and said in a rather sarcastic tone, "Well, it's better to marry than to burn, you know."

"The only man I want to marry is you." The words caught in her throat as she realized she had made herself suddenly vulnerable by such a rash confession.

Emitting a slightly sardonic chuckle, he said, "Marry me? Good Lord, lass, do you have any idea what you're saying? Do you realize who you are and who I am? Marry me? Why, that's ridiculous. You are an Almonester, a member of the crème de la crème of this city, while I . . ."

"That's only an accident of birth," she argued.

He laughed again. "An accident of birth, is it?"

"What has that to do with me and the way I feel about you?" she insisted, wondering why he had chosen to refer to their social status rather than to his being married—if, in fact, he really was.

"Let me tell you, my girl, that we are all the products of the accidents of our births," he replied, laying his hands on her shoulders. "I'm a dirt-poor Irishman fresh off the cattle boat, trying to eke out a living in this unfriendly city that resents me for being what I am."

"I don't care about my family or this city or my social position or anything else," Micaela declared, her voice about to crack under the strain of her emotions. "The only thing I care about, Patrick Lynch, is you! How can you punish me for that? I would give up everything for you. What can I do to make you believe me?"

"You're talking nonsense and you know it," he said curtly.

"We don't have to stay here," she went on. "We could go away. We could go to Mobile or Savannah or even New York City."

Patrick frowned and stared at her quizzically. "Why did you mention New York?"

"I don't know. Why?"

"Because it's the one city we *couldn't* go to. Now is as good a time to tell you as any—if you haven't heard already. I have a wife and child in New York."

She had not really believed Pierre when he told her about Patrick's supposed family. On hearing it from Patrick himself, she was stunned and felt her knees grow weak and tremble.

"I suppose I should have told you before," he admitted, his tone softening, his blue eyes gazing at her with sympathetic concern. "I should have told you at the ball on New Year's Eve. That way you wouldn't have wasted your midnight kisses. It was a serious mistake, waiting until now to tell you, and I apologize —for whatever good it does."

"Is this your way of telling me without seeming cruel that you don't really want me?" she asked.

"That I don't want you?" he repeated incredulously. Seizing her, he pulled her close and buried his face in her hair. "I do want you," he whispered. "God knows I do." His warm lips planted a string of kisses on her brow, her closed eyelids, and the edges of her ears. "It's just that I can never make you my wife. A fine girl like you deserves the best—a real husband, a real marriage. You can't have that with me."

"Oh, Patrick, Patrick," she cried in desperation, caressing his strong back and shoulders.

"My wife stayed in New York. She was afraid to come here with the boy because of the yellow fever. We lost a daughter in England, and it broke her heart.

If we lost our small son, I'm afraid it would kill her. I thought if I could build up a good practice here and prove to Emily that New Orleans isn't as unhealthy as she thinks, she might see things differently and eventually join me here."

"Do you miss her?" Micaela asked.

"Yes, sometimes I suppose I do," he allowed. "After all, we have been married a few years. She *is* the mother of my son. I am obliged to honor our vows."

"Do you love her?"

"Love?" he mused. "That's a difficult word to be specific about. It means different things to different people. Perhaps someday when you're older you'll understand all the different shades of that word. In a way, yes, I suppose I do love Emily, although it's not your 'grand passion' kind of love. It's a special relationship. I'm sorry if I hurt you by deceiving you. I had no intention of that. Perhaps if things were less complicated, if there wasn't this difference in our ages and social status . . . if I wasn't married with a family . . . perhaps we could stand some chance together. But as things are, it's best to forget each other."

Gazing up at him with tear-glazed eyes, Micaela said, "I thought you loved me. I wanted to believe you did."

"I did, and in my own way I still do," he assured her. "But you've got to understand—"

Impatiently she interrupted him. "I understand all about your wife and child."

"I love them, too, but in a different way," he went on. "You see, I married Emily when I was a youth, scarcely much older than you are now. I was in England trying to work and study at the same time. I was alone and lonely. The English don't take too kindly to an Irishman in their midst. Emily was kind to me. She was a friend when I had none. When I was kicked by a horse and in danger of losing my leg, it was she who nursed me until it was better. If it weren't for her, I'd have only one leg instead of just a limp. We developed affection and respect for each other. Eventually we married. Perhaps if we had known more about each other, or if the circumstances had been different, we might not have stayed together."

Overcome by the storm of emotion building up inside her, Micaela clung to him despairingly and began to cry.

"Oh, Patrick, I love you so much. Can't you see? Don't you realize . . . ?"

"Yes, I see," he replied sadly. "I realize."

"I can't go through with this marriage to another man," she protested.

"I can't help you, lass." He shook his head. "That's between you and your mother."

"I want only you, Patrick. Don't you understand?"

"There are few times in our lives when we get what we want. Life is mainly enduring the compromises we're forced to accept."

"But I want more than that," she insisted tearfully. "I've got to have more."

"Then I wish you well," he said, kissing her tenderly. "Believe me, lass, I wish you well with all my heart."

On the way back to the shop where she had sent Binnie to look for the gloves, Micaela was grateful, after all, that her mother had insisted she wear the heavy veil. It now concealed her red, swollen eyes and tear-streaked cheeks. She hoped that Binnie would not realize she had been crying and that she wouldn't break down again in the carriage on the way back to Versailles.

How hopeless it all looked now. There seemed to be no way to extricate herself from the oncoming tide of events that appeared destined to sweep her up and pull her under. With Patrick so definitely married, there was no chance of his saving her. In view of his present state, he could offer no escape from the union that her mother and the Baron de Pontalba were so eagerly engineering. If only Celestin would develop an intense dislike for her . . . But even if he did refuse to marry her, what was left? Another arbitrary marriage with another suitor selected by her mother? Undoubtedly. At best, the alternatives looked grim.

"You didn't leave no gloves in that store, Miss Micaela," Binnie informed her, vexed that she had been sent on a wild-goose chase on such a hot day.

"I know. I'm sorry," Micaela said, turning her face away from the slave so that she couldn't see the fresh tears trickling down her cheeks.

17

UNABLE TO SLEEP even after downing several cups of cognac, Captain Armand Dulac parted the flaps of the field tent and wandered out into the hot, dry Portuguese night. Earlier in the evening the young sublieutenant with whom he shared the tent, Celestin de Pontalba, had been summoned to Marshal Ney's headquarters and still had not returned. Dulac could not help wondering why the marshal had suddenly sent for his youthful subordinate—a rather unusual occurrence—athough he was aware that Ney and the youth's father were old friends. He hoped that, whatever the reason for Ney's request, he would not lose the young aristocrat from his staff. Pontalba had proved a valuable asset to the unit, and besides, Dulac would have hated to part with such an excellent chess partner.

To date, the Spanish-Portuguese campaign had been disastrous, a bloody, devastating, wearisome, and ultimately futile effort. Dulac, like Ney himself, was disgusted by the manner in which Messena, another of Napoleon's famed but older marshals, was conducting it. Throughout the entire operation Ney had been deeply resentful of Messena's authority, giving the former smuggler and fruit seller turned army officer only minimal support. Messena had marched them across the vast Iberian Peninsula, over miles of bleak, barren countryside with few remaining inhabitants. During the trek they had scarcely been able to obtain food for the troops or fodder for the horses and were constantly harassed by savage guerrilla attacks as well. Forced to camp in burned-out villages, they had to deal daily with despair and disappointment among the troops.

After undistinguished skirmishes along the route at such places as Ciudad Rodrigo, Almeida, and Busaco, the emperor's Grand Army ultimately found itself at Torres Vedras and up against a vast chain of impregnable fortifications designed to block all approaches to Lisbon.

For six weeks Messena had sought a way through or around the fortifications, but knowing that he did not have enough men to storm Torres Vedras, and unable to progress further, he was forced to order a retreat. Without fuss or bother, the army turned around and began its long march back to Spain once again.

It was during this retreat that the sullen and cantankerous Michel Ney had pulled himself together and finally supplied Messena with the kind of support for which he was known. With Ney virtually taking over command of the retreat, Wellington, their crafty and capable British opponent, found his troops confronting a resolute rear guard every morning, much to his dismay.

Now that they had reached the Spanish-Portuguese border, Dulac began to fear that Messena's pride would flare up and that he would seize the leadership from Ney and insist on staying in Portugal to mount another offensive later in the year. The proud old field marshal wanted revenge against Wellington, the man who he felt had injured his reputation. In any case, Dulac knew there was nothing he could do except obediently curb his impatience and wait in this desolate, burned-out, Godforsaken country until a decision was reached. Like all military men, his duty was to follow the orders of his superiors.

As Dulac strolled among the cluster of tents where his men lay sleeping, he felt the hot, dusty wind on his face and listened to the horses quietly munching on their meager rations of straw and hay. His soldier's eye and ear were ever alert for the possibility of danger from the Portuguese guerrillas hiding in the surrounding canyons and hills. Carried on the wind was the odor of fire-demolished farms and rotting animal carcasses, which sickened him faintly. All his life he had been a soldier, having run away from his detested stepfather's farm at twelve to join the army. In the subsequent years, more than two decades, he had known little else.

Starting as a lowly groom, he had cared for the sweaty, lathery mounts of the cavalry and learned all he could. At a very young age he had become an expert with all manner of weapons. Beginning in the dragoons, a heavily armed, mounted infantry unit, he had quickly progressed when his diligence, skill with weapons, and dedication attracted the attention of higher-ups. His greatest advancement had occurred, however, when Napoleon, with his notions of equality, took over the army. Almost at once Dulac had sprung from the humble enlisted ranks to that of a commissioned officer. With Ney's Sixth Corps he had distinguished himself at the battles of Austerlitz, Jena, Eylau, and Friedland and ascended to the rank of captain, which he now held.

Because of his dedication to the Grand Army, Dulac had little time for other things, including a wife and family. In his mid-thirties, he now found himself with only his beloved vocation for consolation. Aloof and somewhat reserved, he devoted himself almost obsessively to duty. Only because of their love of chess and their continuous association on the battlefield had he opened himself up slightly to young Pontalba.

Celestin de Pontalba, on the other hand, was the complete opposite of Dulac. He had not come up through the ranks but had begun as Ney's aide-de-camp; for a time he had even been Napoleon's personal page. From all indications, he had served both illustrious leaders well. His record was distinguished for one so young, and since his assignment to the Fifteenth Light Cavalry Regiment, he had conducted himself well and discharged his duties in fine fashion. In fact, Dulac admired the determined and thorough way he set about things, bent on carrying out orders to the letter. If anything, young Pontalba was too dedicated. Dulac wished he would devote more time to their chess games.

Ordinarily this subordinate would have been a target of Dulac's contempt. When the captain had first seen him, he had decided that Pontalba was more than likely another spoiled, pampered son of a wealthy and landed aristocrat who had been sent to the army to while away a few years respectably before retiring to the country, where he could forever reminisce about his days in the emperor's service. With his huge, vulnerable-looking dark eyes, slender nose, and perfect bow of a mouth, he seemed far too pretty for a fighting man. His body, though wiry and surprisingly strong, was slender and lithe, with an innate grace that Dulac found somehow disquieting.

At first the seasoned captain had treated his new junior officer with an indifference bordering on disdain, constantly testing and observing him, expecting ineptitude and cowardice. Instead, young Pontalba had proved intelligent, brave and cooperative, a valuable addition to his staff, who distinguished himself at the battles of Ciudad Rodrigo, Almeida, and Busaco. Although the aristocratic sublieutenant had not been wounded so far, his epaulets had been blackened by artillery fire at Valladolid. In spite of his privileged background, Pontalba had an inner strength and toughness not readily apparent, but which he could call upon when necessary. Dulac's initial contempt and skepticism had soon been transformed into respect and admiration.

Dulac had also discovered during the course of their association that the young sublieutenant was not just a highly competent officer but an agreeable companion as well. The latter admission was not an easy one for the seasoned cavalry captain, who generally despised the aristocracy. The two men drank together, although Pontalba was a light drinker, fenced, and played cards and chess. Only at the latter did Pontalba excel, although Dulac was determined to improve his game and eventually hoped to beat him more often.

Satisfied that nothing was afoot in the hills overlooking the army's campsite, Dulac returned to his tent and decided to try to sleep once again. He unbuttoned his blouse with its double row of gleaming buttons, draped it carefully across the back of a camp chair, and inspected his bare flesh in a small metal field mirror by the light of a lantern. His powerful chest, taut, muscular, and covered with thick black hair, was etched in several places by prominent scars. Dulac smiled as he fingered the former tears in his flesh, reminding himself that no matter how his opponents had managed to scar him, their fate had been far worse. How different his body looked, he mused, from Pontalba's, whose alabaster-white, nearly hairless skin had yet to be broken by a single blade or a musket ball.

Sitting on the edge of his cot, Dulac poured cognac into a metal cup and downed it in a single swallow. Just as he was about to fill the cup again, he heard footsteps approaching the tent and knew by their rhythm that it was Pontalba returning.

Pushing the flap aside, the sublieutenant saluted crisply and entered the tent. "Good evening, sir," he said. Military courtesy was one of the areas in which he was never remiss, even to the point of carrying the formality a bit too far in their personal relationship.

"Good evening, Pontalba," Dulac replied, automatically returning the salute. He was anxious to learn why Ney had summoned the young officer to his headquarters, but did not wish to appear too eager to find out. "How is our good commander this evening?" he asked.

"As good as can be expected under the circumstances, sir," Pontalba replied. "A retreat is always disheartening, no matter how skillfully it is conducted. Nevertheless, he sends you his regards."

"Poor Ney," Dulac said. "He knows it is impossible to continue to maintain the troops in such a sterile country, but Messena is reluctant to continue the retreat."

"He longs for a showdown with Wellington."

"One can't blame him for wanting to vindicate his honor."

"Do you think that if Marshal Ney were to defy

Messena, he might be relieved of his command by the emperor, sir?" Pontalba asked.

"I hope not," Dulac said, reaching for the cognac bottle. "You'd like a drink, wouldn't you?"

Pontalba nodded. "I could use a little cognac right now."

"Really?" Dulac raised his eyebrows ever so slightly, knowing this was his chance to find out why the commander had summoned Pontalba. He filled a cup to the top, handed it to him, and asked, "Why so?"

"Because of the news I've just had," Pontalba replied.

"Nothing bad, I hope?"

Looking downcast, the young officer said, "I must leave for home tomorrow."

Surprised, Dulac repeated, "Home tomorrow? You mean, to France? What's wrong? Is it the family?"

"No, my family is well." Pontalba took a hearty swig of his drink. "My father has just written Marshal Ney requesting my release from the army at once. Since he and the marshal are good friends, Ney will undoubtedly comply."

Mystified, Dulac asked. "Why is your father taking you away just when your career looks so promising? His reasons must be extraordinary."

"Not at all. His reasons are quite ordinary. He merely wishes me to marry."

"Marry!" Dulac exclaimed. "Good Lord, many officers marry without resigning from their regiments. Why on earth can't you just take a leave, marry, and rejoin us? Allowing time for a decent honeymoon, of course."

"The particular girl my father has selected for me lives in America," Pontalba explained. "He wishes me to sail to Louisiana and join her and her mother at once."

"An American?" Dulac mused. "How odd. I can understand your father wishing you to marry well, but surely there must be suitable girls in France . . ."

"He has settled on this one, possibly because her mother and he are first cousins. Besides, I am told that one day she will inherit a considerable fortune."

It was readily apparent to Dulac that Pontalba was upset at the prospect of leaving. "When do you go?" he asked.

"Tomorrow morning."

"Well," Dulac began, tracing the rim of his cognac cup with his index finger, "needless to say, I regret to see you depart."

Glancing at the older officer with dark, soulful eyes, Pontalba said, "And I dislike going as well, sir. I have so thoroughly enjoyed and profited from our association."

"Well, thank you, Pontalba." Dulac was genuinely moved but a little embarrassed by the compliment. "I consider it a privilege to have had you on my staff. I'm just sorry the campaign has gone so badly."

"It's not your fault, sir," the young sublieutenant protested. "Nor is it the fault of Marshal Ney. He's a brilliant leader and has conducted this retreat admirably well."

"Unfortunately, it *is* a retreat," Dulac said wearily.

"True, sir," Pontalba agreed. "If the Spanish and the Portuguese hadn't had help from Wellington and the British, we'd have easily defeated them and made the Iberian Peninsula part of the empire in no time. Their own armies are no match for us."

"But their guerrillas are a bunch of wild-eyed fanatics," Dulac reminded him. "The Grand Army isn't accustomed to such savage adversaries."

"Then we must learn to adapt ourselves to less conventional types of warfare, sir. I believe an army must be flexible."

"That, my boy, is easier said than done," Dulac pointed out, waving a hand at the youth's face. "Armies are notoriously conservative."

Far into the night the two men continued talking, sharing the bottle of cognac and playing chess until Pontalba, who was not really concentrating on the game, complained of a severe headache, excused himself, and fell into bed.

At dawn Dulac awoke and thought, for a moment, he heard Pontalba sniffling in his cot on the opposite

side of the tent. His first instinct was to get out of bed
and see what was wrong, but he restrained himself,
not wishing to embarrass the young officer if indeed he
really was crying. Dulac knew that Pontalba would
have great difficulty accepting his father's demands
that he quit the army and marry, but from his past
association with the sublieutenant he did not expect
him to actually break down and cry. Still, he understood how heartbreaking it would be for him to leave
the unit to which he was so devoted and that he had
served so valiantly through a long and arduous campaign. Resigning a commission just when one's military
career looked so promising would have been devastating to anyone as dedicated as Pontalba.

Raising his head, Dulac peered across the tent and
saw that Pontalba, naked to the waist, was lying on
his stomach, his tousled head of curly black ringlets
buried in his folded arms. This time Dulac's sympathetic impulses were so strong that he could not allow
himself to remain indifferent. Swinging his feet over
the side of the cot, he rose and went to Pontalba's
side.

"Lieutenant . . . ?" he said, gently placing his hand
on the youth's bare shoulder.

Without lifting his head or acknowledging his fellow officer's presence in any other way, Pontalba
sought Dulac's hand with his own, and when he found
it, he gripped the fingers tightly, desperately.

18

IN PREPARATION FOR the impending arrival of
Celestin de Pontalba, who would be traveling solely in
the company of his mother, the Baroness Jeanne,
since his father was not free to accompany them,
Louise evicted the tenants of her townhouse opposite
the central parade grounds, brought some of her
slave artisans and craftsmen from the Bayou Road
plantation, and completely redecorated the residence.

When the renovations were finished, Louise moved herself, Micaela, and their personal slaves from Versailles to the house in which Micaela had lived as a small child.

Glancing around at the new furniture and decorations, Louise put her arm around Micaela and said, "It looks truly lovely, doesn't it, dearest?"

"I don't see why you had to go to so much bother," Micaela replied.

"It's very important. We must make a good impression on the Pontalbas. For your sake . . ."

"For my sake?"

"Yes, of course." Louise smiled, smoothing her daughter's gleaming red hair. "A good painting must be properly framed. Just as a fine jewel needs the proper setting."

In preparing the proper "frame," Louise had spared no expense, nor had she stinted on Micaela's clothing for the all-important visit. Box after box of the finest dresses, hats, shoes, and gloves arrived daily from the various stores. Joylessly Micaela modeled each new article for her mother while Louise decided which frock was right for what occasion.

As Binnie helped her into a dress of imported blue French calico with a white lace collar at the neck, Micaela sadly recalled the day of the fitting for this dress. That had been the last time she had seen—or perhaps would ever see—Patrick. Gazing at the frock in the elegant new gilt-framed mirror in her bedroom, which still smelled of fresh paint, she wished it could be Patrick for whom she would wear it and not the young French nobleman whom she had no desire to meet.

Since leaving Versailles, she spent her days moping listlessly about the townhouse, gazing at the bleak, depressing, weed-infested parade grounds across the way with its ankle-deep mud and shaggy sycamores, wishing that it had a few flowers or some neatly pruned trees to lift her spirits. She had little appetite, scarcely touched her meals, and avoided talking to anyone if she could. Even a visit from Claire Villegrande did little to cheer her up.

"School is going to be awful without you this year, Micaela," Claire said.

Micaela felt an inner sense of helplessness and outrage that others controlled her life, that her future was completely out of her hands, and she tried to express these feelings to Claire.

"But that's the way it is," Claire responded with a resigned but unhappy shrug. "The way it's always been."

"But why?" Micaela persisted. "Why does it have to be that way?"

"No one knows why. In any case, there's little we can do about it."

In her realistic moments Micaela faced up to the fact that there was virtually no possibility of a continued relationship with Patrick Lynch, and at times she convinced herself that if she could not marry him, it made no difference whom she did marry. If she chose not to marry Celestin de Pontalba, her mother would only force some other equally uninteresting suitor on her. From his portrait and what she had heard about him, Celestin seemed more appealing than any of the local swains, and if forced to make a choice, she considered him definitely superior. The idea of being coerced to wed a young man like Alexandre Mouton or Octave Blanchard was repugnant to her. Even the nunnery would be preferable to that. At other times Micaela wished she had more of a religious bent and could seek refuge as a novitiate, but she knew she would never last a week in that setting.

Whenever she contemplated the possibility of marriage in a cold and dispassionate way, she realized that it did offer certain avenues of escape. If she married Celestin, she would leave New Orleans and live in France, thereby avoiding all reminders of Patrick and their painful, short-lived affair. Also, she would no longer be under her mother's domination. A third and important consideration was that her mother would probably settle Micaela's share of her father's estate on her, enabling her to have an independent income. She knew that her mother had been discussing the subject of financial arrangements in her meetings with LeBreton, which undoubtedly pertained to herself. Thus, in the final analysis, becoming Celestin's wife might not be too unpalatable.

In spite of all these rationalizations, Micaela still was not able to summon much enthusiasm for her meeting with the Pontalbas.

Almost immediately upon their arrival in New Orleans, Jeanne de Pontalba sent Louise a calling card announcing their presence in the city, and Louise replied with a suggested date and time for their first visit.

Promptly at the appointed hour, Celestin and his mother arrived in a carriage. Binnie was told to inform Micaela, who was moping in her room.

"He's here, Miss Micaela," Binnie announced, bursting into the room in a flurry. "Your mama sent me up to make sure you was ready and lookin' your best for Monsieur Celestin and his mama."

"I'm ready," Micaela mumbled glumly, and started for the door, but Binnie blocked her path so that she could first appraise her appearance. Micaela was wearing a dress of pale green Marceline silk with a skirt so full it had required an entire bolt of the shiny fabric for the single outfit. Her waist was cinched by a tournure, commonly referred to as a 'tchuny,' and the folds of the silk skirt were draped over it, giving a fullness to her hips that, in turn, made her waist seem even tinier by comparison.

"No, you ain't," the teen-aged slave said in her high-pitched voice. "You sit down there a minute and let me fix you up."

Obediently Micaela sat on the bed while Binnie touched up a few of the pomaded red curls and brushed her cheeks with mullein leaves to give them a heightened pinkish glow.

Standing back, Binnie appraised her at arm's length. "There! Now you looks just fine, Miss Micaela."

Taking a deep breath, Micaela descended the stairs and entered the parlor, where Louise was already conversing in an animated fashion with a tiny, birdlike woman who Micaela automatically assumed was Bar-

oness Jeanne. Casting a quick, furtive glance about
the room, she was surprised to see no one else present
except Flore, who was holding the baroness's blue
cape and bonnet. She wondered where the much-
heralded Celestin was.

"Micaela, dear, come and meet your cousin Jeanne,
the Baroness de Pontalba," Louise said, motioning her
to join them.

From the gold damask chair in which she was sitting, Jeanne extended her dainty hands to Micaela,
drew her close, and pecked both her cheeks in a perfunctory salutation.

"Micaela! How nice to see you!" Jeanne exclaimed.
"What a lovely young lady you've become. I remember you as a tiny little girl in your father's arms, the
day you went sailing up in that balloon with him!
How exciting that was! Don Andrés, dear man that he
was, was always full of such madness. But how he
adored you! And how much you've grown to resemble
him!"

"Pleased to make your acquaintance, madame,"
Micaela murmured, and curtsied politely.

"Look, Louise," Jeanne continued. "Truly, she has
Don Andrés's eyes, the shape of his face, and, of
course, his red hair. Ah, that hair!"

"She has nothing of me or my side of the family in
her," Louise lamented.

"I must have Celestin meet you at once," Jeanne
gushed, and instructed Flore to retrieve him. "He's
down in the patio, entranced, I think, by that parrot
of yours."

In a few moments, responding to his mother's sum-
mons, Celestin entered the parlor twirling a brilliant
blue parrot feather between his fingers.

"Micaela, this is your cousin Celestin." Jeanne
smiled proudly at her son.

"How do you do, sir?" Micaela said, and once again
curtsied politely. She realized immediately that the
miniature had been a faithful likeness. Celestin de
Pontalba did indeed possess the large, soulful dark
eyes, the classical nose, and the well-shaped mouth of
the portrait, although his hair was shorter than she

had imagined and not as curly, and his skin less pale. He was quite slender and appeared taller than his actual medium height because of his stiff, military posture. Although he forced a smile as he took her hand and brought it to his lips, he had an air of unhappiness and resignation about him.

"Charmed, mademoiselle," he said.

Louise invited them all to be seated and instructed Flore to serve some refreshments.

Using a delicately embroidered lace handkerchief to dab at her forehead, which was framed by tiny spit curls, Jeanne remarked, "I'd forgotten how frightfully hot New Orleans can be at this time of year."

"Yes, it is rather warm," Louise agreed.

"In France the summers are more mild," Jeanne said. "Aren't they, Celestin, dear?"

"Oh, yes," he replied.

"Celestin's been in Spain lately," Jeanne continued.

"Portugal, Mama," he corrected.

"I understand you are an officer in the emperor's Grand Army, Lieutenant Pontalba," Louise said. "That must be quite exciting."

"Celestin loves it!" Jeanne cried.

"Army life suits me quite well," he offered solemnly.

"But it wasn't always that way," Jeanne said. "When Celestin's father first arranged for his commission with our dear friend Marshal Michel Ney, Celestin was not very happy about it, I tell you—"

"You exaggerate, Mama," Celestin cut in.

"Once Celestin adjusted, he became quite fond of all that pomp and circumstance, didn't you, dearest?"

He looked at her askance. "The army is far more than mere pomp and circumstance, Mama."

"It must have been rather hot in Spain also, was it not, Celestin?" Louise asked.

"I scarcely had time to notice the weather, Cousin Louise," he replied. "I was rather occupied with more serious matters."

"Oh, dear me, I didn't mean to underestimate your duties." Louise was slightly flustered by his humorless attitude.

"Tell Cousin Louise about the time you were wounded at Valladolid," Jeanne urged. "I was frantic when I got the news . . ."

"It was nothing," Celestin scoffed. "How you exaggerate, Mama! Some artillery fire merely blackened my epaulets, nothing more."

"But you could have been killed, dearest."

"Really, Mama," he reproached. "You're exaggerating again."

At that moment Flore appeared with a pitcher of fruit punch and a ginger cake fresh from the oven that filled the room with the odor of fragrant spices.

"Celestin just adores ginger cake," Jeanne squealed.

"Lately, sweets have been upsetting my stomach," he remarked, eyeing the cake with disinterest.

The strained small talk continued until Louise finally suggested that Micaela take Celestin for a stroll. "Perhaps along the levee so that he can see the river and all the foreign ships that call at our city these days."

"I can assure you, Cousin Louise," he said, "that I've seen quite a few 'foreign' ships lately, more than I cared to. British ships were sailing in and out of the Lisbon harbor with supplies for their troops and for those of the Spanish and the Portuguese. If we could have cut off the enemy fortifications, we could easily have defeated them, even though we were outnumbered, and Spain and Portugal would have become part of the French Empire."

"I think Louise's suggestion is splendid," Jeanne interjected blithely. "Why don't you two go for a little walk?"

"Binnie will accompany you," Louise added.

Realizing her mother's true purpose was to send them off alone so that they could get to know each other, Micaela reluctantly agreed, and the two of them took their leave.

Together they strolled along the levee, Binnie a discreet distance behind, and Micaela pointed out the various sights and landmarks. She thought it was ridiculous that they had to be accompanied by a chaperone, after her escapade in the bayou with Patrick, but such was the hypocrisy of Creole life. Appearances counted for everything.

Celestin gallantly attempted to feign interest in what she was saying, although his distracted expression made it plain that he was simply performing a duty, just as she was, and probably under protest at that. It was obvious that neither he nor Micaela felt at ease with the situation into which they had been forced by their respective families. Eventually, interrupting her patter, he came right to the heart of the matter that was on both their minds.

"I suppose you are aware of why our parents have thrown us together like this, aren't you?" he asked bluntly.

Although she was surprised by his directness, Micaela was nevertheless relieved that at last the matter was out in the open.

"Yes, I suppose I am," she admitted.

"Well, how do you feel about it?"

"I'm not sure it matters how *I* feel. I think my mother has made up her mind that it's time for me to marry, and that's that."

"My father feels the same way."

"But how do *you* feel about it?" She was beginning to sense the first stirrings of a possible sympathetic rapport between them.

Celestin shrugged. "I think it makes little difference how I feel," he answered in a resigned tone. "My father cares little for my feelings or opinions. He has simply decided that it is time I had a wife, and since he has yanked me from my army unit and sent me all the way across the Atlantic, I rather imagine he hopes I will choose you for my bride. In any case, he is determined that I marry soon. Of that I'm certain. If I choose not to marry you, I am sure he will present me with a steady procession of girls until my resistance finally weakens and I decide on one of them."

As terribly bleak and unromantic as was the situation he painted, Micaela realized that hers was quite comparable, perhaps even worse. Louise was equally determined to see her married, and if not to Celestin, to someone else. Louise, too, would hammer away at her objections, if she offered any, until they were useless.

"My mother is quite similar to your father in many ways, I think," she remarked.

Celestin smacked his fist into his open palm. "Ah, why can't they just let us alone?" he complained. "At this time of my life I would have much preferred pursuing a military career. I was a sublieutenant in the Fifteenth Light Cavalry Regiment. My record was rather good, if I may say so. I was forced to resign my commission to come here. When I return to France, I hope to resume my military pursuits, but I know it will be impossible. My father no longer wishes that for me. He prefers that I remain at Mont L'Eveque and administer our lands and property."

"Why do you allow your father to rule you so completely?" she asked.

"Why do *you* allow your mother to rule you?" he countered.

"But it is so much easier for a man to assert himself. A girl has fewer opportunities."

He shrugged again. "Perhaps. But you have not met the baron. He has a will of iron. It is not easy to oppose him. When he was young, he was also a soldier, in the service of the Spanish king, although he is, of course, French. He fought Indians here in the Louisiana Territory. He's used to giving orders and being obeyed. It's been like that ever since I can remember. He's been a kind and affectionate father in his own way, but it's difficult for him to conceive that one might have ideas that differ from his. The baron is rather inflexible, I'm afraid."

"How like my mother he sounds!"

"Well, they are cousins. The same blood courses through their veins."

"Yes, I suppose it does."

"Tell me about yourself," he said. "I'm sure you must have many beaux."

Micaela shook her head. "No, not many."

"No one you care about?"

Somewhat hesitantly, she replied, "There was someone once."

"And what happened?"

"Nothing. It's over now. You see, he was unsuitable."

Puzzled, Celestin frowned. "You mean he wasn't a proper gentleman?"

"No, he was a fine gentleman. It's just that the circumstances were unsuitable."

With the two young people gone, Louise and Jeanne were able to dispense with polite chitchat and get down to more serious matters.

"Recently I've been meeting with Monsieur LeBreton," Louise remarked casually.

Jeanne's face brightened with recognition at the mention of the attorney's name. "Really? And how is dear François? I understand he is one of the most successful lawyers in New Orleans."

"Yes, he's very well esteemed," Louise affirmed.

"You must give him my regards the next time you see him."

"I have been looking into matters concerning my late husband's estate," Louise continued. "I am trying to arrange things carefully in the event that Micaela should decide to marry soon. After all, I should like my daughter and the young man of her choice to be comfortably situated."

"Yes, of course," Jeanne agreed, anxious to hear more details.

"It appears as if, should Micaela marry, her dowry would be close to forty-five thousand dollars, which is her initial share of her father's estate."

Having expected a much larger sum to be assigned to her future daughter-in-law, Jeanne frowned. "From what I've heard about Don Andrés's fortune, I would have imagined her share to be considerably more."

"Much of his estate, LeBreton informs me, is what is known as paraphernal property under Louisiana law," Louise informed her cousin, well aware that such legal terminology would be incomprehensible to Jeanne. "And, therefore, Micaela would not be entitled to it. However, I intend to add to the forty-five thousand dollars an additional eighty-five thousand dollars from my own personal funds."

Suppressing a smile of relief, Jeanne said, "Well, Louise, that is most generous of you."

"Yes, I think so, too."

Louise's expectant expression told Jeanne that she now awaited details of the baron's contribution to his son's marriage. Hesitant to discuss such matters without her husband's prior approval, Jeanne nevertheless felt obliged by Louise's earlier disclosure to say something.

"I suppose, should Celestin decide to marry, the baron would attempt to match whatever dowry his son's bride were to bring with her," Jeanne offered, not wanting the Pontalbas to be outdone by the Almonesters.

"I can assure you, dearest Cousin, that I would consider no less from the family of any young man who elected to marry my daughter," Louise declared.

"There's no reason why you should," Jeanne told her.

"I know." Louise smiled. "I am very well aware of my daughter's worth."

19

SCARCELY THREE WEEKS were allotted to the courtship, which both mothers regarded as superfluous but socially required. While Micaela and Celestin were getting better acquainted, Louise and Jeanne tackled the wedding arrangements with glee. Once it had been decided that their two offspring would marry, there was no reason to delay. If either Micaela or Celestin had expressed any wishes in the matter, they would have been disregarded. There were many reasons for haste; some were voiced, others not. The most frequently mentioned were Louise's desire to return to her ailing husband and the Pontalbas' wish to go back to Mont L'Eveque.

A few days prior to the wedding, set for October twenty-third, LeBreton presented the completed marriage contract to the two mothers for their signatures. Because the baron had been unable to accompany his wife, he had conferred his power of attorney on her before her departure from France.

"Dear me, I do hope I'm doing the right thing," Jeanne fretted nervously, pen in hand. "I would feel so much better if my husband could read these documents first."

"I can assure you, Baroness, they are of the highest order," LeBreton intoned.

"There's nothing for you to worry about, Jeanne," Louise added.

"If these contracts aren't to his liking, the baron will be furious," Jeanne sighed.

"How could Cousin Joseph possibly be furious about anything that you yourself said is the soul of fairness?" Louise demanded.

"That's how it appears to me," Jeanne replied, "but the baron may have other ideas."

"I doubt that, Madame," LeBreton said.

"Sign them and be done with it," Louise nearly snapped, her patience waning rapidly.

"Very well," Jeanne agreed, and placed her signature on the documents.

"There!" Louise smiled. "You've done exactly what I have done and no more. You have simply agreed to match the sum of Micaela's dowry with a similar settlement on Celestin. That's all. I've been most generous, and you've been most generous as well."

"Why don't we drink a toast on it?" LeBreton suggested, rolling up the heavy parchments and tying them with a silk ribbon.

"Excellent!" Louise said, and called for Flore to bring them a bottle of champagne.

On the morning of the wedding the sun was hidden behind thick black clouds that produced a steady downpour, turning the streets into muddy rivers.

"They say that rain on a weddin' day means a marriage with lots of tears," Binnie groaned as she gazed out the window of Micaela's room. Both she and Flore had been assigned to help Micaela into her elaborate white silk wedding gown, but preparations were not proceeding with much enthusiasm, either on the part of the bride or on that of her servants.

"Now, you hush your mouth, hear?" Flore reprimanded Binnie. "Ain't gonna be no tears except tears of joy. Ain't that right, Miss Micaela?"

"I suppose so," Micaela listlessly agreed, having earlier resigned herself to going along with her mother's plans, knowing that opposing her would gain nothing. She had decided to be numbly obedient, an automatic doll, and to allow her mother to direct things as she wished. About Celestin himself she had mixed feelings. Certainly he was good-looking and polite, but he seemed as little interested in her as she was in him, which produced a strained, disconcerting relationship between them. His one characteristic that bothered her the most was his seeming willingness to be dominated by his parents, especially by his father. Apart from that, he was certainly as fine a prospective husband as anyone else she knew, perhaps better than most. Under the circumstances, things weren't as bad as they might have been, although she knew that marriage to him would never erase the memory of Patrick Lynch, no matter whether their future together would be happy or not.

Micaela, her huge bridal bouquet of white and pink roses and magnolias in her lap, rode the short distance to the cathedral in an extravagantly flower-decorated coach. Accompanying her were Louise, Flore, and Bernard de Marigny, one of Louise's most distinguished relatives, who had agreed to give the bride away in place of her deceased father. Marigny was one of the wealthiest and most powerful men in New Orleans, and Louise considered his presence an honor. Binnie and some of the other house slaves followed behind in another carriage. It was their job to see that Micaela's long gown and trailing veil did not get mussed or soiled with mud.

"Binnie, I want you and the others to see that Miss Micaela's skirts never touch the ground," Louise had ordered. "If there's so much as one spot on her gown, I'll have you all whipped. Is that clear?"

"Yes, ma'am, Miss Louise," Binnie had replied.

As they approached the cathedral Micaela observed that in spite of the foul weather, the banquettes were lined with spectators. They cheered at the sight of her flower-festooned carriage and shouted congratulatory messages as the wedding party rode by.

The carriage passed a narrow alley, and Micaela caught a glimpse of a man with a slight limp hurrying down the banquette, long rolls of paper tucked under his arm as he tried to protect them from the rain. Realizing that the man was none other than Patrick Lynch, Micaela gasped audibly and clutched her throat, startling everyone in the carriage.

"What's wrong, child?" Flore asked solicitously.

"Nothing," Micaela muttered.

"Just nerves, I'll bet," Marigny laughed.

"Of course," Louise agreed. "All brides are nervous before the wedding."

As Celestin crossed in front of the altar in the hushed cathedral and took his place at Micaela's side, his thoughts were not on the solemnity or the joy of the occasion. When the organ began to play again, he longed to hear instead the sound of trumpets and snare drums, or even the roar of muskets and artillery, the clanking of sabers, the thundering of horses' hooves. Instead of the sweet smell of orange blossoms, magnolias, and jasmine, he yearned for the acrid scent of gunpowder and smoke. For him the wedding was nothing more than a charade, a ritual, a formality to be endured. He viewed it as an obligation that was destined to happen sooner or later. He was going through with it to fulfill his duty to his father, just as he had done all his life. He hoped that if it turned out well and his father was pleased with both him and Micaela, he might be permitted to return to his cavalry unit. He adored that life and felt it was the only one for him. In the cavalry he had status and recognition and, above all, the only real freedom he had ever known from his father's tyrannical will. There, within the rigid military structure that proved so stifling to many, he had been able to breathe freely for the first time. He loved everything about it: the sweaty, skittish horses, the formations, the dazzling uniforms, the charges, the excitement, the camaraderie, the danger. Ever since his adolescent days as an aide-de-camp to the emperor himself, he had loved all of it, but his most recent assignment was, without question, his favorite. He relished being an officer in the Fifteenth Light Cavalry Regiment and serving under Captain Dulac. Never had he encountered a superior whom he admired more. Dulac, with his extraordinary skill with weapons and horses, his confidence, and his courage, was the sort of man he aspired to be but knew he never would or could become. Dulac was peerless.

Celestin thought of how ironic it was that he had balked when the baron had first announced his plans to send him to the army. Celestin had been full of fear and dread at that time. His father had caught him embroidering a scarf for his great-aunt, Madame Miró, one day and had yanked it out of his hand, upsetting his embroidery kit and spilling its contents all over the floor.

"Why did you do that, Papa?" Celestin had asked, badly shaken.

"There are too damned many females in this household who are pampering and coddling you," his father had raged, "Your mother, your aunt, the maids. Too damned many women around here! I want you to be tough, a fighter like I was. Otherwise you'll never survive in this world. Once in a single day I killed more than one hundred savage Indians. That's what a man's supposed to do—not this embroidery nonsense! I want you to become proficient at guns and swords, not at sewing. Today I'm writing to my good friend Michel Ney. I'm going to ask him to find a place for you in the army. Maybe there you'll give up this nonsense your head seems to be filled with lately!"

Before he had departed, choking back tears, Celestin had received a basket of pears from his father, each one rubbed to a glow by the baron's own hands. The gesture has seemed almost one of apology.

"Goodbye, my son," he had said, avoiding Celestin's eyes.

Much to everyone's surprise, not least of all the baron's, after some initial trauma Celestin had taken a definite liking to military life. When he was required to be away from the army, even on leaves to Mont L'Eveque, it was evident that he missed its Spartan life-style and rigid discipline.

Decorated with elaborate floral bouquets from floor to ceiling, St. Louis Cathedral had probably not witnessed a more expensive or glamorous wedding than that of Micaela Almonester and Celestin de Pontalba. Louise had felt obliged to give her only child a wedding on a grand scale. After all, the girl's father had been one of the city's most prominent citizens and had received the enormous honor of being buried inside the cathedral, only a few feet from the altar where his daughter was exchanging her vows. Hasty invitations had been sent out, and although an air of scandal still hovered about Micaela's expulsion from school, nearly everyone had accepted. The front rows of the church were filled with the cream of Louisiana society.

Watching Micaela and Celestin kneeling before the distinguished priest Father Antonio de Sedilla, Louise, in an honored position in the front row, breathed a secret sigh of relief that at last she had done her duty and seen Micaela married well. Not only had a potential scandal been cleverly averted, but she had also managed to marry off her daughter to a handsome and titled young Frenchman and to secure a generous settlement for her from the usually tight-fisted baron.

"Just let Baron Joseph try to break the contract I have drawn up," LeBreton had chuckled when Louise voiced certain apprehensions about the legality of the marriage contract. "The old fox will then find out how ironclad it is."

"I hope so," Louise had said. "My cousin is a very shrewd and clever man."

LeBreton had grinned and pinched her cheek. "Not half so clever or shrewd as we, dear Louise."

Once the long nuptial Mass was concluded, Micaela and Celestin marched glumly down the aisle arm in arm, each preoccupied with his or her private thoughts.

At the reception that followed, only Louise and the imported French champagne sparkled. As for the bride and groom, it was difficult to decide which one seemed more languid or unhappy.

Pierre, always the dandy and today resplendent in a claw-hammer coat and a black satin waistcoat embroidered with extravagant birds of paradise, sidled up to his aunt and said, "One would think you were the bride, Aunt Louise. You're the only giddy one in the wedding party."

"That's because I'm the only one who realizes what a real triumph this wedding is," Louise replied. "As far as I'm concerned, it's the coup of the century."

Nodding toward Micaela, who was standing listlessly across the room beside her equally listless groom, Pierre remarked, "Your daughter might be sipping fine French champagne, but I think it's Irish whiskey she'd rather be tasting."

Rapping his knuckles sharply with her fan, Louise snapped, "How dare you say such a thing? I think you're drunk. Perhaps you'd better leave before you cause both of us any embarrassment."

"Perhaps you're right, dear Aunt," Pierre conceded with an indifferent shrug. "Weddings always depress me, anyway."

Almost immediately after the reception, the couple departed for France aboard a large passenger ship, accompanied by their respective mothers and Binnie and Flore.

On the ship Micaela and Celestin were to share a single first-class cabin. Jeanne had timidly suggested separate accommodations for the newlyweds, but Louise would not hear of it.

"The adjustment is always difficult even in the best of circumstances, but aboard ship it will be impossible," Jeanne had said.

"I agree that it is a difficult adjustment, but the

sooner they get accustomed to each other, the better," Louise had answered. "Aboard ship is no worse than any other place."

The cabin was small and cramped and precluded any sort of privacy. Sensing Micaela's possible discomfort the first night out, Celestin voluntarily left their quarters so that she might undress with only Binnie present to help her out of her clothes.

While she readied herself for bed, he nervously paced the spacious deck, inhaling the pungent salt air and enjoying the fine misty spray, cool on his cheeks, and attempted to prepare himself for his first night with his new bride. Earlier Jeanne had taken him aside and cautioned him to treat Micaela with great care and tenderness. "Above all, tenderness," she had stressed. "You must always be very gentle. You must remember that just a few months ago she was behind the walls of a convent while you were with the army— two very different worlds, you must admit."

Although Celestin had been in the army a few years, he was still virginal, having successfully shunned both his companions' invitations to visit various brothels and the advances of whores, camp followers, and *vivandières,* who were especially attracted to him because of his good looks. Before he left for the army, the baron had warned him of the terrible diseases that could be contracted from such women. Abstinence had been his strict policy. Even Dulac's urgings to join him for a night of carousing at some lively bordello had not swayed him.

In spite of Binnie's protests, Micaela had elected to wear a heavy flannel nightgown instead of the lace-trimmed silk one the slave encouraged her to put on.

"That one you got on is for an old maid, not a bride on her first night," Binnie said.

"This is the one I choose to wear, and I will hear no more about it," Micaela decreed.

When the maid had gone, she knelt, rosary in hand, on the gently rocking cabin floor and began to say her prayers, extending them far beyond their usual brief length. It was her hope that Celestin would come in and find her praying and thus be put off by it, thereby postponing the consummation of their marriage. Since the ceremony her thoughts had been constantly on Patrick, and, unreasonable or not, she could not bear the prospect of intimate relations with any other man —including her new husband.

Idly gazing at the deck through the porthole in her cabin, Louise caught a glimpse of Celestin leaning over the rail, staring at the dark sea. Realizing that Micaela must be alone, she hastily threw a cape over her nightgown and went to her daughter's stateroom.

"Listen to me, dearest," she said, sitting on the edge of the bed and taking Micaela's hand in hers. "Like me, you are a very strong woman. This quality can be very intimidating to some men and not at all to your advantage in your relationships with them. Now that you are married, you must remember to suppress your natural inclination toward independence and place yourself under your husband's will. It's important that he feel comfortable with you and want to be with you. Marriage can give great joy, but it can also extract great sacrifices."

With a frown Micaela repeated, "Under my husband's will?"

"Yes," Louise said. "It is a wife's duty to subjugate herself to her husband. Just as God rules man, so does a man rule his wife."

"Why does it have to be that way?" Micaela asked. "I don't think I like it."

"Because that's the way God intended it," Louise replied with certainty. "Now, go call Celestin inside. He'll catch his death of cold walking around out there in that chilly sea air."

Reluctantly following her mother's advice, Micaela summoned Celestin back into the cabin. While he undressed quietly in the dark, Micaela, in bed, feigned sleep, so that when he climbed in beside her, he lay as far from her as possible, apparently not wishing to disturb her.

Neither of them slept very well on their wedding night.

Part Two

20

DURING THE FIRST few days at sea Micaela suffered the usual discomforts of first-time voyagers, but once she had become accustomed to the dip and roll of the ship, acquired her sea legs, and got her stomach under control, she began to realize that the social advantages of a long voyage could be considerable. There were many opportunities to meet important and influential people. Both Louise and Jeanne encountered several passengers on board whom they had known in Paris, and they presented Micaela and Celestin to them. As the only newlyweds aboard, the young couple was looked upon with great fondness and considered something of a novelty. Many of the older passengers sought them out and seemed delighted to make their acquaintance, perhaps recalling their own youthful days.

As a result of this shipboard socializing, Micaela and Celestin received many invitations to visit their fellow passengers when they arrived in France. Micaela had been worrying that her life might be lonely away from New Orleans, especially with her mother so preoccupied with her ailing husband, but she was relieved to discover that an active and potentially exciting social life could be hers in the French capital, a compensation for what would surely be a dull and disappointing marriage.

Although she and Celestin had been sharing the same bed for days, he did not press her to fulfill any sexual obligations, and she went to sleep each night thinking, not of her husband sleeping quietly beside her, but of Patrick Lynch, thousands of miles away, whom in all likelihood she would never see again.

Eventually the ship docked at Le Havre. Micaela and Celestin, with their respective mothers and the two slaves, continued to Paris, where they registered in the bridal suite of one of the better hotels. Both Jeanne and Celestin expressed their eagerness to return to Mont L'Eveque, the Pontalba family château situated about ninety miles northeast of Paris, but Louise insisted that her daughter and son-in-law must first get to know the French capital and meet her friends at a series of dinners and receptions she had planned in their honor.

"It would be unthinkable for Micaela and Celestin to leave now," she argued. "My friends would be insulted if they didn't get the opportunity to meet them."

"Yes, of course, Louise, dear," Jeanne conceded, and was forced to return home alone.

Micaela was more than excited by her first encounter with the French capital, she was thrilled and ecstatic; she could scarcely take in the size of the city, to say nothing of its bustling activity, chic sophistication, and vitality.

"And to think I believed that poor little New Orleans was the center of the universe!" Micaela laughed as she threw open the casement windows of their hotel suite and gazed at the city spread out before her as far as the eye could see.

"Yes, I suppose Paris does have a certain charm," Celestin agreed rather indifferently. The military activity in the city was the only thing that interested him; otherwise he seemed thoroughly bored with everything else.

"I adore Paris!" she exclaimed, like the giddy schoolgirl she had so recently been. "I want to get to know all of it. Every corner. I want Paris to be as familiar to me as New Orleans, as the back of my hand."

"Paris is a big city. After all, it's the most important one in Europe. Probably in the world," Celestin said.

"New Orleans is a muddy little provincial town. You cannot compare them."

When they were not being entertained by Louise and her friends or by the people they had met on the ship, Micaela would coax Celestin to show her around Paris, although he would have preferred to return to the country or to socialize with the cavalry officers at the Cafe de Roy.

"How beautiful and elegant these stately chestnut trees are that line the boulevard," she remarked to him as they rode in an open carriage belonging to her mother. "Will they grow in Louisiana?"

"I doubt it."

"You're probably right. I'm sure that if they would, Pierre would already have planted hundreds at Versailles."

Circling the Bois de Boulogne, they passed a number of fine carriages, many carrying stylish, well-groomed women attired in the latest and, to Micaela, somewhat daring fashions. The Empress Josephine had introduced dresses of very thin fabrics cut low across the bosom, which exposed a great amount of the wearer's flesh. These gowns had caught the feminine fancy and were now being widely worn in all levels of society. Frequently the horses pulling the carriages of these stylish women had their manes and tails braided or clipped in decorative patterns, and the drivers were adorned with fresh carnations.

"What a lovely idea!" Micaela commented when she saw the carnations, her eye constantly on the alert for all things new and different.

On their ride about the city it was obvious to her that Napoleon had ambitious plans for Paris that included a host of new buildings, elaborate public gardens, and many arches and monuments commemorating his victories. As a result, an enormous amount of construction was in progress, much of it in the Greek revival style Patrick favored so much. When they passed the various construction sites, including one on which the half-completed Arc de Triomphe was under way, Micaela grew sad and thought of how much more she would have enjoyed her tours of the city if Patrick had been her guide instead of Celestin, who seemed to have little interest in anything that was not directly connected with the military. Fortunately, this type of influence was everywhere and kept him sufficiently engrossed, so that he didn't insist on returning immediately to Mont L'Eveque, as Micaela had feared he might.

The city was like an army camp. Little French schoolboys marched to school in quasi-military uniforms; dashing dragoons with drawn swords lined the marble stairs of the opera; furniture was decorated with Napoleon's favorite eagles and Roman standards. The streets, cafes, and restaurants were crowded with boisterous grenadiers, hussars, dragoons, and trumpeters in their fancy red and gold uniforms, shiny boots, golden tassels, and high hats ornamented with feathers and gleaming insignias, giving the entire city an aura of panache and glamour.

Micaela soon learned that Celestin's favor could be more easily obtained if she bartered an afternoon call on a friend of her mother's for a trip to the Champs-de-Mars so that he might attend a military ceremony on the celebrated parade grounds. A ball at the home of an acquaintance from the ship might be traded for an afternoon of watching the emperor review his troops before the Palais Royal. Micaela did not mind going to the Palais Royal; in fact, she liked it, not just for its regal atmosphere but also because of the vast gardens that surrounded it. Scattered throughout the well-tended gardens were fifteen restaurants, thirty cafes, seventeen billiard saloons, twenty-four jewelers, six booksellers—including one who specialized in erotic books—a dentist, a foot doctor, an abortionist, a silhouette cutter, a money-lender, and several bordellos. Although Celestin strongly disapproved of frequenting the area because of the large number of prostitutes and beggars who accosted strollers, Micaela loved to walk up and down the many paths.

"This is hardly a proper place for a woman of your station to be seen in," he warned her.

"Proper, proper," she repeated impatiently. "I'm tired of everyone worrying about what's proper and what isn't. I'm too intoxicated with Paris to pay attention to such nonsense."

One day when they arrived back in their hotel suite after a junket to the gardens, they found a basket of fresh apples from Mont L'Eveque waiting for them, each piece of fruit polished and wrapped in individual tissue paper, along with a note from the baron addressed to his son.

"Your father has certainly been most attentive," Micaela remarked as she bit into an apple while Celestin read the letter. "He's been sending us fruit and flowers and candy practically every day since we arrived. It's as if he were courting us or something."

"I suppose he is, in a way," Celestin said, folding the note. "You see, dearest, he'd like us to come to Mont L'Eveque."

"I don't suppose it would hurt if we went for a short visit."

"We are expected to live there."

"Live there?" she echoed, aghast. "But I want to live in Paris. I want to stay in Paris forever."

"That's quite impossible, Micaela," he declared. "My place is at Mont L'Eveque with my father."

"With your father? Your place is with me. I'm your wife," she argued, adding in a different, almost disdainful tone, "At least in *name* I'm your wife."

The provocation implicit in her words was not wasted on Celestin, although his mind was still on the contents of the note in his hand, a disturbing message he was reluctant to convey to Micaela.

"There's something else in the baron's letter I feel obliged to discuss with you," he said slowly.

"What's that?"

He hesitated. "I don't exactly know how to tell you."

"Tell me what?"

"You see, the baron has received a letter from someone in New Orleans, which concerns the circumstances of your dismissal from the Ursuline Convent school. The person who wrote the letter alleges that you were involved with a certain 'gentleman' . . ."

"Who wrote such a letter?" she demanded.

"It wasn't signed," he replied.

Micaela rubbed her handkerchief between her sweaty palms and felt her pulse accelerate as she wondered how she was going to explain away these accusations.

"You certainly aren't going to believe anyone who lacks the courage and decency to sign his or her name to a letter like that, are you?" she said, speculating that the author was most likely Renée Houdaille.

"I don't want to."

"Well, then, you shouldn't."

"Then I have your assurance that these accusations are false?"

"How dare you suggest otherwise?" she snapped. "Really, Celestin, you've offended me."

"I'm sorry, dearest," he apologized, placing his arm tentatively around her shoulders. "I have no wish to offend you. Ever."

Later, to compensate for having hurt her feelings, he ordered a carriage and took her to the Boulevard du Temple, where she delighted over the tightrope walkers, acrobats, and street musicians.

On arriving in another section of the city, they alighted and walked along the Seine, which was crowded with floating laundries, mills, and coal barges. Although the weather was chilly, many of the poorer residents of the city were bathing in its waters. Naked and unashamed, they stood soaping themselves or drying their hair over a scrap-wood fire.

Celestin took her into parts of Paris she had not previously seen, parts that were crowded, busy and brawling, full of the clatter of carts and wagons and of the ring of horses' iron shoes striking the cobblestones. In these sections open sewers carried much of the city's refuse and often ran red with the blood of freshly slaughtered animals, since butchers did their killing on the sidewalks in front of their shops. Stray pigs grew fat and healthy on the heaps of garbage that filled the gutters.

As they toured the out-of-the-way areas, Micaela wondered how much longer she could persuade Celestin to put off their going to Mont L'Eveque. Not only

had she no wish to leave the excitement of the capital
and bury herself in the country, she also dreaded facing any questions her father-in-law might have concerning the allegations in the anonymous letter.
Handling the matter with Celestin had been no problem, but she feared that convincing the baron of her
innocence might prove more difficult.

Hoping to forestall their departure to the country,
Micaela suggested they go to the Cafe de Roy together
one evening. At first Celestin was surprised. He had
expected her to suggest a place like Frascati's, where
she liked to sit and sip on fruit ices while watching the
couples on the public dance floor, but, delighted by
her suggestion of his favorite military hangout, he
readily acquiesced.

Among the various cafes of the city, the Cafe de
Roy was unquestionably the most popular haunt of
army officers, who often brought their wives, mistresses, or girlfriends with them. Although many officers in Napoleon's Grand Army had begun life in
humble or less than humble circumstances, while others, like Celestin, bore more genteel credentials, military life had proved a great equalizer and reduced
class consciousness. Everyone from corporal to colonel
mingled freely at the cafe. Celestin, for all his diffi-
dence in most social situations, relaxed in its smoky,
noisy atmosphere and seemed to gain confidence and
stature the moment he and Micaela crossed its threshold. Coming upon an officer in the hussars who had
served under Marshal Ney, he asked if the man, a
leathery-skinned survivor of Marengo, Austerlitz, and
the German and Polish campaigns, had any news of
his company commander, Captain Armand Dulac.

"I suppose that if relations between our emperor
and the czar break down—as indeed it looks as if they
might—Captain Dulac, like most of the other cavalry
officers will be heading toward Russia," the grizzled
hussar replied. "I'm sure that the prospect of crossing
thousands of miles of first-class cavalry country will
put old Dulac in an excellent fighting mood."

Celestin's dark eyes brightened at the thought of
the cavalry's fighting its way across the vast steppes of

Russia, and inwardly he began to fume over the fact that his career was curtailed at such an important time by his father and his recent marriage.

When they returned to the hotel, he was in one of his particularly glum moods. Sensing that he wished to be alone for a while, Micaela summoned Binnie from the adjoining room in which she slept and asked her for assistance in disrobing.

While she was in the bathroom with the maid, Celestin plopped himself in a chair, picked up a leather satchel containing a ball of yarn and some needles, and began knitting, one needle furiously clicking against the other. Later, when Micaela emerged in her long flannel nightgown, she was dismayed to find her husband engaged in what was regarded as strictly a female pastime. Even Binnie had to suppress a snicker as she exited from the room, leaving them alone for the night. It astonished Micaela to see a man with such zeal for military life—almost an obsession—equally enamored with knitting, but she was discovering that Celestin was a man of many contradictions and ambiguities.

"Will you be coming to bed?" she asked as she slid beneath the covers.

"Later," he answered, barely taking his eyes from his knitting.

"You were upset tonight when you heard about the possible Russian campaign, weren't you? You want to participate in it, don't you?"

"Yes," he answered after a moment's hesitation.

"I'm sorry, Celestin," she said. "Sorry if our marriage keeps you from the things you seem to hold so dear. I was watching the way your face glowed at the cafe tonight when you were talking about your Captain What's-his-name . . ."

"His name is Dulac."

"You had so much enthusiasm."

"Did I really?" he replied indifferently.

At last he extinguished the lamps, undressed in the dark, and crawled into bed beside her. For the first time since they had been married, he moved close to her and slipped his arm beneath her waist.

"Micaela," he said softly, "I'm afraid that perhaps this marriage isn't all you expected."

"It's all right, Celestin," she replied. "Whatever disappointments there are, I am responsible for them as much as you are. We both know it wasn't made in heaven."

Drawing her close to him, he sighed, "Ah, Micaela, Micaela . . ." and planted a tentative kiss on her lips.

Thinking that perhaps she had hurt him earlier, she encircled him with her arms and laid her head on his chest, a gesture he perceived as one of encouragement. Clumsily, with little regard for her feelings or her lack of excitement, he proceeded to act out his inept notion of lovemaking. Roughly, almost in a desperate frenzy, he yanked up her nightgown, accidentally covering her face with its voluminous skirt until she felt as if she would smother before she could pull it away from her. Raising up onto his haunches, he attempted to force her legs apart, and when they were sufficiently separated, plunged his erect manhood into her with one fast, deep thrust, causing her to cry out in pain.

"Oh, dearest, I'm sorry," he whispered hoarsely.

After the initial thrust he began to move quickly in and out with a jerky rhythm and a kind of frenetic energy, not allowing her to fully adjust to his plunging presence inside her. In what seemed like only seconds he was consumed and contorted by a succession of spasms that engulfed his entire body and elicited repeated shudders and groans from him.

In a state of exhaustion, he rolled off her and collapsed, sweating profusely and gasping for breath, but smiling blissfully through it all.

A few minutes later, as though suddenly aware of her presence beside him, he leaned over and kissed her. Surprised by the taste of salty tears on her cheek, he said, "Don't cry, darling. The first time for anything is always difficult. Next time it will be better. I promise you."

21

IN THE MORNING when she awoke, Micaela saw that Celestin was already dressed and hurriedly gathering their things together.

"You'd better get up, dearest," he said. "We have to say goodbye to your mother before we leave. There isn't much time."

"Leave? You might tell me where we're going," she retorted, knowing that it was undoubtedly to Mont L'Eveque.

"Home," he answered simply.

"Home?" she repeated.

"Yes. To Mont L'Eveque."

"For how long?"

"We're going to live there."

"But I want to stay in Paris," she protested.

"Don't fret, dearest. We'll come back to Paris again."

"But I want to *live* in Paris."

"That's impossible," he said firmly. "Our place is at the château. I am obliged to help my father in the administration of his estates. I can't do it from Paris."

Micaela could see from his adamant stand that it would be impossible to dissuade him, so she climbed out of bed and called for Binnie to help her into the imported French blue calico dress.

When they arrived at the Castillons' large home on the fashionable Rue St. Honoré—such homes were referred to by the French as *hôtels privés,* or private hotels—Louise was dismayed by the abrupt announcement of their departure from the city.

"I'm sorry you're leaving so soon," she said. "There are so many more people I want you to meet. I regret that because of my husband's illness I have not been able to devote more time to you, but alas . . ."

"It's all right, Mama." Micaela touched her arm.

189

"Let me say goodbye to Jean-Baptiste. Is he well enough to see me today?"

"I'll go with you, dear," Louise offered, taking her daughter by the hand. "Will you excuse us, Celestin?"

"Of course." He nodded and prepared to wait in the vestibule until mother and daughter returned.

When they entered her stepfather's room, Micaela was shocked at his appearance and wondered how a man who had once been so handsome and vital could have deteriorated to such a point.

Closing the door behind them, Louise took Micaela aside and spoke quietly but emphatically.

"Be careful of the baron when you get to Mont L'Eveque," she warned. "I hear he's received some anonymous letters containing slanderous accusations against us. He's very clever and may try to trap you into making certain admissions. Tell him nothing. If he proves too difficult for you, let me know. I can handle him."

"Yes, Mama," Micaela agreed.

Changing her tone completely, Louise greeted her husband and said to Micaela, "Now, go kiss him goodbye before you leave."

En route to Louise's home Celestin had casually informed Micaela for the first time that they would have to leave Binnie in Paris.

Aghast at such an idea, Micaela had cried, "What! Leave Binnie behind?"

"Yes. She can stay with your mother. You won't be needing her at the château. We have a large staff of servants far more capable than she."

"But I want Binnie with me," Micaela had protested. "I need her. She's been with me since I was a child. She's more than a maid, she's my companion."

"Nonsense. She's no companion at all. She's an ignorant, uneducated girl. You can get along without her very easily. Besides, there is no room for her in the servants' quarters, and frankly, I don't know how well the staff would accept her presence. After all, unlike them, she *is* a slave and not free to come and go as she chooses. We French are fiercely independent, even French servants. They would find the presence of a slave in their midst demoralizing."

"She's like a part of my family," Micaela had said in Binnie's defense.

"Hardly, dearest."

Having felt it was necessary that she give in on the issue, at least for the time being, Micaela was now forced to bid a sad farewell not only to her mother and stepfather but to Binnie as well.

"I don't like you goin' off with nobody to look after you, Miss Micaela," the slave girl wept, hugging her mistress in the vestibule of the lavish home.

"It's all right, Binnie," Micaela soothed. "We'll see how things work out. Perhaps you will be with me quite soon again."

As the coach drove down the Rue St. Honoré a fine drizzle began, and by the time they reached the outskirts of Paris, the rain had turned into a heavy downpour that continued relentlessly throughout the coach ride to Mont L'Eveque. As they left Paris farther and farther behind, Micaela became increasingly despondent while, conversely, Celestin seemed to grow happier, a look of relief apparent on his handsome, sensitive features.

"Ah, this sweet country air," he said ecstatically, opening the window of the coach and allowing the rain to pelt his face.

"Please, Celestin, close the window," she urged, refusing to share his joy. "It's chilly."

After several hours in the coach they came to a river, which Celestin proudly identified as the Oise. At that point the road paralleled the winding river for a considerable distance, until it finally veered away and was swallowed by a dense forest enclosing it on both sides.

"This forest is on Pontalba land," he boasted. "It's full of the finest game."

"Really?" she responded indifferently.

Eventually she was lulled into a light sleep by the gentle swaying of the carriage as well as from the fatigue of the trip, and she closed her eyes and rested her head against the back of the seat. Celestin slipped his arm around her, and pulling her close to him, kissed her forehead tenderly.

Sometime later she awakened with a start when the carriage turned sharply into a narrow, badly rutted lane and encountered a flock of noisy, honking geese herded by a peasant girl drenched from the driving rain. The girl and her geese quickly scattered to avoid the path of the coach.

"Dearest, we're almost home," Celestin announced.

At the end of the long lane winding through the woods they came to a wooden bridge over a deep, muddy moat choked with lily pads. Seeing the moat, Micaela thought for an instant of the hyacinth-clogged bayous she had explored with Patrick, and experienced a sinking feeling in her stomach. Several white swans huddled together on the edge of the ditch, as if trying to protect one another from the rain.

The coach rumbled over the bridge and into the courtyard of the château. Mont L'Eveque, rather than being a single château, was actually a group of buildings enclosed by the moat. In addition to the main edifice, there was a chapel, a guest house, stables, and a long, narrow greenhouse. The château itself was square and blocklike, the plainness and severity of its basic design relieved by windows and doorways arched and decorated in the typical Gothic style. The four corners were softened by rounded turrets, each having a pointed, conical roof.

Celestin ordered the coachman to stop in front of the entrance, and extending his cloak to protect Micaela from the rain, helped her out of the carriage.

"We're here at last," he said with a smile, his wet black curls pasted to his forehead.

The first person to greet them was a shabbily dressed gray-haired man who emerged from the greenhouse, trowel in hand, and hurried toward them. Micaela assumed he was one of the gardeners until, much to her astonishment, he embraced Celestin fervently and called him "son."

"Dearest, let me present to you my father, the baron," Celestin said proudly.

Before taking her hand, the baron dropped the

trowel and wiped his hands on the dirt-spattered gardener's smock he was wearing.

"Charmed, my dear," he said as he raised her fingers to his lips. Through the fabric of her gloves she could feel the rough, calloused skin of his hands.

"Likewise, I'm sure," she murmured, and curtsied politely. How different he seemed from what she had been led to expect. In spite of his humble, unassuming appearance, he did have a rather formidable air about him, and on closer inspection she doubted that anyone would ever truly ever mistake him for a gardener.

For a few moments there was an awkward silence as daughter-in-law and father-in-law looked each other over, broken only when Celestin said, "Please excuse us, Papa. I must take Micaela out of the rain. I know that Mama and Aunt Celeste are anxious to see her."

"Yes, go on. Take your bride inside," the baron agreed. "But come to the greenhouse as soon as you can."

"The greenhouse?" Celestin echoed.

"Yes. There are some new things I want to show you. I have some delightful surprises." Affectionately he pinched his son's cheek.

"Perhaps Micaela would like to see them also," Celestin suggested.

"No. Come alone. It's too wet for Micaela."

Celestin led Micaela through the high, arched front doorway into a cold, vaultlike vestibule. Jeanne rushed forward to greet them, bestowing kisses on Micaela's cheeks.

"Welcome to Mont L'Eveque," she fluttered. "I've been waiting for you a long time. How naughtly of you to tarry in Paris so long!" With that she rang for the servants and instructed them to bring in the young couple's baggage.

As Jeanne and a maid helped Micaela out of her wet things she was struck by how tiny and insignificant Jeanne appeared, dwarfed by the château's high, vaulted ceilings and huge granite walls covered by old and valuable tapestries.

"Mama, will you take Micaela to meet Aunt Celeste?" Celestin asked. "Papa is waiting for me in the greenhouse."

"But aren't you going to say hello to her yourself?" Jeanne reproached.

"I'll see her a little later, Mama," he replied, obviously impatient to return to his father.

When Celestin disappeared out the front door into the driving rain again, Jeanne took Micaela by the hand and led her down the cold, drafty hall to a large parlor in which a warm, cheerful fire was burning in the marble fireplace. An elderly, white-haired lady was seated in a rather worn-looking green armchair, crocheting. She looked up from her work and smiled as Jeanne approached with Micaela.

"Micaela, this is my aunt Celeste, Madame Miró," Jeanne said.

"How do you do, my dear." Madame Miró extended a bony hand speckled with brown spots. Celeste Miró, widow of the one-time governor of Louisiana, had raised her niece since childhood, and Jeanne was as devoted to her as if she had been her natural mother.

"Charmed," Micaela murmured.

"I know who you are," Madame Miró beamed. "You are the daughter of Don Andrés Almonester. I would have guessed it even if no one had told me. I see so much of him in you, child. Ah, how my husband and I loved your dear father! What a wonderful man! Don Andrés did more for New Orleans than anyone else. Mont L'Eveque is a long way from home for you, isn't it? Well, I hope you'll be happy here. Sometimes it's not easy."

"Shame on you, Aunt Celeste!" Jeanne scolded. "What on earth do you mean by saying such a thing?"

"It's true, Jeanne," Madame Miró insisted. "You know that far better than I."

Celestin hurried through the mud and wet grass to the greenhouse and dashed inside, closing the door quickly. Overhead, the rain pounded unmercifully against the many panes of glass, creating a terrible din. Because of the stifling, humid heat inside the glass structure, he began to tug absentmindedly at his collar. This greenhouse was Joseph de Pontalba's special sanctuary, where he spent hours cultivating all manner of fruits and vegetables as well as herbs and spices. He even maintained a section for rare medicinal plants about which he had learned during his years as an Indian fighter in the territory west of the Mississippi.

In the rear of the greenhouse, the baron, transferring potted strawberries from one container to another, looked up and smiled when he saw his son hurrying toward him. Immediately plucking a ripe, plump berry, he offered it to him, and when Celestin smiled with delight, pushed it gently into the youth's eager mouth.

"Remember how I fed you strawberries when you were small?" he said. "You used to love them. During those young years you spent away from me with your mother and Aunt Celeste in Spain, I missed you so much. I vowed then that I would always do everything in my power to see that you had strawberries whenever you wanted them."

"Oh, Papa, you attach too much importance to it," Celestin laughed, wiping his mouth on the back of his hand, a childish gesture that secretly delighted his father.

"I attach importance to all your wants and needs," the baron declared.

"What did you wish to see me about, Papa?"

"So that is the bride we sent you all the way across the Atlantic to marry, is she?" The baron twisted his thin-lipped mouth disapprovingly.

Puzzled by his father's tone and feeling somewhat apprehensive, Celestin asked, "What's the matter? Doesn't she please you, Papa? She's very nice. Really . . ."

"Oh, the girl is all right," Pontalba replied, dismissing her with an indifferent wave of his hand. "It's the marriage contract that displeases me."

"In what way?"

"Ah, what a clever fox my dear cousin Louise is. And what a stupid fool your mother was to play right into her hands. Your mother signed that loathsome

contract without so much as a single second thought."
The baron scowled. "You are familiar by now with the
provisions set forth in that contract, are you not?"

"Yes, I think so," Celestin answered hesitantly.
Legal matters had never been easy for him to comprehend, much to his father's chagrin. "Micaela was to
receive forty-five thousand dollars as her share of her
late father's estate and—"

"You may stop right there," the baron interrupted
him. "Surely common sense tells you that forty-five
thousand dollars is a mere pittance. Don Andrés Almonester's estate was worth many times that amount.
By law Micaela is entitled to a minimum of one half
of his fortune."

Perplexed, Celestin frowned. "Then I don't understand . . ."

"Through some kind of devious legal maneuvering,
Louise and those various attorneys of hers—Saint-
Avid here in Paris and that LeBreton fellow in New
Orleans—somehow managed to declare most of Don
Andres's holdings paraphernal property."

"What is that?" Celestin asked.

"It is a complicated legal term for property which
is retained by the widow and therefore not subject to
the normal division of an estate. In short, my dear
cousin Madame Castillon has cleverly succeeded in
keeping nearly all of Don Andrés's holdings for herself and doling out this mere pittance to her daughter."

"But Cousin Louise has agreed to add eighty-five
thousand dollars of her own money to the forty-five
thousand dollars," Celestin said. "I think that was
rather generous of her."

The baron slammed his fist down hard against the
potting bench, jarring the plants. "Good Lord," he
cried, "are you as big a fool as your mother? Don't
you realize that Louise gives her daughter that eighty-
five thousand dollars only if I match it with a similar
sum?"

Celestin was thoroughly confused. He hated to have
his already somewhat uncertain marriage plagued by
such complex financial dealings, all of which seemed
rather crass to him.

"If you'll forgive me for saying so, sir, it doesn't seem unfair to me."

The baron shook his head in dismay. "It will be difficult to forgive you for such unabashed ignorance."

"Surely we aren't too poor to spare eighty-five thousand dollars," Celestin argued. "I have seen the revenues from our holdings—"

"That's not the point," the baron cut in angrily. "Our wealth is in our land and not in goods or properties that are easily or advantageously converted into cash. The point is that Madame Castillon has deeply insulted us by inserting such a condition into the marriage contract. The very idea that I am obliged to make any payment at all is the height of effrontery. Many people would be willing to bestow far more than her relatively paltry contribution on a daughter just for the privilege of marrying into this family. After all, we are a long, illustrious line. I cannot believe that your mother would be so stupid as to affix the Pontalba name to such an outrageous document."

"Perhaps Mama was unaware of its contents," Celestin suggested.

"No, she was quite aware. But, like you, your mother was persuaded by Cousin Louise into thinking the conditions of the contract were quite reasonable. This action of Madame Castillon's is an unforgivable insult. But enough of that woman. I am not without a means of dealing with her. She will find a formidable adversary in me."

"Papa, I hope you will not hold anything against Micaela."

"Mothers and daughters are of one flesh," the baron snapped.

"But, Papa . . ." Celestin started to protest.

"Enough of both of them." Then he continued in a far more genial tone. "Come down this aisle with me, Celestin. I have carefully nurtured the most delicious Brussels sprouts especially for you. You must taste them. The leaves are so delicious and tender. Remember how you have always loved them?"

After a brief chat with Madame Miró, Jeanne conducted Micaela on a tour of the gloomy, musty-smelling castle. Although its four stories contained an enormous number of rooms, very few were currently in use.

"We manage to live in just a few rooms," Jeanne explained. "The baron says it's becoming frightfully expensive to maintain this old château. Thrift is very important to him."

After leading her daughter-in-law up a winding staircase inside one of the four cylindrical turrets, Jeanne unlocked a door on the second floor that led to a group of rooms more musty and stale-smelling than any she had toured so far.

"This is the apartment you and Celestin will share," Jeanne announced.

"Which is the maid's room?" Micaela asked, surveying the sparse and shabby furniture.

"Maid?" Jeanne repeated.

"Yes, Binnie," Micaela replied. "I was forced to leave her in Paris with Mama, but I want to send for her as soon as possible."

"Oh, you won't need a maid," Jeanne laughed. "We have enough servants here. I don't think the baron would look favorably on another mouth to feed. Besides, he doesn't like us to rely too much on servants, not for most things. He believes that people, no matter how high their station in life, must learn to be self-sufficient. I'm afraid you may have to make some difficult adjustments under the baron's roof. We all have had to, even Celestin."

"I shall be most unhappy without my maid, Binnie," Micaela insisted. "I know that."

"Oh, you'll get over it," Jeanne said, dismissing her objection with breezy indifference. "You'll probably find you never needed her in the first place. You American girls are so spoiled by all your slaves running after you, catering to your every wish. Here it's quite different."

From the moment the carriage had pulled into the courtyard at Mont L'Eveque, the baron monopolized

his son's attention, scarcely allowing him time for anyone else. Celestin felt uncomfortable with the situation
and wished his father would demand less of him. It
was readily apparent that Micaela was unhappy in her
new surroundings, and he wanted to spend more time
with her to help her make the necessary adjustments,
but he was finding it impossible. Before leaving Paris,
he had known she would miss the capital and its many
diversions but had hoped that in time she would come
to love Mont L'Eveque as he did. Such did not seem
to be the case, however.

In the bucolic wilderness Micaela could find little
with which to occupy herself, except for reading—she
had picked up several novels as well as books of poetry
and plays at the stalls along the Seine—and walking
about the grounds, feeding bread crumbs to the swans
in the moat or throwing bones to the noisy hounds
caged up behind the stables. She tried to sketch, but
her drawings were invariably of buildings in Paris or
New Orleans, which she did from memory and filled
her with discontent and longing.

In the evenings the entire family gathered around
the fireplace in the parlor, the only warm room in the
house. Celestin played chess with his father, Madame
Miró and Jeanne did needlework, and Micaela read or
sulked. Occasionally Madame Miró questioned her
about New Orleans and people whom she had known
there many years past. The old woman's questions
evoked the same feeling of unbearable nostalgia that
her sketches did.

One evening the baron called Celestin into his study
and locked the heavy oak double doors behind them.
From a drawer in his massive rosewood desk he took
out a recently executed document and presented it to
his son.

"I want you to read this," he said.

Celestin did as he was instructed, and when he
finished, he stared at his father incredulously. "Does
this really say what I think it does?"

"It merely states that although I will bestow the
eighty-five thousand dollars on you as stipulated in
the marriage contract, you will immediately turn that

sum back to me," the baron explained. "It also commits you to secrecy in the matter."

"But if Micaela or Cousin Louise should learn of this . . . ?"

"The only way they can learn about this pact of ours is from you or from me. No one else knows. They will find out nothing from me, I assure you. If they hear about it from you, the consequences will be dire, as you just read."

"I read that I am threatened with disinheritance," Celestin said, a disbelieving tone in his voice.

"It more than threatens," the baron corrected. "It guarantees."

"But if through some accident Micaela or Cousin Louise should learn I've returned the money to you . . . ?"

"Conceivably they could go so far as to insist on an annulment of the marriage," the baron told him. "And they would be within their rights."

Celestin paled at the mention of the word "annulment." "I wouldn't want that," he said, fearing the disgrace that might be heaped on him if he returned to the army and his fellow officers learned of it. Annulments for such men automatically implied sexual inadequacy, whether or not that was the case.

"Neither would I," the baron agreed. "So we must guard against such a possibility."

"How, Papa?"

"By getting the girl pregnant," his father stated bluntly. "And fast."

Celestin considered his father's answer carefully before he spoke. "If Micaela becomes pregnant, may I then return to the army?"

The baron looked at him in surprise. "Right away, you mean?"

"No, I mean after the baby is born and we are certain that everything is all right."

"I'm not sure that everything will ever be 'all right,' " the baron said, "but we'll discuss that issue at the proper time. There is always the possibility that you might return to the army. Yes, I haven't closed my mind to the idea altogether. Meanwhile, you have a bride who at this moment is probably in bed and anxiously awaiting you—or so I should hope. So sign this document and be off."

22

IF MICAELA FOUND life at Mont L'Eveque difficult when she first arrived, she soon discovered that it became progressively worse, rather than better. Unlike her mother and the Parisians she had recently met, the Pontalbas led a secluded, practically reclusive life in their country château, seeing virtually no one; entertaining—if such a word could be used with respect to this family—was almost nonexistent. Their chief social diversion was Mass in the chapel on Sunday, at which time the peasants from the surrounding farms were invited to participate. Excursions away from the estate, especially to Paris, were considered almost unthinkable. With each day that passed, Micaela felt more and more like a prisoner in isolation. Whenever she suggested a trip away from Mont L'Eveque, she encountered great resistance.

"Why should we leave this delightful countryside to go to that corrupt, immoral pigsty of a Paris?" the baron would say, curling his thin lips in disgust. "Paris has nothing to offer."

"Paris has the opera, the theater, cafes, restaurants, and marvelous parks," Micaela would argue. "Above all, it has life."

"You mean frivolity, madame," the baron would return. "Foolishness and wantonness."

"There's enough life for us right here," Jeanne would add, siding with her husband as she always did, even when he was wrong or unreasonable, a pattern Micaela found maddening.

The baron ruled his little fiefdom with such an autocratic hand that at times Micaela thought she was living under the feudalism of the Middle Ages. It was difficult for her to believe that the French had fought a long and horribly bloody revolution against just this form of tyranny only a few decades earlier. The baron would ride imperiously across his many acres, the peasants would bow and scrape and doff their hats to him as they would to a monarch, and it was obvious that Baron Joseph relished every moment of it.

From Celestin, Micaela learned that her father-in-law had extensive holdings, not just around Mont L'Eveque but in other parts of France as well, and these estates had to be visited from time to time. Celestin was frequently expected to act as his father's emissary to these distant properties, collecting rents from the peasants and handling minor matters.

Despite his autocratic airs, the baron was a man of oddly austere tastes. He preferred to dress in the simple clothing of the middle class and to dine on game from his own forests or on meat from livestock raised on the premises and on vegetables from his garden or greenhouse. Time not spent on the administration of his lands was consumed by gardening, which seemed to be his great passion, although he also enjoyed an occasional game of chess with his son.

The women of Mont L'Eveque, Jeanne and her aunt, seemed reasonably content to busy themselves with the routine of running the château. Jeanne was a bit of a neurasthenic, who at times required a great deal of rest and complained of chronic fatigue.

Celestin's role of servant to his father's will caused Micaela deep distress, not simply because he was away on business for the baron a great deal but also because he was often forced to neglect her and leave her on her own. Although they didn't share that many interests, he did try to help make her life in the country more bearable.

One activity they enjoyed together was riding, and Mont L'Eveque had an excellent stable. Because of Celestin's experience in the cavalry, he was an expert judge of horseflesh. Unfortunately, when he was away, the baron forbade her to ride alone; his excuse was that she was too unfamiliar with the countryside and its possible hazards, as well as that it was not proper for a young married woman to go riding by herself.

At night, when she and Celestin lay together in the large, musty-smelling bed, he tried to be ardent and tender, but despite his efforts, his lovemaking was awkward and hurried, as if he were driven more by a compulsion to prove himself than by an actual need or desire for her. Micaela was finding it increasingly difficult to respond to him and took to fantasizing that it was Patrick Lynch making love to her instead of her husband, a fantasy that was not easy to trigger or to sustain. Fortunately, an unresponsive wife was not considered undesirable, so that her reluctance to encourage intimacy between them was not regarded as a flaw in their relationship. If anything, a disinterest in sex on the part of a wife was deemed noble and virtuous and could often increase a husband's esteem.

As for Celestin, he seemed neither happy nor unhappy with Micaela. The marriage for him was little more than an inevitability that he tolerated amiably. The only time she saw any true enthusiasm or happiness on his face was when he spoke about his life in the army.

Hoping to point out to him exactly how much his father dominated his life, one day as they were riding through the Pontalbas' vast pear orchard, she remarked, "Sometimes, Celestin, it's as if your father gives you no credit for having a mind of your own."

Frowning at her, he asked, "What are you talking about, Micaela?"

"I'm talking about the way your father seems to run your life totally—*our* life."

"You may not believe this, but Papa means well. Everything he does is ultimately for me—for us."

"I'm not so sure."

"You didn't want to leave Paris and come here, so you've made up your mind not to like Mont L'Eveque, and you blame the baron for everything that doesn't suit you. It's unfair."

"Can't you see that I'm bored and lonely?" she complained. "There's nothing for me to do and no one to talk to except your mother and Madame Miró. You and I haven't met anyone new since we left Paris. I miss the people there. I miss the activity. Sometimes I feel as if I'm being buried alive here!"

"Paris is full of shallow, superficial people posing as intellectuals and artists and various other things they're not," he argued. "Here people may not be sophisticated, but at least they're genuine."

"How would I know?" she retorted. "I never see anyone but your family and the servants." She realized with dismay that her attempt to convince Celestin of his father's iron-handed rule had failed.

When they returned to the château, Jeanne greeted her son with a kiss and handed him a letter that had come for him. He glanced at the handwriting on the envelope and seemed to recognize it at once. Barely excusing himself, he left Micaela and his mother standing in the vestibule and went into the study, closing the doors behind him.

"Dear me," Jeanne said, and put a hand to her cheek. "I wonder why he did that."

The letter was from Armand Dulac in Dresden, and just seeing the cavalry captain's scrawl on the envelope was sufficient to arouse Celestin's great longing for his former life. As much as he loved Mont L'Eveque, it could not begin to offer him the excitement and satisfaction he had experienced in the Grand Army. The reason why he felt the way he did was something he really could not fathom.

Seating himself at the rosewood desk, he began to read the letter.

I am not one for writing, but since one of my men was returning to his village in the Oise district, I decided to take advantage of his trip and send this note with him. I needn't tell you that the Spanish-Portuguese campaign was a disaster, although, as you well know, our regiment under Ney's expert command made a fine showing in the retreat. Now we are camped at Dresden with the emperor, who is at this moment making plans for an invasion of Russia, an excellent country for cavalry warfare. The Cossacks are reputed to be very skilled mounted fighters, but they have yet to face the cavalry of the Grand Army. We'll see how good they are after that. Ah, Pontalba, if only you were riding with us! Naturally they have sent me a replacement, but he cannot measure up to you. In any event, I will not belabor a chapter that is apparently closed in your life. I am sure you are occupied with other matters at present and perhaps wish to hear no more of the army. Reliable sources, who met you in Paris at the Cafe de Roy, told me that your bride is most attractive. Lucky man! I hope one day soon to see you again, but in the meantime, receive a fervent hug from your friend and fellow officer.

Sadly Celestin folded the letter, started to drop it on the desk, then changed his mind and slipped it inside his shirt.

At the urging of the Pontalbas, Micaela went to Mass at the château chapel on Sundays, although she would have preferred to attend services in one of the nearby towns.

One Sunday, after she had been at Mont L'Eveque for about two months, she awoke feeling weak and nauseous, but her in-laws refused to accept her protests and forced her to get up, dress, and accompany them.

The chapel was as cold and drafty as the château, and despite her heavy cape, which she pulled around her, Micaela began to shiver uncontrollably during the reading of the Gospel. At a nudge from Madame Miró, Celestin put an arm around his young wife and attempted to warm her, but her chills seemed to grow worse. Silently he helped her out of the pew and down the aisle.

Back at the château, Micaela headed straight for bed, and as she climbed the spiral stairs to their second-floor apartment, she suddenly felt faint and clutched at the stony wall for support. Spots danced before her eyes and the blood slowly drained from her head.

Concerned about her despite the whispered admonitions from his father during Mass that she was merely acting up because she didn't want to leave her warm bed, Celestin followed her up the stairs and, fortunately, was right behind her when she collapsed. He caught her in his arms, nearly losing his own balance under the impact of her dead weight. Shouting excitedly for the servants to help him, he carried her to their apartment and put her to bed, suggesting that they send for the doctor.

"Ridiculous," the baron scoffed at this idea when the rest of the family returned from Mass. "She's not ill. Her blood is merely thin from living in the tropics all her life. She isn't used to the French climate. I shall make her a tonic at once from some of my plants —it will thicken her blood. She'll be fine in no time." With that, he left immediately for the greenhouse.

Later Celestin attempted to administer a spoonful of the freshly concocted tonic, but Micaela shoved away the foul-smelling, murky green liquid with a shudder.

"But it's good for you," he urged. "It will help you and make you feel better. The baron's herbal remedies are exceptional. They have seen me through many illnesses."

Averting her head in disgust, she said, "Please, Celestin, take it away."

The following day Micaela forced herself out of bed and again fainted, not once but twice, the second time nearly striking her head on the corner of the dressing table, which terrified not only Celestin, who had witnessed the fall, but Madame Miró as well. It was she who stubbornly insisted that the doctor be called, and this time Celestin ignored his father's open opposition and went into the village.

"She needs no doctor," the baron fumed. "You're all coddling that girl too much. Soon she'll be running all of us."

"She will never run you, dear," Jeanne advised her husband.

Celestin and the doctor returned while the argument was still going on. With only the most cursory of questions and examination, the doctor pronounced

Micaela pregnant, a diagnosis that seemed to astound everyone.

"I can't believe it!" Jeanne cried.

"The doctor's a fool," the baron snapped.

"I don't see why you're so surprised," Madame Miró chuckled. "Young couples become parents every day. Why should Celestin and Micaela be any different?"

Celestin greeted the news of his wife's condition with a strange mixture of elation and misgivings. Elation because he had satisfied his duty to produce an heir for the Pontalba line, and misgivings because the child might bind him even more closely to the family and prevent his returning to the army in spite of his father's promise to allow him to resume his military career if Micaela became pregnant.

From the very beginning Micaela's pregnancy proved to be a difficult one, so much so, in fact, that the Pontalbas gave in and allowed her to send for Binnie. A room was prepared for the maid next to the master bedroom in the couple's apartment, thus keeping the young black girl separated from the other servants.

Eventually the fainting spells subsided and the doctor permitted Micaela to leave her bed, but the persistent, nagging nausea that had accompanied the fainting spells did not disappear. Even the odor of food was intolerable to Micaela, and, unable to eat, she grew increasingly pale and weak.

"If you don't eat somethin', Miss Micaela, you're gonna waste away to nothin' and die," Binnie warned. The slave was overjoyed to be united with her mistress again and was almost too conscientious in her care for her.

"You've got to force yourself to eat, dear," Jeanne urged. "If not for your own sake, then for the sake of your unborn baby."

Because it was a favorite of his, Celestin thought fresh fish might appeal to her, so he went to a nearby stream and caught several trout, which he instructed Binnie to poach for her mistress. But when Micaela lifted the silver cover from the serving dish, she let out a groan of anguish and reached frantically for the chamber pot, into which she promptly vomited.

That evening, as Celestin was preparing to sleep on the daybed that had been placed in their bedroom for him because of Micaela's present state, she called out to him weakly. In an instant he was at her side.

"What is it, dearest?" he asked anxiously.

"Celestin, please take me away from here. I want to go back to Paris," she pleaded, her voice an almost inaudible whisper. "I want to see my mother."

"We will go after the baby is born," he assured her, patting her hand affectionately.

"No. I want to go now. I must see my mother. Does she even know I am ill?"

"We didn't want to worry her. You know how distressed she is by poor Castillon's illness."

"Please, Celestin, you *must* take me to see my mother." She longed for the sanctuary of her mother's home and was beginning to believe that if she had to remain in the gloomy château much longer, she would surely die. "Promise me you will."

"Such a trip is out of the question, particularly in this foul weather," he said, glancing out the window. "And especially in your condition."

"Then send for her and tell her to come at once," she begged. Micaela knew that if Louise saw the present state of her daughter's health, she would find some way to get her out of the château and back to Paris. Thank God, Micaela thought, my mother is a strong-willed, resourceful woman and not a wishy-washy, spineless creature like Jeanne.

"The baron has forbidden your mother to enter this house," Celestin finally replied, hating to convey such an edict but knowing he had to inform her sooner or later.

Shocked, Micaela gasped, "What! How dare he?"

"He's very angry with her about the marriage contract," Celestin explained. "He feels she has insulted his dignity."

Micaela had been well aware of the baron's hostile attitude toward her ever since her arrival and had suspected that the marriage contract might have been a factor. Now she was certain.

"But I am ill," she said. "He can surely overlook such petty matters at this time."

Celestin shook his head. "You know how stubborn he is. Besides, I don't think he regards the marriage contract as a petty matter."

"Petty or not, this is no time for him to be stubborn," she argued. "At least go to him and ask him to allow Mama to visit me."

"It would be useless, dearest."

"Do you refuse to ask, him, Celestin?"

"I know his answer."

"Then you refuse to do this for your wife, who at any moment could die, and with her your unborn child?"

"You know the baron," was his answer.

"I know that no one is such a heartless monster."

"Please, Micaela, you're being unreasonable."

"Very well, if you won't do it, I shall have to ask him myself," she declared, adding, *"If* I am ever strong enough to get out of this bed."

The following day Micaela forced herself to eat some food, keeping it down by sheer strength of will. With Binnie's assistance she managed to make her way down the winding stone steps and into the baron's study. He was astonished to see her and rose from behind his massive desk.

"What has happened?" he asked.

"I must speak to you, sir," she said quietly.

He pulled up a chair and helped her into it, then sat down again. "What is wrong?"

"I want to see my mother," she blurted out, too weak to bother with subtleties.

Looking at her coldly, he said, "Madame Castillon is not permitted here."

"Then I would like to go to her in Paris," Micaela declared. "Celestin has refused to arrange such a trip for me. Now I am asking you to do so, since you are the one who has forbidden my mother's presence at Mont L'Eveque."

"You know perfectly well that your present condition precludes such a trip," he answered. "And even if you weren't ill, I wouldn't allow it. Your mother has insulted the dignity of this family. Until she is willing to make some kind of restitution, she cannot see you, either here or in Paris or anywhere else."

"Are you telling me I am a prisoner?" she cried, aghast at his words.

"Define it as you wish, my dear."

Not having the strength for an out-and-out confrontation, Micaela was obliged to pursue another route. "Very well, sir, what must my mother do to regain your favor?"

"Regain my favor?" he mused, obviously pleased that she seemed to be capitulating to his demand. "She must assign you your rightful share of your father's estate, that's what she must do. The paltry sum in the marriage contract is a mere pittance, an insult. Your true share is many times that amount."

"I have no need for it now," Micaela replied ingenuously. "When Mama dies, it will all be mine, anyway."

Agitated, the baron came out from behind his desk and stood over her. "Don't you see, you silly goose, this is more than a matter of need? It is a matter of pride—my son's pride, the pride of the Pontalba family. All that is yours belongs by law to my son. In cheating you, your mother has cheated Celestin of his rightful dowry. After all, he is your husband, your lord and master. You must never forget that. Now, do you understand why I am forced to be so severe? I refuse to allow you or anyone else in my family to associate with Louise Castillon until she has made amends for her grievous insult to us."

"But, sir, I am very ill," Micaela insisted stubbornly. "Surely you would rescind such an order in my present state?"

"I would not do such a thing even if you were about to die," he returned, his voice almost a hiss. "And that, my dear, is final."

23

WHILE COLLECTING RENTS on the baron's out-lying farms, Celestin learned, in a chance encounter with a soldier from his old regiment, that Armand Dulac had been sent by Marshal Ney on a mission to Paris. Since Celestin found himself approximately mid-way between the French capital and Mont L'Eveque, he impulsively decided to go on to Paris instead of re-turning home, hoping for a reunion with the cavalry captain whom he held in such high esteem.

En route he was beset by conflicting emotions: ela-tion at the prospect of seeing Dulac again and guilt about leaving Micaela behind when he knew how much she desperately longed to return to Paris. When his father had invoked the cruel edict barring his young wife and her mother from seeing each other, he had wanted to intervene but could not bring himself to do so for fear of provoking the baron's wrath. He knew how obsessively determined his father was to retaliate against the so-called duplicity in the marriage contract. Baron Joseph was a strong adherent to rigid beliefs and principles and unswerving in his fixation that Louise surrender what he felt rightly belonged to the Pontalbas. The devious means he had had to employ to avoid payment of the eighty-five thousand dollars had irked the baron and goaded him to seek further reprisals. He had resolved to force his crafty cousin to capitulate to his demands no matter to what lengths he had to go. Of that Celestin was certain.

When he arrived in Paris, Celestin decided that the best place to begin looking for Dulac was the Cafe de Roy, and as he headed in that direction he recalled with a twinge of remorse how much Micaela loved the lively cafes, even the Roy with its air thick with to-bacco smoke and its noisy military men. How pale and thin she had looked before he left, hardly able to tolerate any food other than an occasional Creole dish Binnie had been able to persuade her to eat.

"There ain't hardly nothin' she can keep down, Master Celestin, no matter what I fix," the maid had complained. "If Miss Micaela don't start eatin' soon, I don't know what's gonna happen. She's gonna waste away to nothin'. She ain't but skin and bones as it is. Instead of eatin' for two like she should be doin', Miss Micaela ain't eatin' enough to keep one alive."

"Try to do your best to force her to eat while I'm away," he had enjoined Binnie, and left feeling helpless and dismayed.

Alighting from the carriage, Celestin entered the cafe, crowded as always with soldiers. Making his way through the throng, he anxiously searched for Dulac. After asking several fellow cavalrymen about him, he stumbled on a lieutenant in the dragoons who informed him that Dulac was in a fencing studio a few blocks from the cafe.

Celestin proceeded to the studio at once. In the doorway he was accosted by a gypsy woman in filthy rags who held a repulsive ape on the end of a chain.

"Please, sir," she said in a whining voice, fanning out a deck of cards, "my ape will tell your fortune. Let him pick the cards of your destiny."

Impatiently he brushed her aside, causing the ape to become excited and wave its long, spidery arms and bare its enormous teeth threateningly at him.

Inside the fencing studio, a small group, mostly military men, were avidly watching two adversaries as they saluted one another with their weapons and stood en garde, the afternoon sunlight flashing off their shiny steel blades. Celestin recognized Dulac at once as the captain rapped his opponent's rapier, provoking him to attack. There were three passes in rapid succession, with no touch either way, but one came so close to Dulac's unprotected chest that Celestin winced. The match was evidently only an exercise, and hopefully, neither man would be skewered. Celestin knew that Dulac enjoyed a reputation as one of the finest swordsmen in Europe, but he had never had the opportunity of seeing him in a match and was fascinated to observe how closely Dulac studied his opponent, the lightning manner in which he moved, and the grace with which he handled the rapier. Celestin, who considered himself barely competent with a blade, fervently wished he could achieve Dulac's skill and dexterity.

As the match progressed, Dulac's opponent drew his weapon back as if preparing to deliver a cut, but with amazing speed the cavalry officer swerved to the side and successfully avoided it. The opponent then charged in with a low hand aimed at Dulac's heart, but the captain stepped back and parried. His adversary deceived the parry, and the point of his weapon lunged forward and caught itself in the fabric of Dulac's shirt. Dulac retreated quickly, but the other fencer pressed him, allowing him no time to plan a retaliative strategy, and lunged short. Dulac beat the blade to the right, riposting with a deadly thrust to the face, which his opponent parried bravely without retreating, forcing Dulac back. The officer slipped and fell backward, head over heels, but recovered miraculously in a reverse lunge as his staunch opponent thrust down at him. With a swift movement of the wrist Dulac brought his blade up and beat the other man's weapon so high he lost his grasp on it and watched in dismay as it tumbled from his hand. The spectators laughed, and seeing that the match was ended, quickly moved in on the two adversaries, congratulating each for superb swordsmanship.

Wiping the sweat from his forehead, Dulac looked around and spotted Celestin in the crowd. He shoved his way through to the youth and threw his powerful arms around him.

"Pontalba!" he cried, as much with joy as with surprise at seeing his junior officer again. "What in the hell are you doing here? I thought you had retired to your country estate to watch the hay grow and your pigs get fat!" He laughed, slapping Celestin heartily on the back.

Gracefully easing out of Dulac's embrace, Celestin said, "Sometimes I have to come to Paris on business."

"What kind of business does a country squire have in this city?" Dulac questioned jovially. "But no matter, I'm so happy to see you. How is married life treating you, my boy?"

"Fine," Celestin assured him. "Fine indeed."

Moving away from the group of fencing enthusiasts crowding about them, Dulac focused his entire attention on Celestin.

"Come, we must have a drink together," he urged. "At the very least."

The two men seated themselves in the Cafe de Roy, and while they drank, Celestin listened raptly to Dulac relate the cavalry's escapades in great detail.

"Ah, Pontalba, you should never have left the regiment," Dulac sighed. "How much you are needed. How much we have all missed you. Your replacements have not been worth their salt. I've never had so competent a junior officer in my life as you, my boy. And I probably never will. You must end this dreary life in the country and come back to the army. The Russian invasion will be our most fabulous adventure yet. At last we will have opponents in the Cossacks truly worthy of our fighting skills. You must not miss Russia."

"It's impossible for me to leave, Dulac," Celestin replied regretfully. "You see, my wife is pregnant. We're going to have a baby."

Dulac's face grew serious. "Well, that does change things, doesn't it? How soon is the baby due to arrive?"

"In a few months."

"Yes, that changes things considerably," Dulac repeated, a note of definite disappointment in his voice.

From the Roy they went on to other cafes, steadily becoming intoxicated and Celestin drinking far more than he ever had before. In the early hours of the morning they had lost count of the number of bars and cafes they had visited and found themselves in a truly low-life establishment full of pimps, pickpockets, and whores, not far from the extensive gardens of the Palais Royal that Micaela loved so much.

Leaning close to Celestin, Dulac put his arm around the youth's shoulder and asked in an intimate tone,

"Tell me, my boy, how long has it been since you've had a really good piece of ass?"

Although embarrassed by such a question, Celestin was sufficiently inebriated to answer it truthfully and without hesitation, as few soldiers would have done. "A long time," he admitted. "You see, my wife's been under the weather with the baby and all . . ."

"Good!" Dulac roared. "Come with me. Let's get out of here. I know just the place to fix you up."

Over Celestin's rather ineffective protests, Dulac dragged him out of the dive and to the Jardin des Capucines, one of Paris's most notorious brothels. On the way they stopped a street vendor and bought what Dulac referred to as "French letters." When Celestin inquired what they were, Dulac merely chuckled and replied, "You'll find out, my boy. You'll find out very soon."

Inside the plush, garishly decorated whorehouse, Dulac was welcomed as an old friend by the madam and her girls. A few minutes later, Celestin realized that his former captain was arranging for him to bed down with one of the whores, and he grew uneasy. Taking him aside, he confided, "My God, Dulac, I can't do that. I'm a married man."

Overhearing him, the madam and several of the girls broke into gales of raucous laughter.

"Our best and most frequent clients are married men," the overpainted madam assured him.

"And the best lovers," one of the girls added, grabbing at his crotch and giggling when he jumped.

"But if I should contract a disease . . ." he fretted, recalling his father's stern lectures.

"My girls happen to be the cleanest and safest in Paris," the madam informed him indignantly. "The most important men in Europe come here. No one has ever contracted a disease in my establishment. I would not permit such a thing."

The women were all so heavily rouged and powdered that Celestin had no idea if they were clean or not, and as for their being "safe" from disease, there was no way of knowing that until much later.

Extracting one of the "French letters" from his

pocket, Dulac said, "You won't catch anything if you slip this over your cock."

On closer inspection Celestin discovered that the object Dulac held was a fish bladder. The thought of wearing one of these foul-smelling things repelled him.

"Go on, take it from him and put it on," the madam urged.

"No disease and no unwanted brats," one of her girls remarked.

"Better not be any unwanted brats," a bare-breasted whore named Françoise piped up. "I've already got one brat to keep, and that's enough."

Taking Celestin by the arm, a girl named Jacqueline began to lead him upstairs. "Come on, my little man, let me show you a good time," she coaxed.

When Celestin started to resist, Dulac jumped in to egg him on. "Go ahead, Pontalba, have some fun!"

Jacqueline dragged the young aristocrat into a plush bedchamber filled with gleaming mirrors, including one on the ceiling, directly over the bed. Erotic murals depicting orgiastic couplings covered the walls. Employing all the forceful persuasion of her profession, she finally succeeded in divesting him of all his clothes and getting him into bed. His youth enabled her to arouse him quickly despite his lack of cooperation. Once he was in an erect state, she slipped the fish bladder over his distended manhood.

"Please," he begged as she began to straddle him, placing one foot on either side of his hips. "I am a married man. I am soon to be a father. I should not do such things."

"Do what?" Jacqueline giggled playfully as she slowly lowered herself onto the masthead of his desire.

In the adjoining room, Dulac and another whore named Colette secretly observed Celestin and Jacqueline through a hidden peephole in the wall.

"I was afraid that in his embarrassment he might make her extinguish the lamp," Colette said. "You know how these shy ones are."

Thoroughly aroused by what he was seeing through the peephole now that Celestin had finally surrendered to his basic drives, Dulac began rubbing his rapidly distending crotch.

"I'm glad they didn't," he grunted hoarsely. "Then we wouldn't be able to watch them."

While Dulac's attention was riveted on the erotic twistings of the two naked bodies in the adjoining room, Colette knelt before the powerfully built cavalry officer, unbuttoned his trousers, and pulled them down over his hips.

"Ah, what a voyeur you are, Captain," she chuckled. "Why is it that I cannot bring about such a state of excitement in you all by myself? Am I not as provocative to you as Jacqueline and your young friends are?"

As though to silence her, Dulac grabbed her head and shoved it into his groin, never taking his eyes from the peephole.

24

MICAELA CALLED FOR Binnie as she attempted to raise herself and get out of bed. She had become so weak that any minor exertion was even too arduous.

"Oh, Binnie, what am I going to do?" she cried when the maid appeared. "What am I going to do? Somebody has got to do something. Somebody has got to help me!"

"I'm tryin' to do all I can, Miss Micaela," Binnie responded. "Yesterday I done cooked you at least a half dozen different dishes, and you didn't touch none of them."

"I can't, Binnie. I can't. Don't you understand? I'm too sick."

"You ain't never gonna get yourself well if you don't eat nothin'," Binnie warned.

"God knows, I want to get well, but I just can't eat," Micaela complained. "I can't even bear the mention of food."

"The baron keeps on askin' if you is takin' that tonic he made for you."

"For God's sake, tell him I am."

"He'd be mighty angry if he knew you was havin' me pour it out."

"Let him be mad, then!"

Taking a tray with a cup and saucer from the night stand beside the bed, Binnie remarked, "At least you manage to keep that tea an' honey I fix for you in your stomach. It's a good thing, because if you didn't take that, you'd most likely be dead by now."

"Sometimes I feel as if I'll never live to see the birth of my poor baby if I don't get away from this place," Micaela moaned despairingly, unconsciously placing her hands over her bulging abdomen.

"I don't see how you is ever gonna do that unless you suddenly sprouts wings and flies," the black girl said, shaking her head. "You ain't in no condition to go travelin', and even if you was, that baron would never let you out them big doors. He's mighty mean. He's just about the meanest man I ever seen in my whole life."

"Yes, he's a monster," Micaela readily agreed. "And a self-righteous monster at that."

"He's plenty mad at your mama, I can tell you that."

"He's using me to punish her," Micaela sighed. "I must escape from him and get away from here. Celestin's no help at all. He sides with his father in everything, even though he swears he loves me and wants the best for our child. And yet he does nothing to assist me out of this terrible situation. Whenever I need him, he's off to God knows where."

From beneath the pillow she removed a letter she had written.

"Binnie, listen to me carefully," she went on. "You must help me get this letter to my mother in Paris. Do you understand?"

Puzzled, the black girl stared at her mistress. "How you expect me to do that, Miss Micaela?" she asked.

"Somehow I will contrive to send you into town on an errand for me. You must go to the inn where the

coaches bound for Paris stop. Leave this letter with
the innkeeper and tell him to see that it gets to Paris
on the next coach."

Looking at her doubtfully, Binnie said, "I'll do
whatever you say, Miss Micaela, but it ain't gonna
be easy with that baron so suspicious of everythin' we
do."

From the first, Baron Joseph had objected to the
black maid's presence at the château, and he tolerated
her only because of Celestin's pleadings on Micaela's
behalf. But he distrusted Binnie completely, and as a
result, kept her under his personal surveillance.

When, from the greenhouse windows, he saw her
hurrying across the bridge over the moat, he dropped
what he was doing and pursued her.

Catching up with her, he demanded, "Where are
you going?"

Looking at him with trepidation, the maid responded, "Into town, Master Baron."

"What for?"

"Miss Micaela gave me somethin' to do for her."

"What?"

"Just somethin'," she answered evasively.

Spying an envelope in the bottom of the open net
reticule she carried on her arm, he said, "To post that
letter for her?"

"What letter?"

"The one in the bottom of your reticule. Let me see
it at once."

"I ain't got no letter," Binnie lied.

"Give it to me, I said, or I'll thrash your black hide
here and now!" he threatened, his gaunt face becoming red with anger.

"I told you, Master Baron, I ain't got nothin'," she
insisted.

Furious, he snatched the reticule from her, ripped
it open, and withdrew the letter.

"That's Miss Micaela's personal letter," Binnie
wailed.

"It may have *been* Miss Micaela's, but it's mine
now," he hissed, quickly tearing it open and reading

the contents while Binnie stood there alarmed and helpless.

When he finished, he regarded her darkly. "If you tell your mistress that I have taken this letter from you, I'll skin your black hide right off. Is that clear?"

"Yes, sir, Master Baron," Binnie sniffed, thoroughly intimidated.

Celestin returned from his jaunt to Paris in a state of great elation, but his joy evaporated the moment he laid eyes on the sleeping Micaela, who was thinner, paler, and more gaunt than when he had left. Not having the heart to wake her, and badly shaken by her appearance, he hurried downstairs to his father's study, where he found the baron recording entries in his account books.

Looking up, the baron exclaimed with surprise, "Well, my son, you're back! You were gone longer than I anticipated. Did you collect the rent from that miserable wretch Beauvais? It's three months past due. If he doesn't pay soon, I shall have to evict him and all those snotty-nosed brats of his."

"Papa, there is something more important I must talk to you about." Celestin spoke with great urgency. "I have no time to worry about Beauvais and his back rent."

The baron eyed him suspiciously. "Your escapades in Paris? You see, I know that's where you've been."

"No, it's about Micaela. I'm worried about her. I've just come from our apartments, and she looks so ill . . ."

Ignoring his son's anguish, the baron asked, "Tell me, Celestin, do you still wish to return to the army?"

Slapping his forehead in exasperation, Celestin replied, "What on earth has that got to do with what I have just said?"

"I thought you might be anxious to get back to your old cavalry regiment," the baron continued in the same even tone.

"Yes, I would like to, but at the moment I am far more concerned about the health of my wife and our unborn child. Have you seen her recently? My God, she looks like death itself. I think that talk about any other matters at this time is inappropriate."

"Yes, you may be right," Baron Joseph conceded. "Actually, it's precisely your wife's state of health I had hoped to discuss before you became, shall we say, overwrought."

"What do you intend to do for her?"

"Do for her?" the baron repeated. "Before we talk about what measures we will follow to improve her condition, there are some papers I must explain to you first."

Celestin was flabbergasted. "Papers? What papers at a time like this, for God's sake? Haven't we had enough of papers?"

"Specifically, I refer to a project of testament," his father calmly replied.

"What is that?"

"Since you have never studied law, I wouldn't expect you to know. However, a project of testament is a document which will appoint you Micaela's sole heir, should she die."

"Die?" Celestin echoed in a thin voice.

"In that way you will receive all the properties and other belongings of Don Andrés Almonester which rightfully belong to Micaela, and thus to you as her husband, but which her mother has cleverly appropriated," his father explained. Reaching into a cubbyhole in the desk, he removed a sheaf of legal papers. "This document is quite straightforward," he continued. "It simply grants you everything you should have gotten when you married the girl. It's very simple, but be sure to read it carefully. All that Micaela is required to do is sign it."

"How can she sign anything in her condition?" Celestin protested.

"That, my son, is your responsibility. I want you to get her signature on these papers, and I don't care how you do it. Once that is accomplished, then we shall talk about what to do for her."

"She'll never sign," Celestin asserted.

"I grant that it will probably take all your powers of persuasion," the older Pontalba said, "but I have every confidence in your eventual success. Do not disappoint me."

25

ALTHOUGH INITIALLY REPELLED by the prospect of urging Micaela to sign the so-called project of testament, which amounted to nothing more than a special kind of will if she happened to die in childbirth, Celestin had no choice but to agree to his father's goadings.

Propped against a mound of pillows, Micaela gazed at her husband through hollow, sunken eyes and attempted a wan smile, scarcely noticing the stack of formal-looking papers he had brought with him. Her skin was so pale it was almost translucent, making the contrast to her red hair more vivid than usual.

"Hello, dearest," Celestin said, sitting on the edge of the bed and kissing her forehead tenderly. "How are you feeling today?"

"I don't know," she replied, shaking her head discouragingly. "I can't remember what it's like to feel good . . . What are those papers you have?"

"These? Oh, nothing. Just a little something for you to sign."

"I couldn't possibly sign papers today. I'm far too weak to read that many pages."

"They're just routine. You don't have to read them, for goodness' sake. All you have to do is sign them."

"But I don't want to sign anything unless I know what it's all about," she protested.

"They're just some papers."

"What kind?"

"A mere formality."

"What kind of formality, Celestin?" His evasiveness and hesitancy to explain them began to arouse her suspicions.

"Well, they're kind of like a will," he replied, sheepishly avoiding her questioning gaze.

"A will?" she repeated, a worried frown creasing her smooth forehead. "Do you think I'm going to die?"

"Of course not, dearest," he said quickly. "It's just that the baron thinks it's best we have everything in order . . ."

"Yes! Everything in order in case I *do* die. That's it, isn't it?"

"We all may die at any time, and it's important that we look ahead."

"But I'm the one who's ill!"

"You'll be better soon. I know you will be, dearest." He patted her pale cheek. "That's why these papers are of no importance. Please sign them and let's be done with it. Perhaps then, we may get other concessions from the baron."

"Such as?"

"I don't know exactly, but your signing them will help weigh things in our favor with him."

"You mean regarding Mama?"

He nodded. "Possibly."

After deliberating a moment, she said, "All right, I'll sign them if that will permit me to see my mother. Besides, I'm too weak to argue. Give me a pen and I'll sign my 'will.' "

Almost immediately afterward, Micaela's health took a sudden turn for the better. Much to Binnie's relief, her mistress ravenously devoured the special Creole dishes she prepared, then asked for more. Micaela's weight began to increase, her pallor disappeared, and her energy returned. Her newfound strength seemed nothing short of a miracle.

The baron, of course, attributed her astonishing improvement to the special tonic he had concocted for her from rare Indian medicinal plants, but what neither Binnie nor Micaela told him was that, at Micaela's direction, Binnie had tested the tonic by mixing it with milk and feeding it to one of the cats. After the cat had a convulsion right before Binnie's eyes, they agreed to discard the noxious solution and replace it with colored water. When the baron visited Micaela to check on her progress, he was none the wiser, although he seemed perplexed by her restored health.

In the last three months of her pregnancy the baby became increasingly active, and Micaela looked almost radiant. Weary of battling her father-in-law's ban against seeing her mother, despite having signed the will, Micaela decided to forego the fight and conserve her energy for the time being. For the sake of the baby, she vowed to remain as serene as possible. Once the baby was born, however, she would again pursue her rights, determined that Louise would see her grandchild no matter what.

While waiting out the days of her confinement, Micaela sought out what few pastimes existed at Mont L'Eveque. She went for long strolls through the autumn-hued forests and visited the tenant farmers and their wives, who cheerfully patted her distended belly, gave her advice, and prognosticated on the sex of her unborn child. She fed the swans in the moat, picked ripe fruit from the trees in the orchards, and generally led a pastoral existence, quietly biding her time.

Madame Miró tried to interest her in needlework, just as the nuns at the Ursuline Convent had done in the past, but this did not appeal to Micaela. Instead, it was Celestin who took up needle and thread and sat around the fire at night, patiently embroidering clothes for his expected child, much to his father's chagrin.

"Can't you let your mother and Aunt Celeste do that?" he asked.

"It relaxes me," Celestin replied as he bit the thread in two and knotted the ends.

The one activity from her earlier life that Micaela revived and thoroughly enjoyed was sketching. She strolled about the grounds, capturing on paper the various old buildings at Mont L'Eveque, and occasionally took a carriage ride to the neighboring village, where she found the architecture quaint and picturesque.

"Your fingers may not be well suited to the needle-crafts," Madame Miró remarked one evening while Micaela was finishing a sketch she had started earlier in the day, "but you do have a talent for drawing, especially buildings. Of that I have no doubt."

One of her favorite and most wishful projects was the search for a site on which a little theater could be erected at Mont L'Eveque, something she had begun to dream of lately. She knew that her father-in-law would vehemently oppose any plans she might have for such an addition, but she reasoned that if he would not permit her to go to Paris and attend the theater there, she would try to bring the theater to Mont L'Eveque. Her inspiration for this project was, of course, her cousin Pierre. Thinking of the ill-fated Versailles theater brought back painful memories of Patrick Lynch, and as she walked along the banks of the Oise she found herself daydreaming of him again and wondering whether he would ever vanish completely from her thoughts.

One day near the approach of winter Celestin, who was greatly distressed by reports of the dreadful failure of Napoleon's Russian campaign and by his own inability to receive any news of Armand Dulac, took Micaela rowing on the cold gray waters of the river as a distraction for both of them. She had become increasingly bored and discontent as her childbirth date rapidly approached.

As they drifted around a bend in the river, the boat lurched slightly with the current and Micaela experienced a sharp pain in the lower back. From all she had gleaned in her conversations with the farmers' wives and the servants in the château, she felt certain that the baby was on its way.

"Celestin, I think we'd better go back," she said.

Preoccupied with other thoughts, he asked absently, "Why? Are you not feeling well, darling?"

"No, I'm feeling fine. It's just that I'm experiencing a bit of a chill."

"Very well." He quickly turned the boat around and headed back up the river.

Once in her apartments at the château, Micaela dismissed Celestin, summoned Binnie, and ordered her to lock all the doors.

Puzzled, the maid said, "Lock all the doors? What for, Miss Micaela?"

"Because I'm about to have my baby."

"Oh, Lordy!" Binnie squealed. "I'd better run and tell Master Celestin so he can go fetch the doctor!"

"No," Micaela declared adamantly, her face full of fierce determination. "I don't want him to know. I don't want anyone to know, and I don't want the doctor either. You and I are going to deliver this baby, and no one must know a thing until it is all over. Is that clear?" Micaela wanted to add that she had become more distrustful of the Pontalbas since she had signed the will, but she was reluctant to discuss such matters even with Binnie.

"You and me?" the maid repeated, her eyes wide with fear and astonishment. "I ain't never birthed a white baby before. The only ones I ever helped was black."

"All babies are born the same way, white or black. Now, go get a clean, sharp knife for the cord, some strong twine, some clean blankets and towels, and a basin of hot water." Her visits to the farmer's wives had provided her with a mental list of what equipment was needed for a delivery.

Binnie nodded mutely.

"When you return," Micaela went on, "knock three times, and I'll unlock the door and let you in. Now hurry!"

Despite the excruciating pain and apprehension engendered by the entire birth process, Micaela had to suppress her fears and muster up all her remaining courage in order to control the nearly hysterical maid.

Nevertheless, mistress and slave managed successfully to deliver what appeared to be a normal, healthy baby boy. Only when Binnie had the squalling infant bathed and wrapped in a blanket did Micaela finally allow herself to relax completely and to try to recover from the incredible ordeal she had undergone.

"Go tell Master Celestin he has a son," she directed.

The moment Celestin heard the incredible news, he promptly fainted and had to be revived by Binnie and the other servants. When he was on his feet again, he raced up the winding staircase and berated Micaela for not informing him beforehand so that he could send for the doctor. He was stunned to realize that she had accomplished something as traumatic as the delivery of a baby, assisted only by an ignorant black maid.

"How could you do such a thing?" he reproached her. "It's barbaric. My God, you both could have died!"

"Yes, Celestin," she replied weakly, cradling her infant son close to her, "but we didn't. Just think, if we had, my whole fortune might have been yours. You and your father would have liked that, wouldn't you?"

"How can you say such a thing?" he bellowed, obviously stung by her words. But his cries fell on deaf ears.

The baby proved healthy indeed, and excited plans for his baptism were being executed by Jeanne and Madame Miró. Micaela seriously disrupted the proceedings, however, when she insisted the child be christened Andrés, after her late father.

Aghast, Jeanne firmly announced, "That simply isn't done, Micaela. The first son is never named for anyone on his *mother's* side. Firstborn sons are always named for someone on the father's side, preferably the father himself or the grandfather. Anything else would be considered disgraceful, besides hurting poor Celestin greatly. He wants this baby to be called Celestin after him. If you are so anxious to name a child Andrés, do it for your second or third son."

Annoyed, Micaela decided to confront Celestin with the situation, and was surprised to find him willing to compromise from a standpoint she had never anticipated.

"If you will agree to name this first son of ours after

me," he said, "I will personally write to your mother in Paris and invite her to the christening."

"Do you mean that?" Micaela asked, her eyes wide.

"Yes. I promise."

"But the christening is to be here at Mont L'Eveque. You know your father's decree," she reminded him, inwardly astonished but pleased that for once he was finally willing to oppose his father. Could he be growing up at last? she wondered.

"I will take care of my father," he replied, although he hadn't the slightest idea how to go about it. "It's the baby's name I leave up to you."

The prospect of seeing her mother again after so long a period of forced separation delighted Micaela beyond measure. Spontaneously she threw her arms around Celestin and kissed him.

"Celestin his name is, and Celestin it will be!" she cried.

On the day of the christening, the baron was informed by an excited servant that the carriage of Madame Castillon had arrived at the château and that the lady was determined to enter. At first Joseph de Pontalba flew into a rage, demanding to know what right Louise had in coming to Mont L'Eveque uninvited, and ordered her turned away, but later, suspecting that Louise's presence had been instigated by his son, he decided to see the woman herself and hear her story.

Going straight out to her carriage, he once again reiterated, in as calm a manner as he was able to effect considering the highly charged emotional issue that existed between them, the demands that had to be met if she wished to enter the château and see her daughter and new grandson.

"You have cheated and wronged us badly, madame, and you know it," he asserted. "Until you are willing to make amends and restore the honor of my family, you will not be permitted inside."

"You must be joking," Louise countered.

"I assure you I am not."

"But Celestin himself invited me."

"I know nothing of such an invitation," he replied, certain that she was lying.

"I have the letter at home."

"That is no concern of mine, madame."

Louise sighed resignedly. "All right, what do you want of me? What must I do to satisfy you to allow me to see my child and grandchild?"

"You must agree to make proper restitution."

"And if I don't?" she challenged.

"Then have your coachman turn the carriage around and go back to Paris."

At that moment the sound of a baby crying was heard from inside the château, and Louise gasped and clutched her bosom. "My God . . .!"

"I beg your pardon, madame?"

"Very well, I'll come to terms with you. You're a hard man, Cousin Joseph, but I am weary of this whole matter and want to be done with it. I am too exhausted from the years of caring for my dying husband to fight you any longer on this issue. Tell me exactly what it is you want, and I will do my best to see that you get it. Only please, I beg you, if you have any Christian charity in your stony heart, allow me to see my daughter and grandson on this special day."

"Then I have your word, Louise, that you will settle on Micaela what is rightfully hers?" he persisted.

Pausing thoughtfully a moment, Louise nodded. "I will agree to assign her half the income from my Louisiana properties. Is that sufficient to satisfy you?"

"She is entitled to more than half, since she is the heir of both her father and her late sister, but I won't quibble over such technicalities. To celebrate this joyous occasion of the christening of our new grandson, Celestin Junior, I will graciously accept your offer."

She smiled. "How kind of you, dear Joseph. Now may I get out of my carriage and come inside?"

"Of course, dear Louise," the baron agreed with a gallant flourish.

26

ATER THE CHRISTENING, Louise, overjoyed at seeing Micaela once more, to say nothing of her new grandson, returned to Paris. Almost immediately she called on her trusted lawyer, the brilliant and resourceful Saint-Avid, and informed him of her capitulation to the baron's demands.

"For the sake of my daughter's happiness and peace of mind, I have given in to the Baron de Pontalba and agreed to turn over half the income from my Louisiana properties to Micaela and her husband," she explained.

Saint-Avid raised eyebrows that were as dark and bushy as his beard. "Well, you have been most generous."

Louise shrugged. "I had no choice. Prepare whatever papers are necessary and I will sign them. It is good to have this unpleasantness finished, even at such a price."

"Very well, madame, if that is your wish," Saint-Avid replied. "Still, permit me to say that if we had fought the Baron de Pontalba in the courts, such concessions as you have made in order to see your daughter again would not have been necessary. I am certain we could have beaten him."

"I have no strength for such a fight. Castillon is too ill. The doctors fear he may go at any moment," Louise said with a weary sigh. "Therefore, simply prepare the papers."

Knowing that the baron was pleased not only by the birth of his grandson, who would continue the Pontalba line, but also by the assignment of half of Louise's Louisiana income to Micaela, and thereby to Celestin, Jeanne felt the opportunity was ripe to help forge a lasting peace between her husband and Micaela. It distressed her to see him and his daughter-in-law at odds when all of them lived under the same roof.

Joining Micaela as she wheeled the infant around the grounds of the château in a new and very fancy carriage Louise had sent from Paris, Jeanne told her how pleased the baron was with the recent turn of events.

"He's absolutely delighted," she said. "He's hardly raised his voice to anyone lately."

"Why shouldn't he be delighted?" Micaela returned, indifferent to her mother-in-law's effusiveness as she paused to adjust the hood of the carriage so that the sun stayed out of the baby's eyes. In spite of the Pontalbas' objections, she had insisted on caring for the baby herself as much as possible, especially taking him out in his carriage. She believed it was good not only for the baby but for herself as well. The fresh spring air and sunshine gave her an inner strength and made her feel extraordinarily healthy. She had learned from experience that she needed every ounce of strength she had in order to cope with the Pontalbas. "My mother has conceded quite a lot to him."

"Well, yes, I suppose she has," Jeanne reluctantly acknowledged.

"There's no question about it," Micaela affirmed.

Her experiences at Mont L'Eveque had taught Micaela a great deal about the Pontalbas and had also hardened her general outlook on life. No more was she the naive, innocent schoolgirl fresh from the Colonies. Even though she was isolated from the sophistication of Paris, she had acquired a certain cynical worldliness since leaving New Orleans that made her more assertive and sure of herself in her dealings with her in-laws.

"I was just thinking," Jeanne continued, "that now is a good time for you to ask the baron for any favors you might wish."

"Favors?" Micaela repeated. "What sort of favors?"

"Well, Celestin informs me that you have a keen interest in the theater."

"Yes, I do." Micaela wondered what the birdlike woman had in mind.

"You know, I have always thought it might be nice

to have a little theater of our own here at Mont L'Eveque," the older woman said.

"Really? I would never have suspected that." She was surprised by such a suggestion from Jeanne and curious as to what had prompted her to make it. The Pontalbas' mode of living was so austere that anything as potentially extravagant as a private theater seemed incongruous.

"Oh, yes," Jeanne assured her. "I should love a theater of our own on the grounds. Celestin tells me you share the same sentiment."

Recently Micaela had dismissed the idea of a theater, considering it a ridiculous fantasy, but now, encouraged by Jeanne, she decided there could be no harm in approaching the baron on the matter, especially when he was in a receptive mood.

Feeling she had little or nothing to lose, Micaela returned to the château, turned little Celestin—already nicknamed Tin-Tin by everyone—over to Binnie, and sought out her father-in-law. The servants directed her to his study, where she found him at his desk going over some large ledgers.

Seating herself in a chair opposite him, Micaela promptly related her idea for a theater, making sure to add that Jeanne, too, was enthusiastic about such a prospect.

The baron pondered her words a few moments before he spoke. "As you well know, my dear, I am not much given to theatrical entertainments. I regard it all as frivolous and inconsequential. But if a little theater at Mont L'Eveque would make you happier, I am willing to consider such a project. After all, none of us is exactly unaware of your discontentment."

Having apparently secured her father-in-law's permission for a theater—and far more easily than she had expected—Micaela wondered whether she might dare to suggest Patrick Lynch as the architect for the proposed theater. If he were to accept such a commission and come to France, she wasn't sure what effect his presence would have on her or on her marriage. Since the birth of little Tin-Tin, the child had become the central focus of her attention, although

Patrick was by no means absent from her thoughts.

One evening at dinner in the cavernous dining hall, where the entire family was expected to gather every evening, the baron, seated at the head of the long oak table, brought up the subject of the theater. Everyone seemed either indifferent or in accord, but no one opposed it.

"It will be the first new building on the grounds of Mont L'Eveque in over one hundred years," Baron Joseph announced.

"We must be certain that it will be architecturally compatible with everything else," Celestin said.

"Who will design it?" Jeanne asked, signaling to one of the maids to refill her crystal wine goblet. At meals Micaela's mother-in-law drank more wine than anyone else.

"I'm sure one of our local architects will be capable of doing the job," the baron replied.

"Oh, no," Micaela protested, and everyone at the table turned to look at her. "It requires a special architect to design a theater. I'm sure there is no one in the entire Oise district who knows the first thing about it. The man must be a specialist."

Staring at her skeptically, the baron said, "A specialist in theaters?"

"Certainly there would have to be specific considerations, Papa," Celestin pointed out. "A theater requires special equipment, special designs . . ."

"This will be a *simple* theater, nothing extravagant," the baron stated.

"Simple theaters require the same special knowledge on the part of the architect that the more complicated ones do," Micaela told him.

"How do you know so much about it, dear?" Madame Miró asked.

"I was at Versailles when my cousin Pierre was involved in a similar project."

"Ah! And does Versailles have its own theater now?" Madame Miró lifted the wine goblet shakily to her lips.

"No. The project was abandoned before its completion."

"Oh, how unfortunate," Jeanne said. "Why?"

Micaela shrugged. "There were problems."

"What kind?" the baron asked.

"Personal problems," she answered.

"I'm not surprised, after some of the stories I've heard about Pierre Delaronde," Jeanne remarked.

"What sort of stories?" Micaela was indignant at her mother-in-law's innuendoes.

"Oh, nasty ones," Madame Miró answered for her niece. "They say he dares to live openly with his black mistress, right under his poor parents' noses."

"I know nothing of Pierre's personal life," Micaela lied. "Ever since I was a child, he's always been kind to me. Kindness is very important."

"Oh, my, yes, it certainly is!" Jeanne agreed.

"Getting back to the theater project," Celestin said, waving his fork impatiently, "who designed Pierre Delaronde's theater, Micaela?" After Tin-Tin's birth he had seemed more relaxed, perhaps because at last his father had gotten what he wanted from Louise, and perhaps because he himself was no longer uncomfortably positioned between father and wife, but Micaela still sensed that he was basically unhappy.

"An architect recently arrived in New Orleans," she replied. "An Irishman named Patrick Lynch. He's obviously very talented, or Pierre wouldn't have engaged him. Pierre is very particular."

"About some things," Jeanne sniffed.

"Still, I'm certain somebody can be found right here in France," the baron said, savoring the aroma of fresh cauliflower, which he had raised himself, as a maid placed the dish before him. "Bringing an architect all the way from America seems needlessly expensive."

"What harm could there be in writing this Mr. Lynch and asking him for his fees?" Micaela proposed, looking around the table for some sign of support.

"None, I suppose," the baron conceded, spooning a generous serving of the cauliflower onto Celestin's plate. "If you do contact him, be sure that he includes his estimated travel and living expenses in any prices he quotes."

At the earliest opportunity Micaela penned a letter to Patrick, informing him of her present life, the baby, and the baron's plans for a theater.

"If you are interested in undertaking the project that I have attempted to describe," she wrote, "please send my father-in-law, the Baron de Pontalba, sketches of the proposed theater and an estimate of all costs involved."

She kept the letter deliberately impersonal in tone, not just because the baron would undoubtedly find some way to read it, as he did all her correspondence, but also because she had decided to proceed cautiously where Patrick was concerned, taking one step at a time.

While the domestic scene at Mont L'Eveque appeared relatively peaceful for the moment, France was undergoing an opposite reaction. Napoleon's Russian campaign had proved to be an unmitigated disaster, and as a result of that defeat and the earlier Spanish-Portuguese debacle, the French Empire was in danger of crumbling fast. It looked as if Napoleon himself might soon lose his throne.

Strangely unconcerned about the agonies besetting his nation, Baron Joseph preferred to busy himself with his greenhouse and his gardening, carefully nurturing his current favorite, a dwarf persimmon that was already filled with smooth red fruit. He had relegated more and more of the administration of his holdings to Celestin, leaving himself free to pursue his avocation. Privately, he was glad the Grand Army had met defeat in Russia and that Napoleon was having great difficulty in raising new armies to battle the enemies who were determined to crush the French emperor once and for all. Perhaps that would finally end his son's longing to return to the military life he adored, a desire that had continued unabated despite his marriage and the birth of his son. Aware of his earlier promise to Celestin and knowing he would be forced to honor it one day soon, the baron had been secretly hoping for some kind of outside intervention in the matter. Hopefully, the overthrow of Napoleon and the collapse of the Grand

Army would provide exactly what he had been praying for.

"I suppose you've heard the news?" Celestin said, entering the greenhouse and quickly closing the door behind him to conserve the humid heat inside. "The emperor seems certain to be overthrown despite his recent victories at Lützen, Bautzen, and Dresden."

The baron shrugged indifferently. "I'm not surprised. The people of France are tired of war." Gently pushing his son aside as he carefully snipped the end of a branch of the dwarf persimmon, he changed the subject by asking, "Did you see the Widow Bouvier?"

"Yes," Celestin sighed.

"Well? Did she pay up?"

"The poor woman has no money and a dozen children to feed."

"Yes, and each fathered by a different farmhand," the baron remarked snidely.

"You shouldn't talk about her that way," Celestin reproached. "The Widow Bouvier seems to be a morally righteous woman to me."

"What do you know?" the baron scoffed, snipping off another tiny branch after he had stepped back and carefully appraised the general shape of the tree. "Tomorrow I want you to return to Madame Bouvier and collect her overdue rent. Is that clear?"

"How can you be so concerned with trivialities when our nation is in such turmoil?" Celestin wondered impatiently.

"One thing is certain: the turmoil will soon end. Then the emperor will have no further need of his Grand Army, which is draining this country dry. Nor will he have need of you," the baron added, watching his son carefully so that he might plan his next move.

Somewhat shocked, Celestin said, "What do you mean? Napoleon is now attempting to establish a new army to head off that British dog, Wellington. He can use every able-bodied man he can get. I'm an officer, a proficient cavalryman."

"You know as well as I do that the emperor and his Grand Army are finished," the baron snapped. "That recent Leipzig defeat, which you neglected to mention when you were naming that string of so-called victories, was the beginning of the end."

Indignant, Celestin cried, "France will always have a great army!"

"Possibly, but it will not require your services. You now have responsibilities, and serious ones, right here at home."

"You once said that if I succeeded in persuading Micaela to sign that will when she was ill, I would be permitted to return to the army. I assumed you would take the responsibility for my wife and son while I was away."

The baron raised his eyebrows. "I said that?"

"You inferred as much."

"Well, yes, perhaps I did, but I meant depending, of course, on the situation."

"The situation now is that the emperor is in desperate straits because of the lack of men. Besides, there is no real need for me here. Anyone can be a rent collector. I serve no useful purpose. You are the master of Mont L'Eveque. I am merely your deputy."

"Have you forgotten that one day you will be the baron?" his father reminded him. "Inheriting my lands and my title?"

"I think I truly prefer the army to the life of a country squire," Celestin asserted.

"Nonsense," his father snapped. "Don't let me hear you speak such foolishness. I sent you to the army to get you away from your coddling mother and aunt and to make a man out of you. I never intended that the military would be your lifelong career. It has served its purpose, and we are done with it—both of us. I will hear no more about it. You will not return to the army. Not now, not ever."

Aghast, Celestin blurted out, "What do you mean?"

"Just that."

"But—" he started to protest.

"The subject is closed."

Instead of confronting such a pronouncement with anger and defiance, Celestin seemed shattered by it, accepting it without further protestation, as he had all the other edicts issued by the baron in the past.

"I see," he said quietly. "Then that's how it is, is it?"

"That's how it is," the baron affirmed. Then, plucking a ripe persimmon from the tree, he smiled, turned to his son, and forced it between his lips. "Don't be so glum," he chided. "It may be the end of the emperor, but it's not the end of you. Your life is just beginning. Someday you'll be grateful to me for curbing this foolish impulse of yours to run off and rejoin the army. So I want you to cheer up and for today, at least, enjoy these fine persimmons."

27

PATRICK'S REPLY TO Micaela's letter was prompt, cordial, and polite, but more impersonal in tone than she had expected. In it he explained that despite the setback his career had suffered because of Pierre's efforts to discourage his friends from engaging him, he had managed to come through some rather difficult times with his optimism intact and was presently receiving a fair number of commissions. He regretted that he could not become involved in the theater she proposed, because it would necessitate his being away from the United States for a considerable period of time, during which he would be unable to supervise several projects currently in progress. He wished her well, congratulated her on the birth of her son, and assured her that she would always occupy a special place in his memory. As a sort of afterthought, he added that he had finally managed to persuade his wife to leave New York and come to live in New Orleans.

"I think that Emily is at last convinced that New Orleans is no more unhealthy than New York," he wrote, signing the letter "With fondest regards, Patrick."

Believing the reply was impersonal enough to be shown to her father-in-law, and not really concerned how he or Celestin might interpret the "special place"

in Patrick's memory that she might occupy, Micaela
went to the study to inform the baron that the New
Orleans architect had declined the offer to design the
proposed theater and that he might now begin seeking
out a local architect for the project.

Although the desk was open and various letters and
papers were scattered about, no one was in the room.
One sheaf of papers, official-looking documents tied
with a purple ribbon and lying in the center of the
desk, caught her eye. Assuming they were the project
of testament she had been coerced into signing during
her severe illness, she decided to untie the ribbon and
read them, convinced that they concerned her every
bit as much as they did the baron or Celestin. At the
time they had been presented to her, she had been
nearly delirious and had signed them without having
first read their contents. For a long while she had had
a lingering curiosity to know exactly what the conditions of that document were, and now seemed to be a
perfect opportunity to find out.

As with all legal papers, the language was formal
and unnecessarily complex, and it was easy to lose the
thread of a sentence while trying to unravel what it
meant. Nevertheless, Micaela persisted, and as she
read, she realized that this was not the will at all but
an entirely different document. This one also concerned her, she soon discovered, though more indirectly, and she had had no prior knowledge of its
existence. In short, it seemed to be a secret promise
from Celestin to return immediately the eighty-five
thousand dollars the baron had promised to settle on
the young couple as stipulated in the marriage contract.
Micaela trembled with outrage and indignation as she
read it a second time to be sure she had correctly understood the stilted, formal wording. In essence,
Celestin had secretly released his father from an obligation to both of them—Micaela and himself—without
so much as giving her the slightest indication that such
a transaction had occurred. But how could this be?
she wondered. The document she held in her hand
threatened Celestin with disinheritance if he ever di-
vulged the contents of the secret contract. The baron,

who had used the cruelest of means to extract money from Louise, was, according to these papers, denying his son and daughter-in-law a sum as comparatively small as eighty-five thousand dollars. How petty and despicably ungenerous of him! Furious, Micaela threw the papers back on the desk, deliberately neglecting to retie the purple ribbon, and left the room.

Beneath dark, rain-threatening skies Celestin waded through the dank marshes, rifle in hand, trailed by a pair of water spaniels. He was waiting for a flock of wild ducks to appear overhead, but despite everything, his mind was not on the sport of duck hunting. Instead, his thoughts were occupied with the realization that his military career was indeed over. He had lost his one opportunity to throw off the yoke of his domineering father and establish his own life and identity. Of that he had no further doubt. Napoleon's attempt to fight the coalition of France's enemies had ended in a debacle. The French senate was calling for a Bourbon king to return to the throne, and Napoleon's own commanders were urging him to abdicate. The days of glory for the Grand Army were as remote as yesterday's sunset.

Looking back, he realized that his marriage had been a trap set by his father to curb his discovery of freedom in the army, and he resented it but did not blame Micaela at all. He never had. In some ways they had both been victims of opportunistic parents. She was trying her best to be a good wife and mother and to adapt to a mode of living she disliked and for which she was unsuited. In her own way she, too, was being stifled. Knowing the feeling well, he understood her discontentment and restlessness. He had hoped that the birth of their son would alleviate some of her unhappiness, but it hadn't. Often in the morning when he awakened, he almost expected to find her side of the bed cold and Micaela gone. Granted, it would not be easy for anyone to escape from Mont L'Eveque, but he had learned, in the almost two years they had been married, that she was a most resourceful woman. She was free to visit her mother in Paris if she chose, and he would not be surprised if one day she left and didn't return to the château. Probably the only reason she endured life there was because of little Tin-Tin and because she clung tenaciously to the hope that one day things might be different. He could not bring himself to speculate how much longer she would tolerate the present situation. Beset with his own problems and frustrations, he acknowledged that he had not been the husband she deserved and which he should be if he wanted to hold on to her. If she left him and the marriage disintegrated, he dreaded the consequences. The baron's anger at such a failure on his part would be unrelenting.

Pausing a moment in his trek through the marshes, he felt himself sink nearly to his knees in the soft mud. For a moment he wished he would continue sinking until the black ooze covered the top of his head. Raising his eyes, he scanned the gloomy, turbulent skies for a formation of ducks but saw nothing. Who was truly to blame for his unhappiness? he wondered as he resumed trudging through the swamp, cattails brushing his coat and leaving their fuzz behind. Certainly not his wife or his son. His father? No, not even the formidable baron. I am the one, he finally admitted to himself. There is much in myself I must overcome.

Above the tops of the trees a flock of low-flying ducks suddenly appeared. He raised his shotgun, took careful aim, and fired. One of the ducks plummeted to the ground, landing with a splash about fifty yards in front of him. The dogs rushed forward in quick, excited pursuit.

As Celestin put the limp duck in his knapsack he thought of Armand Dulac and how proud he would have been of that shot. Dulac was a crack shot as well as an expert swordsman, and on the practice range he had tried to imbue Celestin with some of his expertise. Yes, the army had offered him the chance to mingle with men who, in different circumstances, would have been considered his social inferiors. Celestin was positive that in the normal course of his life as the son of a country noble he would never have met anyone like Dulac. And how much poorer his life would have been if he had not crossed paths with that daring and capable fighting man.

When he faced it squarely, Celestin realized that next to the loss of his freedom and independence, what he would miss most about the army, above all else, was Armand Dulac.

Late in the afternoon it had begun to rain hard, and when Celestin, dripping wet in his hunting clothes, returned to the château, he deposited his day's game with the servants in the scullery with orders to pluck and clean and prepare the ducks for the evening meal, then hurried to his apartment to change.

In his stocking feet he padded up the winding stairs to the rooms he shared with his wife, having left his muddy boots in the kitchen for the servants to clean. The moment he turned the knob and entered the bedchamber, he could see that Micaela, who was sitting in an armchair with an opened book in her lap, although she was not reading, looked profoundly upset.

"Hello, dearest," he said, moving toward her and kissing her cheek. Beyond them, in the nursery, he could hear his son noisily shaking the sides of his crib, anxiously trying to capture the attention of his newly arrived father. "How was your day?"

"All right," she answered coldly.

"Mine was good. I managed to bag six ducks."

Micaela made no response and continued to stare blankly at the book in her lap.

"Are you upset about something?" he asked, beginning to take off his muddy clothing. He had been on the verge of calling for Binnie to remove the clothes to the laundry, but from his wife's expression he decided it might be best if they were not interrupted, at least not until he discovered what was troubling her.

"Yes, I'm upset," she replied, and lifted her eyes to meet his gaze.

"What is it?" he asked solicitously. "Aren't you going to tell me?"

"There are many things I can forgive, but today I discovered something that is more than I am willing to pardon."

He was stunned by her answer. "What on earth are you talking about, Micaela? There must be some misunderstanding."

She proceeded to tell him about the document she had found on his father's desk in the study.

"You had no business snooping," he said lamely.

"Snooping!" She repeated, outraged at his response. "I have a right to know about anything that concerns me!"

"It means nothing," he soothed, attempting to minimize the situation by forcing a smile. "We have no need of that money from the baron, anyway. We have more than enough. All our wants are taken care of, aren't they? You will even have your little theater, I promise you that."

"To hell with the money and the damned theater, too!" she exploded, throwing the book across the room. "It's principles I'm talking about!"

"What principles?"

"No, you really don't know, do you?" she muttered, more in dismay than in anger. "You have no idea what I'm talking about because in spite of all your father's grand talk, neither one of you understands the first thing about honor and decency."

Attempting to calm her, he said, "Please, Micaela, you're making much too much out of this. It's only a few pieces of paper, not worth getting excited about."

His remark only served to inflame her. "Only a few pieces of paper!" she stormed. "That just shows what little regard you have for me and what that document implies. Your father has nothing but contempt for me and our marriage. When I read it, it was as if a great dark cloud had descended over our marriage."

"Dearest, you're going to frighten Tin-Tin if you don't lower your voice," he admonished. In the nursery, the baby, upset by the sound of their agitated voices, had already begun to cry.

"I don't care," she snapped.

"That document means nothing," he insisted.

"Then why was it drawn up?" she demanded. "Why did you sign it?"

"The baron ordered me to sign it."

"The baron ordered you to sign it," she mimicked disdainfully. "That's the whole problem. You do anything he tells you to do—no matter what. You are too weak to stand up to him."

"I'm sorry, dearest. Tell me what I can do to make things up to you."

"How can I tell you something like that?" she cried in exasperation. "And *why* must someone tell you everything? Why can't you think for yourself? Act for yourself? How long is that father of yours going to dominate you—dominate us—our marriage? How long, Celestin? You tell me that!"

Shaking his head forlornly, he confessed, "I don't know, Micaela. I just don't know."

"You don't know because you're weak. You've always been a spineless creature, and you'll probably be that way for the rest of your life—weak and spineless!"

Unable to control her emotions any longer, she burst into tears and fled into the nursery.

28

THE FOLLOWING MORNING Micaela awoke in the chilly bedroom and knew instinctively, without checking Celestin's side of the bed, that she was alone. In the gray morning light she saw a note pinned to his pillow.

Dearest Micaela,

I have departed this morning for Mignot to look after some properties of the baron in that region. I am sorry I cannot tell you at this time when I shall return, because I do not know myself. One of the purposes of this absence, apart from the baron's business, is to clear my head so that I may contemplate my life and overcome my weakness. I have been aware of this characteristic for a long time, but only when you pointed it out to me last night with such anger and loathing did I vow to take some

measures to change. It is a difficult challenge, but
one which I am determined to master. I pray that
with God's help I may achieve my goal. Know that
in my own way I love you and our little son very
much. A special embrace for both of you.

Your Celestin

Micaela's first reaction to the note was indignation
mixed with pain, but later, when she considered the
reasons for his actions, she felt less resentful about his
flight and accepted it with the hope that this "retreat"
of his might eventually help him and their relationship.

After several weeks Celestin's prolonged absence became conspicuous and a subject for concern at Mont
L'Eveque.

"What on earth can be keeping him for so long at
Mignot?" Jeanne asked Micaela one day, barely concealing the anxiety in her high-pitched voice. "I have
asked the baron, but he gives me no satisfactory answers. Celestin has never liked being away from home
for long periods, except, of course, when he was in the
army. He loved it then. Sometimes I think he yearns
for those army days of his more than any of us realize.
Have you had no word from him as to when he plans
to return? I am becoming quite worried."

"He did say he might be gone a long time," Micaela
replied, her eye on Tin-Tin as he played on the sweeping green lawn with Binnie. "And that there are some
pressing things he must think about while he is away."

"Well, *I* think he'd better think about getting back to
his family," Jeanne said crossly, shading her eyes from
the sun with her hand as she gazed at the bridge over
the moat, almost as if she expected to see Celestin
cross it at any moment. "A husband and father cannot
go running off whenever he chooses. It simply isn't
done. I shall tell the baron to write him at once and
insist that he return immediately. I am sure he has accomplished long ago whatever he was sent to do."

"He'll return when he's ready, I'm sure."

"You sound as if you don't care when he comes
back," Jeanne remarked in a slightly reproachful tone.

"Well, I don't want him to come back if he doesn't feel ready."

"Ready for what?"

"Ready to be the husband and father he should be," Micaela answered casually, snapping open her parasol and raising it to keep the sun off her delicate complexion.

"You mustn't judge him too harshly," Jeanne cautioned, coming to her son's defense. "After all, he's still quite young. One mustn't expect too much of a man in his early twenties. He's trying to do his best under the circumstances, and, all in all, I would say he's doing rather well."

"Would you?"

"Things have never been easy for Celestin, especially with his father."

Turning to her mother-in-law, Micaela observed, "I am coming to the conclusion that things are not easy for anyone at Mont L'Eveque."

Celestin had been away for almost three months when Micaela received word from Louise that Jean-Baptiste had finally succumbed to his lingering illness.

"It is almost a relief," Louise wrote. "No one knows more than I how that poor man suffered. I thank God that his misery is over at last."

In her note of condolence Micaela casually mentioned Celestin's long absence, and when Louise learned of it, she viewed the current rift in her daughter's marriage as a possible means of bringing her back to Paris. Micaela could live with her and help assuage the loneliness she felt after Castillon's death. After all, she reasoned, if the girl's husband had openly deserted her, she was no longer obliged to remain at his parents' home.

Summoning Flore, she ordered her to pack for a trip to Mont L'Eveque.

When Louise drew up to the château, she considered herself fortunate to encounter the baron working in his vegetable plot before she saw anyone else. Quickly dispensing with the usual irrelevant pleasantries, she came right to the point of her visit.

"I am not going to mince words, Cousin. Your son has deserted my daughter, and I demand to know what you intend to do about it."

Attempting to make light of her concern, the baron brushed the dirt off his trousers and replied, "I don't think you can correctly call my son's temporary absence a desertion. To the best of my knowledge, he has never stated an intention not to return."

"Errant husbands seldom do," she countered.

"I have every reason to believe that Celestin will be back soon," he assured her, leaning on his hoe.

"When?" she demanded.

"I'm certain he won't be away much longer."

"Let me warn you, dear Cousin," she said, speaking very slowly and distinctly from behind the thick black mourning veil that covered her face, "that if he has not returned one week from today, I shall bring this matter to the attention of my attorney, Monsieur Saint-Avid."

The baron knew Louise had good grounds on which to base a case of desertion and consequently sue for the return of everything settled on Micaela as part of the marriage contract, and he was greatly disturbed by the mention of the lawyer's name. Saint-Avid was reputed to be one of the cleverest lawyers in Paris.

"I can assure you, dear Louise, that this matter hardly warrants the attention of your attorney. It's a mere trifle, and you are making far too much of it. I realize that in this deeply sad time of your life it is difficult to perceive things in their proper light . . ."

"My grief has not distorted my perceptions in the least, dear Joseph."

He gave her a weak smile. "Celestin is merely on a kind of extended holiday."

"But without his wife," she reminded him.

"In any case, I will contact him at once and see that he returns before your deadline of next week," the baron promised.

"Be sure you do," Louise urged. "Or I shall be forced to take the measures I just mentioned. But I didn't come here to threaten. Is Micaela inside?"

Assured that she was, Louise entered the château. A few moments later the baron dropped his hoe and rushed to the stables, ordering the groom to saddle a horse for him. As soon as the animal was ready, he mounted and galloped toward Mignot.

Arriving there in record time, he inquired of his son's whereabouts from several peasants and finally located him in an unoccupied gamekeeper's cottage on Pontalba land.

Celestin, looking bewildered and somewhat remorseful, admitted his father inside with a sheepish "Hello, Papa."

"So this is where you've been hiding out, is it?" the baron looked around and spotted a pillowcase that Celestin had apparently been embroidering in a fancy floral pattern. He fingered it contemptuously. "Is this how you've been spending your time?" he growled.

"I must keep busy at something," Celestin replied helplessly.

"Well, I have not come here to discuss needlework," his father said shortly. "Tell me, when do you plan to return home?"

"When I feel ready, sir."

"Oh? And when will that be?"

"When I've found some of the answers I've been searching for."

"And do you expect to find them here?" the older man asked skeptically. "In this gamekeeper's cottage? Among your needlework?"

"I am trying to find them within me," Celestin answered evenly, refusing to be provoked by his father's attitude. "I must have an atmosphere of peace and serenity in which to think. This place provides me with that."

"Nonsense!" the baron snapped. "Enough of this adolescent silliness. Get your things together. You are returning to Mont L'Eveque with me at once. You've been sulking like a petulant child ever since I told you that you couldn't return to the army."

"Well, you *did* promise . . ."

Ignoring him, the baron continued. "It's time you snapped out of it and accepted your responsibilities like a man. You have a duty to your wife and son as well as to your mother and me."

"Micaela understands what I'm trying to do. It was she who gave me the courage. I'm certain she agrees wholeheartedly."

"She may agree," Baron Joseph conceded, "but her mother does not."

"What does her mother have to do with it?"

"Madame Castillon has learned of your flight and is threatening legal action if you do not return. I don't have to tell you she has good grounds on which to establish a case of desertion."

"When are Micaela and I going to be able to live our own lives without interference from either you or Madame Castillon?" Celestin demanded, his calm giving way to rising agitation. "When? Answer me that!"

"Individuals must sacrifice their own selfish interests for the good of the greater family," the baron replied in an unctuous tone. "Marriage is never the simple union of two people. It is the merging of two families, two clans. A person must put the best interests of the family above his own."

"And who is to determine what the so-called best interests of the family are?" his son challenged.

"Those with wisdom and experience." Baron Joseph was rapidly becoming annoyed at this unaccustomed display of defiance.

"I see." Celestin nodded, folded his arms across his chest, and rocked back on the heels of his boots.

Wagging a thin finger in his son's face, the baron warned, "If you do not return to your wife at once, the consequences may be dire. Madame Castillon is threatening to take certain measures which could be very damaging to us and might create a potential scandal. Not at any cost will I allow a blemish to be foisted on the name of Pontalba. Is that clear?"

Old, unwelcome feelings of being trapped and defeated began to stir inside Celestin, and he struggled valiantly but unsuccessfully to resist them.

"All right," he said at last. "I'll go back to Micaela, if that's what you demand."

"It's not what I demand. It's simply your duty."

"Yes, my duty," Celestin murmured, more to himself than to his father.

The baron smiled, pleased by his son's acquiescence. "Now you're behaving more rationally, like the Celestin I know and love. Are you ready to accompany me back to Mont L'Eveque now?"

"I'm not going back to Mont L'Eveque."

"But . . . ?"

"I said I would return to Micaela. I made no other promises."

"I'm afraid I don't understand." The baron frowned in disbelief. "How can you return to Micaela without going back to Mont L'Eveque?"

"Send Micaela and little Tin-Tin to me," Celestin directed.

Aghast at such a suggestion, the baron cried, "Send them *here?*"

"I don't care where. Any place except Mont L'Eveque. I feel that if we are to have a successful reconciliation, we must do it by ourselves—away from Mont L'Eveque. When I am satisfied that we have established a new and firmer foundation for our marriage, perhaps we'll come back. But not before."

Satisfied for the moment that he had obtained the major concession he sought—namely, Celestin's reconciliation with Micaela—the baron was now willing to compromise, especially when he could see, much to his surprise, that his son was adamant. It was not a good time to press for more demands.

"Micaela and your son certainly cannot share a gamekeeper's cottage," he said.

"Why not?"

"Because your wife is not accustomed to such humble surroundings. In fact, at times her ideas are a bit grandiose." The Pontalba patriarch sighed heavily. "As you well know, since the birth of the baby she's become quite demanding, insisting on that silly theater of hers and much more."

"If they don't come here, then where do you propose we go?"

After several moments of contemplation the baron brightened and replied. "There is some business with a bank in Geneva that I have to transact soon. Perhaps you would like to do it for me—as my agent?"

"Go to Switzerland?" Celestin mused. "Yes, that sounds quite satisfactory. I think Micaela would like it there."

"Good." The baron allowed himself a wide grin. "Since you seem to have an aversion to Mont L'Eveque, at least for the moment, I shall send Micaela and Tin-Tin and that damned maid of hers to you in Geneva, once you have found suitable housing for them."

"Fine!"

The baron reached out and embraced his son. "Don't linger in Switzerland too long," he cautioned. "I shall miss your presence more than you know. And your mother and Aunt Celeste will count the days until you and your family are back where you belong. Remember that we all love you very much."

Unmoved, Celestin freed himself from his father's embrace. "Goodbye, Papa," he said, and avoiding the older man's eyes, reached for his embroidery.

29

THE SIGHT OF an autumn-tinged Geneva, its serene, intensely blue lake and snow-covered Alps creating a majestic grandeur the like of which she had never imagined before, greatly pleased Micaela. The carriage wound through twisting cobblestone streets lined with cafes, restaurants, and fine shops until it reached the outskirts of the city, where it began its ascent into the Alps, twisting back and forth on the narrow mountain road, the wheels groaning on their axles, the horses puffing and sweating.

Binnie, who had never seen mountains before, stared out the coach window in awe of the towering, snowcapped peaks.

"Where are we goin', Miss Micaela?" she asked apprehensively.

"I have no more idea than you do," Micaela replied. "I simply gave Celestin's letter with the directions to the coachman."

About halfway up the mountain they came to a rustic chalet with a steeply slanted roof and deep, overhanging eaves, perched like an aerie on a ledge. The carriage rumbled to a halt before the entrance.

"Lordy, Miss Micaela, is this where we is fixin' to live?" Binnie asked, wide-eyed. "Way up here in the sky, like the birds?"

"For a while," Micaela answered, mulling over what she would say to Celestin when they met. She didn't know whether to reproach him for the way he had run off or simply to forget it and start anew, hoping for the best.

The clatter of the carriage brought Celestin out of the chalet in one bound. Throwing open the carriage door, he helped Micaela out and embraced her fervently.

"Oh, my dearest, my darling, how I've missed you!" he cried, his dark eyes brimming with joy. "How wonderful it is to see you again!"

"We've missed you, too," Micaela replied in a rather cool tone. Then she took little Tin-Tin from Binnie and presented him to his father.

"Tin-Tin! Oh, my son!" Celestin was nearly overcome with emotion before covering the child's face with kisses. Tin-Tin squirmed, began to cry, and waved his tiny arms at Binnie for help.

Later that night, when Celestin and Micaela were alone in their bedroom, he said, "Can you ever forgive me, dearest?"

"Yes, I suppose I can. This time." She had agreed to the reconciliation in Geneva more for their son's sake than for her own. Louise had tried to persuade her to leave Celestin altogether and bring the child to live with her in Paris, but after thinking it over, Micaela had declined. She had no desire for her son to grow up apart from his father. For a large portion of her young life she had known what it was like to be a near orphan, and she had no wish for Tin-Tin to repeat her experience. Since Tin-Tin's birth she had instinctively begun to put her own desires aside and give him first consideration. If she had been convinced that Celestin had deserted her permanently, she probably would have gone to Paris as her mother wished. There was no question in her mind that that was where she preferred to live, but for the boy's sake she would remain with Celestin and see how things progressed, at least for the present.

"Do you think you can be happy here?" he asked, stirring the fire on the hearth with a poker and raising a shower of bright orange embers.

Micaela shoved aside the unbleached canvas curtain and gazed down the mountain slope at the lake below. A delicate mist was rising off the water, gradually enveloping the chalet in a cottony stillness.

"For a while," she answered.

Before they retired for the night, Celestin added more logs to the fire. "That should keep us warm," he said.

When they were in bed, he lost no time in taking Micaela in his arms.

"How I've missed you, dearest," he whispered, his lips caressing her ear as he spoke. "I've suffered without you and little Tin-Tin. You don't know how painful it was for me to leave you the way I did. When you accused me of being weak, it wounded me deeply, and yet I knew you were right. I *was* weak, and I knew I had to do something about it. I had to be alone to decide what steps I could take to cure myself of that affliction."

"And are you stronger now?" she asked.

"Yes," he said without hesitation. "The fact that we are here together, away from Mont L'Eveque, is proof. The baron came to Mignot, you know, and ordered me home, but I refused. I told him that you and I must have our own life, away from him and the château."

"Good." Micaela was pleased to hear this.

"It wasn't easy," Celestin continued. "He attempted to dissuade me, but I remained resolute. Eventually he gave in to my demands. It was the first time I can ever remember his doing that. It's a beginning and I feel good about it."

"So do I." She hoped he would stick to his decision to assert himself with his father. If he did not, she doubted whether the marriage would last. From the beginning the marriage had survived because neither of them was under any romantic illusions. They had been ordered to marry and they had obeyed. Their lack of expectations had been the key to the survival of their union, but Celestin's voluntary subjugation to his father's will had placed severe strains on Micaela's patience.

"Oh, dearest . . . dearest," he murmured, snuggling close to her. Almost immediately aroused by the smoothness and warmth of her body, he fumbled nervously with the hem of her cotton nightdress, attempting to slip his hands beneath it. "I know now that I cannot live without you," he declared as he planted his eager mouth over hers, kissing her avidly, his fingers sliding upward along the inside of her thighs. After a few perfunctory caresses he crawled on top of her and tried to part her legs, but his haste and eagerness made him unintentionally rough and clumsy, and when he impulsively plunged into her, Micaela was unprepared and cried out.

"I'm sorry, dearest, I didn't mean to hurt you. It's just that it's been so long and——"

His attempted apology ended abruptly, and he began to thrust his throbbing manhood rapidly in and out of her, oblivious to the fact that Micaela lay motionless and unresponsive beneath him. His desire was consumed very quickly in a series of spasms that convulsed his entire body and left him sweaty and breathless.

"You were wonderful, dearest," he muttered hoarsely. "Wonderful."

During their first week or so together at the chalet their lovemaking was almost a nightly occurrence, as though Celestin were driven by some compulsion to prove that his desire for her had not waned. Micaela, for her part, would have preferred proof of another kind.

After a few months had passed, Micaela confided to Binnie that she was certain she was pregnant again.

"Oh, Lordy, Miss Micaela, I hope it ain't like the last time," the maid fretted.

"I hope not, either," Micaela sighed apprehensively, remembering the trauma she had suffered in carrying Tin-Tin.

When she revealed to Celestin that a second child was probably on the way, he attempted to affect some semblance of elation, but inwardly he was dismayed by the news and its implications. A second child would totally obliterate whatever dim hope he had of returning to the army.

"Celestin, I must go to Paris and stay there during this pregnancy," she said. "It is only by the grace of God that Tin-Tin and I survived the first. If I have trouble this time, I want to be near good doctors and clinics. I refuse to take chances with my life or the life of our new child, or to be confined either here in Geneva or at Mont L'Eveque."

Somewhat stunned by her pronouncement, stated in such forceful terms, Celestin felt bound to object. "But dearest, the Swiss doctors are extremely competent. The clinics in Geneva are the best in the world."

"I prefer to go to Paris."

"But the journey from here to Paris is long and arduous," he countered. "It would be dangerous to undertake it in your condition. I think we had better remain in Geneva for the duration."

Looking at him in such a way that he could not mistake the seriousness of her intention, she declared, "If you do not take me to Paris, I shall go without you. And I shall not stay with my mother."

Celestin was puzzled and confused. "If you do not stay with your mother, then where will you stay? Certainly not in a hotel for months?"

"I will get a house of my own."

"You cannot stay in Paris alone, a married woman without her husband," he protested. "It would be a scandal!"

"In that case, then, I trust I can count on you to come with me."

"How can we possibly manage in Paris?"

"We shall have no problem. The income from the New Orleans properties which Mama assigned to us is more than ample to meet our needs and keep us in a very comfortable style."

"But the baron controls those funds."

"From now on, the baron controls nothing," she said testily. "We have declared our independence from him. Or have you forgotten your promise?"

"Still, dearest, he will be very angry."

Micaela shrugged indifferently. "Let him be angry. What does it matter? You assured me that you would no longer let him dominate our lives."

"I know I did, but . . ."

"And he won't," she asserted. "Are you coming to Paris with us or not?"

"Yes, I suppose so," he replied, still unsure of his commitment.

She smiled. "Good. I'm proud of you, Celestin. I shall tell Binnie to begin packing at once."

When Louise received the news that her daughter and son-in-law were coming to live in Paris, she was overjoyed and thankful. Through her various agents she found them a comfortable home on the Rue du Houssaie, not far from her own.

Micaela's second pregnancy progressed smoothly, with none of the problems of the first, and she was ecstatically happy to be living in the French capital. It seemed as if a dream was finally being fulfilled, or at least partially fulfilled. The real dream was to live in Paris with Patrick Lynch, but she knew that was a ridiculous fantasy and should be forgotten.

For the first six months her pregnancy was hardly evident, and she was able to frequent many theaters, restaurants, and cafes, renew old acquaintances, and attend parties and balls. Louise was still in mourning for Castillon and as a result could not entertain on the lavish scale she might have wished, but she did give occasional small, quiet dinner parties and afternoon teas to reacquaint her only daughter and son-in-law with Parisian society, and vice versa.

On his part, Celestin loathed Paris and its life-style, and was tense and unhappy most of the time.

"It's just not proper for me to be frittering away my days here in Paris," he complained, "and leaving the baron with the full responsibility of administering our lands. He will have no time for the gardening he loves so much."

"You're really not happy here, are you?" Micaela said as she adjusted a cushion on the gray damask settee in the drawing room.

"It's just that I feel I belong at Mont L'Eveque. After all, dearest, I *am* the next baron. I do have my duty and obligations."

"And you would like us all to return there, wouldn't you?"

"Yes, especially since your pregnancy seems to be progressing satisfactorily this time."

"Regardless of that, I feel I must stay near my mother now that Castillon is dead. She is very lonely."

"Your mother has a great many friends to support and comfort her in her grief. I'm confident she'll get along fine."

"If you feel such a strong need to return to Mont L'Eveque for a while, I urge you to go. I don't want to see you so unhappy." She paused, then added, "But I am staying in Paris."

"I don't know what I feel the need of," he said, jumping up from the settee, "other than some air. It's stuffy in here, and I'm beginning to get a headache." With that he went out into the hall, grabbed his hat and walking stick, and left the house, heading for the only place where he felt truly comfortable in Paris.

Since the severe defeats and virtual disbanding of the Grand Army, the Cafe de Roy was not the same boisterous, jovial spot it had once been during the heyday of the Empire. This favorite haunt of the military could not dispel the air of gloom that had hung over it ever since the fateful Russian debacle, and which had deepened, in fact, with the recent abdication of Napoleon and his subsequent exile to Elba. Former soldiers seated at the tables quietly sipped their beer or cognac and pondered a bleak future.

On entering the cafe, Celestin spotted a sergeant he knew from the cavalry regiment, sitting by himself. Going straight to the man's table, he asked permission to join him.

"My pleasure, sir," the sergeant said, rising politely.

Much to Celestin's disappointment, the man seemed reluctant to talk about the unit's exploits in the vast, frozen steppes of imperial Russia or in the burned-out rubble of Moscow, conquered by the French in a decidedly Pyrrhic victory.

"It was terrible," the sergeant muttered in his beer. "Terrible."

Eventually Celestin pressed him for news of his former commander, Captain Dulac.

"Ah, now there's a sad case," the sergeant said, shaking his head forlornly.

"What do you mean by sad?" Celestin asked, alarmed at the soldier's tone.

"It was near Smolensk. We were retreating—sick, starving, freezing, and miserable. There was nothing to eat except an occasional dead horse, fallen in the snow, whose flesh we carved and devoured raw. Anyway, Marshal Ney was in charge of the rear guard. We were certain the Russians were determined to capture our emperor and take him prisoner. We could hardly see how they could fail, but Ney was equally determined they would not succeed. With the Russians in hot pursuit, Ney ordered the troops to stand up to them, and stand up to them they did—gallantly, I might add. The marshal himself drew his sword out of the scabbard and fought the oncoming Russians hand to hand. Dulac was right there at his side and did in quite a few Russians himself. Oh, what a night that was—Ney and Dulac battling the Russians blade to blade! We were all so inspired by the fierce fighting spirit of those two officers, we fought more bravely than ever before. Where our strength came from I don't know, sir. It was a miracle. Somehow we managed to hold off the Russians and save the emperor from being taken. But then things went bad for Dulac. During the fighting he received certain wounds . . ."

"Wounds? Were they serious?" Celestin asked anxiously.

"The wounds themselves were not so severe," the sergeant replied, "but they prevented him from moving about sufficiently to protect himself from the bitter cold. You know, when it's cold you must keep stirring about or you freeze. Ah, you can't imagine what it was like—the Russian cold is like no other. As a result, Dulac suffered frostbite. The toes on both his feet had to be amputated."

"My God!" Celestin gasped. "Where is he now?"

"Captain Dulac? Who knows?" The sergeant shrugged. "The army was his whole life. Without his toes he could no longer serve. God knows what has become of him. I hate to think about his present state of mind. As I said, he's a sad case indeed, poor fellow."

30

MICAELA SEEMED RELATIVELY content with her home on the Rue du Houssaie and grateful to be living in Paris, far from Mont L'Eveque. Although the house was attractive, comfortable, and well located, it was nonetheless modest, neither as large nor as elegant as the other residences surrounding it. One day when Micaela expressed her dissatisfaction with the house to her mother, Louise replied, "Yes, I admit it is rather plain, certainly not a *hôtel privé,* but it will do for the present. The most important thing for you now is to get to know people, explore the city, and become established. Later, when you're older and your family is larger, you can move to more elaborate living quarters. After all, you must remember that Celestin is a country boy at heart. You shouldn't overwhelm him with too much at once. Let him get used to this new way of life little by little."

Inwardly Micaela wondered whether Celestin would remain in Paris long enough to accustom himself to living there. Each day he became increasingly restless, and she expected him to depart at any moment.

At Mont L'Eveque the baron, of course, was thoroughly vexed that Micaela had persuaded his son to live in Paris, but for the moment, at least, he realized there was nothing he could do to change the situation. He was well aware that his son's earlier "desertion" could have placed the marriage, and thus the family, in great jeopardy. For the present he was willing to overlook almost anything in order to preserve the precarious union and avoid the scandal of a separation—to say nothing of the loss of Micaela's income from her mother's Louisiana properties. He had been able to make some very profitable investments with that money, and so he thought it gracious of him to allow his daughter-in-law the freedom to enjoy her Parisian fling, if that was what she insisted on, hoping only that it would not prove to be embarrassing or too costly. With a second child now on the way, he feared further extravagance on her part.

When Micaela decided to refurbish the house, she was unwittingly fulfilling the baron's misgivings. She rejected her mother's offer of pieces from her own home, many of which Louise had brought from New Orleans, and insisted on the current rage of decor that duplicated the classical Greek, Roman, and Egyptian lines in low, graceful chaises, slim tables edged in gold, and beds draped with canopies to resemble tents. Fortunately, her condition still permitted her to get about easily, and she spent tireless hours touring the fine stores and craftsmen's shops in search of the proper woods—mahogany, citrus, and ebony were the most popular—tiles, and mirrors. When she wasn't shopping or dreaming up ways to make the Rue du Houssaie home more attractive, she was busy interviewing servants and designing uniforms for them. She also contemplated major structural changes and even went so far as to draw up a few sketches of what she wanted done. Such projected alterations brought Patrick Lynch immediately to mind. She would have loved to have been able to call on him for advice in such matters, but instead, she fantasized how enjoyable it would be if they could work together on remodeling the house. Even now, with the birth of her second child imminent, thoughts of Patrick and their brief but unforgettable relationship made her sigh with longing and nostalgia.

Celestin, for the most part, dutifully endured his new life, considering it a kind of penance for having earlier abandoned Micaela and his son, and only occasionally raised minor objections about his wife's extravagance and what seemed to him an overly active social life for a woman about to be confined to await the birth of a baby. He longed to return to the bucolic serenity of Mont L'Eveque with its green meadows, orchards full of pears and apples, trout-filled streams, and forests and marshes teeming with game. Having led a relatively unsophisticated country existence, he was uncomfortable associating with the urbane aristocrats, intellectuals, artists, and affluent bourgeoisie with whom Micaela seemed so determined to ingratiate herself, much in the same way as her mother had. Celestin regarded his wife's newfound friends effete and somewhat threatening, and he preferred to remain in the background whenever possible. At times he thought his principal function in Paris was to pay the endless stack of bills Micaela acquired in her seemingly obsessive quest for social status. Her closets were bulging with expensive sequinned dresses cut in the fashionable style of ancient Greece, which hugged the body and clearly exposed the breasts, as well as with toques à la sphynx, felt poke bonnets, and pseudo-Greek Minerva helmets. Her pregnancy did not in the least deter her quest for the best. Celestin's sole compensation for this was his young son, with whom he was able to spend a great deal of time because Micaela was often otherwise occupied. Tin-Tin, a cheerful, bright, and extremely active child of almost two, adored being taken through the well-tended, popular Parisian parks by his father and sailing little boats in the pools and fountains. The sails of these boats were emblazoned with the Pontalba family crest, hand-embroidered by Celestin himself.

At night, while Micaela went over various guest

lists and menus with the household staff, Celestin read his son fairy tales and stories about military heroes such as Julius Caesar and Alexander the Great, often falling asleep in the boy's room and spending the entire night surrounded by lead soldiers, horses, and toy cannons.

Although relations between Micaela and Celestin appeared smooth on the surface, it became increasingly clear to both of them that an ever-widening gulf was fast dividing them. Celestin feared that unless they returned to Mont L'Eveque, their marriage would be in serious trouble. Micaela was progressively being seduced away from her duties as wife and mother by the charms of the City of Light and its brittle, sophisticated society. Celestin promised himself that if he and Micaela did eventually separate, he definitely would not leave the children behind.

On the day their second son was born, whom they named Alfred, Micaela's greatest distress was that they would not be able to attend a dinner in honor of the Italian composer Gioacchino Rossini, whose operas were becoming the rage in Europe. Micaela refused to stay in bed for several weeks, as was usually the custom following childbirth among the upper classes, and as soon as she had recovered from her delivery, she gathered her household staff around her and planned her own dinner party for the illustrious and talented Signor Rossini.

"But you've just had a baby," Celestin protested when he heard of her plans to entertain.

"Having a baby is not an illness," she argued. "It's an occasion to celebrate. I want to throw open our home, humble as it is, to all Paris, even though it is not really suitable for entertaining on a large scale."

"You will never be satisfied with this house, will you?"

"No, I won't," she agreed, "but for now it will have to do. At this time of our lives anything too large or too grand would not be appropriate. Later, when we're older and more established, we'll go on to bigger and better homes."

Returning to his original objection, he said, "There

is considerable stress and strain connected with entertaining. Frankly, I don't think it's wise in your present
condition."

"There is stress and strain connected with everything, Celestin—certainly having a baby is no exception, but it's no reason to go into hiding, either.
Besides, my condition is fine," she added. "I was in
seclusion for too long as it was. If you're not seen
about, people soon forget you. Entertaining is one way
of announcing your return to society. It serves many
purposes. If one doesn't entertain, how is one to have
any friends?"

"I doubt if we shall ever have real 'friends' in this
city," he countered. "I don't think that the ambience
of Paris—or at least the sector of Parisian society to
which you aspire to belong—encourages true friend-
ships."

"Nonsense," she scoffed. "Why must you always
repudiate everything I want to do? If Paris is to be our
home, we must make an effort to become part of its
community, just as Mama did when she first arrived
here. You know, it wasn't easy for her, either. That's
why she's been so generous in sharing her many fine
friends with us."

"I belong to Mont L'Eveque. I will never be part of
Paris," he declared. "I'm not even sure I want to be."

Micaela eventually won out, and the gala dinner
party for Rossini and several other luminaries of the
Parisian cultural world was arranged in spite of Celestin's objections.

"Just imagine, Celestin, not only is Signor Rossini
himself coming, but Madame de Staël, Jacques David,
and Barthélmy Vignon have accepted as well!" Micaela cried excitedly when Georges, the butler,
brought her the day's mail.

"I know the writer Staël and the artist David, but
who is this Vignon fellow?" he asked, scarcely looking
up from the needlepoint in his hand. It was his own
design, a complicated scene of a cavalry charge.

"Monsieur Vignon happens to be one of France's
finest architects," she explained. "Don't you remem-

ber? We met him at Mama's right after we arrived in France."

He shrugged indifferently. "I'm not much interested in architects."

"I find them very interesting," she said with a smile.

"I can't imagine why."

Returning her attention to the guest list, she made a small moue. "Still, I am a bit disappointed that Madame Récamier has declined."

"You shouldn't be. After all, Madame Récamier also declined to share the emperor's bed."

"Do you think it's true she's still a virgin and that in all her years of marriage she has never permitted her husband to sleep with her?"

"I haven't the faintest idea."

Since coming to Paris, Micaela seemed to be preoccupied with gossip, not at all like the naive, innocent girl she had once been—or so Celestin thought. The changes in her that he felt Paris had wrought disturbed him beyond measure.

"I wish I knew what wine would be best with the fish course," she mused. "Mama says always to start off with the best wines. Later, when everyone is a little high, it doesn't make much difference what you serve."

"Yes, that sounds like your mother," he remarked.

Ignoring his rather snide comment, she said, "I would like to surprise our guests and serve larks, but it's so hard to find good ones. Mama says Carcellet has the best."

"There's no meat at all on the poor little things."

"The pastries, of course, will be from Toulouse. That's not a problem. And the fish and the stuffed tongue will be from Hymet's. The only big decisions still remaining are the flowers and the candles."

"Yes," he said wryly. "Those really *are* big decisions."

Leaving Micaela to her dinner-party preparations, Celestin held his son Tin-Tin by the hand and walked through the busy Parisian streets toward the park, where he had promised the boy he could sail his boat. He felt relieved to be away from the near hysteria surrounding the upcoming dinner party. Perhaps the headache that had plagued him for days would go away. The change in Micaela from a simple American girl to an ambitious French hostess was difficult for him to cope with, and his method for handling it was simply to remove himself from the house.

In the park, the sun was surprisingly warm for a November day, and the winding gravel paths bustled with mothers and nurses tending their small charges. Celestin had wanted Binnie to join them with baby Alfred, but Micaela insisted that she needed the maid to help her and that the weather was not warm enough to hazard taking an infant only a few weeks old outdoors.

Along one of the quieter paths Celestin came upon a man seated on a bench, apparently dozing in the sun. Somehow the fellow, despite his rather shabby attire looked familiar. Close to perhaps forty and with a generous sprinkling of gray in his dark hair, he appeared ruggedly powerful, the only odd thing about him being the multiple pairs of thick woolen stockings that enclosed his feet, which were stuffed into worn-looking carpet slippers. A pair of crutches lay on the bench beside him. Knowing it was rude, Celestin could not help staring at the casual sunbather, whom he was sure he recognized.

Approaching him, Celestin finally ventured to say, "Captain Dulac?"

Startled, the man on the bench turned in his direction, opened his eyes, and raised his hand to block out the sun. Staring at Celestin, who was holding his son's hand, he mumbled, equally astonished, "Pontalba . . . ?"

"Yes." Celestin nodded eagerly, his face breaking into a wide smile at the prospect of accidentally encountering his old friend.

Dulac leaped up, and tottering precariously, lurched forward and grabbed Celestin in a fierce embrace.

"Pontalba!" he cried. "My God, can it really be you?"

"Dulac! What an incredible surprise!"

Detaching himself from the former cavalry captain,

who seemed reluctant to let him go, Celestin introduced his young son. Tin-Tin clung shyly to his father's trouser leg.

"Go on, Tin-Tin, shake hands with Captain Dulac," Celestin urged. "He is one of Papa's best friends. Papa and Captain Dulac were in the Grand Army together."

Reluctantly the boy did as he was told, although he seemed uncomfortable in Dulac's presence and fixed his gaze on the man's thickly stockinged feet.

"What are you doing in Paris?" Dulac asked Celestin.

"Micaela and I are living here now. I brought Tin-Tin to the park to sail his boat."

"Good, good."

Hobbling on his crutches, the former officer insisted on accompanying them to the fountain, where they renewed their acquaintance while the boy played with his sailboat. The sight of this once intrepid and splendid cavalryman now reduced to limping about like a defeated old man sickened and dismayed Celestin. How cruel life was, he thought. How unbearably cruel.

Although Celestin feared that Dulac might feel uncomfortable discussing the past, the former cavalry captain insisted on relating the horrors of Napoleon's disastrous Russian campaign in vivid detail.

"It was a good one to miss, I tell you, Pontalba," he said, shaking his head. "We were starving and freezing at the same time. The only thing we had to eat was the putrid flesh of our horses, which were shot from under us or died of starvation, poor beasts. I hate to say this, but there were even rumors of cannibalism among our foot soldiers, although I personally never witnessed anything as disgusting as that. We in the rear guard gave the Cossacks a good fight. The Russians expected to kidnap the emperor, but we foiled their plans. If I hadn't been wounded by a Cossack who caught me off guard from behind and left me for dead, I wouldn't have lost my toes."

"What are you doing now? How do you live?" Celestin asked.

Dulac smiled a twisted, ironic smile. "Oh, I survive. I have a studio where I teach all the rich young fools of this city how to fence. It's a living, and at least I'm not out on the street begging with an alms bowl in my hands, like many another old soldier. But tell me, Pontalba, what are you up to?"

Celestin began to relate all the things that had happened to him since they had last seen each other. Restrained at first, he soon poured forth everything, omitting nothing, almost as if he were purging himself by admitting his general discontentment with his life since leaving the army, his troubles with his father, his concerns about Micaela. Finally he paused, suddenly self-conscious, "Why am I boring you with all this?" he muttered. "My troubles must seem trite indeed compared with what you have undergone these past two years."

"I'm flattered you feel free to confide in me," Dulac said.

"Well, I have always regarded you as a good friend," Celestin told him.

Placing one large hand on Celestin's shoulder and giving it a squeeze, Dulac nodded approvingly. "And well you should, my boy, well you should."

Part Three

31

LIVING IN PARIS, Micaela began to feel that she had finally achieved a mode of existence that compensated to some degree for disappointments in other areas of her life. Liberated from Mont L'Eveque with its gloomy rooms, drafty halls, and stony staircases, from the loneliness and boredom of her isolation in the country, and, most of all, from the stifling repression of the Pontalbas' way of life, Micaela was happier than she had been since leaving New Orleans.

Initially her mother had introduced her to her set of friends who, in turn, introduced her to their friends, and so it went. Among these many new acquaintances, Micaela discovered, were some of the most notable and accomplished Parisians of the day. Her reputation as a gracious and charming hostess attracted many to her inner circle, and her wit, intelligence, and beauty —to say nothing of her money—proved valuable social assets. During her years in Paris, Louise had acquired considerable knowledge and taste, much of which she imparted to her daughter, and much of which was expensive, even extravagant by the Pontalbas' standards, as they pointed out at every opportunity.

Despite the distance separating them, Celestin remained in constant contact with his father. One day, undoubtedly influenced by the baron, he complained anew to Micaela about her clothing expenditures just as she was preparing to visit the exclusive fur salon La Reine d'Espagne.

"In order to be a successful hostess, one must dress the part," she replied.

"That's very important to you, isn't it?"

"Yes, it is," she admitted, certain now she would buy the lynx cape she had had her eye on for weeks but felt was simply too costly.

Micaela had also taken to wearing cosmetics and perfume, which she had specially blended for her at Martin's, and wondered what the nuns at the Ursuline Convent would have thought if they could have seen their former pupil with her face "painted." *They should be glad I haven't had it enameled,* she thought to herself, referring to a process many women underwent that left their faces as smooth as a porcelain mask and equally expressionless.

She also loved the delicate French lingerie. Hers was entirely silk and trimmed with the finest Valenciennes lace.

On Monday evenings, along with the rest of the fashionable set, Micaela attended the opera, and on Thursdays, the Comédie Française, both of which she adored. Although serious artistic and cultural pursuits were prominent in her Parisian life, she also enjoyed an occasional gambling spree at the Jockey Club, where her favorite game was passe-dix. On Sundays she regularly attended Mass at Ste. Clotilde's with her mother and the rest of the elite, and afterward, during the season, went out to the races at Longchamp.

The Parisian social season was basically divided into two parts: a "petite" season, which began around Christmas and ended at Easter, and a "grand" season, which began at Easter and continued into early summer, at which time Parisians left the city in droves for the seaside resorts of Deauville and Trouville, for the Alps, or for grouse shooting in Scotland. Both the "petite" and the "grand" seasons were crammed with events of all kinds, and Micaela invariably found herself in the center of things.

Because her life in Paris was filled with so much activity, the years seemed to fly by, relatively happy years, marred only by a steady decline in her mother's health.

In 1821 a third son, Gaston, was born, and the year of his birth marked the tenth anniversary of her marriage to Celestin. Through sheer stubbornness and force of will she had managed to root her life firmly in the City of Light, although there were occasional obligatory visits to Mont L'Eveque, some lasting for months, especially in the summer. Like their father, Tin-Tin and Alfred seemed to enjoy life in the country, which was quite a contrast to their usual city existence.

The baron, hoping to lure Micaela back to Mont L'Eveque permanently, had constructed a small theater at the château. Among Micaela's acquaintances were a number of actors, including the celebrated François Talma, who had been one of Napoleon's favorites, and they as well as other friends were often invited to the country. Many plays were performed in the little theater, Micaela herself sometimes playing various roles. Despite the objections of the baron, there were usually two performances, one for the Pontalbas and their guests and one for the peasants.

In addition to theatrics, Micaela and her sophisticated Parisian friends also enjoyed fox hunting, many of the women following the hunt in dogcarts pulled by Great Danes or Irish wolfhounds, or in boats on the river. Horse shows and the races were also popular activities during their country visits.

In the evening when they were not performing plays, they would often engage in a lively game of charades or dance to Napoleonic quadrilles, Versailles minuets, and Henry IV pavanes, played by orchestras Micaela imported from the capitol.

In the summer when the weather was warm, Micaela and her friends would bathe in the river, the blondes assigned black bathing suits, the brunettes red. Micaela, the only redhead, wore blue or brown. Needless to say, the Pontalbas did not look kindly on these outings, but since she didn't have to reside permanently at Mont L'Eveque, Micaela worried little about what they thought.

Conversely, Celestin grew increasingly despondent with the passage of years, and only his friendship with

Armand Dulac and his time spent with his three sons made life in Paris tolerable for him. When Tin-Tin and Alfred began attending school, and Gaston, still too young to be much company for his father, was the only child at home during the day, Celestin began to return to Mont L'Eveque with greater frequency, and his visits there grew more extended.

"Why does Papa go to Grandfather's so much?" Alfred asked Micaela one day. "Doesn't he like it here with us?"

"Your father grew up in the country," Micaela explained. "He feels comfortable there."

"But Grandfather is so strict," Alfred said.

"Yes, he is rather strict, isn't he?" Micaela agreed.

Quite often on Mondays or Thursdays or on other days of the week Micaela found herself without an escort for the opera or the theater and was forced to rely on various friends. Nevertheless, she worried about gossip and the threat of scandal. If she were seen in public too often without her husband, rumors that the marriage was in trouble would undoubtedly begin to circulate. It was already well known that she and Celestin were not particularly compatible.

Celestin did not enjoy the opera or the theater, at least not to the degree Micaela did, and in addition seemed ill at ease around her witty and urbane friends, with whom he felt he had little in common. He was positive that they, in turn, regarded him as little more than an uninspiring country squire. When his discontent reached the point where he felt the need to unload, Dulac was more often than not the one to whom he turned.

"Sometimes I feel like the royal consort," he complained to the fencing master.

Lovingly polishing the long steel blade of a curved saber, Dulac smiled and said, "Some men might like that role."

"I'm not one of them," Celestin assured him.

Frequently Dulac's feet swelled painfully and his other war wounds plagued him, but he bore the discomforts stoically. "Suffering is a bore," he remarked. "No one wants to hear about it."

"And yet I burden you with all my troubles," Celestin sighed. "How trivial and stupid they must seem."

"Not when they're yours, my boy," Dulac said, reaching out and giving his knee a reassuring squeeze.

There were still times when Celestin felt desperately frustrated and unhappy and went so far as to actually plead with Micaela to return with him to Mont L'Eveque.

"It will be different now," he said. "We're older. We have the children. The baron, too, has mellowed. You have the theater there, and you could invite your friends from Paris whenever you like."

"You know as well as I do that I could not endure Mont L'Eveque when we were first married, and I would not be able to endure it now," she told him. "I'm sorry, Celestin. I know how you long to return there, but I am in Paris to stay."

"Do you think these Parisians who are always hanging around you really care for you?" he asked. "They laugh at your peculiar patois speech and your Creole accent and think it quaint and amusing. They regard you as nothing more than a curiosity, an eccentric American. Only your money and the generous way you spend it attract them to you."

"I am aware that some of what you're saying is true," she admitted. "But if I am unloved in Paris, I am unloved far more at Mont L'Eveque."

In her bid to be a leading hostess Micaela's expenses were very high. The baron took a keen interest in their finances and demanded a detailed accounting every month from his son, who kept the records and paid the bills, albeit entirely with his wife's money. As time passed, Baron Joseph grew increasingly intolerant of his daughter-in-law's extravagance and eventually reached the point where he could not continue to stand by and allow her to indulge her fancies for the sake of preserving the marriage and, thereby, the Pontalba good name.

"Look at this!" the baron cried in exasperation, waving a bill from Micaela's milliner in his son's face. "This bill is an outrage!"

"Micaela needed a wide-brimmed hat to keep the sun off her face at the races," Celestin explained.

"But must she buy a hat at such an exorbitant price? Surely there are less expensive ones. Besides, you shouldn't allow her to go to the races so much. She's betting too heavily and losing too often."

Realizing that his son's objections would have little effect on curbing Micaela's expenses, the baron decided to take the matter into his own hands and confront her directly on her next visit to the château.

"I will be frank with you, my dear, and tell you that you are simply too extravagant," he declared.

Taken by surprise, Micaela said, "Really? Extravagant? I?"

"Yes. Celestin showed me some of your bills. They were outrageous, to say the least."

"Outrageous?" she repeated with a bemused smile. "I don't think they are outrageous at all, Baron. Not when one considers who I am."

"And just who are you, my dear?"

"A woman of intelligence, taste, and culture," she replied confidently. "I also happen to be a woman of means. Let me remind you, dear Baron, that the money I spend is my own."

"Nothing is your own," he snapped. "You are a married woman. You have no property of your own. Everything that is yours automatically becomes your husband's. You know our laws as well as I do."

"As a Pontalba and the future baroness, I feel an obligation to support cultural pursuits and the arts, which I believe are the foundations of civilization, although I am aware that some do not share this view."

"And *I* am well aware of who you are, madame. It seems that from your bills you aspire to support fashion as generously as all those other interests—perhaps more so."

Micaela shrugged, indifferent to his criticism. "One must dress the role life obliges one to play. One's clothes have a great influence on others and how they treat you. One cannot, after all, have one's gold interred in one's grave. Money should be enjoyed to the fullest, not locked away in strongboxes, as it is at Mont L'Eveque."

"Is that your only defense, madame?" the baron fumed.

"I don't feel the need to defend myself," she replied. "I have no intention of altering my life-style in the least. And let me tell you, dear Baron, your days of intimidating me are over."

"Are they?" he retorted, struggling to control his rising anger. "We shall see."

32

FOR THE THIRD time that evening Micaela nervously checked the details of the dinner party with Georges, the butler, and was about to go to her room to dress when Binnie approached to say that little Gaston was ready for bed and wanted to say good night to her.

Entering her youngest son's room, Micaela was surprised to find Celestin, who she assumed was in his room dressing, lying on the child's bed reading aloud while Gaston listened with rapt attention.

"Celestin, you haven't even begun to dress yet, and our guests will be arriving in less than an hour," she chided.

"I guess I've gotten as engrossed in this story as our little one," he said, giving the child an apologetic look and reluctantly closing the book.

"No, Papa, more," Gaston pleaded, slapping at the book with his small hands. "Read more, Papa. Read more."

"I'm sorry. No more tonight, Son. Papa has other things he must do. Besides, a story is much better if you leave some of it for another time."

Attempting to assuage the boy's chagrin, Micaela smoothed his brown curls and said, "Mama will tuck you in, darling."

When she was satisfied that Gaston was about to fall

asleep, Micaela tiptoed from his room and proceeded to Alfred's to say good night to him and from there to Tin-Tin's across the hall. Now that her eldest was thirteen and fast becoming a young man, she felt obliged to knock at his door before entering.

"Just a moment, Mama," he called out in his unsettled adolescent voice.

When he finally gave her permission to enter, Micaela detected a suspicious odor permeating the air. "Have you been into your father's cigars again?" she asked suspiciously.

"No, Mama."

"You aren't lying, are you?"

"No, Mama. I have been smoking, but not Papa's cigars," the boy confessed, removing a still smoldering cigar from beneath the covers where he had tried to conceal it.

"Where did you get *that?*" she demanded.

"Captain Dulac gave it to me as a reward."

"A reward for what?"

"He said I performed splendidly in my match yesterday," Tin-Tin replied. He had been studying fencing under the tutelage of Dulac for several months, with his father's enthusiastic encouragement. Initially Micaela had not approved of this activity for the boy, but when she saw how much pleasure it gave Celestin to take his son to Dulac's studio and how much the boy enjoyed the sport, she reneged and gave her consent. According to all reports, Tin-Tin was developing into an excellent swordsman, a fact that didn't surprise her since he had always been daring and exceptionally well coordinated since birth.

"I shall have to have a word with your father about Captain Dulac and his rewards," Micaela said, kissing him perfunctorily on the cheek, the only overt demonstration of affection he would permit at this age.

When she returned to the master bedroom, Micaela found Celestin struggling with his cravat.

"Why don't you ask Georges to come and help you dress?" she suggested.

"Because invariably when I need Georges, he's busy doing something for you."

"You know, Celestin, busy as I am now, there's something I must discuss with you."

Assuming it concerned the dinner that evening, he said disinterestedly, "Oh? What's that?"

"It's about Tin-Tin. I caught him smoking a cigar tonight."

"I suppose he's got to start learning to smoke sometime," he observed casually.

"Not at thirteen. It's not good for his health."

"He's just amusing himself, that's all. He's not smoking seriously. Dulac gave him that cigar as a kind of joke. It's much too strong for him. He'd be sick after a few puffs." He chuckled. "He deserved a cigar after that match the other day. He handled himself splendidly. You should have seen him. Dulac was most pleased."

"*I'm* not pleased. I haven't said much about this before, Celestin, but I think Tin-Tin is spending too much time with that crippled fencing master."

"Why do you always have to refer to Dulac by his disability?" he reproached. "Especially when you know his name perfectly well."

"I'm sorry," she apologized. "It's just that I'm not sure I approve of Tin-Tin's being around that sort of person when he's at such an impressionable age. Besides, the servants tell me he's been using a lot of bad language lately, and I myself have noticed that he has acquired mannerisms and habits I don't like."

"I suppose you'd rather he spend his time with your fancy friends instead?"

"Why do *you* always have to belittle my friends?"

"Friends?" he laughed. "You call them friends? Do you know what they think of you?"

"Of course I know what they think of me. You needn't repeat your opinions. I've heard them often enough." She paused. "My friends admire and respect me."

"Hah!" he scoffed. "Admire and respect you? They laugh at you behind your back. They consider you nothing more than an upstart American heiress with a lot of pretensions and too much money."

"The finest people in Paris accept my invitations and come here," she said defensively.

"They may be contemptuous of you, but they aren't fools," he replied. "They know you serve excellent food and the best wines. Some of these so-called artistic and intellectual friends of yours can't dine anywhere else the way they do here. They also know you're a generous patron of the arts and other causes —an easy touch, so to speak. In short, they come here because they know what side their bread is buttered on —no pun intended."

Micaela chose not to retort angrily, as she was at first tempted to do, because she realized that would only escalate the animosity between them. Sighing wearily, she remarked quietly, "You know, Celestin, it's a sad thing that our values and interests are so different that they put us constantly at odds with each other."

"We've been mismatched from the start," he conceded. "And we both know it. Actually, I suppose we should congratulate ourselves for staying together as long as we have."

"Sometimes I'm sure you'd like to leave. Isn't that true?"

"Yes, sometimes it is," he admitted frankly. Then he tore the troublesome cravat from around his neck, tossed it on the floor, and scrambled in the drawer for another one.

The dinner party, in honor of Jean François Champollion, a noted Egyptologist who had succeeded in finally unlocking the secret of the Rosetta Stone and thus providing archaeologists with the key with which to translate Egyptian hieroglyphics, went splendidly, as Micaela had hoped it would. Afterward she conducted her guests into the drawing room, where they sipped coffee and cognac and conversed while waiting to see what special entertainment she had prepared for them. Micaela was known for her unusual divertissements. On this particular evening she had prevailed on her special friend, François Talma, the noted actor who had been a frequent guest at Mont L'Eveque, to recite passages from Shakespeare's *Antony and Cleopatra,* in keeping with the Egyptian theme of the party. Talma agreed on the condition that Micaela would play Cleopatra to his Antony.

"What? A red-haired Cleopatra?" she laughed.

"Why not?" Talma urged.

"Cleopatra undoubtedly used a henna rinse on her hair," Champollion said. "They've found henna in the various Pharaohs' tombs, you know."

She nodded. "Yes, why shouldn't I be the Serpent of the Nile?"

"I knew they wouldn't have to twist your arm very hard," Celestin remarked.

While Talma and Micaela were enthusiastically declaiming one of the classic play's most dramatic scenes, they were suddenly interrupted by the unexpected appearance of Flore, who burst excitedly into the room, her cape flying behind her, her bonnet askew.

Micaela was startled by the intrusion and instantly sensed that something was seriously wrong at her mother's.

"Oh, Miss Micaela! Miss Micaela!" Flore cried.

Immediately stepping out of the character of the beguiling Egyptian queen, Micaela hurried toward the servant.

"Flore, what is it?" she asked anxiously.

"It's Miss Louise. She's mighty bad. The doctor told me to fetch you right away. You got to come quick," Flore replied, choking back hysterical tears.

Abandoning her guests, Micaela rushed from the drawing room and down the hall toward the front door, Flore following behind her.

Celestin ran after her. "I'll go with you, dearest," he offered.

"No, no. Stay here with our guests," Micaela said over her shoulder as she hurried down the steps to the curb, where the Castillon carriage was waiting. "Apologize to them for me. Try to explain . . ."

When she arrived at Louise's great house on the Rue St. Honoré, she headed straight for her mother's bedroom and found her obviously dying. The only light in the room came from the flickering flame of a single *veilleuse*.

"Micaela, you've come. Thank God you've come before it's too late," Louise murmured in a nearly inaudible voice, stretching out a bony hand.

Micaela sat on the edge of the bed, clasped the extended hand in hers, and pressing it against her cheek, began to weep. "Oh, Mama . . . Mama . . ."

"Please, dear, no tears," Louise whispered. "I had a good life. I go without regrets. No, I won't say without *any* regrets. My greatest regret is that I was not a better mother to you."

"You were fine, Mama, fine," Micaela tried to reassure her.

"I was barely adequate, but that's beside the point now. I tried to do all I could for you under the circumstances, but it wasn't easy. Maybe someday you'll realize all I was obliged to contend with. Then you'll understand and perhaps, hopefully, forgive me."

"There's nothing to forgive," Micaela insisted.

"There's much to forgive," Louise contradicted. "But I don't want to labor that now. In these later years I tried to make it up to you. I'm sorry for so many things. My one goal in life since the death of your father has been to protect you, to provide for you in every way possible. After my death you will still be taken care of. Saint-Avid has arranged everything. Trust me and believe in me. I have done all I could. In my own way I have done everything . . . everything for you, my dearest child . . . Everything . . ."

Louise squeezed Micaela's hand with surprising strength, held on to it, smiled slightly, and closed her eyes forever.

Following the death of her mother, Micaela was so distraught that Celestin was obliged to handle the entire funeral arrangements himself.

The service was attended by most of the leading figures in the Parisian cultural and intellectual society as well as by the Pontalbas, who made one of their very rare excursions from Mont L'Eveque. En route the baron could not help remarking to his wife and

Madame Miró, with whom he shared the family carriage, "I hope we do not have to stay in Paris any longer than necessary, but I will not leave the city until I learn the contents of my late cousin's will."

"I hear that poor Micaela is beside herself with grief," Madame Miró said.

"I'm sure she will recover for the reading of the will," Baron Joseph commented wryly.

"I never thought Micaela had much love for her mother, if you want my frank opinion," Jeanne offered.

Her aunt disagreed. "I think they grew closer after Micaela moved to Paris."

"With Louise gone, Micaela will no longer have a good excuse to remain in Paris," Jeanne observed.

"She has lost her most fervent champion in that particular fight," the baron said.

"She will never consent to come back to Mont L'Eveque to live,"Jeanne mused. "Never."

"She'll have to if she's given no choice," he replied.

Staring at her husband with a puzzled frown, Jeanne asked, "What do you mean?"

"I mean if she suddenly finds herself with no other home," he answered, although by no means clarifying what he meant for his wife and her aunt.

"But now she will have two homes," Madame Miró said. "Her own *and* her mother's."

"Neither of those residences is *her* home," the baron chuckled. "They belong to our son. At last, with Louise finally out of the way, Celestin will be able to claim what has been rightfully his since the day he married Micaela—namely, all her property."

"That's quite a lot," his wife acknowledged.

"Of course," the baron agreed. "At long last the games, the trickery, the deceit, are over. There will be no more sly deceptions from Louise and her lawyers. No more tricky clauses, no more devious language behind which they can hide. All obstacles have been removed. Celestin will finally get what has been rightfully his from the beginning."

When Micaela had recovered sufficiently from her

grief after the funeral, a reading of her mother's will was arranged. Accompanied by Celestin, the baron, Jeanne, and Madame Miró, she went to Saint-Avid's office. Although the day was bright and sunny, the thick-set, bearded Saint-Avid kept the heavy damask drapes drawn in deference to the family's mourning. When they were all seated around his sprawling oak desk, the lawyer put on a pair of gold-rimmed spectacles, removed the will from a leather briefcase, and began to read it.

The last will and testament of Louise Castillon was a long, complicated document sprinkled with the usual legal jargon that no one in the room except Saint-Avid himself could fully understand. There were innumerable small bequests to various friends, servants—Flore and Raymond were given their freedom and pensions for life—and favorite charities and cultural institutions, the naming of which the Pontalbas endured with great patience. Not until the lawyer reached the portion of the will that enumerated all of Louise's many holdings, both in Louisiana and in France, did everyone suddenly sit up and pay sharp attention. They all knew that Louise had made some astute investments that had increased the original estate of Don Andrés many times over, but they were truly astonished to discover the exact magnitude of her wealth. It was immense.

Gazing over the top of his spectacles, perched precariously on the tip of his nose, Saint-Avid smiled.

"I have saved the best for last," he said.

Continuing with the reading, although not in the same dry tone as before, he made it clear to one and all that Louise had willed her vast estate to her only surviving child Micaela Almonester de Pontalba. For the first time since entering the lawyer's office, the baron relaxed and breathed a sigh of relief. Louise had made Micaela her heir after all, forgoing any surprises. Having endured the many insults and indignities heaped upon him by his dead cousin as well as the eccentricities and extravagances of her daughter had been worth it. By leaving all her property to her daughter, Louise Castillon had made his son one of the wealthiest men in France. It was all he could do to restrain himself from cheering. The long, often humiliating struggle was finally over. Celestin and future Pontalbas would be rich beyond their wildest expectations. His exultation was halted only by the sudden realization that Saint-Avid had not yet finished.

In a voice that barely concealed his suppressed glee, the lawyer announced that the provision naming Micaela as sole heir emphasized that the properties bequeathed to her were to be held and administered exclusively by her and her alone.

"Under no circumstances will there be any participation, meddling, or interference of any kind by my daughter's husband, his family members, or his friends," were Louise's exact words, and the attorney read them slowly and carefully.

The baron was so stunned by this revelation that he could not restrain himself. Leaping out of his chair, he shook his finger angrily in Saint-Avid's face and accused him of lying.

"I demand to see that will myself!" he shouted.

Maintaining his calm, the lawyer passed the document to him. Hands trembling, the baron read it and examined the signatures as well.

"I protest this will," he cried. "My cousin cannot do this under French law. It is illegal. You may be an attorney, Monsieur Saint-Avid, but I am not totally ignorant. The contents of this will are in violation of the civil code established by Napoleon himself. These properties, willed to my daughter-in-law, automatically pass to my son and are under his control."

"I'm afraid, sir, that is not the case," Saint-Avid demurred.

"This document is not worth the paper on which it is written. It will never stand up in a court of law," the baron declared, angrily throwing the papers down on the desk.

"I can assure you, dear Baron, that it will most definitely stand up in the French courts," Saint-Avid replied, calmly stroking his dark beard, unfazed by the nobleman's burst of temper.

"We'll see about that!"

"I guarantee that it is legal and unassailable," the lawyer insisted.

"We shall see," the baron muttered, shaking his fist in the dignified attorney's face. "We shall see."

With that he stormed from the office, grumbling and cursing in a rage, his shocked and stricken family staggering after him.

Inwardly Micaela smiled. Her mother had truly taken care of her, just as she had promised.

33

ONCE THE BARON'S initial rage had somewhat cooled, he realized he had to plan his strategy carefully if he were to wrest control of Micaela's property. Even from the grave Louise had foiled his ambitions yet another time. His first step, he knew, would be to enlist his son to the cause. Celestin's cooperation was essential. Without it there could be no strategy at all.

"Somehow we must force Micaela to relinquish everything to you," he told Celestin. "We have coerced her before and we can do it again. The fact that she's still in shock over her mother's death and grieving considerably makes her more vulnerable and gives us an advantage we didn't have before. Thus, it shouldn't be too difficult. Have I your support in this? After all, you must bear in mind that I am only trying to obtain for you what is rightfully yours. You do understand that, don't you, Celestin?"

"I do, but I also know as well as you that the will absolutely prevents anyone from meddling in Micaela's properties," Celestin reminded his father.

"There must be an answer." The baron tapped his finger nervously on the surface of the rosewood desk. "I am not discouraged by Monsieur Saint-Avid."

Because of Micaela's stricken state and her insistence on quiet and solitude, Celestin had returned to Mont L'Eveque with his family after the funeral, taking his sons with him.

The baron rose from behind his desk and gazed out the window at the three boys romping with the spaniels and the Great Danes on the lawn. Suddenly the ruthless old aristocrat's face brightened.

"I have it!" he declared, turning to his son. "Not only will you continue to stay here at Mont L'Eveque, but the boys will stay here, too. We will keep them from Micaela until she agrees to see things our way. Separating mother from child has been effective before. It will be effective again. Short of kidnapping them, there is no way she can claim her sons as long as they remain with you. A father has complete jurisdiction over his children. On that point of French law I'm certain."

Celestin was dismayed by the solution his father was proposing. "You mean we are going to blackmail Micaela into submission by keeping the boys away from her?"

The baron grinned. "Precisely."

"But still, I don't see how that will break Louise's will," Celestin argued.

"We don't want to break it. Let it stand as it is. What do we care what it says? It can say anything. Words are unimportant. What we want is for Micaela to surrender to you the right to administer her properties and collect the income from them. That power is rightfully yours, and I want you to have it now."

When Micaela received the news that both Celestin and the boys would not be returning to Paris but would remain at Mont L'Eveque indefinitely—or at least until she made certain concessions—she was at first shocked and devastated. It had been difficult accepting the death of her mother, but to realize that her husband and in-laws could take such despicable advantage of her loss outraged her.

Immediately she went to Saint-Avid and related the news to him. Even the worldly, sophisticated lawyer was shocked by the lengths to which the Pontalbas were willing to go to force her to bend to them.

"It's appalling," he said, shaking his head repeatedly.

"Is there nothing that can be done to get my sons back?" she asked.

"I regret to tell you that your husband is well within his legal rights if he wishes to keep the boys with him," the lawyer advised her. "There is very little you can do to counter his action."

As she left Saint-Avid's office she realized that her father-in-law's attitude toward her, which had always been one of disapproval and disdain, had now degenerated to outright hatred. Obviously he was determined to punish her for the terms of her mother's will, interpreting it as yet another attack on the dignity of the Pontalbas. How much better it might have been, she thought as she walked toward her waiting carriage, if she had not been born so wealthy.

Without Celestin and the children, Micaela's life in Paris became bleak and lonely, aggravated by the sense of loss she felt for her mother. Although Louise had not been without her faults and had been responsible for much of Micaela's childhood unhappiness, she had later given her daughter moral support on some of the most important issues of her life. It was her encouragement that had provided Micaela with the courage to make the move to Paris. In spite of her melancholy state of mind, Micaela was determined not to accede to her father-in-law's demands, which she regarded contemptuously as sheer blackmail. She would simply bide her time. He could not keep Tin-Tin, Alfred, and Gaston from her forever. She knew that all three boys loved her and in time would insist on returning to her.

After the funeral, according to custom, she ordered all mirrors in the house draped with black and all signs of cheer removed.

"You know, Miss Micaela, I respected Miss Louise just like she was my own mama," Binnie said, "but I don't think she'd like the way you're turnin' this house of yours into a tomb."

"What I am doing I do out of respect," Micaela replied, covering a gleaming silver tea service with a piece of black crepe.

"I think your mama'd like it better if you went on just like she was still livin'," the maid continued.

"Perhaps," Micaela conceded thoughtfully.

"Here in France it ain't like it was back in Louisiana. Folks here don't set so much store in all the old customs."

"Well, they certainly observe mourning. It's proper and civilized."

"Yes, but not as strict as you do, Miss Micaela. You do nothin' but stay by yourself all the time. You ain't seein' nobody these days, and that ain't like you."

"One doesn't encourage callers when one is in mourning," Micaela reminded her.

"You got to see somebody once in a while," Binnie insisted. "You can't keep on staying by yourself all the time. That ain't good for nobody."

"Perhaps you're right, Binnie."

"I know I am."

Eventually convinced by her maid, Micaela decided to invite half a dozen intimate friends for a quiet dinner one evening. She was careful to see, however, that the table was set with black-bordered china, and she ordered the servants to omit a floral centerpiece and decorations. Among those invited was the noted architect Charles Percier, whose work she particularly admired.

While she was dressing, Georges knocked on her door and presented her with a note from Percier, saying that he had an unexpected foreign house guest and wondered if he might bring him along.

"It's rather short notice," she remarked, staring at the note. "Why did he wait until the last minute like this? Oh, well, it's always nice to have an extra man at the table. Set another place, Georges."

"Then I am to tell Monsieur Percier that it is all right to bring his friend, madame?" the butler asked.

"Yes, of course," she replied with an impatient wave of her hand, and closed the door.

That evening, dressed in a simple black velvet gown, Micaela greeted her guests sedately as Georges announced each of their entrances. As she turned and saw Percier standing in the vestibule with his foreign visitor, she felt her heart begin to pound unmercifully.

"It can't be!" she gasped aloud.

"Is something wrong, madame?" Georges asked.

"Micaela!" a mellow baritone voice cried out, and she was immediately swept into a fervent embrace by a pair of strong and once familiar arms.

"Patrick! I—I can't—I can't believe it!" she stammered. "After so many years . . ."

"Oh, do you two know each other?" Percier asked slyly.

Patrick winked. "Slightly."

Micaela hoped he would continue to hold her, because she felt her knees growing weak and about to buckle under her, and she feared she might faint in front of her guests.

Chuckling, Percier came to her rescue. Taking her by the arm, he said, "I purposely didn't mention my guest's name in that note because I wanted to surprise you."

"You certainly succeeded, sir."

"Well, I didn't mean to shock you," Percier laughed. "You must have thought I was pretty bold to ask to bring a friend to dinner on such short notice, but I couldn't let this chance for a reunion between you two escape. I was surprised when Patrick asked me if I knew you almost as soon as he arrived."

"Oh, Charles, you devil," she scolded, slapping him playfully with her hand-painted fan. "You should have warned me. You had no right surprising me this way. Patrick and I haven't seen one another for . . . How many years has it been?"

"More than fifteen," Patrick supplied.

"Is it really that long, Patrick? Over fifteen years? It seems like only yesterday we were paddling through Bayou Barataria . . ."

"Yes, like yesterday," he agreed, the familiar twinkle in his blue eyes.

Throughout dinner Micaela could scarcely keep her mind on the conversation or tear her attention away from Patrick. She simply could not believe that after all this time he had actually come to France and was sitting at her table.

Still tall and slender, he had changed very little, except for the sprinkling of gray in his hair and the deep furrows etched in his brow. His eyes still exuded the same humor and intelligence, his mouth the same warm, sensuous smile. More to her astonishment was the excitement she felt in his presence. Throughout the meal her thoughts kept drifting back to their moments together in Bayou Barataria when he had held her in his arms while she listened to his soft, seductive Irish brogue, feeling his slightly rough hands caressing her eager young flesh. Fifteen years of separation, of marriage to Celestin, of bearing three sons and enduring various trials and tribulations, had failed to erase any of it or diminish the longing she felt for him.

When dinner was finished, Patrick requested the honor of escorting Micaela to the drawing room. Grasping a lock of her hair, he wound it around his fingers and inspected it, as he had so often done in the past. "Your hair is still as red and lustrous as the fairest Irish colleen," he said, smiling.

During the concert Micaela had arranged for her guests' after-dinner entertainment—a string quartet playing Boccherini, Vivaldi, and Albinoni—Patrick, seated beside Micaela on the gray damask settee, took her hand in his and gave it a gentle squeeze, sending tiny, familiar shivers down her spine. She shifted nervously in her chair, wondering whether her guests might have noticed the flush he was arousing in her.

At the end of the evening she kept hoping that he would loiter behind, even though he had come with Percier and to have done so might have been considered improper, but he departed with the rest of the guests, his lingering goodbye kiss the only indication that he might have felt as she did.

Later, as she was undressing for bed, disappointed that she had allowed him to slip so easily through her fingers, she heard a peculiar sound at her window, as if the glass were being struck by hailstones or tiny bits of gravel. Curious, she drew aside the drapes, and seeing nothing, unlatched the casements and threw them open. Outside, clinging to the balustrade of her balcony, was a man in evening clothes. She was about to

scream for help when a voice cautioned her in a loud
stage whisper, "For God's sake, lass, don't scream!"

"Patrick!" she cried, even more delighted to see him
now than she had been earlier in the evening. "What
on earth are you doing hanging there? You must go
away. How did you get up here?"

"You have a very sturdy rose trellis," he said as he
hoisted himself over the balustrade and onto the balcony. Entering her room through the open windows, he
lost no time in taking her in his arms. "Ah, Micaela,
I couldn't just go off and leave you," he murmured, his
lips warm against her ear. "Not after waiting all these
long years."

"Please, Patrick, you mustn't," she insisted. "If anyone should find out . . ."

"There's no one about at this hour."

"The servants might hear us . . ."

"The servants have all gone to bed," he assured
her. "I watched them turn out their lights, one by
one, in the servants' quarters."

"If word of this should reach my husband . . ."

"It won't."

". . . it would create a terrible scandal."

"Who's going to tell him?"

"Oh, Patrick, really, you must go. Please," she
begged, although she knew her objections were half-
hearted at best.

Still holding her in a close embrace, he pressed his
lips to hers in an eager, demanding kiss. "You know
you don't mean a word of it," he said, and gently slid
her silk dressing gown over her shoulders.

"No, Patrick, you shouldn't," she protested feebly,
attempting to detach herself from his arms but lacking
any real strength or resolve to do so. In her heart she
had no desire to push him away. During all their years
apart she had dreamed of this moment, had prayed
for it, all the while convinced that it would never happen. But it was happening, and she longed just to relax
and allow herself to flow with the tide of her emotions.

A catalyst of searing flame, his tongue probed relentlessly to the very depths of her throat, causing her
to gasp with joy. And when his hands hungrily ca-

ressed her neck and shoulders, sweeping down over and rubbing her pink nipples to a sweetly aching tautness, she began to tremble uncontrollably. This man whom she had not seen for so long had the power to arouse unbearably strong desires in her just by his presence, while Celestin with all his efforts and determination, had never been able to achieve anything close to this.

As Patrick pulled her dressing gown down farther, it slipped over her hips and fell in a rumpled mass at her feet. Naked, she lost all sense of resistance and surrendered to the passions seething deep within her.

Sweeping her up in his arms, he carried her to the bed she had joylessly shared with Celestin. For a single brief moment she had slight misgivings and started to protest. "Patrick, no . . ."

Laying her down on the satin sheets, he quickly stripped off his own formal clothes, throwing them carelessly about the room. His excitement was boundless; he had no wish for anything more than to share his bursting desire with her.

Stretching out on the bed beside her, he made gentle, tender love to her at first, nibbling on her creamy flesh from the top of her head to the tips of her toes, as if he wanted to savor every part of her, every precious second of this long-awaited reunion. Soon she was thrashing about, sighing with an overwhelming need to feel him inside her. Tugging at him, she urged him on top of her. Cradled between her thighs, he raised himself on his elbows and gazed lovingly into her eyes.

"I forgot how wonderful you were," he whispered. "God knows, I've missed you, lass. There hasn't been a day that I haven't thought of you."

"Is that true, Patrick?"

"I swear before God."

"I've missed you, too," she replied breathlessly. "Oh, Lord, how I've missed you!"

When she locked her arms tightly around his neck, he lifted himself onto his haunches and entered her swiftly but gently, causing her to gasp with delight and surprise.

"I'm not hurting you, am I?" he asked. "I'm so eager, it's hard to restrain myself."

Tossing her head wildly from side to side, her hair spreading loosely over the pillow, she said, "Oh, no, no, no. You're not hurting me at all. You feel so good ... so good ..."

He interpreted her reply as encouragement to enter her, and he began his thrusts slowly at first, inserting, then withdrawing nearly to the limit, again and again, causing her to fear the abrupt cessation of a pleasure more intense than she had ever experienced before. He reassured her with softly murmured words and plunged deeper and deeper, accelerating his strokes faster and faster, provoking her to move with a synchronous rhythm and meet his drives with strong upward thrusts of her own.

"Oh, my God!" she heard herself cry out hoarsely. Her gratification was greater than she had ever known, so deep and intense that she felt she would burst from unbearable joy. "It's never been like this before. Never, never, never!"

Her excitement mounted steadily, higher and higher, her gasps and moans mingled with his deep groans of pleasure. They rode the crest together, higher still, until they reached the summit of ecstasy, both crying out in unison, clinging, writhing, clutching each other, their bodies entwined in harmonious spasms.

When they were completely sated, they lay close together, breathless and sweaty, but feeling transported, happy, and fulfilled. Idly she ran her fingers through his hair while he gently stroked her smoothly rounded breasts, tweaking her nipples playfully and smiling.

Despite the quiet contentment of the moment, following the incredible exhilaration of their unfettered passion, Micaela was troubled by thoughts of Celestin. Why had it never been like this with him? Why could it never be this way? Guiltily she wondered if perhaps the fault rested with her.

"Now what do we do?" Patrick asked, gazing at the drapes blowing in the wind from the open window.

"I don't know," Micaela replied, kissing his chest and snuggling up to the warmth of his body. "Let's worry about that in the morning."

34

FROM THAT NIGHT on, Patrick and Micaela saw each other at every conceivable opportunity. Although she welcomed his visits to the house and awaited them with great eagerness, she began to worry about the possibility of damaging gossip if they were seen together too often. Without a formal separation agreement between Celestin and herself, Micaela knew she had to conduct her personal life with great care and discretion. Saint-Avid warned her that even hinted-at indiscretions could be used against her in court by the Pontalbas, should things ever come to that. She felt confident that she could trust Binnie, but she was not nearly so sure of the other servants. As far as she knew, no one except Binnie was aware that she and Patrick frequently spent the night together. Appreciating Micaela's situation, Patrick gladly made his presence in the house as inconspicuous as possible.

"We've been seeing each other for several weeks now," Patrick said one day, "and although I've tried not to pry into your personal life, I can't help wondering where your husband is. You've scarcely said a word about him."

"There's really not much to say," she replied. "Celestin is at his father's country estate."

"And your children?"

"They're with him."

"When are they coming back?" he persisted. "Or aren't they? It's none of my business, but I can't help being a little curious."

"I have no idea what Celestin intends to do."

Patrick frowned and shook his head. "It's very odd for your husband and children to be away and you to know nothing of their return."

"I know it is." She glanced distractedly out the drawing-room window for a moment.

"That doesn't say much for your marriage, now, does it, lass?"

"One might ask where your wife is, Mr. Lynch," she countered, remembering how heartbroken she was when Pierre first informed her that Patrick was a married man. "After all, I don't see her with you in Paris, unless you've got her hidden somewhere."

"Emily's at home. She fears boats and dislikes any sort of travel intensely." He shifted slightly in his seat next to her on the settee. "Besides, she's happy now that she's settled in New Orleans. It took me years to convince her that yellow fever wasn't necessarily going to do us all in. I came to Europe because I had to— for the sake of my health, you might say."

"Your health?" she repeated, surprised.

"I was having some trouble with my eyes. They were badly strained, and I was advised to rest them for a while. I had been doing too much close, detailed work. New Orleans is growing so fast that construction can scarcely keep up with demand. I have more commissions than I can handle, even with my son in the firm now. I've overworked myself a bit, trying to make up for all those lean years when I was struggling. Before I came to Paris, I was in London seeing a doctor, who put me in a dark chamber for a time and had me undergo what he calls the 'cold-water cure.' It seems to have helped quite a bit. I suppose I ought to return to America and get back to work. Before I go, though, I want to do a bit more sightseeing. I love to walk up and down the streets of Paris, taking in all the buildings, good and bad, visiting the museums and the art galleries. There's such a wealth of beauty in Europe. Twenty centuries to borrow from. I get so many ideas here. Basically, an architect must keep an eye on the future with a reverence for the past." He stopped suddenly and broke into a self-conscious smile. "Why am I blathering on so and boring you?"

"You couldn't bore me, Patrick," she said, "even if you wanted to."

"Just because I go on about these old buildings and

museums and the like doesn't mean I'm not going to be with you every chance I get." He put his arm around her and gave her a loving squeeze.

True to his word, Patrick did spend considerable time with Micaela, and as time went on, their relationship steadily deepened and mellowed, as each brought to it the maturity and experience they had gained in the years they had been apart.

After overhearing some rather suspicious remarks by the servants, however, Patrick began to worry about Micaela's reputation and decided to call a halt to his visits at the house.

"I refuse to cause trouble for you," he explained. "I did that once long ago, and I've been sorry ever since."

"Let me worry about protecting my good name," she pleaded.

"No. I'm not coming to the house any more," he said adamantly. "Let the servants think I've returned to America."

Despite her arguments, he refused to change his mind, and they finally agreed to adopt the notorious French custom of the "four-to-five," named so because that was frequently the time during which many fashionable women met clandestinely with their lovers. According to a prearranged plan, Micaela would have her coachman drive her to a dress shop or a tearoom, and then she would slip out a rear exit and hurry to a hotel at which she and Patrick had reserved a room for their assignation. Several hotels existed expressly for just such affairs. The intrigue and secrecy of their arrangement excited and amused both of them, and when they met in their discreet little hotel room, their mutual passion nearly exploded.

"If I had known you would be so wild, I would have begun meeting you in hotel rooms long before this," Patrick chuckled, pleased and flattered by the extremely active part she took in their lovemaking.

"I can leave all my fears and guilts behind at home," she replied, smiling.

"What you mean is that you don't see your husband's presence hovering around the bed," he teased.

"Actually, it was Emily's presence that bothered

me more," she returned, giving him a playful jab in the ribs, which made him wince and grab for her in retaliation. Micaela eluded him and jumped off the bed, running around the room giggling and squealing until Patrick caught her. Then they tumbled onto the bed and renewed their lovemaking with unabashed abandon.

More than merely lovers, Micaela and Patrick were, above all, friends. Micaela enjoyed their shared confidences and experiences, relishing the time they spent together with a feeling bordering on reverence.

One cold and rainy afternoon as they lay in a hotel bed, each writing declarations of love on the steamy windowpanes, Micaela finally confided to Patrick the entire story of her mother's will and the Pontalbas' vengeful reaction to it, explaining fully for the first time the continued absence of Celestin and her three sons. Prior to that day, the subject had been too painful for her to discuss. At first Patrick was amused by the clever way Louise had thwarted the expectations of the Pontalbas and prevented their seizing Micaela's fortune, but realizing Micaela's longing for her children, he grew more serious.

"But do you know what your mother's will really implies?" he asked, as if he had suddenly made a discovery she hadn't been aware of. "It means you are essentially a free woman, financially independent. How many other French ladies—or women anywhere, for that matter—can claim that?"

Puzzled, Micaela said, "What do you mean?"

"I mean that you are free to do whatever you damned well please. You have no need to go groveling on bended knee to your husband every time you need something. You have your own resources, completely under your control. Don't you see what that means, lass? Or have you lived under the oppression of your in-laws too long? I'll wager there's many a woman in Paris who'd gladly change places with you—and it's not just the money I'm talking about. You don't have to depend on anyone, don't you understand, lass?"

"But still, Patrick, financial independence isn't enough. I admit that I'm grateful for what my mother has done, but I need more than the assurance that I have money at my disposal when I want it. For one thing, I need my children more. You can't imagine how much I miss them, even with you here. When you go it will be impossible. I don't want them to suffer because of me. If there were a scandal . . ."

"You need not fear a scandal, either," he firmly assured her.

"But to a woman a scandal is always a threat, no matter what resources she has." She tried to explain her feelings about it. "Even from one's best friends there are subtle slights that might go unnoticed by a man. It has to do with the way others think of you and treat you. Unfortunately, it extends to the children in many cases. Since living in Paris, I've witnessed that sort of social ostracization. It isn't pleasant. I don't want to cause my children any harm. And I don't want to hurt Celestin either, as odd as that probably sounds to you."

"I think I can understand," he murmured, kissing her bare shoulder. Her skin felt cool to his lips, and he drew her closer to him and pulled the covers higher.

"In his own way Celestin has always tried to be kind to me, to do the best he could under the circumstances," she continued. "It's not his fault he's been conditioned to obey his father's will at all costs. The old man is a cruel, ruthless tyrant who isn't happy unless he can dominate everyone around him. Celestin was doomed from the start. He's never been able to liberate himself from his father's iron hand, and he never will be," she added in a voice tinged with sadness. "Some people are weak and some are strong. Celestin, unfortunately, falls into the first category."

Perhaps to relieve the increasing guilt and anguish she was experiencing as her feelings for Patrick intensified, Micaela decided one day to write to Celestin, her first communication in a long time. Seated at her desk, she dashed off a note quickly, fearing that if she lingered over it, she would change her mind. In it she asked him to return to her with her sons, and warned him that she feared the consequences if he abandoned her permanently.

A few days later he responded, saying that both he and the three boys were quite content to make their home at Mont L'Eveque and were able to get along very well without her. At present, he informed her, they intended to stay there indefinitely. He reminded her that her place was with them and that as long as she insisted on remaining alone in Paris, she was an errant wife and neglectful mother who through her stubbornness was placing their marriage in serious jeopardy.

"If you have any love for your sons or me at all, you will abandon this life you are leading in Paris and come at once to Mont L'Eveque," he concluded.

Somehow the curtness of the reply seemed to relieve much of Micaela's guilt and encourage her defiance. When she saw Patrick later that afternoon, she invited him to escort her to the opera the following Monday. It would be the first time they would be seen together in public.

Baffled by this invitation, he said, "But I thought you didn't want us to be seen together by your friends."

"I've changed my mind," she told him. "I've decided to stop punishing myself by remaining at home just because I lack a suitable escort for the opera."

The performance on the Monday they attended the opera was Paisiello's *Barber of Seville,* which Micaela found less lively and amusing than her friend Rossini's opera of the same title, but nevertheless, she enjoyed the work. The evening was greatly enhanced by Patrick's secret caresses after the houselights had dimmed.

The presence of a strange and attractive man in the Pontalba box excited great curiosity among the regular Monday-night subscription holders, most of whom were well acquainted with one another.

During the intermission Micaela chose to remain in her private box, where she playfully fed Lynch chocolate bonbons from silver tongs. Several friends called on her, and she dutifully introduced them to Patrick, whom she referred to as "an old childhood friend," a description they both laughed over later.

One of the intermission visitors was a certain Marquis d'Anthieul, who had a summer home in the Oise district, not far from Mont L'Eveque. He and his wife were acquainted with the Pontalbas and could be counted among the few occasional callers at the château.

"I have not seen the baron since last summer," the marquis said. "I trust he is well?"

"Oh, yes, quite well," Micaela assured him.

"Good." The marquis nodded and prepared to return to his own box at the signal that the curtain was about to rise on the final act. "Nice seeing you again, Madame de Pontalba," he added politely. "And pleased to have met you, Monsieur Lynch. May you enjoy your stay in Paris."

When he had gone, Patrick asked, "Do you think he'll report on us to the baron?"

"Of course," Micaela said. "No one wants to miss the opportunity to relay a tantalizing bit of gossip. Not even a marquis."

"Are you afraid?"

"Not really," she replied indifferently, remembering Celestin's letter with some acrimony.

As the lively music began and the curtain went up, Micaela observed that the opera glasses that had been trained on her box during intermission were once more directed at the stage.

35

AT TIMES THE joy Micaela felt with Patrick was so great that it frightened her and made her dread the emptiness she would be left with when he was gone. Never before had she known such intense emotion or so much happiness. As she thought of his inevitable departure, she grew sad and anxious.

"I feel as if I want to be with you forever, Patrick," she said. "I don't know what I'll do when you're gone. I feel almost desperate."

"You've been through trying times lately—the death of your mother, the difficulties with your husband and his family, the absence of your children. It's been lonely for you," he sympathized. "I can appreciate that."

"Long before you came to Paris—years before—I had a terrible yearning, a need gnawing away at me, that was unfulfilled. Now suddenly, for the first time, I feel whole."

"That's all very flattering for me to hear, you understand," he said with a smile.

"It's the truth," she insisted.

"You know, lass you have a way of making *me* feel good. You've done it right from the start—from that first day I saw you poking your curious little nose about my New Hibernia Hotel." He drew her to him and playfully kissed the tip of her nose.

Despite Saint-Avid's warnings to be exceedingly discreet, Micaela and Patrick were tired of pretense and decided to be more open in their relationship. He called regularly and freely at the house, and they would stroll up and down the streets of Paris, much as she and Celestin had done when they were first married. But with Patrick the strolls seemed so different, so much more exciting. Through his eyes Micaela viewed the city from a fresh, new perspective. As they walked down a street, he would point out particularly interesting buildings and explain the intricacies of their construction.

"Most people build as they live—as a matter of routine and mindless accident," he said. "There is no plan, no great overall scheme, behind it. But impressive buildings are no accident. They successfully unite the two essential principles of architecture: beauty and utility."

"Someday I'm going to have a house built exactly the way I want it," she told him. "What a change that will be from inheriting what was planned for someone else!"

"The design of a house should be dictated by the needs of the owner, not by a compulsion to impress." He put his arm around her and gave her a squeeze. "Just keep that in mind when you build yours."

They came to a small cafe and stopped in for coffee, choosing a seat by a glowing coal stove. Their talk was still of buildings, but this time less impersonal.

"If you feel such an urge to build something," he continued, "you might start by fixing up some of those properties in New Orleans that your mother left you. They're in the most valuable part of the city, you know."

"It's been so long since I was in New Orleans," she said, raising the steaming china cup to her lips. "I'm sure there have been a great many changes."

"It's growing by leaps and bounds. But let me tell you, lass, your mother's properties are in the heart of the French Quarter, and that's still the best real estate. That's where the river is the deepest and where all the big boats tie up. But the trouble is that your mother's properties have been allowed to decay and become run down. They're all badly in need of renovation and repair. If they were modernized just a little, they'd double in value and bring in twice the rent."

"Really?" This was the first time Micaela had given any serious thought to her inherited properties. In the past they had been mere listings on legal papers, not real entities of wood, brick, and cement.

From the cafe they decided to go ice skating in the Bois de Boulogne.

"How much would it cost to fix up Mama's buildings?" she asked as they sat on the snowy bank and laced up their skates. A circle of torches lighted the pond, their reflections shimmering on the smooth ice.

Pleased that she was considering his suggestion, Patrick pondered her question and finally answered, "Between fifty and sixty thousand, I suppose."

"That's quite a bit of money."

He laughed and helped her to her feet. "Not for you, lass."

"But you don't understand," she said, wobbling unsteadily. "My money is all tied up in real estate or other property. I have very little cash."

"Well, have you considered a loan?" he asked, guiding her to the edge of the ice. He stood behind her, placed one hand on her waist, the other outstretched, holding her hand, and eased her into the band of skaters circling the frozen pond.

"A loan?" she repeated as they began skating in a clockwise motion. "No, never. I know nothing about loans."

"You must learn, lass," he said, his breath visible in the frosty night air. "I'm sure there's not a bank in the world that wouldn't want to do business with you."

"But wouldn't a loan require my husband's signature?" A note of discouragement crept into her voice. "That's one French law even Mama couldn't have gotten around."

"Well, you might approach him on the matter," Lynch suggested casually.

"Celestin?" she cried in surprise, almost bringing them to a halt.

"The worst he could do is refuse."

"You want me to go to Celestin?"

"Why not? He's your husband, isn't he?"

"Yes, but . . ."

"Besides, if those Pontalbas are as greedy as you've been telling me, I have a feeling he'll sign in a flash if he knows the loan is to renovate properties which could double in value with a few improvements. There's no harm in asking, you know."

A few days later Micaela decided to follow through on Patrick's suggestion and go to Mont L'Eveque. He was working with Percier on a collaborative project, and she knew she would be seeing little of him. It seemed like a good opportunity to make the trip.

Before she left, she was positive that her reception would be something less than cordial, and she was not wrong. Still, she did not expect the open animosity with which she was greeted.

The baron refused to put her up in the château and assigned her instead to the guest house. He also tried to prevent her sons from seeing her, but that was impossible. The moment the three boys got word of her arrival they rushed to her lodgings, hugged her joyfully, and covered her with affectionate kisses.

"I've got a new jumper," Tin-Tin said excitedly. "You should see us take the hurdles, Mama."

"Just be careful, that's all," she cautioned.

"That tutor Grandpapa engaged for us is awful," Alfred complained. "He's forcing us to study German. I hate German."

"Germany is our neighbor," she said. "Besides, it never hurts to know another language. Look at me. I must be able to speak both French and English equally well, and switch back and forth all the time. I have to admit I wish you boys were studying English instead of German, but I've no say in the matter—at least not yet."

Little Gaston showed her some drawings he had done that were excellent and displayed a precocious talent. They reminded Micaela of her own love of sketching when she was young.

"I shall have them framed," she asserted, kissing his thick tangle of brown curls.

Relations between Micaela and Celestin were badly strained in spite of the boys' openly expressed desire for their parents to reconcile. She did have a chance, however, to discuss the possible loan with him one day while they watched Tin-Tin and his new horse jump a series of hurdles he had constructed in a meadow.

"As you know," she said, "it would require your signature."

"I can see no objection," he replied, "although I would have to think the matter over."

Hoping to keep the subject of the loan confined to them and away from the baron, she urged, "Please do not divulge this matter to anyone."

"I'll try not to," he promised. But in view of past experience, she was not at all confident he would be able to keep his word, regardless of his present intentions.

Throughout her visit the baron was rather obviously

hostile to her presence, although he tried to disguise his true feelings as best he could. He had little contact with her and tried to discourage Jeanne and Madame Miró from socializing with her as well. Curiously enough, he brought a strange, exotic flowering plant to the guest house one day and placed it on a stand near her bed. She thought such a gesture very odd and wondered why he would want to make the guest house more attractive to her while forbidding her to stay in the château.

"I suppose you can see how well the boys are getting along without you?" he remarked.

"I don't find that as readily apparent as you do, Baron," she replied, miffed at such an insinuation.

"As for Celestin," he went on, "he has confided to me that he is finished with you as a wife. From now on, the marriage will exist in name only, although naturally, appearances must be maintained for the sake of the children."

"I prefer to hear that from Celestin himself. So far, he has mentioned nothing of the sort."

"He will," her father-in-law assured her.

"What makes you so sure?"

"Certain stories have reached our ears."

"Stories?" she echoed in surprise.

"Yes, that you have been seen about Paris frequently in the company of a certain foreign gentleman."

"Oh, Patrick," she readily admitted, hoping the blush she felt creeping into her cheeks didn't betray her. "He's an old friend."

"Patrick?"

"Yes. Patrick Lynch, the architect. He's someone I've known for years. He's a friend of my cousin Pierre's as well."

"Married women are not seen in the company of men other than their husbands, even if they are old friends," he observed sternly. "Especially in public places such as the opera and cafes."

"I would like a chance to discuss these matters with Celestin."

"If he wishes to call on you in the guest house, I cannot stop him. The only thing I can do is keep you out of the château. Admitting you to our home would mean I approve of your actions, and, as you know, I most certainly do not."

In the middle of the night Micaela awoke feeling as if she were suffocating. Gasping for breath, she ran to a window for relief, and staring at her reflection in the pane, realized her face was red and swollen. It also itched intensely. The air in the room was saturated with an overpowering perfume so sickeningly sweet that she felt each breath she took filled her lungs with molasses. Although the night air was cold, it provided a welcome relief. As she inhaled, she wondered if the exotic plant could be causing her distress and placed it outside on the doorstep for the rest of the night, not caring whether the cold damaged it or not.

A short while later she closed the window and returned to bed, feeling sufficiently relieved to go back to sleep. In the morning the swelling and redness had subsided and the itching stopped. She made a mental note to tell one of the servants to take the noxious plant back to the baron and advise him not to bring her anything more to brighten up her living quarters.

Baron Joseph's attempts to isolate her from her husband and sons were only moderately successful. The boys continued to see their mother at every opportunity, and Celestin, though more restrained, called frequently enough to arouse his father's displeasure.

Before leaving Paris, Micaela had the bank draw up the necessary papers for the improvement loans, which she brought with her. As Patrick had predicted, the bankers were more than delighted to do business with her. All that was needed was Celestin's signature. She had hoped to get him to sign before the baron learned of her plans, but such was not the case.

One afternoon, as she was watching little Gaston feed the swans at the edge of the moat, the baron, with Celestin close behind, approached her.

"My son has informed me of the loan you wish to make," the baron said abruptly.

Realizing that her husband had betrayed his promise, she turned on him angrily. "Must you tell your father everything?"

Before Celestin could reply, the baron answered for him. "My son trusts me completely and has come to me for advice long before he met you, my dear."

Ignoring her father-in-law, she continued to address Celestin. "I think it's time you began thinking for yourself. I intended this to be a private matter between us. The loan merely requires your signature. I ask nothing else."

"Your mother once used similar words—'I ask nothing more from you.' I believed her and have regretted it to this day," the baron muttered. "How do you intend to compensate Celestin for his willingness to share the burden of your indebtedness?"

"What indebtedness?" she said.

"Sixty thousand American dollars is no piddling sum," the nobleman asserted.

"It is very little when one considers the value of the properties and how much they will appreciate if the needed improvements are made," she argued.

"Tell me, my dear, who has put you up to all this?" the baron asked suspiciously, his voice lowered so that Gaston, who had left the swans and was now avidly following the confrontation between his mother and his grandfather, would not hear.

"No one has 'put me up to it,' as you say," she protested.

"Come now, Micaela, you haven't been to New Orleans for years. How could you possibly know what real estate values are there?"

"Mr. Lynch and I have, naturally, discussed such matters," she admitted. "But the decision to improve the properties is purely mine."

"In any case, Celestin must receive some compensation from you before he will sign," the baron insisted stubbornly.

Turning once again to her still-silent husband, Micaela said, "Very well, Celestin, tell me what it is you want in exchange for signing the loan."

Before his son could reply, the baron interceded. "He wants all your French properties," he announced.

Micaela was stunned by such unabashed avarice, even from her father-in-law. "What?" she cried.

"The house on the Rue Saint Honoré, the properties on the Place Vendôme . . . But why must I enumerate them? He wants all your holdings in Paris. It's quite simple, really."

"What's Grandpapa talking about, Mama?" Gaston asked, tugging at Micaela's skirts.

"Nothing, dear. Run along and play."

"Yes, yes," the baron urged. "Run along, Gaston."

Returning to their conversation after the boy had gone, Micaela said, "I can't give you those even if I wanted to. You know the conditions of Mama's will as well as I do."

"Your mother's will merely forbids your husband or anyone else to administer, control, or otherwise interfere with your property. It does not prevent you from doing as you choose—of your own free will, however," Baron Joseph added. "If you should decide to deed those Paris properties to Celestin, who's to stop you?"

"But they comprise approximately half the estate!"

The baron shrugged and absentmindedly pulled a huge red radish from his pocket, polished it with his handkerchief, and gave it to his son.

"Half seems like a husband's fair share to me," he remarked. "Doesn't it seem fair to you, Celestin?"

Looking sheepish and feeling ashamed of his father's ruthless bargaining with his wife, Celestin stared blankly at the shiny radish. "Yes," he agreed, nervously biting into it. "It does seem fair."

That same day, enraged at the baron's excessive demands and the passivity of her husband, Micaela left Mont L'Eveque without concluding anything. Back in Paris, she sought solace in Patrick's arms, recounting to him her aggravating negotiations with the Pontalbas.

"Extortion, that's what it is," he declared. "Extortion, pure and simple. They're all a bunch of thieves and blackmailers, demanding what they have no right to at all."

"What can I do? How can I deal with them when they are the father and grandfather of my sons as well?" She sighed deeply. "It's so difficult."

After mulling things over, he finally responded, "I'm not a lawyer, but I do think that if you must bribe Celestin to sign for the loan, why not offer the Louisiana properties instead?"

Puzzled by his proposed solution, Micaela asked, "What good will that do? I'll offer them nothing, that's what I'll do. I'll simply forget about the whole thing and let the Louisiana properties rot until they wither away."

"That's stupid. It's like cutting off your nose to spite your face. You must offer the Pontalbas something."

"Not the Louisiana properties," she insisted. "Never. Originally they were my father's. I am much too attached to them to allow them to fall into such unscrupulous hands."

"You mustn't be so silly and sentimental," he reproached. "I think that if you make the correct moves, your in-laws will have a much more difficult time claiming actual ownership on those holdings than on the French ones. In any case, you'd be wise to consult with Monsieur Saint-Avid before you do anything. After all, he protected your mother for many years. I'm sure he can protect you, too—even from greedy sharks like the Pontalbas."

Snuggling close to him, Micaela buried her face in the hollow of his neck.

"Oh, Patrick, what would I ever do without you?" she murmured.

"I'm afraid you're going to have to learn to do without me quite soon," he said with a melancholy sigh. "You see, lass, I must go back to America. Lord knows, I've stayed long enough, much longer than I should have."

He kissed her gently and held her very tight.

36

FOLLOWING PATRICK'S ADVICE, Micaela consulted Monsieur Saint-Avid, who agreed wholeheartedly that she should transfer the Louisiana properties and not the French ones to Celestin.

"By all means, that is the way to do it," the lawyer said, and promised to draw up the necessary legal papers.

When the documents were completed, Micaela notified Celestin and advised him to come to Paris to sign them, adding, "I refuse to travel to Mont L'Eveque and endure your father's insults and humiliations, even though it means sacrificing an opportunity to be with my sons once again."

"I'm sure he'll refuse to come to Paris," she confided to Patrick, who was busy arranging for his passage back to America.

"In this case I think he will."

The architect's prediction proved to be correct. A few days later Celestin presented himself at Saint-Avid's office and hastily scrawled his signature in all the required places.

"There! Done," he said with a satisfied smile, raising his pen from the last of the papers with a flourish.

"Yes, done," Micaela repeated, but there was no joy in her voice.

Fortunately, Celestin had no plans to linger in Paris and informed her that he intended to return to Mont L'Eveque at once. "Do you have any messages for the boys?" he asked.

"Only that I love them and miss them and long to have them with me again," she answered. The rapturous depth of her experience with Patrick could not relieve her intense longing for the children. That was a love of an entirely different nature.

"You could have them with you every day if you

would only come to Mont L'Eveque," Celestin reminded her. "It's a terrible sacrifice you're making by stubbornly insisting on living in Paris."

"I find it amusing that *you* call *me* stubborn."

"You are," Celestin replied with conviction.

Micaela was grateful for her husband's quick departure. Patrick had only a few days remaining before sailing, and they were anxious to spend as much time together as possible. Micaela wanted those last days to be untroubled.

"Sometimes I think my marriage was the cruelest mating in the world," she confided sadly to him as they sat before the fireplace in the drawing room, sipping mulled wine. "Two people who basically don't dislike each other yet no more belong together than oil and water. If only I could feel real hatred for Celestin, it would be so much easier, but I can't. My strongest emotion for him is pity. Frankly, I can't think of two more ill-matched individuals than Celestin and myself."

"No, not unless it's Emily and me," Patrick sighed.

"You aren't anxious to get back to her, are you?"

"I doubt that she's eager to have me come home. I think I cause Emily much grief, not so much by what I do as by what I don't do. I never intentionally try to hurt her—God knows, I don't want to. It's just that I do. As far as returning goes," he went on, "one has one's obligations. As we get older, our lives become more complicated and less under our control."

"Do you think we'll ever see each other again?" she asked wistfully, staring at the flickering flames in the hearth through the deep red wine in her glass.

"We will if we want to badly enough," he replied.

"Oh, Patrick, I want to so much," she said, laying her head on his broad shoulder, near tears at the prospect of his leaving.

"Me, too," he murmured, tenderly kissing her moist eyelids.

Indifferent to the documents assigning him Micaela's Louisiana properties, Celestin had dropped them on his father's desk when he returned from Paris, scarcely giving them a second thought until the baron brought up the subject.

"Have you read these papers?" he demanded, slapping the sheaf of legal documents on the desktop. When Celestin didn't answer, he repeated, "Well, have you read them or not?"

"I'm confused by all that legal jargon," Celestin answered. "You know that, Papa. I have no mind for the law, remember? That's why you sent me to the army."

"That, and for other reasons as well," the baron conceded. "As far as these papers are concerned, there's only one thing you need to read, and that's the name of the lawyer who prepared them."

Celestin stared at his father with a puzzled frown. "You mean Monsieur Saint-Avid?"

"How can you pronounce that name with such remarkable naiveté? Don't you remember who he is?"

Celestin shrugged. "Of course. Micaela's mother's lawyer."

"If you will recall," the baron said in an attempt to prod his son's memory, "he was the one who drew up that insulting will of hers. The moment you saw that loathsome name on these papers you should have immediately been alerted."

"I'm afraid I don't have a suspicious nature, Papa. Another of my failings, alas."

"You'd better develop one if you intend to survive in this world," his father growled. "You shouldn't have signed anything until we had an opportunity to consult a lawyer of our own. Ah, why must you take after your mother instead of me? Neither of you poor creatures would survive if not for me. I despair to think what will happen to you and your mother when I am gone. She allowed my cousin Louise and her lawyer to make fools of us with the marriage contract, and now you let the daughter make fools of us again. I should not have permitted you to go to Paris alone, just as I should have never allowed your mother to go off to New Orleans without me to negotiate the marriage contract. Of course, at that time I had no way of knowing what a ruthless viper we were dealing with in the late Madame Castillon. Now it seems that her daughter is following in her mother's footsteps. But, unlike *your* mother, you are a man. As a result, I expect more from you. Ah, will I never learn?"

"If you'll forgive me for saying so, sir, I see nothing deceptive in those documents," Celestin said. "They appear quite straightforward to me—that is, what I can comprehend of them."

Shaking a bony finger in his son's face, Baron Joseph warned, "Nothing is ever straightforward when you are dealing with Cousin Louise or her daughter. You can be sure that contained in these pages is a trick. Mark my words."

The baron's aspersions against Micaela and her mother and their attorney did not end with the transfer papers. He continued his campaign of slander against them, eventually touching on more sensitive areas.

"I suppose you have heard that your wife has been seen all over Paris with that Irish architect of hers?" the baron remarked one night after dinner when the four adults of the family were seated around the fireplace in the library. Tin-Tin and Alfred were in their rooms studying, and Gaston was asleep.

"Please, don't start with that," Jeanne pleaded with her husband. She and Madame Miró were both knitting, and Celestin, much to his father's annoyance, was occupied with needlepoint.

"Why shouldn't I tell him?" the baron countered. "He's probably the only one who doesn't know."

"The husband is always the last to know," Madame Miró muttered.

"I'm aware of it, yes," Celestin said, keeping his attention fixed on the cavalry scene he was slowly fashioning with colored yarns.

"If you are, then how do you plan to restore your honor?" the baron continued.

"Restore my honor?" Celestin repeated, looking up in surprise.

"Get revenge," the baron clarified. "Certainly you are not going to sit by with your sewing like some silly woman and allow this intruder to insult the Pontalba name, are you?"

"Please, dear," Jeanne begged her husband, looking distressed.

The baron ignored her and went on. "They have even been bold enough to flaunt their relationship in public, embarrassing us before all of Paris. I will not permit you to play around with your needles and yarn and let this lout get away with it."

"Just what do you propose I do?" Celestin asked.

"Nothing," Jeanne put in quickly. "You will do nothing, Celestin. I'm sure that Micaela's relationship with this foreign gentleman is perfectly aboveboard. She is aware of the reputation she must maintain as a wife and mother."

Glaring angrily at Jeanne, the baron continued to address himself to his son. "As a former military officer, must you really ask me what your duty is? Do I always have to lead you by the hand? You must defend your honor in any way you choose, but you must defend it. In short, you must challenge this interloper."

"You mean a duel?" Celestin, wide-eyed, was obviously dismayed at such a prospect.

"What else?" The baron grinned, glad that his son had finally comprehended his point.

Tossing her knitting aside, Jeanne rose to her feet. "No. I will not permit Celestin to engage in any duels. I forbid it." Going over to him, she stood behind his chair and placed her hands on his shoulders.

"You forbid nothing," the baron rebuked her sternly. "Get away from him and sit down. I am the authority in this family. Celestin has recognized his obligation and will carry it out. Won't you, son?"

Before he could answer, Celestin pricked himself sharply with the large needle. A copious flow of blood began to drip onto the fabric in his lap, leaving large red stains.

Informing only his father, Celestin reluctantly left for Paris once again. Hesitating at first, he eventually ended up at Armand Dulac's fencing studio, where he found his friend huddled around a tiny wood stove in the dingy, untidy living quarters behind the main room, sipping coffee.

Surprised to see Celestin, Dulac smiled and immediately extended his hand to him.

"Well, what brings you to Paris, my boy?" he asked, his leathery face reflecting his delight.

Celestin lowered his eyes and stared at the slate floor. "This is very difficult for me to say, Dulac. But if I can't tell you, who can I tell?"

Pleased by the anticipated confidence from his former junior officer, Dulac encouraged him by saying, "Please go on. You have my sworn confidence, Pontalba."

"My wife is seeing another man, or so I have reason to believe," he confessed.

Dulac cleared his throat and spat. "This city corrupts all women. Even the best of them can't be trusted!" he declared angrily. "None of them has a shred of true virtue. Or loyalty, either. Only men can be loyal to one another. Women are fickle and worthless. A man should stay clear of any entanglements with them. They will ensnare you like wild geese in a net. The only thing to do is simply to fuck them and then cast them aside and forget them. It is absurd to expect them to be honorable creatures. They have no concept of honor." Realizing his tirade was making Celestin uncomfortable, he stopped suddenly, then added, "But that doesn't explain why you have sought me out in my humble fencing studio."

"The reason is simple. I wish to revive my dueling skills."

The coffee in Dulac's cup spilled over the brim and into his lap.

"My God, Pontalba, you aren't going to challenge this supposed lover of your wife's to a duel, are you?" he demanded incredulously.

"Why not? I must," Celestin asserted. "Do you think I am so inept with weapons?"

"No. On the contrary, I happen to know you are excellent," Dulac replied. "But a duel is a way for only young hotheads to settle things."

"I'm sure that if your pupils believed that, you would starve, Dulac."

"My pupils are young fools. But you . . ."

"Insults to one's honor are not confined to the young," Celestin said stiffly. "Besides, it is the honor of my entire family that is at stake, not just my own."

Dulac nodded. "So this is your father's idea, isn't it? Just like the marriage?"

"Partly," Celestin admitted.

"In that case, I think you should find out more about this supposed lover of your wife's," the fencing master advised. "Don't accept the word of others. You must obtain the proof yourself, especially before engaging in anything as rash as a duel."

"Do you really think so?"

Struggling to his feet without the aid of his crutches, which were leaning against the bare brick wall, Dulac reached out and put his arm around Celestin. "Yes, I do," he said. "I definitely do."

On Patrick's last night in Paris he and Micaela dined on gourmet fare in a private room at one of the secluded hotels they had often used for their clandestine meetings. Afterward, at Micaela's suggestion, they decided to take a stroll through one of their favorite spots, the gardens of the Palais Royal. Casually they ambled along the winding paths, enjoying the lively atmosphere and inhaling the fresh, crisp evening air. Coming upon a silhouette cutter, they had him shape a remarkable likeness of the two of them with his tiny scissors and admired the results.

It was not until they reached a shadowy, deserted part of the gardens that Micaela began to sense that they were being followed. There was nothing to support her fear, which Patrick scoffed at when she told him about it, except for the occasional rustle of branches or crackle of dry leaves.

"You're being silly," he laughed, giving her hand an affectionate squeeze.

"But, Patrick, I know we're being followed," she insisted. "I can feel someone's presence in the darkness."

"Nonsense," he chided. "Do you think we're about to be accosted by a bandit?"

"I don't know . . ."

"Or do you think your father-in-law or my wife has put detectives on our trail?"

"Patrick, please . . ."

"Come here and kiss me, my silly little goose," he said, pulling her into the shadows and enfolding her in his arms. He was about to plant an eager kiss on her lips when a cloaked figure sprang forth from a clump of bushes. Micaela screamed and clutched at Patrick, who immediately shoved her protectively behind him and prepared to face the intruder.

Suddenly Micaela gasped. "Celestin!" she cried, recognizing none other than her husband.

"Yes, it's I," he acknowledged, stepping out of the shadows and revealing himself.

"What are you doing here? And why are you following us this way?" she demanded, more angry and embarrassed by his tactics than ashamed to be caught by him with another man. "You have no right—"

"Yes, I have no right," Celestin broke in. Turning to Patrick, he removed his glove and slapped him soundly across the face with it.

"Celestin, have you gone mad?" she cried, shocked by this sort of gesture from her normally passive husband.

"If this is a challenge, sir," Patrick said in a surprisingly calm voice, as if he had been expecting just such a confrontation, "I must inform you that I do not participate in duels. If you wish to kill me—and there are those who would say you have every right to—kill me now, because, I assure you, I have no skill with either sword or pistol. In my lifetime I have had no time to master such arts."

"Then just how would you like to defend yourself?" Celestin asked, once more the officer facing the enemy. His military training sustained him in situations of this nature, which were beyond the powers of his civilian mentality.

After a moment's thought Patrick replied, "I've been known to be a pretty good man with the fists, sir."

"Then fists it shall be," Celestin impulsively agreed, whipping off his cloak and throwing it on the ground.

Rolling up his shirt sleeves, he assumed a fighter's stance, raising his fists. "Ready when you are," he challenged.

Patrick hesitated a few moments, which prompted Celestin to taunt, "You aren't frightened, are you?"

"The only thing I'm frightened of, sir," Patrick said slowly as he doffed his own coat and rolled up his sleeves, "is that I may harm you more than I care to."

Feeling compelled to intervene, Micaela placed herself between the two men. The last thing she wanted was a row between husband and lover. "Stop, both of you," she demanded.

Pushing her out of the way, Celestin slapped Patrick again, this time with his bare hand and on the opposite side of the face. "I assure you, sir, I have no fear."

Despite Micaela's desperate protests, the two men circled one another, throwing out occasional test punches until Celestin, aiming at Patrick's face, managed to graze his chin. Patrick retaliated by dealing a blow to Celestin's slender abdomen, surprising him. Recovering his balance, Celestin, angry now, moved in, trying to decide where he wanted to land his next punch. He aimed for Patrick's mouth, but the architect ducked and the blow succeeded only in grazing his ear. For a second Celestin dropped his guard, and Patrick took advantage of the lapse to direct a blow squarely at Celestin's nose. The punch connected solidly. Celestin reeled backward but did not fall or lose consciousness and quickly regained his stance. Moving in closer again, the two men exchanged a rapid series of blows, dodging some, connecting with others, until they were pummeling each other furiously at close range. The fistfight quickly degenerated into a grappling match. For his size and weight, Celestin was faster and harder-hitting than one might have guessed, but he was no match for the masterful architect, who had fought and won several amateur matches as a youth in Ireland. Eventually it was clear that Celestin, despite his fierce determination, was being soundly trounced by his opponent. Blood streamed from his nose and down the front of his shirt, and one eye was already badly swollen.

Finally, in response to Micaela's pleas, Patrick backed off, lowered his fists, and digging into his pocket, offered Celestin his handkerchief.

"Here . . ." he said, his pained expression reflecting the anguish he felt for Micaela's husband.

"Let's get him to a carriage and take him home," Micaela suggested, attempting to support the staggering man.

"Let me go," Celestin protested, shaking her hand loose from his arm. He kept sniffling to try to stem the flow of blood from his nose. "Do you want to fight or don't you?" he said to Patrick, tossing a couple of feeble punches at him.

"That's enough," Patrick answered quietly.

"Giving up that easy, are you?" Celestin needled, his eye swelling so quickly he could barely see out of it.

When Patrick continued to ignore his challenges, he finally lowered his fists and picked up his cloak from the ground. Wiping his face with it, he started to walk away.

"Where are you going?" Micaela called after him.

"What do you care?" he retorted.

"You must come back and let us help you," she pleaded.

"Go to hell, both of you!" he shouted, and stumbled down a narrow path between high boxwood hedges, disappearing into the shadows of the night.

The cabdriver's expression was impassive as Celestin, bloody-faced and disheveled, staggered from the carriage, paid him far more than the actual fare, and crossed the street to the fencing studio.

Dulac was asleep on his narrow army cot when Celestin entered the back room, but he awakened as soon as the younger man lighted a candle in the center of the table.

Startled by his battered appearance, Dulac said, "My God, Pontalba, what the hell happened to you? Were you attacked by a gang of hoodlums?"

Celestin shook his head numbly.

"Let me get you some water to clean up," Dulac offered, swinging his legs, swathed in thick woolen stockings, over the edge of the cot.

Celestin restrained him. "Don't disturb yourself. I'll get it myself." Reaching for a basin under the sink, he went to the pump in the courtyard behind the studio, filled the basin, and returned. "I do have a favor to ask," he said.

"What is it?" Dulac inquired anxiously.

"May I stay here for the night?"

Dulac nodded. "You can stay as long as you want. Let me prepare a place for you to sleep."

While Celestin was applying wet compresses to his swollen eye, Dulac dug out some old army blankets and prepared a makeshift bed on the floor.

"Take the cot," he directed. "I'll sleep on the floor."

At first Celestin protested, but when Dulac continued to insist, he flopped, weak and exhausted, face-down on the cot.

"So you've had your duel, have you?" the older man said.

"Yes," Celestin murmured. His face was buried in the pillow, and Dulac was shocked to realize that his friend was crying. He suddenly recalled another night long ago, in a tent by the Spanish-Portuguese border, when Celestin had received word that he must leave the army to marry.

Hesitating at first, Dulac finally sat on the edge of the cot and placed his hand on the younger man's shoulder.

"It's all right, my boy," he said soothingly.

"No, it's not all right," Celestin muttered, without raising his head. "Why must I be a failure at everything? I'm a failure as a husband, a failure as a son, a failure as an officer . . ."

"You were a damned good officer," Dulac reassured him.

"But I wasn't in Russia when I was needed most," he lamented. "I'm a failure as a fighter. I'm a failure as a man."

With that his emotions overwhelmed him, and he burst into racking sobs that shook his entire body.

Unable to restrain himself, Dulac bent forward and pressed his face into Celestin's black, tousled hair.

"No, not a failure at everything," he whispered hoarsely as he stroked the younger man's slender back. "Not at everything, my boy."

37

ALMOST IMMEDIATELY AFTER the scuffle with Celestin, Patrick departed, leaving Micaela alone with her memories of their joyous time together. Within a very short while she heard persistent rumors that Celestin had not scurried back to Mont L'Eveque with his tail between his legs, as she had supposed, but had been seen in Paris on several occasions by various friends. He made no attempt to contact her, and she did not expect him to, knowing how sensitive and proud he was and how much anguish and embarrassment he was undoubtedly suffering.

"The Tricons' maid told me she saw Master Celestin," Binnie commented referring to the family living next door. "He was walkin' around the Bois de Boulogne the other day lookin' like he just lost his last friend."

If Celestin were really in Paris, as everyone claimed, Micaela felt obliged to seek him out and make sure he was all right. She wondered why her sense of responsibility toward him persisted in spite of the unhappiness he had, directly or indirectly, caused her. She concluded that this feeling was deeply ingrained, resulting from their years of intimate association.

For several days she and Binnie dropped by the Cafe de Roy and made inquiries, but no one there had seen him. Then, remembering his long friendship with Dulac, she decided to go to his fencing studio, disregarding the fact that such places were not considered proper for women to frequent.

When the carriage stopped in front of the establishment, she heard the raucous voices of men shouting encouragement or criticism over the clank of one steel blade striking another, and quickly realized that a match must be taking place inside.

"We ain't got no business here, Miss Micaela," Binnie fretted.

"You hush and let me worry about that," Micaela said. She alighted from the carriage, walked up to the door, and rapped on it sharply.

The sound of clashing swords suddenly stopped, and a few moments later the door opened. Dulac, leaning on his crutches, stared at her curiously. This was the first time they had met face to face, although both were indirectly familiar with the other through Celestin.

"Yes? May I help you?" he inquired politely.

"I am Madame de Pontalba . . ."

"I guessed as much," he acknowledged.

"And you must be Captain Dulac, are you not?"

He nodded. "How may I be of service, madame?"

Micaela glanced past him into the cavernous, high-ceilinged studio, bare of all furnishings. The room exuded the smell of tobacco and sweaty, overheated bodies. There were only about a half dozen young men present, although from the street their shouts had given her the impression that there were more. All were staring curiously in the direction of the door. Two of the men were naked to the waist, covered with perspiration, and one of them was anxiously dabbing at a bloody nick he had received just below the left collarbone. Celestin, however, was not among the group.

"I'm looking for my husband," she said. "Have you seen him?"

"Yes, madame, I have seen him," Dulac replied.

"Is he in Paris?"

"Yes, madame, he is in Paris."

"Where?"

"He is here with me."

Quickly surveying the fencing area once again, she still saw no sign of him. "I don't see him, Captain."

"No, of course you don't," Dulac said. "He's in the back." He indicated a door at the rear of the main room.

"Would you be so kind as to tell him that his wife is here and would like a word with him?" she requested.

"I will tell him, madame," Dulac agreed. "Would you like to come inside and wait? However, as you can see, I am not accustomed to receiving women here . . ."

"I'll wait outside, thank you."

Leaving the door ajar, Dulac hobbled toward the back of the studio. He stopped a moment to confer with the group of men, and as soon as he entered the back room they immediately put on their coats, picked up their foils, and left, each tipping his hat politely to Micaela.

Remembering Celestin's having told her what a distinguished officer Dulac had been, honored many times by Napoleon himself, Micaela felt a flash of pity for this weathered, crippled man. How cruel time was, even to heroes, she thought.

In a few minutes Dulac hobbled back, the thud of his crutches against the bare wooden floor echoing throughout the now empty room.

"Please come in, madame," he invited. "Your husband will be with you in a moment."

With the other men gone, she felt more comfortable about entering the studio. "Thank you, Captain," she said, touching her nostrils with a cologne-scented handkerchief she had extracted from the bosom of her dress, grateful to the sweet aroma of flowers for masking the odors within.

Almost immediately Celestin appeared, badly dressed and looking generally unkempt, some of the cuts and bruises he had received in the fight with Patrick still unhealed. He seemed embarrassed to see her.

"Micaela . . ."

"Will you excuse me?" Dulac interjected tactfully. "I have some water for coffee boiling in the back." He closed the door behind him so that they could be alone.

"Hello, Celestin," she said.

"What are you doing here?" he asked, obviously surprised by her presence at Dulac's studio.

"I've been looking for you," she told him. "I heard rumors that you were still in Paris. When I was unable to locate you elsewhere, I decided to come here."

"Dulac has been kind enough to allow me to stay with him," he informed her.

"You could have stayed at our own home. It's yours as well as mine. I had no idea you intended to remain in the city."

"How could I go home and face the baron looking the way I do?" He indicated the injuries marring his nearly perfect features. One eye was swollen and nearly closed, and his nose was crusted with dried blood.

"Still, you could have come to the house."

"Wouldn't we have made a fine trio—you, me, and your lover?" He let out an ironic laugh.

"Patrick left for America the day after . . . after the encounter," she said, searching for the least provocative word.

"I hope I didn't frighten him away," Celestin remarked sardonically.

"He had already planned to leave."

"I suppose you must be brokenhearted . . . ?"

"I do miss him," she admitted, deciding to be truthful. "He is a dear friend."

"So it appeared that night in the gardens of the Palais Royal."

"He's one of the best friends I have."

"And Dulac is my dear friend, one of the best *I* have," he returned. "That's why I came here to stay."

"You are welcome to come back to the house. I want you to know that."

"Is it because you are lonely?" he asked, skeptical of the invitation. "Or are you feeling guilty?"

"Neither. It's because—whether you believe it or

not—I am concerned for your welfare," she replied. "And for no other reason. You and I know our marriage was finished years ago—if indeed it ever really existed—regardless of the fact that we somehow managed to produce three children. We have never pretended much to each other—thank God for that—and until recently we have always maintained a certain respect and affection in spite of everything. That's what I'd like to preserve, if possible. No matter what my relations are with Patrick Lynch, and no matter what else has happened, I hope we can, and will, remain friends. I am truly sorry that my friendship with Patrick, which, I acknowledge frankly, was improper from the start, has led to the consequences it did. But I am not sorry for the friendship, only for the pain it seems to have caused at times."

"If this is an apology, I accept it," he said. "But I intend to continue staying here with Dulac. I have no plans of ever living with you in the house on the Rue du Houssaie or anywhere else. When my injuries are healed, I shall return to our sons at Mont L'Eveque. You are free to do as you like."

Realizing it would be futile to say anything more, Micaela felt it was time to leave. She had made a gesture, Celestin had rejected it, and the matter was closed.

"Well, I guess that's that," she said, moving toward the door. "Goodbye, Celestin."

"Goodbye, Micaela."

As she stepped outside she glanced over her shoulder and saw that Dulac had emerged from the rear room and was standing with his arm around Celestin, as if he were congratulating him on the position he had taken.

When Micaela returned to the house on the Rue du Houssaie, it seemed emptier and lonelier than ever before. Little by little, everyone appeared to be leaving her—first her mother, then Celestin and her sons, then Patrick. The meeting with Celestin had left her feeling curiously sad yet relieved: sad that the marriage was over and relieved that at last they were finally willing to acknowledge it openly to each other. Somewhere in the back of her mind Micaela had clung tenaciously to the hope that she and Celestin might be reconciled for the sake of the boys, if for no other reason. In the past she had always blamed the baron for the troubles between them, but now she wondered if that had been a correct assumption. Today, for the first time, it was clear that Celestin himself was unconditionally finished with the marriage. His refusal to come back with her and his decision to remain at Dulac's place had swept away all doubts. At last he had made a determination for himself, ironic as that was.

As Binnie was helping her out of the heavy plum silk dress in preparation for her afternoon nap, Georges knocked at the door and handed the maid a letter for Micaela. Recognizing the handwriting as Patrick's, Micaela opened it at once and savored every word. He had arrived back in the United States after a rather uneventful voyage. He was immediately flooded with work. His family was fine. Both Emily and his son had missed him. Not until the end of the letter did he finally express how much he missed her, how deeply he loved and needed her. "There have been so many times since I have returned when I would give ten years of my life just to have you beside me again, even though I know how impossible such a wish is. Destiny, it seems, has always been our enemy, Micaela, my dearest . . ."

Unable to sleep after Binnie left the room, Micaela tossed restlessly in her large canopied bed and contemplated Patrick's letter, recalling with agonized longing their recent days and nights together. She also mulled over the distressing encounter she had just endured with Celestin at Dulac's fencing studio. After weighing both of these things in her mind for a considerable length of time, she sat up and rang for Binnie.

"What're you doin' awake so soon, Miss Micaela?" the maid asked when she entered the bedroom.

"I can't sleep," Micaela replied, getting out of bed and opening the drapes. "Besides, we have packing to do."

"Packin'?" Binnie repeated with a puzzled look. "Where is you fixin' to go?"

"Home," Micaela said with a smile. "To New Orleans."

Part Four

38

As MICAELA DESCENDED the gangplank, Binnie close at her heels, she was astonished to see how much New Orleans had changed in the nearly two decades she had been away. It was obvious to her that the city was no longer a provincial, colonial outpost but one of the most important and thriving seaports of the young, restless, and energetic United States. Located at the mouth of the mighty Mississippi, New Orleans had become the destination of the agricultural products harvested in the fertile upriver valleys. These goods would eventually be exchanged for the manufactured wares of Europe, for which the newly affluent American settlers hungered. The vast river was jammed with a steady flow of traffic, vessels of all kinds and sizes. The streets around the waterfront also swarmed with activity. People milled about, speaking a dozen different languages, and conveyances of every description, from fine carriages to humble wooden carts, traversed the roadways. Elegant-looking men wearing clothes tailored in the latest European styles mingled with rough, free-wheeling traders and boatmen from the north clad in buckskins and furs. Exquisitely gowned Creole ladies, their parasols protecting their complexions, strolled along the banquettes with their black maids, passing Choctaw squaws with reed baskets on their heads and free black women from the West Indies hawking fruits and baked goods.

Hiring a carriage, Micaela instructed the driver to take her, Binnie, and their trunks to Versailles.

"I hope my arrival doesn't come as too much of a shock to Cousin Pierre," she remarked, fanning herself against the muggy, oppressive heat that she had nearly forgotten in her years in France.

"You mean you didn't write him?" Binnie said.

"There wasn't time."

"Shame on you, Miss Micaela," Binnie scolded. "You shouldn't be surprisin' Master Pierre this way."

"It'll do him good," she laughed.

As they rode along the River Road, Micaela observed that many swampy areas once considered unsuitable for human habitation had been drained and were apparently thriving as plantations and small farms. She recalled Patrick's having told her how much the city had grown, but only when confronted with the reality of his words was she truly impressed.

"My, my, Miss Micaela, New Orleans sure has changed," Binnie chortled, shaking her head in disbelief.

"Yes, it has," Micaela agreed.

When they arrived at Versailles, Pierre Delaronde, now gray and slightly paunchy, was stunned by the totally unexpected appearance of his cousin.

"Micaela! My God, I had no idea you were coming!" he cried. "Why didn't you write? I would have prepared . . . planned some kind of welcome . . ."

"Just seeing you is welcome enough," she said, kissing both his cheeks.

When the flurry of excitement over her unexpected arrival had died down, Micaela rested for a few days, recovering from the rigors of a long and arduous sea voyage. Pierre, who had settled into a rather quiet, sedate middle age, had still not married, at least not formally. He and Pelagie continued to live together, although she was officially relegated to the overseer's cottage with their offspring, several of whom had been sent off to school in the North. Colonel Delaronde and Eulalie, as well as the beloved slave Aunt Sally, had long since passed away, but Roland still functioned as butler and Pierre's personal valet.

"I tell you, it's not easy being a planter these days," Pierre told Micaela one evening as they sat on the main gallery. He was now completely in charge of the running of the plantation. "The tension over slavery is growing in this country. The abolitionist movement is gathering steam. I honestly wish there were some way we could survive without slaves, but it's economically impossible." He glanced at Micaela, still not quite believing that she was no longer a schoolgirl but a mature woman with three sons.

"I suppose you know that Mother Germaine has passed on?" he continued. "And your good friend, Claire Villegrande, who used to come here to visit you in the summer, has married a Yankee and lives in Natchez. As for Renée Houdaille, she married one of the richest young men in town and has several children. One of her daughters—I believe her name is Rosine—is said to be a real little beauty and very sweet-natured."

"She doesn't sound much like her mother, then," Micaela remarked, recalling Renée and their intense rivalry.

One day, on the pretext of visiting her inherited properties in the French Quarter, Micaela went up to the city. After a quick inspection of the stores and houses being remodeled, she headed for Patrick's office, which, she discovered, was now located in a sedate building graced by high white columns built in the Greek revival style, one of Patrick's favorite architectural designs and now popular throughout the South. A brass plaque on the door read "Patrick Lynch & Associates, Architects." Inside, she found an office of quiet, pleasing dignity, much as she had supposed it would be.

A young male secretary stood up and greeted her. "Good day, madame. What can I do for you?"

"I'd like to see Mr. Lynch, if I may," she replied, wondering how Patrick would react when he discovered she was in New Orleans. She hoped that she hadn't been too impulsive in calling on him without warning. Surprising Pierre was one thing, but dropping in unannounced on Patrick was another matter.

"Junior or Senior?" the secretary inquired, reminding her that Patrick's son was also with the firm.

She smiled. "Senior, please."

"One moment, madame. Let me find out if Mr. Lynch can see you now," he said, and excused himself.

In a few minutes Patrick himself emerged from a huge, airy, well-lighted drafting room. In his shirt sleeves he looked pretty much as he had in Paris a few months ago, except that his eyes appeared somewhat reddened as if strained.

"Micaela!" he exclaimed, as astonished as Pierre had been to see her. Crossing the reception room, he seized her in a discreet but fervent embrace, apparently unconcerned what his secretary might think. "What are you doing here? I can't believe it!"

"It still seems a bit unreal to me, too," she said, attempting to regain her composure. Being close to him once again made her tremble and feel lightheaded.

Anxious for them to be alone, Patrick instructed the secretary to refer all clients to his son until he returned. Then he escorted Micaela out, hired a covered cab, and ordered the driver to take them around the city.

Once away from the office and sequestered from public sight, they fell into each other's arms and exchanged ardent kisses.

"Oh, Patrick, Patrick," she murmured, clinging to him desperately, "I've missed you so."

"I've missed you, too, lass," he said, burying his head in her soft neck.

Not wanting their passion to erupt in the cab, they attempted to restrain themselves and settle into a dignified, ordinary conversation, at least as far as possible. After some small talk Micaela described her last meeting with Celestin.

"Poor man," Patrick sighed, remembering the blows they had exchanged. "What do you intend to do?"

Hesitating a moment, she finally admitted what she had been constantly debating in her mind throughout the entire ocean voyage. "I'm thinking of getting a divorce."

"A divorce?" he repeated. The idea shocked him. Divorce was an exceedingly rare occurrence, considered scandalous at best. It subjected the family to disgrace and rendered the two principals social outcasts.

"The thought of such an action distresses me, but under the circumstances I see no other way out. The big question is whether or not I have the courage to go through with it."

Patrick shook his head solemnly. "It's a momentous decision, there's no doubt about that," he said, neither discouraging nor encouraging her by his tone. "The very word 'divorce' is an anathema to most people. Even in your position you mustn't be hasty. Think it over carefully before you take any steps. For God's sake, don't be rash or impulsive, lass. As I've often told you, my own marriage isn't the happiest or the best, yet I could never bring myself to inflict a blow as cruel as divorce on poor Emily."

"Whatever I do, it won't be easy."

The carriage proceeded along St. Charles Avenue through the area known as the Garden District. Patrick proudly pointed out the various mansions he had designed for the newly prosperous Americans. All were surrounded by beautifully tended lawns and gardens.

"What lovely homes they are," Micaela remarked with delight. "And how different from the Creole houses in the French Quarter."

Nudging her playfully with his elbow, he said, "You Creoles prefer to live right on the street, selfishly hiding your gardens behind walls, keeping them private for yourselves. The Americans, on the other hand, want the whole world to know who they are and what they've managed to acquire."

"Why have they all shunned the French Quarter and chosen to build in this area?" she asked.

"Because your stubborn Creole friends and relatives refuse to sell land to a Yankee or a foreigner," he replied.

"How foolish . . ."

"In the end, this narrowness of mind is going to be their ruin. Just wait and see. Already the heart of the city is shifting away from the French Quarter. I wish the men who were elected to govern New Orleans had a little more intelligence and less stubbornness. But then, my voice still doesn't count for much. I'm only a lowly Irishman. They just want me to build their houses for them and keep my mouth shut."

"I wouldn't describe you as lowly at all. You've been quite successful, Patrick."

"I guess I have been a bit successful—or lucky— whichever the case may be," he conceded. "Of course, I've also worked damned hard. Sometimes I think I turn to work as the remedy for all my problems. Since I've come back from Europe. I've taken on too much work again, as usual. My eyes are feeling the strain. At night when I leave the office, they're swollen and congested. I try to relegate things to my son, but you know how the very young are. They're not like us. Besides, I have to poke my nose into everything. I have no confidence in anyone, not even in young Pat."

Feeling a momentary twinge of longing for her own three sons in France, Micaela snuggled close to him and whispered, "Yes, I know . . ."

On the recommendation of Saint-Avid, Micaela sought out her mother's American lawyer and cousin, François LeBreton, who had drawn up her own controversial marriage contract. She presented the elderly lawyer with the documents that deeded her Louisiana properties to Celestin and informed him that she was contemplating a divorce.

LeBreton read over the papers and then gave her his opinion. "As far as your husband and the courts of Louisiana are concerned, these papers are worthless. In order to get these properties officially returned to you, you only have to appear in court here, answer a few questions, and swear to certain statements under oath. Regardless of the fact that you are married to a French national and have been living in France, you are still considered an American citizen in the eyes of the American law. I congratulate you, as I often congratulated your dear mother in the past, on employing the services of the superb Monsieur Saint-Avid. He is a brilliant attorney and has made my task very simple indeed by the skill with which he has drawn up these documents. As for the divorce proceedings, I caution you not to rush into such a serious matter."

"Whether I decide to divorce my husband or not, I want to regain these properties legally," she said. "They were my father's, and my interest in them is as much sentimental as it is financial."

A few weeks later Micaela made the necessary court appearance and, exactly as LeBreton had predicted, reacquired all the Louisiana properties willed to her by her mother. In the same decision her husband was stripped of all claims of ownership, and the documents drawn up in France were declared null and void.

When the final word was handed down by the court, Micaela could scarcely wait to tell Patrick the news, since he was the one who had originally suggested she cede to Celestin the American properties instead of the French ones. Because of her own business affairs and because she was still residing at Versailles, they had seen very little of each other since her arrival.

When his employees had left the office for the day, Patrick lay down on a leather sofa, placed cold witch hazel compresses over both eyes, and asked Micaela to pour each of them a glass of sherry from the decanter on his desk.

"Naturally, I intend to repay the bank loan Celestin signed in order for me to secure the funds to remodel the properties here," she said as she placed a silk cushion on the floor and settled onto it, resting her head against the sofa.

"How is the remodeling coming?" he asked. "I've been too busy to get over there to see what progress has been made."

"Everything's fine," she replied. "But still, they're very old buildings. If it weren't so costly, and if I knew what direction my life was going to take, I'd probably tear them down and replace them with new structures."

"I'm sure the city would like nothing better," he laughed, reaching out for her hand and pressing her fingertips to his lips. "Ah, Micaela, Micaela," he sighed. "Let's not talk of buildings. At least not now . . ."

Now that the legal matters regarding the return of her property were concluded, Micaela decided to escape the oppressive New Orleans heat and head north to the cooler air of Saratoga Springs, a fashionable resort in New York that was popular with affluent Southerners. She hadn't really had any serious purpose in mind when she discussed this vacation with Patrick, although it was her fervent hope that he might be able to get away from his family and business and join her there.

In Saratoga Springs the nights were cool, and the air was fragrant with the scent of pine and honeysuckle. Micaela found it delightful.

She had been in the small town located at the foot of the Adirondack Mountains only a few days when Patrick arrived, alone and unexpected, ostensibly to confer with a vacationing client.

"You were crazy to follow me here," she chided, nevertheless overjoyed to see him. "This town is full of people we both know. I swear half of New Orleans was at the races yesterday."

Kissing her playfully on the tip of her nose, he said, "I came to take the waters, lass."

Because there were so many familiar faces—many of them Patrick's clients—their meetings had to be discreet and involved a certain amount of ingenuity and imagination. Their favorite spots for a rendezvous were the many trails through the cool birch and pine woods or the mineral baths, where they would enter separately, engage a private bath and resting room, and then secretly join each other when the attendants weren't looking. In the bath they shared the hot, steaming, sulfurous pool together, happily soaking and splashing about like two children in a single bathtub, each scrubbing and soaping the other, stirring the springs of passion until they swelled into a gushing torrent and one warm, slippery body slid sensuously against the other as they surrendered themselves to an abandoned, watery embrace that fused them solidly together, physically as well as spiritually.

Later, as they lay peacefully entwined on a very narrow massage table covered with freshly laundered linens, she wondered aloud, "What if we ever forget to lock the door and one of the attendants comes in on us?"

"I'd tell them you were my sister," Patrick replied, and Micaela burst into laughter, beating him playfully with her fists.

One day they impulsively decided to leave Saratoga Springs and go to Niagara Falls. They caught the train and were relieved to discover that all of the passengers aboard were total strangers.

"I can't believe we're so lucky," Patrick remarked as they entered their private compartment.

In Niagara Falls, for the sake of appearances, they requested separate rooms at the hotel, but made certain they were on the same floor. As soon as Patrick was sure the hall was clear, he would scurry into Micaela's room, often in his robe, and slip beneath the cool sheets of her bed. Their lovemaking reached new, rapturous heights that delighted them both and left them breathless and shaken.

Almost immediately after they arrived, they rushed to see the falls and stood awestruck before the majesty of the roaring waters. Below them at the turbulent base of the falls, a delicate rainbow arched gracefully across the mists.

Snuggling close to him, Micaela murmured, "I feel as if we are on a honeymoon."

Later, back in the hotel, Patrick said, "You know, I've never promised you marriage, Micaela. You understand that, don't you?"

She was certain he was referring to her remark at the falls, which she had meant to be casual and humorous and nothing more.

"Why do you bring that up now, Patrick?" she asked.

"So that later there will be no recriminations, no misunderstandings, no bitterness."

"There won't be," she assured him, still troubled by his words. "I promise you."

"And remember, I'm not encouraging that divorce of yours. Whatever you do is purely your own decision."

She nodded, accepting his words yet wishing that somehow things might be different.

"Ah, if only we could stay here forever and didn't have to go back to New Orleans," he lamented, echoing her own thoughts.

"Yes, that would be lovely," she agreed warmly. Then she regarded him with a serious expression in her face. "Patrick, regardless of what you say, I am going through with the divorce. As soon as I get back to New Orleans, I'm going to call on LeBreton and tell him to initiate the proceedings. I know it won't be easy, and there may be many unpleasant repercussions, but I believe I'm strong enough to withstand them. My greatest, and perhaps only, fear is for my sons and what effect a divorce might have on them and their futures. I don't want them to suffer because of me. They are my major concern."

"Suffering is inevitable," he sighed, perhaps recalling much of his own life. "It is part of the human condition."

39

WHEN CELESTIN WROTE his parents of Micaela's sudden departure for New Orleans, which he learned of one day through a chance encounter on the street with Georges, the news aroused surprisingly little reaction at Mont L'Eveque. By now the Pontalbas were accustomed to their daughter-in-law's fierce independence and rebellious nature, and they regarded the trip as simply another of her whims. If they were unable to dominate her, they were slowly managing to wrest from her control what they desired: her American properties, her three boys, and Celestin. Essentially, all that remained were her properties in Paris, and Baron Joseph was confident that, considering her impulsive departure from France, he would be able to seize them as well. Soon, if all went as he hoped, she would be reduced to a pathetic, powerless creature, stripped of everything she owned, forced to abandon her arrogant ways and submit to her superiors.

On the heels of Celestin's news an official letter from LeBreton arrived, informing the baron that the Louisiana courts had declared Micaela's American properties hers and hers alone, denying all claims to them by her husband or anyone else. The letter caused a minor furor at the château, but, in retrospect, its contents seemed inconsequential in comparison to a second letter from none other than Micaela herself. In it she announced that after much deliberation she had decided to seek a divorce from Celestin. "My mind is irrevocably made up," she wrote.

Throwing the letter down on his desk, the baron smashed it with his fist. "This time she has gone too far!" he cried. "This time I shall not stand idly by while she debases the honor of this family. This time, by God, I shall have revenge!"

"A divorce in our family . . ." Jeanne moaned, sniffing, and dabbing at her teary eyes with a delicate handkerchief Celestin had embroidered and given to her as a gift. "Such a thing is beyond my comprehension. If she were really to dare to go through with a divorce, I don't think I could survive the scandal. I would die of shame and disgrace. Oh, the brazen hussy! Even to contemplate such a thing is shameful in itself. I never liked her from the start. Even at seventeen she was too worldly for my poor Celestin. I cannot bear a divorce in this family. We *must* stop her!"

"I promise you, my dear," the baron said, taking his wife by the arm, "there will be no divorce."

"How can we stop her?" Jeanne wailed. "She is in America and we are in France. An ocean separates us. Already she has persuaded the American court to snatch away the properties she signed over to Celestin and that were rightly his from the beginning."

Picking up a pen, the baron tapped it thoughtfully against his open palm. "The woman is clever and cunning, like her mother, but this time she won't get the better of us. I can promise you that. Tomorrow I shall go to Paris for a talk with the French minister. He is an old friend. We must try to work through him. That is the first step."

When the baron arrived in Paris the next day, he headed for his son's house on the Rue du Houssaie, expecting to find him there. He was shocked to learn from the butler that Celestin had not been living in the house for a long time.

"Then where is he?" the elderly nobleman demanded. "Where has my son been staying all this time?"

"I believe he may be at the fencing studio of a certain Captain Dulac, sir," Georges suggested, and gave Baron Joseph directions on how to get there.

Living at Dulac's studio, Celestin eventually discovered, much to his dismay, that he was no more comfortable there than he had been at Mont L'Eveque or with Micaela in their own home. His relationship with the former cavalry captain had somehow deteriorated, becoming a source of tension and unhappiness; he felt more confused and unsure of himself than ever before. There were even moments when he actually yearned to be with Micaela again in spite of all their difficulties and the bitterness between them.

Dulac, of course, was well aware of Celestin's discontent but chose to pretend not to notice it. His patience was boundless where his friend was concerned, and he was prepared to wait until Celestin reciprocated his strong feelings. Dulac was willing to forgive him anything. He was certain that if he was sufficiently patient and waited long enough, Celestin would finally come around. In the meantime, he did his best to amuse and distract Celestin with tales of his army adventures and the various campaigns in which he had fought, often plying his younger friend with cognac, wine, and fine cigars, gifts from his fencing pupils. Frequently they would go to the cafes for reunions with other veterans of the Grand Army and would revive old times, bemoaning the present state of affairs. Although Celestin had loved anything connected with his days in the service, lately it took all the persuasion Dulac could muster to get him into the proper spirit at these reunions.

"Those days are lost forever," an old dragoon mourned one afternoon, staring at his cognac.

"Vive l'empereur!" a carabineer cried, raising his beer mug.

Celestin remained silent.

When they returned to the studio, he went directly to bed, complaining of a stiff neck and a severe migraine headache.

Laying his crutches aside, Dulac hobbled to the army cot on which Celestin slept, and sat on the edge. Wordlessly he began to knead the tense muscles of the younger man's neck, shoulders, and upper back, as he had done many times in the past when Celestin had similar complaints. This time, however, Celestin was unable to relax, and despite the slow, even rhythm of Dulac's massage, he finally shoved him away.

"Not now," he said.

"Very well," Dulac replied, and rose.

After a few minutes' contemplation Dulac sighed wearily. "You're free to go, you know. The door is not locked. You are not a prisoner. If you are unhappy, I prefer that you leave. I have no hold on you, Pontalba. You owe me nothing. Is that clear?"

Without raising his head from the pillow, Celestin mumbled, "Yes, it's clear."

"Good."

"And I'm sorry," Celestin added.

"What have you to be sorry for? From the beginning I suspected that perhaps it was a mistake. I guess I always knew you wouldn't stay, but I kept deluding myself. I have been expecting you to fly off, like a bird released from its cage."

"Please don't be angry with me," Celestin said, extending his hand to Dulac.

The older man took it, murmuring, "I could never be angry with you . . ."

At that moment they were interrupted by an insistent pounding on the door.

"Who the hell can that be?" Dulac wondered, reaching for his crutches. "I'll be right back."

While Celestin waited anxiously for his companion's return, he strained to hear the conversation in the adjoining room.

A few minutes later Dulac hobbled back into the room and announced that Celestin's father was waiting for him in the fencing studio.

"I told him you were asleep and not feeling well, but he's demanding to see you," he said.

"I can't talk to anyone now," Celestin moaned, clutching his temples.

"I think you'd better," his friend advised.

With Dulac's help, Celestin dressed and, visibly trembling, went out to face the baron.

When he saw his son, the baron's stern face registered little. "Celestin . . ."

"Papa . . ."

"I should like a word with you privately."

"I'll close the door, sir," Dulac offered, hovering in the doorway between the studio and the tiny living quarters.

"No, it's all right, Captain," the baron said brusquely. "My carriage is outside."

Once he and Celestin were in the carriage, he ordered the driver to circle the Bois de Boulogne until he directed him otherwise, and then addressed himself immediately to the reason for his sudden visit.

"I'm sure you are aware that your wife is seeking a divorce in America, are you not?" he began.

"Yes," Celestin mumbled, his head throbbing so badly he thought it would split in two momentarily. "I know about it."

"I'm sure you agree that we cannot permit this to happen," the baron continued.

"The marriage was finished years ago for all intents and purposes," Celestin replied, closing his eyes against the harsh sunlight, which seemed to intensify his agony. "What difference does it make?"

"Many marriages end the day they begin," the baron said sharply, struggling to control his temper. Celestin's seemingly indifferent attitude was rapidly angering him. "But that is no reason for divorce. Many types of accommodations can be reached, compromises made, but divorce is not one of them. It is a disgrace —totally unacceptable. A divorce in the Pontalba family cannot and will not be tolerated."

"We couldn't stop her even if we wanted to. When Micaela is determined to do something, no one can change her mind."

"Oh, really?" the baron scoffed.

"Yes, that's true. We are powerless to move against her while she is in America. You saw how the court there ruled on the property transfer. It declared my ownership null and void."

"On the contrary, we are not powerless at all. Perhaps we are in matters of real property actually situated in the United States, but not in domestic matters such as divorce. We must bring this to the attention of the French minister. He can block her efforts through diplomatic channels. Do I have your permission to consult him?"

Celestin gave an ironic laugh. "When have you ever required my permission for anything?"

"I can make no moves without your cooperation," his father declared. "Shall we prepare to call on the minister or not?"

Celestin sighed. The pain in his head was fast becoming unbearable. Dulac's massage had only aggravated it, and riding with his father was escalating it past all endurance. Clutching his temples, he groaned, "Do just as you wish, sir."

"Good." The baron reached into a bag he had brought from Mont L'Eveque and produced a huge shiny purple plum, which he pressed into Celestin's hand. "I knew I could count on you to be sensible."

Celestin dropped the plum as if it were a red-hot ember, yelled for the driver to stop the carriage, and fled into the woods by the side of the road, where he began vomiting uncontrollably.

The meeting of the Pontalbas with the French minister in charge of Franco-American affairs was awkward and embarrassing for both Celestin and his father. The minister outlined the steps necessary to block Micaela's divorce proceedings and informed them that the process would be more complicated and costly than either had probably anticipated.

"No cost is too great if it will stop this shameful and humiliating act my daughter-in-law is attempting to perpetrate in her madness," the baron assured the official.

As explained by the minister, the strategy would include a communiqué sent to the governor of Louisiana, informing him that Micaela was the wife of a French citizen, and in the eyes of the French law, herself a citizen of that country. A dissolution of the marriage, therefore, would not fall under the jurisdiction of the courts of the State of Louisiana, but under the French courts instead.

"I believe we can get the Louisiana courts to accept that," the minister assured them, adding, "Since, as you have informed me, this is a case of a wife deserting her husband and children."

"That is correct," the baron affirmed.

"The consequences of desertion could be dire for Madame de Pontalba. Is she aware of that?" the minister questioned.

"I'm sure she must be," the baron replied. "She has very capable lawyers in America."

"Although I realize it is a very personal matter, I must ask you, first of all, whether or not you have considered trying to persuade her to return. That seems to be the best initial course of action to me."

"Yes," the baron said, "we have done everything in our power to persuade the woman. Before coming to see you, I obtained the necessary authorization for us to confiscate all of Madame de Pontalba's French property. As a deserted husband, my son now has unquestionable claim to it—unless, of course, my daughter-in-law chooses to return, which, it appears, is highly unlikely."

Later, after leaving the minister's office, Celestin expressed surprise that his father had already apparently taken steps to seize Micaela's French properties.

"She might come back," he said. "One never knows with Micaela."

"Nonsense," the baron scoffed. "She is gone for good, and I say good riddance. She has followed that lover of hers. Well, this time we'll fix her. Not only will we block her divorce so she cannot marry her lover, we will seize her properties in Paris as well, and there is nothing she can do about it. Nothing at all."

Until the various legal maneuvers were concluded, the baron remained in Paris, staying with Celestin at the Rue du Houssaie house. When it came time for him to return to Mont L'Eveque, it was clear that he expected his son to accompany him.

"Ah, you should see the grapes," he exulted. "The vines are so full they can hardly bear up under the weight of their delicious fruit. Their flavor will be exquisite, I can assure you. We have had just the right amount of rain this year."

"I think I prefer to remain here," Celestin told him.

"Alone in this house?" the baron asked, curious as to whether his son intended to return to his friend's fencing studio.

"I don't know. I may possibly stay at Dulac's." Although Celestin was far from comfortable there, at this point Dulac's quarters seemed preferable to either the château or the house. There were too many reminders of failure at both residences.

"Frankly, I don't think that's a suitable place for you," the baron said with a scowl. "You must bear in mind that if we are going to issue a legal ultimatum ordering your wife back to your domicile—which is officially Mont L'Eveque—you must reside there. Micaela is clever and will seize upon anything she can to use against us. We must not slip up anywhere."

"Then I have no choice, do I?"

"None."

Once again Celestin knew he was being forced to capitulate to his father's will, and he wondered, bewilderedly, how much longer it would be that way.

40

ANXIOUS TO SHARE once again the intimacy they had enjoyed so much at Saratoga Springs and Niagara Falls, Patrick informed Micaela of an invitation he had received to confer with a wealthy Cuban entrepreneur in Havana about the possibility of building a resort hotel there, and naturally asked her to go with him.

"As for the hotel project, I have a hunch nothing will come of it," he said, "but it might be a nice chance for us to be together again."

When Micaela agreed to go, Patrick accepted the Cuban's invitation, and the two of them set sail for Havana.

Just as Patrick had predicted, his Cuban host was not as serious about the hotel as he had claimed, and discussions never went beyond the preliminary stages; but Micaela and Patrick were grateful for the opportunity to be with each other away from the prying eyes and gossipy tongues of their New Orleans neighbors.

When they returned, it was again necessary to part and take up their individual lives, Patrick returning to his family and firm, Micaela to Versailles.

Arriving at her cousin's plantation, she found a letter from LeBreton waiting for her.

"Bad news?" Pierre asked, observing her rather pained expression.

"It's the Pontalbas," she said. "They've succeeded in blocking my divorce by getting the French Minister of Foreign Affairs to intervene. LeBreton has received a communiqué from the governor, stating that because I am a French subject, the courts of Louisiana cannot act on any domestic issue in which I am involved."

"Including a divorce, naturally?"

"Naturally," she affirmed, handing her blue-flowered cloak and silk gloves to Binnie and following Pierre outside to the main gallery, where they seated themselves beneath the shade of the striped awning. After a few moments Roland brought them a tray bearing sloe gin drinks. As a rule, Micaela did not drink, but on this day she decided to make an exception.

"It sounds to me as if there's some political machinations going on behind the scenes," Pierre speculated.

"I've no doubt that the baron has a hand in this. I'm sure he considers divorce proceedings against his son an affront to the entire Pontalba family."

"From his actions in the past I would say you are right."

"Oh, Pierre, what shall I do?" she cried, her voice suddenly full of anguish. "Will I never be free of that hateful family, whose only wish is to strip me of all I possess, including my pride and dignity? When LeBreton first began proceedings, it all looked so hopeful. I thought that at last I would be released from the stranglehold the Pontalbas seem to have on my life."

"Oh, I'm sure it's not as hopeless as you think," he said, adding another piece of precious ice to their drinks.

"What can I possibly do now?" she asked.

"I suppose you might appeal to the governor in person," he suggested.

"What good would that do? You already saw LeBreton's letter."

Contemplating a moment, he declared, "Well, then, go over the governor's head and take the matter to the President."

"The President?" she repeated. "You mean President Jackson?"

"Why not? He's known the Delaronde family for years," Pierre informed her. "He and Papa were great friends. I'm sure he'd be happy to help in any way he could."

"Do you really think so?" she asked hopefully.

"Of course." He smiled, adding more gin to his glass.

The more Micaela thought about the prospect of calling on President Jackson in Washington and asking him to intervene in the divorce proceedings, the more appealing it became, especially a few days later, when she called on LeBreton and learned he had received further communication from the Pontalbas.

"What this is, Micaela," the lawyer began, referring to the thick sheaf of legal papers on his desk, "is a judgment declaring your husband, Celestin de Pontalba, a victim of desertion by his wife and granting him full legal rights to all her belongings. If you fail to return to his domicile, which in this case is Mont L'Eveque, within a specified period of time, you not only forfeit all your property but also relinquish complete and total custody of your offspring to your husband as well. That's the whole situation in a nutshell."

"Does that mean I would never be able to see my sons again?" she asked anxiously. She was willing to forfeit the property if that was what was necessary to rid herself of the Pontalbas, but abandoning her sons to them was decidedly another matter.

"Yes, that's possible," LeBreton said. "It would be up to your husband. If he chose not to let you see your children, there would be nothing you could do about it."

Micaela shook her head in dismay. "That's too high a price to pay."

Discouraged and disheartened, she left the lawyer's office and went to Patrick's, where she found him huddled over a drawing board in the huge drafting room. It seemed that no matter how many assistants he hired, including his own son, he still felt compelled to do much of the fine detailed work himself.

"What's wrong?" he asked, seeing that she was visibly upset.

"I must talk to you, Patrick."

"All right," he said, sliding off the high stool. "Let's go into my office."

Once inside his private quarters, she unburdened the latest development in her struggles with the Pontalbas.

"What shall I do?" she sighed. "I'm at my wit's

end. I want a divorce, but I won't want to risk losing my children."

"Do what you think is best for you and your sons," he advised, clasping her hands in his. "You know how I feel about you, but you also know how little I can offer you."

"I know that you give me greater happiness than I have ever had in my life."

Pressing her fingers to his lips, he said, "Ah, Micaela, you deserve so much more. If only I could provide it for you."

Complaining that his eyes were tired from concentrating on the plans he had been rendering all day, he suggested they go for a ride so that he could rest them for a while, and Micaela willingly agreed.

While they snuggled together in a closed carriage, he ordered the driver to take them past her houses and stores opposite the Place d'Armes, on which he had been supervising the renovations.

"Let's forget domestic troubles for a bit and see how things are progressing," he suggested.

Micaela agreed that the buildings looked much improved despite their advanced age, but said that the parade grounds on which they fronted had degenerated into a weed-covered eyesore.

"It's worse than ever," she complained. "A disgrace to this city. Those sycamore trees look as if they haven't been trimmed in years!"

"They haven't been," he affirmed. "I'm afraid that the Garden District is totally eclipsing the French Quarter in beauty."

Forced to agree with him, she asked, "Can nothing be done about it?"

"The French Quarter is dying on its feet, and all because of Creole indifference. Since the Creoles refuse to sell property in the Quarter to the Yankees, they are forced to buy land above Canal Street and consequently devote all their time and money to glorifying the Garden District. The entire commercial heart of this city is shifting away from the Quarter to Canal Street and beyond. I've told you that before. If the Creoles aren't careful, the incredible beauty and elegance of the whole French Quarter will soon fade away and be just a memory."

"Still, in many ways it *is* the choice section of the city," she argued.

"Of course. The river is deepest there and provides an excellent berth for large oceangoing vessels. But if the Creole fathers, such as your own relative, Bernard de Marigny—"

"He gave me away at my wedding," she recalled.

"If men like Monsieur de Marigny don't wake up and allow the Americans access to all parts of the city, they're going to be a sorry lot, I tell you."

Later Micaela returned once more to the subject of her divorce and the difficulties she was having.

"Well, you can't lose anything by going to see President Jackson," Patrick concluded.

Before he got out of the cab, Micaela told him that during their ride she had decided to go to Washington to see the President, as he suggested, and would leave in a few days.

"I wish you the best," Patrick said, kissing her deeply one last time.

Having lived in France for nearly all of her adult life, Micaela had grown accustomed to the restraint and formality of the French way of doing things. Thus, when she arrived in Washington, the brash, uninhibited frontier spirit that the Jackson regime had recently brought to the nation's capital came as somewhat of a shock to her.

"Goodness!" she exclaimed as she and Binnie were roughly jostled on the sidewalk.

"I ain't never seen folks like these," Binnie remarked. "White trash, if you ask me."

The same boisterous informality pervaded the staff of the White House as well, and her reception there was so hearty and enthusiastic it bordered almost on rudeness. Micaela presented the letter of introduction from her cousin Pierre to Jackson's secretary, Andrew Jackson Donelson, a nephew named in the President's honor.

The blustery young Donelson practically snatched

the letter out of her hand and said, "Let me see what Old Hickory has to say about this."

"Do you mean President Jackson?" she asked.

"Shucks, ma'am, he likes folks to call him by his nickname," Donelson told her.

A short while later she was ushered into the President's own Oval Office and greeted effusively by Andrew Jackson himself.

"Mrs. Pontalba?" he said, extending his hand. Obviously he had no time for European forms of address such as "madame." "How do you do?"

"Fine, thank you, Mr. President," she replied.

"This is indeed a great pleasure," he said, waving her into a seat. Jackson was a tall, slim man with a great mane of silvery hair and a ramrod-straight military posture that reminded her of many of Celestin's associates from the Cafe de Roy. How similar soldiers seemed to be the world over, she thought to herself. Jackson bore a deep longitudinal scar on his forehead, said to have been inflicted by a British officer during the Revolutionary War, and his skin was badly pitted, evidently from a case of childhood smallpox.

"I can assure you that the pleasure is mine as well, Mr. President."

"You know, I shall never forget your uncle, Colonel Delaronde, and his great kindness to me during the War of 1812. Do you remember it, or were you too young, my dear?" he asked.

Flattered, she replied, "I was married and living in France at that time, sir."

"In any case, the Battle of New Orleans was practically fought right in the colonel's backyard—what's the name of that plantation of his? It has slipped my mind at the moment."

"Versailles, Mr. President."

"You'll have to excuse me," he apologized. "I never was any good at fancy French names. Anyway, when I caught a British musket ball and was wounded, they took me up to your uncle's place. It was a real pretty house, as I remember, with all those big oak trees. Your uncle got a surgeon to patch me up, and he did a real good job—probably saved my life. The colonel insisted that I stay right there until I was recovered. I got to know and love that Delaronde family. They were grand folks. I always remember the colonel and his missus with great respect and devotion—what was her name?"

Micaela smiled. "Eulalie."

"That's right," he said, snapping his fingers. Then, shifting stacks of papers about on his desk, he asked, "Now, then, what may I do for you, young lady?"

Micaela related her situation to him as LeBreton had instructed her to before leaving New Orleans. Jackson listened with an obviously sympathetic ear and nodded several times, murmuring, "I see, I see."

When she concluded, he shook his head sadly. "Ah, divorce. What a terrible thing it is," he lamented. "As you may or may not know, my own dear late wife— God rest her gentle soul—obtained a divorce from a man who abused and mistreated her in a most shameful way. I cannot tell you the grief and suffering that accursed divorce caused her. There was no end to her misery. People would not let her forget it. Of course, my being in public life, as I was, only made matters worse. My political enemies, lowly scum that they were, used the divorce issue against me. If you want to know the truth, I think that's what caused the good woman's death long before her time. May God forgive her tormentors, as I know she forgave them. I never can or ever will."

"I'm so sorry . . ." Micaela murmured.

"So think carefully about your situation, my dear," he went on in a less personal tone. "As for *my* helping you in this case, I must take that up with my Secretary of State."

They continued to chat for a few minutes until Donelson intervened to remind the President that he had an important Cabinet meeting.

"I'd much prefer talking to you than to a bunch of stuffy old men," Jackson said, excusing himself and telling Donelson to see that Mrs. Pontalba came to dinner at the White House before she left Washington. "We can't permit such a charming lady to slip away from us so easily."

Dinner at the White House proved as informal as everything else in Jackson's Washington, but once she became used to it, Micaela appreciated its honesty and verve and found the atmosphere delightful in its own way. Because the President was a widower, his niece, Emily Donelson, acted as his official hostess.

During the meal Jackson, who, Micaela observed, ate most sparingly, learned the she had an interest in horses and insisted she visit the White House stables and view his prize steeds.

"I enter them in races under my secretary's name," he confided to her in a whisper. "Folks say it isn't dignified for the President of the United States to have racehorses, but I say fiddlesticks to that!"

Later, as they were crossing the vast expanse of lawn bordering Pennsylvania Avenue on their way to the stables, he informed her that he had discussed her case with the Secretary of State after the Cabinet meeting.

"I wish I could use my powers as President to aid you, but I regret that I cannot," he said. "You see, the divorce you seek is a state matter, not a federal one. The French foreign minister has intervened—at your father-in-law's request—with the governor of Louisiana. Although I believe that the office of the President must be a strong one and must exert the greatest influence in governing this country of ours, I also believe that the states exist as fundamental units, free to do as they choose in regard to domestic matters—divorce being one of them. As much as it distresses me to admit this, I am powerless to help you, my dear. The Secretary of State feels you would be best advised to deal with this matter in the French courts."

Disheartened by the news, yet understanding Jackson's position in the matter, Micaela thanked him for his advice and sympathy and impulsively kissed him on the cheek, which brought a slight blush to his face.

"It's been a long time since I've been kissed by such a pretty redhead," he told her with a broad grin.

That night she left the White House happy for the

experience but feeling that she had now exhausted all possibilities. Never before had things seemed so hopeless.

41

RESIGNED TO THE fact that she could not obtain a divorce in the United States, Micaela realized that any attempts to do the same through the French courts would be equally hopeless. The baron's powerful and highly influential contacts in the French Government would enable him to succeed as well in blocking the divorce in France.

When she arrived at Versailles, she found a thick envelope waiting for her, which Roland said had arrived a few days earlier from France. Instantly recognizing her oldest son's nearly indecipherable handwriting on the envelope, she lost no time in tearing it open. The letter turned out to be a desperate plea for help.

Dearest Mama,

You must return to France at once if I am ever to escape the terrible tyranny Grandpapa inflicts on us. There is no one to whom I can turn for help. Alfred and Gaston are too young, although they are as unhappy as I. Grandmama is his ally in all things, not because she wishes to be, but because she is too timid and frightened to oppose him. Great-aunt Celeste is too aged to burden with such matters, and Papa is robbed of all spirit. You, Mama, are my only hope.

Tin-Tin went on to say that the baron was threatening to send him to a very strict military school in the suburbs of Paris and that this plan had the solid backing of his father.

I have not the slightest interest in the military and will prove to be a miserable student if forced to enroll. I often contemplate running away, but where would I go? Also, I have no money of my own, so how would I live? Ah, Mama, if only you would return to Paris! I understand how miserable you were here and how happy you must be in America, where you were born, but I do so wish you were here to aid me in my desperation.

When Micaela finished reading the letter, she sighed and laid it aside. How much her son's words echoed her own sentiments; how much his situation reflected hers. It deeply distressed her to think that her children were forced to endure the same domination to which she had been subjected.

"What does Master Tin-Tin have to say in his letter?" Binnie asked, sensing that whatever the news was, Micaela had been profoundly affected by it.

"What does he say?" Micaela replied. "He says that he feels desperate and wishes to escape the tyranny of his grandfather."

"Ain't nobody could live with that baron," Binnie said, shaking her head. "He's a mighty peculiar man. He scares me, Miss Micaela."

Enclosed in the same envelope with Tin-Tin's letter was a packet of drawings by Gaston, which further displayed his extraordinary artistic talent. Each sketch had a brief message scrawled across the top: "I love you, Mama," "I miss you, Mama," or "Love and kisses from your Gaston."

There was also a note from Alfred as well, which more or less reiterated the same feelings his older brother had expressed, as well as relating the news that the baron had told him and his brother that their mother no longer loved them and had forsaken them forever. He, too, ended with a plea for her to return to France and take them away.

With tears in her eyes, Micaela gazed at the two letters and the packet of drawings. For the first time she suddenly realized that she was to blame for the misery her sons were experiencing. Obviously they needed her very much, and she felt terribly selfish for being away from them at this crucial period in their lives.

"Oh, Binnie, what am I to do?" she bemoaned. "My sons need me in France, and yet I feel a great longing to stay here. If only I knew for certain that I could help their situation by returning!"

"Do what your conscience tells you, Miss Micaela," the maid counseled.

Consulting a calendar, Micaela calculated that if she returned to France immediately, she not only would be responding to her sons' desperate pleas for help but would also be arriving in time to prevent the Pontalbas from seizing her Paris properties. If all went well, her arrival in France would easily precede the deadline set in the judgment. The trip might be worth the arduous effort.

During the next few days Micaela hurriedly concluded her business affairs and booked her passage to France. One of the most difficult things about leaving New Orleans would be the separation from Patrick once again. Although they had not been able to spend a great deal of time with each other, at least not in New Orleans itself, their moments together had been that much more precious. Even if she did not see him frequently, it was comforting to know that there were only a few miles between them and not an entire ocean. The farewell would not be easy.

"I understand," he said when she explained her plans to him. They were standing among a clump of willows at the edge of the river, and he was holding her in his arms. "I have always put my family before myself. I could hardly expect you to do otherwise."

"Oh, Patrick," she sighed, tears brimming in her dark eyes. "Sometimes I have a terrible feeling I'll never see you again. Every time we part, I think it's the last time."

"You mustn't cry, lass," he soothed, tenderly kissing her moist eyelids.

"I can't help it."

"Sometimes I wish I didn't cause you so much unhappiness," he said regretfully.

"You give me my only happiness. That's why I so hate to leave you."

"I often think you'd be a lot happier if you'd never met me."

"Don't say that!" she cried, placing her fingers over his lips.

A large oceangoing vessel sailed slowly past them, reminding Micaela of her imminent departure, and she clung to him more desperately than ever.

42

THE ATLANTIC CROSSING seemed unbearably long and tedious to Micaela, and she spent most of her time confined to her cabin, displaying little interest in the shipboard social life that in the past she had always enjoyed.

When she landed in Paris, weary and fatigued from the voyage, she looked forward to sleeping once again in her own bed at the house on the Rue du Houssaie. However, on arriving there she discovered, much to her astonishment, that all the doors and windows were chained and padlocked.

"Who done such a thing, Miss Micaela?" Binnie asked, as equally dismayed as her mistress.

Micaela knew instantly that it had to be the work of the Pontalbas. "Come," she said to Binnie. "We must go and find a locksmith at once."

Despite Micaela's pleading and cajoling, the locksmith to whom they appealed refused to cooperate and advised her that she had to consult the police and obtain written permission to enter the house before he or any other legitimate locksmith in Paris would touch the locks.

"But it's *my* property," she argued, her voice reflecting her mounting indignation, although she knew it was senseless to battle with a tradesman about such a matter.

"I'm afraid that's not how it appears, madame," the locksmith said, and tipped his hat to her.

Her next stop was Saint-Avid's office. She explained the situation to the lawyer and demanded that he procure whatever legal orders were necessary to remove the barriers preventing her from entering the house.

"Under the circumstances, I regret to say, Micaela, that it's simply not possible," he replied, stroking his thick beard.

Micaela was stunned. It was a rare occasion when this lawyer, perhaps the most capable in Paris, admitted his helplessness in a given situation.

"But I must get into my house," Micaela insisted. "It is *my* house, after all."

"The first thing you must do in order to accomplish that is to comply with the judgment and return to your husband's official domicile," Saint-Avid explained patiently.

"But the house on the Rue du Houssaie *is* his domicile."

"I'm afraid it's not," the lawyer said, shaking his head. "He has declared Mont L'Eveque his official residence."

"That's his father's home," Micaela scoffed. "Not his."

"In order to issue that judgment and force you to return to Mont L'Eveque, the baron signed over one-twentieth of the ownership of Mont L'Eveque to Celestin. That is the minimal portion he must have ownership of so that it can be considered his official residence."

"It's enough that I have been forced to come back to France. I will *not* go to Mont L'Eveque. That is asking too much."

"If you refuse to live with your husband at Mont L'Eveque, you forfeit your Paris properties—all of them, not merely the house on the Rue du Houssaie."

"I do refuse!" she protested. "Let my father-in-law throw me in jail for housebreaking, if he wants, but I will reclaim my own house. By God, I will!"

"I know I can't stop you," the attorney said. "All

I can do is inform you of the laws governing this case. In any event, I wish you well."

Combing the seamier sections of Paris with the reluctant Binnie, Micaela searched for someone skilled in the art of picking locks. Such a person was not easy to find, but near the Rue du Temple she encountered a gypsy hag with a fortune-telling ape, who referred her—for the right price—to a bleary-eyed man smelling of cheap wine; he made his living swallowing live frogs for the amusement of tourists in the Latin Quarter. After considerable negotiating, the frog-eater, a former burglar, agreed to remove the locks and chains for a rather steep fee.

Micaela beamed triumphantly when the front door finally swung open. "In my own house at last," she sighed as she stepped over the threshold. The ex-burglar hung around until Micaela gave him a few extra francs.

"I don't like havin' nothin' to do with folks like that no-good lockpicker who busted these locks for you," Binnie fussed when the man was out of sight. "Nobody's safe with folks like that loose on the streets."

"Don't worry, I'll have all the locks changed and new bolts installed," Micaela told her.

"Locks and bolts don't mean nothin' to some folks," Binnie ranted.

Ignoring her, Micaela went on. "Let the illustrious Baron de Pontalba have me arrested, if he so chooses. Let him suffer the real disgrace of having his daughter-in-law languish in jail. I'll see that it gets in all the newspapers. I'll create more of a scandal than a divorce ever would. He'd love that, I'm sure."

"I wouldn't put nothin' past that old baron," Binnie muttered, heading toward her quarters in the rear of the house.

A few days later Micaela learned from Saint-Avid that the baron had carried out his threats and enrolled Tin-Tin in the suburban military school. At once she dashed off a note to him, advising him of her return to Paris. Then she asked Saint-Avid to find a way to have the letter delivered secretly.

Very soon afterward Micaela was awakened one night by a persistent knocking on the front door.

"Who can that be?" she mumbled sleepily, ringing for Binnie.

The maid appeared, trembling with fright. "I knew we shouldn't have messed with that frog-eater man!" she wailed.

Since they were still alone in the house—the baron had discharged all the servants Micaela had so carefully selected and trained—Micaela announced that she would go to the door herself and picked up a lighted candle from her night stand.

Through a peephole in the door she observed Tin-Tin standing nervously on the steps. At first she was startled by his uncanny resemblance to his father at a similarly young age. Then she placed the candle on a small table and opened the door. "Dearest!" she cried, and threw her arms around him. "Oh, my dearest first-born baby!"

They held each other for several moments; then, arm in arm, they strolled down the hall to the darkened drawing room, the flickering candle lighting their way.

"Oh, Mama, I'm so glad you've come back," he said. "I've been so miserable at that school. You can't imagine what a monster Grandpapa has become."

"Yes, I certainly can," she assured him, lovingly brushing a dark curl from his forehead.

"I detest the military with all its rigid discipline and silly, senseless rules," he complained. "I don't care how glorious Papa and Captain Dulac say it is, I hate it. The part about swords and guns and horses is all right, but I have no time for the rest of the nonsense. I want nothing to do with army life. Papa and Captain Dulac are welcome to it, if that's what they want, but it's not for me."

"Your father would be disappointed to hear you talk that way," she chided.

"To hell with him," Tin-Tin muttered.

"Shame on you! Such language—and about your father!"

"I have lost all respect for him," the boy declared. "Tin-Tin!"

"Well, I have," he went on, greatly agitated. "How can I have respect when he allows Grandpapa to rule all of us, including himself, like a tyrant? He raises no objections. He does nothing to oppose him. All he does is mope around, complaining of his headaches and other ailments, avoiding everyone—Alfred, Gaston, and me most of all—and shutting himself away with his needlework and his military books. He doesn't even play chess any more."

"Enough, Celestin," she said sternly. Regardless of her own private feelings, she was determined not to encourage his disrespect for his father, even though she sympathized with him and recognized that his complaints and criticisms were valid.

The following day Tin-Tin burned his uniforms and textbooks from the military school in the drawing-room fireplace, creating a great blaze on the hearth. His rebellious spirit secretly delighted Micaela, but discretion prevented her from openly displaying her approval.

"With your permission, Mama, I'd like to go out and be fitted for some new clothes," he said, gazing at the hearth as the last brass-buttoned tunic was consumed by flames.

"All right, darling," she agreed, "but try not to be too extravagant."

Until all the legal entanglements had been settled, Micaela decided to maintain an unobtrusive presence in Paris and not publicize her return. She saw the Tricons and several other close friends but, for the most part, led a quiet life, allowing Tin-Tin, however, to do as he pleased. His frenetic social life more than made up for whatever she might have been missing.

With his Titus haircut, plum-colored tailcoat sporting leg-of-mutton sleeves and extra wide double lapels, and tight black silk breeches, straight from the pages of *Messager,* the leading men's fashion magazine, he cut quite a swath in Parisian society. He played cards for high stakes at the Club des Princes and the Club des Étrangers, ogled the courtesans as they rode in their elegant fiacres and cabriolets through the Bois, and rubbed elbows with dandies, whores, actors, and pickpockets at the Cafe Burel or the Cafe Valois, or with money men, stock speculators, and army contractors at the Cafe Chartres. He soon joined the ranks of a group of affluent young men who were known rather contemptuously as *les bouffes*. This frivolous band centered their activities around the Théatre Italien, where they drank and gambled during the performances and chased the ballet girls all through the intermission.

Whenever he expressed misgivings about the sort of life he was leading, Micaela, knowing that the Pontalbas might intervene at any moment, advised, "Enjoy yourself while you can, darling."

His frantic pursuit of pleasure and frivolity became increasingly costly, but Micaela paid his bills and gambling debts uncomplainingly and continued to give him a generous allowance as well.

When Binnie tactfully questioned her wisdom one day, she answered blithely, "What good is my money if my children can't enjoy it? My only regret is that Alfred and Gaston are still imprisoned at Mont L'Eveque. But I shall make it up to them when I get custody of them."

"You are shamelessly spoilin' that boy, Miss Micaela."

Micaela curled her lip disdainfully. "You know, Binnie, you are starting to sound just like the Pontalbas."

One day a letter addressed to Celestin in a rather untidy hand was delivered to the house. Certain that it was personal and not business, Micaela debated whether to send it on to Mont L'Eveque or to open it. Knowing that she would most likely have a long and bitter struggle with the Pontalbas if her divorce suit ever reached the French courts, and suspecting that the letter might be from another woman, and thus valuable evidence, she felt obliged, for her own protection, to read it. Surprisingly, she had received no word from the Pontalbas, especially considering Tin-

Tin's flight from the military school, an occurrence to which they had thus far not responded. She was certain that they knew she was in Paris, just as she was also sure they were busy planning their next moves against her. Still smarting over their having padlocked her own house against her and confiscated her other properties, she wondered what their strategy might be. Feeling she owed Celestin very little respect or loyalty, she ripped open the envelope.

Glancing first at the bottom of the page, she saw, not a signature, as she hoped but the letter D, and wondered who would sign correspondence in such a mysterious fashion. Could Celestin have been carrying on a clandestine affair after all? If so, it would be good news as far as the divorce suit was concerned. The letter, however, appeared to be written in a large masculine scrawl.

Dearest Pontalba,

Even though you asked me not to contact you, I cannot restrain myself. Since you left me, you are constantly in my thoughts, and try as I may, I cannot purge them from my mind. You warned me that your father is suspicious of our relationship and that we all may suffer considerable harm if I persist in trying to maintain it, but I say to hell with your father and to anyone else who tries to drive a wedge between us. When you left my place in Paris, you said it was forever. I say you simply cannot cast aside our great bond of affection, which I believe still exists between us.

Recently I have heard the name Celestin de Pontalba bandied about in the cafes, so I know you have returned to Paris, and from what I understand you have made yourself highly visible in the leading social circles. Since you have not come to see me, I assume you are once again at your home, and thus that is where I address this letter.

You said you have certain weaknesses that you have long tried to overcome. Well, my boy, we all have weaknesses, myself included as you know perhaps better than anyone. Do not detest that part of yourself—or any part—but accept all in good grace, just as I have come to accept that part of me which still achingly longs for you. I hope this letter reaches you, because I am anxious for you to know how much I care for you and want to see you in spite of everything. The door to my studio, as always, is open to you day or night. With my deepest love and affection—D.

Seeing the word "studio" and the letter D, Micaela at once dispensed with the idea that the letter had been written by a woman, and muttered, "Dulac." Although its intent seemed veiled and somewhat ambiguous, its tone was both revealing and disturbing. She did not consider it a casual expression of mere friendship on the part of one man for another. Its implications were of a far deeper and darker nature than Micaela was familiar with or wished to admit to herself. Her initial impulse was to destroy it, if not out of common decency, then out of concern for her sons, but then she folded it carefully, slipped it back into the envelope, and placed it in the wall safe in her bedroom.

Eventually she received the word from the Pontalbas that she had been waiting for ever since her return from the United States. A letter from the baron's attorneys informed her that not only had she broken the law by trespassing when she forcibly took possession of the house, she had committed an even graver infraction by encouraging Tin-Tin to desert his military school and live with her in Paris, where according to all reports, he was fast becoming a wastrel and a playboy. The attorneys went on to say that as a consequence of her actions, the baron had seen fit to strike his firstborn grandson from his will, thus disinheriting him completely and preventing him from assuming the title of baron upon the death of his father.

"He can't do that! I won't stand for it," she cried aloud, enraged at her father-in-law for punishing her sons for her decision not to return to Mont L'Eveque.

As always, when crises arose in the long-standing battle she had been waging with her in-laws, Micaela went straight to Saint-Avid for counsel. The attorney patiently informed her that whether it was fair or whether she approved, the baron had the right to disinherit his eldest grandson if he chose to.

"There is nothing you or I or anyone else can do about it," he said regretfully.

Undaunted by the lawyer's pronouncement, Micaela was determined to pursue the matter and requested that Saint-Avid write the baron, demanding a face-to-face meeting with him and herself.

"I don't think that's wise, Micaela," Saint-Avid advised.

"It's the only way," she insisted.

"But you may be playing right into his hands."

"I don't care."

"Then you're sure this is what you really want to do?"

"Yes," she replied, resolved to fight the issue in person. "It's now or never."

43

MUCH TO MICAELA'S surprise, the baron promptly responded to Saint-Avid's request for a meeting. He agreed to confer with Micaela in person, but only if she would consent to certain stipulations, namely, that she come to Mont L'Eveque alone, unaccompanied by anyone except her personal maid.

"I absolutely refuse to speak to lawyers or other parties," he wrote. "Or go to Paris."

Micaela had hoped for a mutually agreeable meeting place somewhere between Paris and the baron's Oise district estate, but his conditions were not so unreasonable as to force her to change her plans. She ordered Binnie to prepare for the trip.

"Why we got to go there, Miss Micaela?" the maid

protested in a whining voice. She disliked Mont L'Eveque every bit as much as her mistress did.

"Cheer up," Micaela exhorted. "It will only be a short visit. We won't even be staying overnight."

"That's good."

"And if all goes well, it may be the last time we will ever have to journey there."

"That's just fine with me," Binnie replied.

While Binnie was gathering a few necessary items for the trip, Micaela went to the safe in her bedroom and searched for the letter Dulac had written to Celestin which she intended to take with her.

My trump card she thought as she tucked it into her bag.

The October rains had been unusually heavy throughout northeastern France, and the carriage in which Micaela was riding got bogged down in mud several times en route to the Oise district, so that she and Binnie arrived at the château much later than originally planned.

Instead of being relegated to the guest house, as she fully expected to be, this time Micaela was put in a chamber directly above the baron's study, reached by a winding stone staircase enclosed in one of the four turrets. Micaela did not relish the idea of being so close to where her father-in-law spent so much time. Another drawback to her quarters was that they lacked a satisfactory room for Binnie, and as a result, the maid had to be housed some distance from her mistress. However, Micaela was too grateful for being in the château with her two younger children to voice any complaints.

A servant brought Micaela word that she might lunch with the family in the main dining hall if she wished, but she declined the invitation, electing to eat in her room and asking that her sons, who were occupied with their tutor at the time of her arrival, be permitted to dine with her.

Much to her amazement, the baron did not deny her request for the boys to join her, and both Alfred and Gaston, looking rather solemn and unhappy appeared at her door for the meal. During the course of the luncheon they aired many of the same complaints and grievances about life at the château that they had expressed before.

"Grandpapa doesn't allow me to do my sketching," Gaston said, displaying his latest work, which had been accomplished without the baron's knowledge.

"What does he have against sketching?" she asked, distressed to think that anyone would try to suppress his artistic gifts.

"He thinks it's a frivolous pastime, unfit for boys of my station," Gaston replied.

"Grandpapa is afraid he'll run off to Paris to art school," Alfred offered.

"He is, is he?" Micaela remarked.

"He's threatening to send me to military school," Alfred announced. "And he won't let me ride any more."

Micaela was appalled by such news. "Won't let you ride?" she repeated.

"He's afraid I'll try to run away from here the way Tin-Tin did from that horrible military school," Alfred explained.

"I hate it here, Mama," Gaston said, leaning toward his mother and putting his arms around her. "Why can't we come to live with you, too, like Tin-Tin?"

"I'm trying every way I can, darlings, to have you both with me," she replied. "Unfortunately, the laws do not favor your mother. I don't have the necessary control over the situation, but I am struggling very hard to get it. You must believe me. When I do, you and Alfred may come to Paris and live with me."

"Frankly, Mama, it can't be too soon for me," Alfred sighed.

"Me, either," Gaston added.

After lunch, when the boys had gone off to their studies and Micaela was alone, she heard a soft knock at the door.

"Who is it?" she called out.

"Celestin."

It was their first contact since she arrived. Surprised, Micaela rose and opened the door inviting him inside.

Entering somewhat hesitantly, Celestin stared at Micaela and said, "Well, you're looking quite well."

"Thank you," she replied coolly. "You're looking well yourself." It was not entirely true. Although he retained much of his youthful good looks, he was thin and pale and had a decidedly haggard air about him.

"How is Tin-Tin?" he asked.

"Fine. Enjoying Paris to the utmost."

"So I've heard."

"Really? From whom?" Micaela wondered who the spies carrying such reports to him might be.

"No one in particular," he answered evasively.

"The boy *is* a bit of a rake, I must admit," she chuckled, positive that the informer was the Marquis de Anthieul once again. Tin-Tin had mentioned encountering him at the Club des Étrangers.

"There are other purposes to life besides the relentless pursuit of pleasure," Celestin said. "I want my son to be aware of them."

A trace of a scowl crossed her brow. "Did you come here to reproach me about Tin-Tin?" she demanded.

"No. I came simply to pay my respects."

"I see." She nodded skeptically.

"And to give you this," he added, removing a crumpled piece of fabric from his pocket. When he smoothed it out, Micaela saw that it was an elaborate depiction of a bowl of chrysanthemums, meticulously executed in needlepoint.

"It's lovely," she remarked unenthusiastically. His expertise at the various needlecrafts had never appealed to her.

"Usually I prefer more vigorous scenes, but I thought flowers suited you better."

"Better than what? The cavalry?" she quipped, referring to his predilection for cavalry scenes in his needlepoint.

"I intended it as a sort of peace offering."

"Really?" She stared curiously at the design, feeling both admiration for the skill with which it had been executed and annoyance that he might expect something so inconsequential to smooth over their long-standing grievances.

"Yes," he replied. "And as an apology for any wrongs that I might have done you in the past."

"Such as?" For the first time she realized that over the years there had been too many wrongs, too many injuries, for which nothing could compensate, certainly not a feeble apology in the form of a piece of needle-point. The real issues were far greater, and she would not allow them to be minimized or brushed aside.

"Well, I don't really want to be specific," he hedged. Then, seeing that he had failed to placate her, he decided to change the subject. "I suppose you know why the baron agreed to meet with you?"

"I know why *I* want to meet with *him*."

"About his cutting Tin-Tin out of his will, no doubt?"

Impatient with him and thinking he was behaving in an overly coy fashion, she snapped, "You know perfectly well that's what it's about. Naturally, I wish I could avoid a direct confrontation with the baron. I'd much prefer to express my wishes in this matter to you and have you act as spokesman with your father, but I know all too well how futile that would be. After so many years I've finally learned."

"I'm sorry—"

"You're always sorry," she interrupted sharply, cutting him off. "That's the trouble. There are only so many times a person is permitted to be sorry. After that, apologies are meaningless."

"I suppose you're right," he conceded. "Do you remember, years ago, before our reconciliation in Geneva, when I wrote you from Mignot and told you I was going to do my best to overcome my weaknesses? Well, ever since then I've been trying, but I'm afraid I haven't been very successful. But to get back to Tin-Tin and the baron's will . . ."

"Yes, let's do that," she encouraged, not wishing to rehash the past.

"I want you to know that I tried to change his mind, tried to dissuade him from such an action—I really did—but I could do nothing."

"You have never been able to do anything as far as your father is concerned. That is why I have been forced to come here today to intercede in our son's behalf. Do you have any idea how devastating this is to Tin-Tin? Do you realize what a humiliating blow it deals to your son?"

"Yes, of course I do."

Unable to contain her irritation any longer, she cried, "If you do, then why on earth don't you do something about it? Why am I forced to be the one? He's your son, too. You are his father, for God's sake! It should be up to you to protect his rights. What have you been doing all these years? Why have you abdicated your role and left me responsible for everything? I'll tell you what you've been doing, you've been fiddling around with your silly needlepoint and your chessboard and your ridiculous obsession with your army days, thinking all the time of that Captain Dulac—" The words were out before she could stop them.

Celestin's pale face blanched slightly at her sudden mention of the fencing master. "Why do you bring Dulac into this?" he asked.

For a moment she was tempted to tell him about the letter but decided against it, feeling she might have greater need of that piece of information later, in her dealings with the baron. Ignoring the question and his baffled expression, she went on. "You've denied your responsibilities and have refused to be a father. You've refused to be a husband as well. You've refused to be a man." With that she took the piece of needlepoint with its many colored chrysanthemums and flung it at him.

"Micaela!" he gasped, stunned by her action.

"Don't 'Micaela' me!" she stormed. "Do you know whom you remind me of? All those silly, perfumed colonels in the time of Louis the Sixteenth, that's who!"

Bursting into tears of anger and frustration as well as of shame that she had lashed out at him in such a vicious way, Micaela turned from him and ran across the room, throwing herself across the bed.

Celestin made no attempt to go after her and comfort her. Instead, heading for the door, he said with surprising calm, "Sometimes there are things in our nature we cannot change, even if we want to."

She was still shedding soft, repentant tears when Binnie entered the room and announced that the baron had sent up a servant to inform Micaela that he now wished to see her in his study.

Pulling herself together with amazing strength and speed, Micaela prepared to meet her adversary of many years and prayed that the encounter with Celestin had not taken the edge off her determination and fighting spirit. This was one confrontation for which she would need all her resources and that she resolved would not end in defeat.

Rising from behind the huge rosewood desk, the baron greeted her in a reasonably polite manner, considering their mutual and long-standing antipathy.

"Thank you for coming to Mont L'Eveque, madame," he said.

"It's not with much pleasure that I have come here today," she replied, accepting the seat he proffered and adjusting the copious bustles of her dark green taffeta dress.

With a forced smile he remarked, "Have you ever come here with any pleasure?"

There was a huge bowl of out-of-season fruit on the desk, each piece a prize specimen of its type. Gallantly he passed the bowl to her, but she refused.

"I have not come here to enjoy your fruit, sir."

"Ah, but you must," he insisted. "At least try a few of my cherries. They are so plump and juicy. Celestin adores them. I grew them myself from dwarf trees I cultivated in my greenhouse."

She ignored his deliberate interjection and continued.

"I have come here in behalf of my eldest son, whose rights and welfare are very important to me."

"As indeed they should be," he agreed, absentmindedly plucking a cherry from the bowl and placing it on the sill of an open window. A blue jay quickly swooped down, snapped it in its beak, and flew away. The baron smiled.

Anxious not to waste time, she came right to the point. "Surely you can't be serious about disinheriting Tin-Tin of all that is rightfully his by birth?"

"I assure you, madame, I have never been more serious in my life."

"It's a despicable thing to do, if you ask me!" she blurted out. "The most despicable thing you've ever done!"

He grinned smugly. "I rather expected you to say something like that."

"Punish *me,* if you feel compelled to punish someone, but do not make my sons the victims of your wrath and vindictiveness."

"On the contrary. My so-called wrath and vindictiveness have not been taken out on Tin-Tin because of you, as you accuse me of having done, but because of certain acts committed by the youth himself. He has seen fit to embarrass me by running away from school and thereby forfeiting a career in the military and choosing to live the life of a profligate and wastrel in Paris—albeit with your sanction, encouragement, and sponsorship. I assure you that is the sole reason for my actions. If he makes such choices, then he must be prepared to suffer the consequences. In this life, madame, we must all take responsibility for our actions."

"What a cruel and vengeful nature you have, Baron Joseph," she said with barely concealed contempt.

"I simply mete out justice," he declared blandly, "undistorted by emotion."

". . . and an ice-cold heart," she added. "If, indeed, you have any heart at all."

He shrugged. "Say what you wish. It will change nothing. Nothing at all."

"If you are so adamant, why did you ask me here today?"

"Because there are other matters to discuss. First of all, I must know whether you intend to pursue a divorce here in France despite your unsuccessful attempts in your own country."

"Yes," she answered without hesitation.

"You do?" he replied calmly, as though asking her to reconsider.

"Yes, I do," she affirmed emphatically.

"You realize, of course, that such an undertaking would be absolutely futile?"

"I realize no such thing."

"Well, I can assure you it will be. The grounds would have to be extraordinary."

"My lawyer and I believe we have such grounds." Saint-Avid had not been nearly so positive as she sounded at the moment, but then, he didn't know of Dulac's letter to Celestin and its implications, either.

"Really?" he scoffed.

"Yes. You see, sir, a certain piece of evidence has recently fallen into my hands."

The baron was unable to conceal his surprise. "Evidence? What sort of evidence?"

"A letter."

"May I know more?" He could scarcely contain his enormous curiosity.

"More?"

"Yes. The contents of this letter and by whom it was written."

She reached down into the high bosom of her dress and produced the letter from Dulac. "You may read it for yourself. But be warned, sir, that this is merely a copy. The original is in my lawyer's safe." She felt it was necessary to deceive the baron in this way for fear that otherwise he might try to destroy the letter once he got his hands on it.

Glancing at her dubiously a moment, he took the letter, unfolded it, and began to read. Almost at once he recognized the potentially damaging nature of its contents, even though the author, whom he was quite sure was Dulac, was guarded in what he wrote. His hands trembling, he declared, "This letter is a fraud! A fraud!"

"I can assure you it is not," she replied.

Leaping to his feet, his face scarlet and the veins of his thin neck pulsating, he cried, "Of all the devilish schemes you have concocted, this is the most contemptible! I did not think that even you would sink to such depths! This is the vilest kind of blackmail!"

"Call it what you will, sir," she said, unfazed by his outrage and indignation.

"Surely you would not destroy the lives of your sons by allowing a letter of this nature to be introduced as evidence in court?"

"My eldest son is disinherited and therefore no longer a person of importance. Who knows what measures you might invoke against my two younger sons? I feel it is well worth the risk to put such a document on public record."

The baron cast about desperately for some line of defense. "What about your friends? A scandalous divorce could ruin your reputation and social standing in Paris. We all know how important your position in society is to you. Think, too, how it would reflect on Tin-Tin."

"I am confident that my friends would understand," she replied nonchalantly. "They are quite sophisticated. I don't believe for a moment that they would desert me, regardless of the potential scandal of a divorce and certain revelations made about my husband during the proceedings."

"Oh, you are shameless!" the baron cried, slapping the desk. "Shameless!"

"Say whatever you like. Soon, when I am granted a divorce—and I have no doubt I will be—you will be free of me and I will be free of you. This distressing bond that has bound us together so unhappily for so long will be broken at last."

Shaking a long, bony finger at her, he accused, "You did not come here today in the interest of your son. That was merely a pretense. You came here to blackmail me."

"May I remind you, sir, that I came because you requested me to come?"

"You fabricated that letter in order to force me to reinstate Tin-Tin in my will. If I do that, you will drop everything, won't you? Well, I can assure you, madame, that I will not be blackmailed! Never! Do you hear me? Never!"

Despite her determined efforts to remain unper
turbed by her father-in-law's outbursts, Micaela later
found herself deeply disturbed and suffering from an
excruciating headache. She had come to Mon
L'Eveque expecting the worst, and she had not been
disappointed. If anything, the confrontation had ex
ceeded her most dreaded expectations. She had fully
anticipated the showdown with the baron, but not the
one with Celestin. Somehow, peculiarly, the encounter
with him, though far less dramatic, upset her more.
She had struck out angrily at him for things that, she
realized, he could not help, and she sincerely regretted
her actions.

Unhappy over her mistress's suffering, Binnie
dipped a handkerchief in cologne and tied it in a tight
band around Micaela's head, an old Louisiana headache remedy.

"See what happens when you get yourself all riled
up?" the maid chided. "I knew it was no good coming
here. I just knew it."

"It couldn't be avoided."

"I hope you done finished what you came for so we
can go home."

"The man is a demon," Micaela declared, referring
to the baron. "A devil!"

"I done told you that already," Binnie muttered.
"Over and over."

To add to Micaela's anguish and misery, dark and
ominous clouds suddenly filled the late-afternoon sky
and culminated in a violent and steady downpour that
showed no sign of abating. The road to Paris would
be virtually a swamp, and she had no desire to make
the long trip under such conditions, especially at night.
Much to her dismay, Micaela realized, gazing out the
turret window of the guest room, that she would be
forced to spend the night in the detested château.

"Damn!" she swore aloud, startling Binnie, and
clutched her throbbing head.

When Micaela awoke in the morning, she saw that
the rain had stopped, although the sky was still cloudy
and gray. Crawling out of bed and ringing for Binnie

she was determined to return to Paris even if the carriage sank in mud up to its axles.

"Go to the gardener's cottage and inform the coachman to prepare for our departure," she instructed Binnie when the maid appeared.

"Yes, ma'am," the black woman replied, also anxious to leave the château.

When she had gone, Micaela, impelled by a strange, intuitive foreboding, turned the key in the door and locked it; then, still in her yellow silk robe and negligee, she sat on the edge of the bed and idly brushed her hair.

A few minutes later she was startled to hear the key fall on the stone floor; apparently it had tumbled out of the keyhole spontaneously. Puzzled, she shrugged, dismissed it from her mind, and went back to brushing her hair. A moment or two passed. Then the door flew open, and the baron, looking wild-eyed and disheveled, stood on the threshold. He had his own key and had obviously dislodged hers when he attempted to enter the room.

Micaela gasped and clutched her robe tightly around her. "What do you want?" she demanded. "You have no right bursting in on me without knocking."

Indicating the rose-velvet-covered prie-dieu beside the bed, over the top of which her rosary was draped, he directed, "Kneel, madame, and commend yourself to God."

Shocked, Micaela repeated blankly, "Commend myself to God? What on earth are you talking about?"

Locking the door behind him with the same key with which he had let himself in, he announced, "You are about to die."

Stunned, Micaela dropped the hairbrush and reached out to the bedpost for support.

"You must be mad!" she exclaimed.

"I have endured all I am going to endure from you," he declared, extracting a pair of pistols from his belt and aiming both barrels directly at her. "I will not permit you to humiliate and disgrace my family any longer. I have taken all I can. The end has come for you. Implore God to forgive your sins and be grateful that I am granting you such a privilege before you die."

"You are truly a madman! Get out of here and leave me alone, or I shall be forced to scream for help."

"You will not scream. You will do as I say." He advanced toward her in a half stagger, half strut.

"Get out of here," she ordered, more angry than frightened.

"Madame, you are quickly exhausting my patience," he warned, shaking the pistols at her menacingly.

"Get out of here!" she cried, her voice rising steadily. "Get out of here!"

"Do as I say!" he commanded, his dark eyes full of rage.

Micaela emitted a piercing scream, crouched before a chest at the foot of the bed, and defensively crossed her arms over her chest.

"Do as I say," he repeated.

Almost on the verge of hysteria, she pleaded, "Go away and leave me alone. Please. Remember, I am the mother of your grandsons. I beg you . . ."

"Pray I said!" he shouted at her.

She tossed her head defiantly. "No!"

"Very well, then, you leave me no choice." With that he squinted, took careful aim, squeezed the trigger, and discharged one of the pistols.

The bullet struck Micaela's right hand, which was covering the left side of her chest directly above her heart, and shattered several fingers before it passed into the soft breast tissue beneath. Almost at once a stream of blood began to pour down the front of her robe.

Desperate and terrified, she dove for the safety of a nearby alcove, but the baron pursued her, and panting and sweating profusely, fired again.

The second bullet struck her chest but was stopped by a rib from penetrating any deeper.

With the first pistol still smoking and filling the room with the acrid, pungent odor of gunpowder the baron leveled the weapon directly at her head and took careful aim. Micaela's screams for help were drowned out

by the ear-shattering blast of the third shot, which, by
some miracle, went wild and struck the wall a fraction
of an inch above her.

Her negligee and robe sopping with blood, Micaela
struggled to keep from fainting. Despite the agonizing,
searing pain in her breast and mangled hand, she
somehow managed to reach the door, but as she frantically turned the knob, she realized it was locked.

"You cannot escape me," the baron warned, stringy
locks of white hair clinging to his sweaty forehead. "I
have the key safely in my pocket."

Taking great care to aim properly this time, he
raised the second weapon and pointed it at her.

"Please, dear God, no!" she shrieked, and as she
fell to the floor hoping to evade the next shot, she
felt a cold, hard metal object beneath one knee. Gripping it with her uninjured hand, she realized it was the
key that had earlier fallen out of the lock.

In a lightning move she rose, inserted the key in the
lock, turned it, and once the door was open, threw
herself out into the hall and down the flight of spiral
stairs. Blood splattered the surrounding walls as she
rolled to the landing below.

At the foot of the staircase her unconscious body
nearly collided with Binnie, who was responding to her
mistress's frantic cries for help.

The black woman's shrieks summoned Celestin and
some of the other servants to the turret stairs, with
Jeanne and Madame Miró close behind. Fortunately,
Alfred and Gaston were still sleeping in another part
of the château and were not disturbed by the commotion.

At the sight of Micaela lying bloody and unconscious in Binnie's arms, Celestin recoiled in horror and
covered his face.

"Micaela!" he cried. "My God, Micaela! What's
happened? Oh, my God, what has happened?"

Before anyone could say another word, a loud pistol
report thundered from the room at the top of the
stairs.

"Oh, Lordy!" Binnie wailed.

Celestin gasped but managed to summon up enough

courage to dash up the winding stairs. Cautiously entering Micaela's chamber, he saw his father slumped in a chair a smoking pistol gripped in his hand.

"Papa!" he cried, running to the old baron.

"Strawberries . . ." the baron croaked in a nearly inaudible whisper, a strange smile playing over his thin lips. "I always want my Celestin to have strawberries . . ."

And with that he tumbled lifeless out of the chair and collapsed on the cold stone floor.

44

WHEN MICAELA AWAKENED and focused her eyes on the white wall opposite the bed, barren except for a single crucifix, for a few confused and fuzzy moments she thought she might have been back in the infirmary at the Ursuline Convent. And when a nun in a white habit entered with a basin of water and announced that she was going to bathe her, Micaela's confusion was further heightened by the uncanny resemblance the sister bore to Sister Lucille.

The nun smiled, placing the basin on the night stand next to the bed. "And how are we feeling today, Baroness?" Going to the windows, she opened the curtains and allowed the morning sun to stream into the room, prompting Micaela to shade her eyes with her hand against the bright light.

As she attempted to sit up, a sudden, excruciating pain shot through her chest like a fiery lance, and she was forced to bite her lips to stifle a cry.

"Let me help you, Baroness," the nun said placing a pillow behind her back.

Had the nun really called her Baroness? Micaela, despite her confusion, was sure she had heard correctly. It was the second time in a matter of a few moments that the nun had addressed her by that title. A myriad of questions flooded her mind. If she were really a baroness, then it followed that Celestin must be a baron. And if that was true, what had happened to Baron Joseph? She dreaded to speculate what the answers might be.

Micaela was glad the nun had opened the curtains. The sudden burst of sunlight helped erase the last vestiges of the horrifying nightmare that kept recurring whenever she slept. Once more the enraged baron was standing over her, a pair of pistols aimed at her head, a look of hatred and steely determination on his half-crazed face. He pulled the trigger and fired. There was a loud report, a puff of acrid smoke, the sudden, searing pain that took her breath away, the blood gushing down the front of her nightgown.

Overcome by the emotion that the memory of the dream evoked, she closed her eyes, shuddered, and began to weep.

"Now now, Baroness," the nun soothed, patting her sympathetically. "Everything is all right. You mustn't cry."

The sister's words were reassuring but failed to stop either the stabbing pain Micaela felt with every breath or the relentless throbbing in the bandaged hand beneath the covers.

When the nun finished bathing her and combing her hair, the doctor appeared. An intense, businesslike man, he carefully lifted the blood-caked linen bandages from her chest and inspected the wounds underneath.

Unable to look at her injuries, Micaela turned her head aside and asked apprehensively, "Is anything wrong, Doctor?"

"I'm terribly sorry, Baroness," he said apologetically, shaking his head.

"About what?"

The physician sighed. "Sorry we were unable to remove the bullet from your breast. We probed and probed but couldn't get it out. However, it's my feeling that this wound will heal satisfactorily, anyway, whether we remove it or not."

"Are you quite sure?"

"Yes, I am," he assured her, turning his attention to

her right hand. Carefully he unwrapped the linen strips that bound it and exposed the mangled flesh.

For a second Micaela steeled herself and managed to glance down at her hand. When she realized that most of two fingers were missing, each remaining stump throbbing in unison with every beat of her rapid pulse, she uttered a cry of despair. "Oh, no! My hand . . . my hand!"

"Fortunately, we were able to save much more of your hand than we expected," the doctor told her. "For a time we feared it might be necessary to amputate the entire lower arm."

"Oh, no!" Micaela gasped, tears streaming down her cheeks.

"You must be strong, Baroness," the doctor admonished. "And brave. Years ago I was a surgeon with the Grand Army. Your wounds are slight compared with what I saw then."

There were many questions Micaela wished to ask him, but he was gone before she had the opportunity to organize her thoughts.

Later in the day Tin-Tin burst into the room with an armful of flowers. He attempted to embrace her, but Micaela cried out in pain when he touched her, and he released her at once.

"I'm sorry, Mama," he apologized. "Please forgive me. I didn't think . . ."

"It's all right, darling," she said, forcing a smile. "I'm happy to see you."

"How are you, Mama?"

"The doctor tells me I'm getting along all right."

"You're looking well. Really you are, Mama."

Leaning close to him, she grasped his hand in her free one and said quietly, "Listen, Tin-Tin, you must tell me about your grandfather. Everyone is suddenly addressing me as Baroness and I'm wondering why."

He lowered his extravagantly long lashes over his dark eyes. "Don't you know?" he asked sadly.

Micaela shook her head, her eyes imploring him to tell her more. "No," she murmured.

"Grandpa is dead. After firing at you and thinking he'd killed you, he took his own life."

"Oh, my God!"

"Papa is the new baron."

"How is your father taking all this?" she wondered anxiously, knowing the low tolerance Celestin had for stress. "I have had no word from him."

"Papa has had a complete nervous collapse," he announced solemnly. "Grandmama has arranged for him to be cared for in a private sanitarium."

"Poor Celestin," she sighed feeling a twinge of guilt for the way she had attacked him on the day of the shooting. "I must go see him. Poor, poor Celestin."

"You can't, Mama," he cautioned. "Not yet. Not until you're stronger."

"I know I'll be fine soon. I'm strong now. I will not be defeated by a few bullet wounds. If they would stop giving me that awful medicine which fogs my mind and turns me into a sleepwalker, I'd be much better. The pain isn't so bad that I can't tolerate it."

"Dear Mama," Tin-Tin murmured, kissing her forehead. "You've always been so brave."

"I wasn't always. I had to learn to be, you know. Necessity is the mother of much of what we turn out to be. In any case," she went on, "the part I'm concerned about now is the possible scandal. Has there been anything in the newspapers as yet? The medicine they give me makes me lose all track of time."

"I'm afraid so," he replied, shaking his head. "They're full of speculation about Grandpapa's motives for his actions. The papers have printed some of the most slanderous things—truly rotten. I've been trying my best to keep them from Grandmama and her aunt, but it's difficult with the servants all talking and everyone asking questions. I hear the news has already reached America."

"What are the stories they're printing?"

"It's awful, Mama. They're saying that Grandpapa shot you because of a lover you had."

"Nonsense."

"They're saying he killed himself because he couldn't bear the disgrace he felt you brought on the family."

"We must stop any more tales right away."

"But how can we?"

"We can do anything we make up our minds to do," she asserted. "Enough of this business. Tell me, Tin-Tin, how are your brothers? I've been worried about them."

"They're terribly upset, naturally. Alfred is taking the whole thing much better than Gaston."

"That's to be expected. After all, he's older."

"Not just that, Mama. The same day the tragedy occurred, poor Gaston found a favorite blue jay, which he had been feeding for weeks dead beneath the window of Grandpapa's study. He was most distraught."

A few days later Micaela persuaded the doctor to release her from the clinic so that she might return home.

"I have a very capable maid," she assured him. "She can care for me as competently as the sisters here."

"But there is a danger of a delayed infection with that bullet still in your breast, Baroness," he argued.

"If there is even the slightest problem, Doctor, I promise you that I shall return at once."

"Very well, Baroness, on that condition I will allow you to go. But you must understand that it is not with my approval."

"I understand, Doctor," she said with a smile, and prepared to leave at once.

Micaela's first desire was to visit Celestin at the sanitarium, which she had learned from Tin-Tin was on the outskirts of Paris. Jeanne had tried to prevent anyone from discovering Celestin's whereabouts, but Tin-Tin had obtained the name of the institution and its location from Madame Miró. Before departing for there, however, Micaela insisted on stopping at the offices of the city's leading publisher, despite Tin-Tin's protests, and stormed into his cubicle with a copy of the newspaper containing one of the offending stories.

"How dare you print such scurrilous filth about me and my family?" she demanded.

Confronted by the subject of the lurid account, the

stunned publisher attempted to defend himself. "I'm sorry, Baroness, but it is the obligation of a newspaper to give the public the news," he said nervously.

"I agree, but this is not news." She shook her bandaged right fist at him menacingly, her red curls swirling about her face. "It is vicious rumor, conjecture, gossip whatever—but it is not *news*."

"I'm sorry, but—"

"If I see any more of this rubbish in your paper, you may be certain that I shall contact my attorney and bring suit against you, which will put you and your publication out of business."

Confident that she had successfully intimidated the publisher from printing further stories about the incident, she proceeded on her way.

"I'm sure he will pass the word along to his cohorts and we will have no more trouble," Micaela said to Tin-Tin as she settled back in the carriage for the ride to the secluded sanitarium.

When she arrived and announced that she was the Baroness de Pontalba, she was reluctantly taken to see her husband. Unlike Micaela or his father, Celestin had suffered no physical wounds from the tragic event, but he looked far worse than if he had.

As he and Micaela walked about the well-tended grounds, she noted that he shuffled along the gravel path between neatly trimmed boxwood hedges with the gait of an old man, his head bowed, his shoulders drooping, a far cry from his former bearing as a cavalry officer. He was pale and wan and so thin that he almost appeared severely ill. A burly male attendant was assigned to watch him at all times because, unknown to Micaela, the doctors at the institution believed he might be suicidal.

"If you don't mind, sir I would like to speak to my husband alone," she said to the chaperoning attendant who followed close behind.

"I am under strict orders, Baroness, never to leave the baron's side," the attendant replied.

"I'm giving you new orders to leave us, and I will take complete responsibility."

"You must speak to the baron's doctors first, Baroness."

"Leave us, please. At once," she repeated firmly.

"Very well, Baroness." The attendant nodded and withdrew.

When they were alone, Micaela took Celestin's bony arm and steered him to a nearby bench. He seemed so passive and withdrawn, she felt he could have been led anywhere by anyone.

"Where is Tin-Tin?" he asked. "Did he come with you?"

"Yes," she replied. "He is waiting in the carriage."

"I want to see him."

"He will be here later. First, you and I must talk."

"You know, Micaela," he said in a listless voice, "I cannot believe you are here. I cannot even believe you are alive, for that matter. I cannot believe all that has happened. It overwhelms me. It is too much. My mind cannot accept it. I had been thinking that they were lying to me, that you must surely be dead. After all those shots . . ."

"I assure you I am very much alive. Badly wounded, but alive."

"I suppose you have heard about poor Papa?"

"Yes," she answered quietly. "Tin-Tin told me."

Covering his face with his hands, he began to weep like a desperate, heartbroken child, his body shaking with uncontrollable sobs. "Poor Papa," he sobbed. "Poor, poor Papa . . ."

45

NORMALLY NOT ONE to be defeated or even seriously disheartened by the various traumas of life, Micaela slowly began to realize that the events of that fateful October morning at Mont L'Eveque had taken a heavy toll. The old baron's suicide, Celestin's mental breakdown, and her own narrow escape from death had left her badly shaken and bewildered. She did not grasp the full impact of the tragedy until she had been back in her house in Paris for a few weeks. What had once been a pleasant, peaceful home became, inexplicably intolerable to her.

"I don't understand it," she said to Binnie one day. "Suddenly I cannot bear to live in this house."

"Why not?" the maid asked with a puzzled frown. "You never used to mind it."

"I don't know. Somehow I feel as if it's too small, as if the walls are closing in on me."

"Small?" Binnie repeated incredulously. *"This* house?"

"I feel as if I need more room, a different place, perhaps. It's almost as if there are phantoms here from which I must escape."

"You sure are talkin' nonsense, Miss Micaela," Binnie replied, shaking her head in dismay. "I ain't seen no phantoms."

In an attempt to combat her uneasiness and restlessness, Micaela went on a sudden shopping spree, contacting every real estate agent in the city and insisting on seeing his grandest mansions. To humor her, one agent showed her the magnificent three-hundred-and-eighty-five-room mansion built by Louis XIV for the Duc du Maine; much to his astonishment, she decided to purchase it.

"Are you sure this place is for you, Baroness?" the agent exclaimed, trying to hide his disbelief.

"Quite sure," she affirmed, and asked him to draw up the papers as soon as possible.

Although the enormous house had been badly neglected and thus had fallen into disrepair it was opulently appointed and much of its grandeur was intact.

"Mama, I know you are a baroness now, but don't you think this is carrying things a bit far?" Tin-Tin protested when he saw the house for the first time.

"No. Not at all," she replied, so excited by her purchase that she couldn't wait for her two younger sons to see it, too.

As soon as the doctor thought it advisable, she sent for them to come and live with her in Paris. Since the baron was dead, there was no longer any opposition to such a move. Jeanne relinquished the boys without a fight.

"Is this where we're going to live, Mama?" Alfred asked, astonished when he saw the size of the dwelling.

"It looks more like a hotel than a house to me," was Gaston's opinion.

"When I get it fixed up, it will be glorious, boys," she declared. "Wait and see."

"*If* you get it fixed up," Tin-Tin put in. "It will be frightfully expensive to restore it to its original condition."

"Since when did *you* start worrying whether or not something was expensive?" she laughed turning to her eldest son.

The three boys wandered up and down the endless corridors and stairs, exploring the multitude of rooms. Hours later they were certain they still had not inspected all of them.

Shaking her head, Binnie said, "I declare, Miss Micaela, I don't know what you was thinkin' when you bought this place."

"I was thinking that I am now not only the Baroness de Pontalba but also one of the richest women in Paris as well," Micaela replied. "As such, I must have a residence in keeping with my position. That's what I was thinking."

"I never thought I'd hear you talkin' this way," Binnie remarked unhappily.

"Your social position could be easily maintained with a much smaller house," Tin-Tin reminded her.

"Perhaps," she conceded, "but I like the challenge this mansion represents. Restoring it to livable conditions won't be easy."

As soon as she took possession of the house, Micaela wrote to Patrick, telling him of her fabulous purchase and requesting his professional assistance in remodeling the mansion. As far as she was concerned, she said, he was the only architect in the world with both the imagination and the practicality to accomplish the restoration she required. She was careful to assure him that she expected to pay his current fees in

full as well as his expenses while in Paris if he undertook the job and would underwrite his travel costs to
come to Paris to give her an estimate.

Sealing the letter, she said to Binnie. "I'm sure he
won't come, but it's worth a try."

"You just can't get that man out of your system,
can you, Miss Micaela?" the maid responded in dismay.

"That's impertinent," Micaela snapped.

"Well, it's true, ain't it?" Binnie returned, flouncing
out of the room.

Much to Micaela's surprise, she received a reply
from Patrick in which he told her that he was planning
a voyage to England in the very near future.

"When my business is finished there, I will come to
Paris and look over this great house you have purchased," he wrote.

Micaela anxiously waited out the time, which
seemed like an eternity, until he finally arrived at the
house on the Rue du Houssaie.

Racing down the staircase and flinging herself into
his arms, she cried, "Patrick! You've come at last! Oh,
Patrick! . . . Patrick!"

"Micaela . . ." he murmured pressing his lips into
her loose-flowing hair.

"Oh, dear . . ." She looked behind him to make
certain he was alone. "Is Emily with you?"

"No," he replied. "I couldn't persuade her to come
with me, although it's been many years since she's
seen her family in England. One of these days I'm
sure she'll make the trip. She's still terrified of sea
voyages."

Later, as they rode in her carriage to the Duc du
Maine's former residence, Micaela asked him, "Did
Emily know you were coming to Paris?"

"Yes, I told her."

"Did you say you were coming to see me?"

"I don't know if I was that specific."

"If you did tell her, would she be upset?" Micaela
persisted.

"Upset?"

"By the fact that you were calling on me?"

"No. You see, Emily is much too English and is therefore class-conscious in her thinking. It would never occur to her to suspect that anything improper could go on between a French baroness and an Irish hod carrier."

"Well, you're here strictly on business, anyway," she said, her lips forming a playful smile.

"Am I?" He grasped her chin between his thumb and forefinger.

"Aren't you?"

"Perhaps," he chuckled, kissing her lightly. "But I do intend to combine business with a little bit of pleasure."

After they reached the mansion Micaela personally conducted him on a tour, but before it was half completed, he called it to a halt. "I refuse to see another room," he announced.

Micaela was stunned and a little disappointed. She knew he was perfectly capable of spending hours tirelessly inspecting important buildings, cathedrals, and museums. If he wasn't overwhelmed by her new purchase, she at least expected him to be reasonably impressed by its size.

"But why? I don't understand . . ."

"Because you've been a terrible fool, that's why." He turned on her almost angrily. "You have bought what is undoubtedly the world's greatest white elephant. You must have been mad. Unless you are planning to open a hotel, I suggest you forget about remodeling this place. It would be absolutely impossible. You couldn't make it habitable even if you spent your entire fortune on it."

Feeling helpless and dumbfounded, Micaela asked, "What do you propose I do, then?"

"I suggest that you dismantle and remove all the valuable fittings and trim and decorations. They are the only items worth saving. Then you should demolish the house and build yourself one that has reasonable proportions."

Aghast, she repeated, "Demolish it?"

"Yes." He nodded firmly. "This is a museum, a palace, a public building a hotel, but never a home. It can never be made livable for you."

At first Micaela was indignant at his proposals, but later, when she reconsidered what he had said, she was forced to admit that he was indeed correct. It had been a foolish, impulsive purchase, undertaken during a period of great turmoil and upset in her life.

In less than a week Patrick had brought in, with Micaela's consent, an army of wreckers who leveled the grand edifice to the ground, but not before all the better doors, windows, hardware, shutters, chandeliers, mantels, paneling, ceilings, and stairways had been carefully removed, cataloged, and crated.

While the demolition was under way, Patrick labored day and night on plans for a new house for Micaela—also grand and elegant, but considerably more modest in size—to be constructed on the property she had purchased on the fashionable Rue du Faubourg St. Honoré.

Before Patrick could complete his work, he suffered a recurrence of his former eye problem and was forced to abandon the project and turn it over to another architect, a man named Visconti. Much to Patrick's and Micaela's mutual dismay, he departed for England soon after to undergo treatment for the nagging condition.

"I'll be back as soon as I can," he promised, holding her in his arms, his blue eyes now hidden behind smoked lenses.

In contrast to her working relationship with Patrick, her meetings with Visconti were stormy, perhaps influenced more by her disappointment over Patrick's leaving and his inability to participate in the construction than by any real deficiencies on the part of the other architect.

Eventually the new house was finished, complete with formal gardens and fountains in the rear, stables, and a carriage house filled with an array of coaches and special horses, including a night horse that was used solely for evening excursions to the theater, the opera, and other social events.

"Now I must have a housewarming to end all housewarmings!" Micaela declared excitedly as she went from room to room, especially admiring the elegant fittings that had been salvaged from the Duc du Maine's mansion and skillfully integrated into the overall design of the new house.

"If I know you, Miss Micaela, you will," Binnie predicted.

"And Mr. Lynch will be the guest of honor, if he is well enough to make the trip from London."

Recently he had written that his eyes were much improved after undergoing a new treatment.

"What about Master Celestin?" Binnie asked.

"I shall invite him, naturally."

Several months ago Celestin had been discharged from the private sanitarium. Following the advice of his doctors, he had not returned to Mont L'Eveque but had leased an apartment in Paris on the Rue du Malakoff, where he lived in near seclusion, except for a couple of servants, and occupied his days with needlework, books on military subjects, and chess.

From time to time Micaela called on him and brought him plants and other small gifts she hoped might brighten up his living quarters. Even though they were now legally separated, she still felt a great sense of responsibility toward him, generally overseeing his welfare and needs since his mental breakdown.

Fingering the lacy leaves of a luxuriant fern she had given him, which seemed to be thriving in his care, she remarked, "Well, Celestin, you seem to have inherited your father's green thumb."

"Yes, poor Papa," he said wistfully.

"Do you want to hear about my new house?" she asked, hoping to focus on a less gloomy subject.

"How is it coming along?" he inquired with only minimal interest.

"It's finished, and it is absolutely perfect."

"You must be very happy."

"Yes, I am, and I'm having a housewarming soon. I'd like you to come."

"Oh, I couldn't do that," he said, shaking his head.

"Why not?"

"There would be too many people."

Since the tragedy he rarely ventured from the apartment, except for occasional forays to the Cafe de Roy or outings with his sons. Even though Micaela was the one who still carried a bullet in her breast and had lost two fingers, the aftermath of the shootings seemed to have proved psychologically far more devastating to Celestin.

"You've always been more resilient," he remarked to her after she expressed her impatience with his gloominess and depression. "The most resilient woman I know. And the strongest."

"As I recently told Tin-Tin, I wasn't always so strong," she replied. "I've had to learn to be that way in order to survive."

When Patrick finally returned to Paris, claiming he no longer needed smoked glasses, Micaela began preparations for the housewarming party.

On the day when it was to take place, the capricious Paris weather presented clear skies and balmy temperatures.

That same afternoon there was a luncheon for all the workmen, artisans, and craftsmen involved with the construction of the house, over which Patrick genially presided, amusing the men with jokes and entertaining anecdotes while Micaela plied them with food and wine. She prayed the evening would be as successful. After the scandal of the shootings and her separation from Celestin, she hoped that this new house and the party to celebrate its completion would not only reestablish her as one of Paris's leading social figures but also portend a happier existence in the future.

"I hope nothing goes wrong," she confided to Binnie later as the maid was helping her into a new beige silk gown with a natural waistline and extended bustles that emphasized the hips, purchased from Lerot, the city's leading couturier.

"If it does, it does," the maid replied philosophically. "Don't do no good to worry about it."

At last darkness fell, and the new house, aglow with the soft, romantic light of Venetian lanterns strung about, was prepared to receive its guests. Red velvet carpets stretched from the street to the front entrance, flanked on either side by torch-bearing lackeys in immaculate black livery. Micaela stood at the top of the marble stairs, her three sons at her side, and greeted her visitors; they were announced by a major-domo who, before stating each name, struck his staff against the marble floor of the foyer. To Micaela's delight, the cream of Parisian society turned out, glittering with jewels, furs, and fine silks and satins. The guest list was quite varied and included members of the Bourse, a silk manufacturer from Lyons, a shipbuilder from Le Havre, a wine king from Bordeaux, several armorial Jews, a few Protestants, groups from the Catholic aristocracy and from both the Empire and the Royalist nobility, as well as the usual sprinkling of artists, writers, and musicians, whom Micaela particularly favored. Among the latter contingency were the author Balzac, who had dared to present life as it really was; the rather odd philosopher Alexis de Tocqueville, who had just recently toured the United States and returned extremely pessimistic about its future; the painters Delacroix and Corot; the famed violinist Paganini, who was rumored to have made a pact with the devil in order to play with such extraordinary skill and beauty; the dramatist Augustin Scribe, and the immensely popular Italian composer Gaetano Donizetti, whose tunes were on everyone's lips.

The elaborate ten-course dinner was followed by dancing, initiated by Micaela, who whirled over the highly polished floor of the magnificent new ballroom in the arms of her guest of honor.

"I must give you credit, lass," Patrick said as he nuzzled her while they were dancing. "This is quite a party you have gotten up."

"It's in your honor."

"In honor of what? My farewell?"

"I hope not," she said with an exaggerated pout.

Pleased that she regretted his leaving, he smiled and pulled her close to him.

The evening concluded in the vast formal gardens with a ballet performed by the corps of dancers from the Opéra. The presence of the lithe and graceful young ballerinas about the house fascinated Tin-Tin who pursued them avidly, while his brother Alfred discussed gold futures with a stockbroker from the Bourse. Gaston, still too young for romantic pursuits or business, roamed around making precise but rapid sketches of the house and the guests.

As the climax of the ballet a cage of white doves was released. The birds fluttered over the heads of the delighted guests and landed, cooing softly, in the branches of the trees.

The grand finale was a thrilling display of fireworks that exploded with brilliant flashes of color in the clear Parisian sky, ending with sparkling and sputtering replicas of the American and French flags.

It was dawn before the last guests finally departed and Patrick led Micaela off to bed, the perfect conclusion to what, in her opinion, had been an exciting and highly successful evening.

The vivid memory of their past lovemaking inflamed their senses and erased their fatigue, filling them with an intense and immediate desire for each other.

As Patrick took her in his arms, Micaela saw her own yearning reflected in his light blue eyes. A rush of languor seethed through her as his strong hands began to caress her smooth creamy shoulder, dipping down tantalizingly into the bodice of her gown but careful to be gentle with the injured breast.

His breathing accelerating, he unhooked her gown and slipped it off her shoulders, planting little nibbling kisses in the hollow of her throat and on her already taut pink nipples. Then he slid the dress over her gently round hips and removed the rest of her clothing, all the while cherishing her with his lips, his tingling caresses, his loving, steady gaze.

Trembling, she clasped him even closer and felt his hard, erect manhood pulsating against her. He swept her off her feet in one lithe motion and carried her to the bed. While she waited impatiently, longing for him to the point of frenzy, he cast off his own clothing and then joined her, cradling her tenderly. Her response was immediate and fierce as she threw her arms about him, her eager fingers digging into his muscular back. The urgency of their ardor quickly united them into one, their much-denied love desperately demanding fulfillment.

As he began to slide slowly in and out, Patrick whispered endearments and demands in her ear, but Micaela was too consumed by the overwhelming passion swelling within her to concentrate on the words he was saying. His mellow voice and musical brogue were like additional hands, extra fingers, another pair of lips, caressing her, exciting her, lifting her to ecstatic new heights.

Their stormy, tumultuous drives climbed to a peak and were about to erupt with an intensity that was deeper and more fulfilling than anything they had known before. She met each of his urgent thrusts with her own, rising higher on the waves of rapture, clinging to his tense, sweaty back, and crying in a husky, choked voice, "Oh, Patrick! Patrick! God, how I love it when we're together! How can I ever live without you? How can I? Tell me you love me, Patrick. Tell me! Please tell me!"

46

THE HOUSEWARMING HAD been a great success, and even though the architect Visconti received official credit for the imaginative design of her new residence, Micaela saw traces of Patrick's creative genius almost everywhere. These many reminders of her Irish lover intensified her longing for him and made her wish for more nights like the one they had spent together just before his departure for America.

Eventually, through drive and determination, Micaela managed to reestablish herself as one of Paris's leading social figures, overcoming both her physical injuries and the scandal and tragedy of Mont L'Eveque. Her dinner parties and balls were celebrated not only for the glittering guest list she assembled but also for the charm, spirit, and imagination she always displayed as hostess.

Despite her seemingly complete recovery from her wounds, Micaela was still haunted by specters of the ghastly event. On occasion the nightmarish scene was reenacted during her sleep and sent her screaming from her bed. Loud, unexpected noises jarred her severely and caused her to faint more than once. At other times the bullet fragments still lodged in her breast produced exquisite pain and tenderness, and the amputated digits, which she had learned to conceal cleverly by wearing gloves stuffed with cotton for the missing fingers throbbed unmercifully, especially when the weather was damp, and often robbed her of a night's sleep.

As for Celestin, he continued to live the life of a near recluse, seeing few people other than Micaela. Quiet, solemn, and mild-mannered, he had become increasingly introspective and seemed to have difficulty coping with the world beyond his immediate environment.

All three of the boys were rapidly approaching various stages of manhood. Gaston, whose main passion in life, so far, was art, longed to attend art school, but despite her patronage of the arts and her own artistic inclinations, Micaela couldn't make up her mind whether to permit him to enroll. He still seemed too young and innocent for such a bohemian environment.

Of the three, Alfred was the most practical-minded, and it was to him whom Micaela turned over the management of most of her business affairs, although she maintained a hand in all transactions he undertook. With Alfred in charge, she had more free time to pursue her other interests.

While Alfred was the most serious of the three boys, Tin-Tin continued to be the most frivolous and lighthearted, showing no inclination toward settling into a stable existence. His life was devoted to an ongoing whirl of parties, dances, gambling, drinking, chasing the ballet girls at the opera, and general carousing. Reports of his conduct eventually reached Celestin and greatly distressed him, although he tended to view the matter rather philosophically.

"I'm afraid our eldest son has become a bit of a playboy," he remarked to Micaela during one of her visits, after she had recounted Tin-Tin's latest exploits to him. Since the tragedy, they had remained on relatively amicable terms and rarely, if ever, spoke of it, maintaining a certain distance between them that belied their years of marriage.

"I'm confident he'll settle down one of these days," she assured him. "You'll see. There's nothing sadder or more pitiful than an aging playboy. I'm sure Tin-Tin is aware of that."

"I hope you're right," he sighed.

"I have to be," she declared.

In the late 1830s and early 1840s industrialization began to spread throughout France, producing, for the first time in the nation's history, a large working class. During the reign of Louis Philippe, who was nicknamed Citizen King because he favored the middle classes, the workers' discontent escalated day by day, threatening to overthrow the king and erupt in a violent revolution against the middle and upper classes. Many of the wealthy aristocrats—Micaela among them—feared that such a revolt might prove as bloody and devastating as that of 1789. Although it was close to a half century since the first Revolution, memories of the frenzied bloodbath were still sufficiently strong to cause the privileged classes some alarm.

When a workers' insurrection occurred during a week in June, Micaela took Alfred and Gaston and fled to London, where she planned to wait out the political strife in France. Tin-Tin stubbornly refused to accompany them, insisting that if there were going to be some excitement, he didn't want to miss it.

Micaela had not been in the British capital very long when she received a letter from her cousin Pierre in New Orleans. At first she assumed it was the usual inquiry as to their health and safety, and read it with little more than routine interest until she realized it contained some shocking news.

As you may have undoubtedly heard by now, Patrick Lynch and his wife recently decided to go to Baltimore by ship. After safely navigating the Florida Keys, their vessel was caught in an unexpected and terrible storm near Cape Hatteras and was wrecked on the shoals. Lynch's wife, as well as many of the other passengers, was drowned, despite his heroic efforts to save her—or so they say. His grief is said to be intense . . ."

Micaela could scarcely believe what she had read and scanned those lines a second time. Was Emily really dead and Patrick a widower?

At first she tried to take this news in stride, telling herself that too many years had passed and too much had happened in both their lives for this latest tragedy to affect their relationship, which she had long ago relegated to the status of an affair, with few expectations of anything more.

Nevertheless, barely two weeks after receiving Pierre's letter, Micaela ordered Binnie to begin packing her things.

"Packin'?" the maid said, astonished. "What for? Where we goin'?"

"To America," Micaela replied.

"America?" the maid repeated. "But we ain't been in London but a few months."

"What's that got to do with it?"

"Nothin', but I sure wish you'd make up your mind, Miss Micaela," Binnie complained.

"I have," Micaela declared. "Now get moving."

Part Five

47

MORE THAN FIFTEEN years had passed since
Micaela had last visited the United States. Polk was
now President, and America was on the brink of war
with Mexico. Just as America had changed, New Orleans, too, had undergone considerable revisions—not
all for the better. The French Quarter looked even
shabbier and more neglected, many of its loveliest
structures slowly crumbling. Even Micaela's own rows
of buildings fronting the central parade grounds, which
she had renovated years earlier, were once again in
need of repair. As for the parade grounds themselves,
they seemed even more run-down, if such a thing were
possible. The sycamore trees, their branches tangled
and unruly, the bark peeling and shaggy, had apparently not seen a gardener's pruning shears for years,
perhaps not since the last time Micaela had looked at
them and shaken her head in dismay. It distressed her
to realize that nothing had been done in all this time
to upgrade the very heart of the Quarter. The fact that
most of her life had been spent in France did not
diminish her strong attachment to the city of her birth.

Beyond Canal Street, however, lay the burgeoning
Garden District with its sweeping green lawns and
well-cultivated gardens, and it saddened Micaela to see
that area maintaining its elegant position over the
French Quarter.

After having left her cousin Pierre's plantation in
order to inspect her own properties, Micaela strolled
wistfully about the square, carefully lifting the skirt

of her ruffled violet barège silk gown that covered a stiff hoop and lacy petticoats. She observed that the benches on which lovers had once shyly courted and black nursemaids had watched their white charges at play were gone, as was the delightful fountain that had sparkled in the warm sunshine, dispensing cheer and providing a home for schools of glistening goldfish. The only fixture remaining from her childhood was the curfew cannon, whose booming report each dusk had cleared the blacks from the streets and sent them scurrying back to their masters.

With Binnie in tow, she walked up one side of the square and down the other, noting that while the St. Ann Street side was devoted to fruit stalls and hardware and liquor stores, the St. Peter Street side sported bars, cafes, and restaurants, such as the Quatre Saisons and Victor's, where customers sipped strong chicory-laced coffee, orange flower water, or cognac and played dominoes or chess. On the floors above the commercial establishments were living quarters, occupied by Micaela's tenants. The balcony railings were draped with dingy laundry, and blighted plants in cracked pots struggled to survive on the small galleries. Slovenly women stared blankly at passersby on the street below; old men puffed on corncob pipes.

Standing before the venerable St. Louis Cathedral, at whose altar she had knelt years earlier and exchanged vows with the curly-haired, cherubic-faced Celestin, fresh from Napoleon's cavalry, Micaela surveyed the scene through the thin black veil attached to her tiny violet silk hat. Slapping her hands on her hips, she exclaimed, "What a disgrace!"

Binnie shook her head in sad agreement. "It sure is, Miss Micaela," she said.

"I don't intend for it to stay this way."

"What're you fixin' to do about it?"

"I'm not sure, but I'm going to do something," Micaela resolved. "Come on, Binnie, there's somebody I've got to see."

It required several visits to Patrick's office to catch him in, and with each, Micaela's heart raced excitedly in eager anticipation at the prospect of seeing him again. Since she landed in New Orleans, her uppermost thoughts had been of him, but her sense of propriety forced her to seek an acceptable reason for a visit.

"Mr. Lynch, Senior, doesn't come in often, and when he does, it's usually just for a few hours," the young male secretary explained. "Mr. Lynch, Junior, now oversees the majority of the firm's work."

When at last they finally did meet, Patrick, older and grayer but still handsome, seemed stunned as well as delighted to see her. Restrained in front of the young secretary, he clasped her hand and pressed it to his lips, allowing her fingers to linger there longer than was customary. "Welcome home again, Baroness," he said.

Prompted by the black armband around his sleeve, she felt obliged to comment, "I was shocked and sorry to hear about the terrible tragedy you recently suffered."

Looking genuinely bereaved, he shook his head sadly. "Yes, terrible it was."

A brief but cordial exchange followed. Micaela felt that more than that would have been inappropriate under the circumstances, so she proceeded to the ostensible purpose of her visit, explaining to him that she was appalled at the disgraceful condition of the French Quarter in general and her own buildings in particular.

"If it's feasible," she went on, "I'd like to tear down my buildings fronting the square and erect modern and highly innovative new structures in their place. Perhaps if I begin to improve the Quarter, others will hopefully follow suit and revitalize that section of the city."

"It's a lovely old area, and I'd hate to see it fall into further ruin myself," he replied. "Some of the most intriguing architecture in all of New Orleans is there. I'd like to help to reverse conditions, if possible."

"I'm glad to see we are of one mind on this," she said with a sly smile.

"We usually are, aren't we?" He reached out and

tenderly squeezed her arm, causing a sudden and un-expected effusion of warmth to flow through her.

During the next few weeks they conferred fre-quently at his office and exchanged various ideas on the improvement of the buildings around the central square. Although their meetings were crisp and busi-nesslike, the lifelong attraction between them fre-quently surfaced and seemed as strong as ever, although his state of mourning obliged them to limit their expressions of affection to warm smiles, kisses of greeting and farewell, a touch on the forearm, a hand laid gently on a knee.

Micaela had been greatly influenced by her expo-sure to French architecture and modes of living, and incorporated much of what she had learned and ex-perienced into her thinking.

"I should like the whole square to have the marvel-ous atmosphere of the Palais Royal," she said. "Nat-urally on a much more modest scale, but with the same ambience—if you know what I mean."

Occasionally as they conferred, Patrick made a few rudimentary sketches, which seemed to cause him some difficulty. This caught Micaela's attention at once and greatly concerned her, for in the past he had sketched readily and fluently. Often he looked preoc-cupied and talked to her while lying on the leather sofa in his office for as long as an hour, compresses over his eyes.

"Do you remember the corner of the Place des Vosges in Paris?" she asked. "You know, it's the ar-caded square built by Henry the Fourth."

He nodded. "Of course I do, lass. It's lovely."

Delighted that he remembered it, she said, "That's the sort of character I would like the square to have."

"Fine. I'll try to do some sketches for you, but please don't rush me."

"No. Of course not," she murmured. "I have lots of time."

The sketches took him much longer to complete than they would have years ago, but Micaela was de-lighted when she saw them. He might have lost his speed, but none of his talent or ability. He had given the buildings graceful arcades, just as she had envisioned.

"Oh, Patrick, these drawings are marvelous!" she exclaimed, impulsively throwing her arms around him. For a moment he looked up at her beaming, enjoying her delight with him and his work, and then his expression suddenly clouded and he gently detached himself from her embrace.

"Of course, you realize that if you want these arcades, you're going to have to ask the city to cede to you several feet of land on either side of the Place d'Armes," he warned her.

Micaela frowned. "Do you think that will be difficult?" she asked.

Patrick considered a moment. "I'm not sure," he replied. "I suspect that the rivalry between the Creoles of the French Quarter and the Anglos of the Garden District is sufficiently strong so that you won't have too much trouble."

At that time the city was divided into different municipalities, each with its own mayor and council. The French Quarter fell within the jurisdiction of the First Municipality.

"Mayor Crossman and his council are all for improving the First Municipality," Patrick continued. "It will mean, of course, going before the city council and presenting your requests."

"I have no hesitation about that."

"I think there's very little in this world that gives you pause." As Micaela snuggled close to him, chuckling at her own audacity, he put his arm around her and gave her a squeeze and a kiss on the forehead. "With that spirit of yours and that glorious red hair, you definitely should have been Irish. In fact, sometimes I honestly believe there was an Irishman in that Creole woodpile!"

At the next meeting of the city council Micaela stood before the mayor and the council members and presented her project to them in a crisp, concise manner, which earned their attention and respect.

"And so, gentlemen, all I am asking for is a mere

two feet on either side of the square," she concluded.

During this period Americans in general, regardless of their backgrounds, were still greatly impressed by European titles, and having a bona fide, home-grown baroness in their midst flattered the men on the council. After some slight debate they agreed to cede to Micaela the strips of land she required for her proposed arcades.

Having accomplished this, Micaela went on to her next request a short time later at another council meeting, at which she asked for a twenty-year tax exemption on her properties. This concession proved far more controversial and was therefore not readily forthcoming.

"That is too much to ask," the mayor huffed. "Even for you, Baroness."

"But, gentlemen," she said, addressing the group at the long conference table before her, "I am making a substantial contribution to the beautification and improvement of this city—at great personal expense, I might add. In order to finance this project, I will be forced to sell one of my plantations."

"How you finance your project is not the concern of this council," one of the men snapped.

"Specifically, Baroness, what is the city to receive in exchange for granting you the tax exemption you request?" another member questioned adjusting the glasses on the tip of his nose.

"What will the city receive in exchange?" she repeated. "Everything, gentlemen. Everything. The shops lining the arcades will be the most elegant in the city, and the proposed dwellings above will be luxurious showplaces housing the finest people in the South. I personally shall select the tenants. My new businesses and apartments will revive life in the French Quarter and bring back the trade which has been lost to Canal Street. The Quarter will once again be the vibrant heart of New Orleans that it once was and which it must be again. Visitors from all parts of the world will flock here. Businesses will thrive. You must have faith in my plans, gentlemen."

Eventually Micaela received the tax exemptions she

desired, but the mayor and the council had not yielded easily, forcing her to return to meeting after meeting before they capitulated. She was positive they would hold her to the letter of the agreement between them.

Pierre loved the city as passionately as she did and was an enthusiastic supporter of all her endeavors, using his influence with the other planters to aid her. Because of his strong backing, Micaela felt obliged to spend a few days at Versailles and inform him of her progress.

"I have instructed Patrick Lynch to draw up the plans," she announced when she returned to Versailles, finding Pierre in the rose garden, where he was supervising the slaves who were pruning the individual bushes Eulalie had loved so much.

Pierre grinned. "So the old flame still burns, does it?"

"This time we've kept things impersonal." Except for a few innocent exchanges of mutual affection, relations between Micaela and Patrick might indeed have been called impersonal. Despite the strong feelings she still had for him and was certain he bore for her, she had restrained herself from pressing any demands on him. Presently he seemed to be caught up in other matters, although she had no inkling of their nature. When they were together he often seemed distracted, as if his thoughts were elsewhere, and she didn't want to overwhelm him with her own emotions.

"We work well together," she added, "so why shouldn't I select him for the job? Besides, he's quite receptive to my ideas."

"I'm sure he is," Pierre remarked wryly.

She ignored his comment and continued. "The only thing that worries me about working with Patrick is that he seems to have so much difficulty lately in getting things done. I suppose it's because he's still grieving for poor Emily. I do believe his grief is sincere."

Pierre arched one eyebrow. " 'Poor Emily,' is it now?"

"I certainly never had any hard feelings toward her," Micaela asserted. "Just as Patrick never had any toward Celestin. Both marriages were acts of fate.

Neither of us, Patrick or I, had any control over our destinies. Nevertheless, just living with a person day after day inevitably fosters a certain affection, certain feelings, certain bonds . . ."

"Well, let me tell you something," Pierre replied in a sober tone. "Rumor has it that your Mr. Lynch has fostered a certain interest in a Miss Rosine Wright since the death of his wife."

Micaela was stunned. "Patrick has never mentioned her name to me."

"That doesn't surprise me."

"Who is this Rosine Wright?"

"She happens to be the daughter of your old school chum Renée Houdaille," he told her. "Renée married a wealthy man named Walter Wright and now lives in the Garden District."

"Then this Rosine is fairly young, isn't she?"

"Yes. Such a choice seems consistent with Mr. Lynch's tastes in the past. The girl has frequently been seen coming and going from the Lynch residence. Despite the fact that the house is supposed to be in mourning."

"Well, I'm sure it means nothing."

"One can never be sure about these things," Pierre said turning away from her and giving his attention to a particularly unhealthy-looking rosebush.

48

A FEW DAYS later, as Micaela was casually leafing through *The Daily Picayune,* she chanced to come across a tiny wedding announcement tucked into the bottom of one of the columns: Miss Rosine Wright, daughter of Walter and Renée (nee Houdaille) Wright, was to wed the distinguished architect Mr. Patrick Lynch. The lines of bold face type seemed to scream out at Micaela, and she could not bear to read any further. So this was why he had seemed so distant, so reserved, so distracted! And all the time she had assumed he was suffering from grief and confusion and had forced herself to exercise patience and restraint in their relationship!

"Oh, what a great fool I've been!" she cried aloud, and threw the newspaper across the gallery. In a rage, she ran to the French windows and nearly collided with Binnie, who was bringing out a frosty pitcher of brown-sugar lemonade.

"My goodness, Miss Micaela!" the maid gasped, frantically trying to balance the pitcher on the tray. "What's got into you?"

"Read that," Micaela demanded, pointing to the newspaper on the gallery floor.

"You know I can't read. You got to tell me what it says."

"I—I—can't," Micaela sputtered. "Not now."

"It must be about Mr. Lynch," the black woman correctly guessed.

"How did you know?" Micaela asked, surprised.

"How do I know? 'Cause he's the only person who could get you all riled up like this," Binnie answered frankly.

"He's going to marry a girl young enough to be his daughter—no, his granddaughter!"

Binnie took the news in stride. "The younger they can get them, the better the men like it," she commented.

"That's why he's been so slow with the plans for my buildings," Micaela speculated as she paced back and forth along the gallery. "He's been like a snail. I've seen nothing of them so far. I didn't want to press him because I was afraid he was already overworked. But what has he been doing instead of working on the plans? He's been courting this—this child! To make matters worse, she's the daughter of my worst enemy at school."

"After all these years, you still gonna carry on about somebody you knew at school?"

"Renée Houdaille was always awful to me, and now her very own daughter is marrying Patrick," Micaela lamented.

"Ain't nothin' you can do about it," Binnie said

with a resigned shrug. "If Mr. Lynch is fixin' to get hisself married, he's gonna get hisself married."

"Damn you, Binnie, get away from me!" Micaela cried in exasperation and yanked off her slipper and tossed it at the maid. Binnie ducked, and the shoe sailed through the open French windows and struck a porcelain figurine above the mantel, smashing it to bits. Micaela ran inside, attempted to pick up the pieces, and burst into tears.

Later, when she had regained her composure, she decided to go up to the city and confront Patrick directly about the matter.

Before she left Versailles, Pierre spotted her heading toward the carriage and tried to dissuade her from her mission. "If you think you can change his mind, let me advise you that this trip is futile," he said. He had interrupted a game of billiards with Pelagie, who had developed into a challenging partner in the game over the years, and still held his cue in his hand.

"I have no such intention," Micaela informed her cousin. "My visit to Mr. Lynch today will be strictly business."

"Business, my foot," Pierre scoffed. " 'Hell hath no fury like a woman scorned,' " he quoted.

"Contrary to what you might think, dear Cousin, it *will* be strictly business," she insisted, beginning to convince herself that she would confine her encounter with Patrick to just that.

"Business?" Pierre mused, twirling the cue in his hand. "I'll bet you're going to fire him, aren't you?"

"Perhaps."

"Well, it won't be the first time he's been fired by someone in our family. Just keep an ax out of his hand, that's all," Pierre commented wryly, referring, of course, to the little-theater incident years earlier.

"Whatever I do, he deserves it," she fumed.

"Ah, what was I just saying about a woman's vengeance?"

"It's not vengeance that moves me to fire Lynch— if I do. I've been impatient with him for some time now, but I was willing to overlook things because of our friendship. Now, of course, I feel differently."

"Of course you do." Pierre nodded knowingly.

"The delays have been excessive," she continued. "I'm anxious for the construction to start, but so far I've seen almost nothing except a few sketches. For all I know, he hasn't even begun the plans."

"From what I hear, Mr. Lynch has fallen on hard times—at least professionally."

"What do you mean?"

"I mean that lately I've heard nothing but complaints about him, many similar to yours. People are either withdrawing their commissions or bypassing him completely and hiring other architects. No one seems to know what's wrong. His son is trying to hold the firm together, but he hasn't got his father's gifts or experience. The whole city is puzzled by what's happening to him. As an architect, Lynch is second to none and has—or had—an excellent reputation throughout the state. It's hard to figure out the reason for his decline. Surely we can't blame it all on Miss Rosine Wright."

Ruffled by the mention of her young rival's name, Micaela said, "His personal troubles are no longer a concern of mine."

With that she stepped into the waiting carriage, and Pierre returned to the house and his game of billiards with Pelagie.

When Micaela arrived at Patrick's office, the secretary informed her that Mr. Lynch was not in and might not appear at all that day. "Perhaps someone else could help you, Baroness," he suggested politely.

"No," she replied. "I've come to see Mr. Lynch. I prefer to wait for him at least for a while."

"Just as you wish, Baroness," the secretary said, and went about his work.

Micaela had been there for nearly an hour and a half by the time Patrick finally entered the office. He looked tired and harried, not at all the way she expected a prospective bridegroom to look. In fact, his appearance was so startling that for a moment it served to abate her steadily escalating rage.

"Micaela! What a surprise!" He seemed genuinely happy to see her. "Please come in."

He attempted to take her arm and escort her into his private office, but she shook his hand loose. He regarded her with a puzzled frown as he shut the door behind them.

"I won't be staying long," she said, attempting to control her temper and maintain a cool, businesslike tone. "I have merely come to tell you that I wish to terminate your services."

"What?"

She nodded. "I have decided to take my project elsewhere. My lawyer, Monsieur LeBreton, will settle with you for the work you've done so far."

Stunned by this abrupt dismissal, he asked, "Am I entitled to know why you've decided to take this rather rash action?"

"The delays have been excessive," she replied. "Inexcusable, really."

Gazing questioningly into her eyes, he asked, "Is that all?"

"I simply find your performance unsatisfactory at this point. In the past I've been quite happy with your work, but no longer. I had hoped that my buildings would be well under way by now, but they're hopelessly delayed. That's why I'm dismissing you."

"You're dismissing me because you think *I've* dismissed *you*," he said. "That's the real truth, isn't it?"

"Absolutely not."

He grabbed her firmly by the shoulders and shook her. "Come on, be honest with me, lass."

"Take your hands off me," she demanded, prying at his strong fingers.

"Listen to me!"

"There's nothing to say," she insisted.

"There is," he countered, a note of sadness suddenly penetrating the anger in his voice. "There are things happening to me that you don't understand . . ."

"I understand all I need to."

"If only I could explain . . . if only you knew what I've been going through . . ." He shook his head in anguish and released her from his grip.

"I must be going," she murmured, edging toward the door suddenly feeling cruel and heartless in her actions but at the same time angry and impatient with herself for allowing these emotions to take hold of her.

A few days later Micaela took Patrick's basic sketches to Samuel Stewart, a well-known builder, and told him that she had become dissatisfied with Patrick and wished him to take over the project.

"I'm not surprised Baroness," the portly builder said. "Many have become impatient with Mr. Lynch lately. Of course, you must remember I'm not an architect."

Over a period of weeks Stewart and Micaela conferred several times, and when he had a good idea of what she wanted, he brought in an architect named Henry Howard, who had designed some of the finest buildings in the South.

Howard, a slender, reticent young man, listened carefully and noted all of Micaela's ideas on a pad, promising to incorporate them into the plans.

When Howard's sketches were completed, he invited Micaela to his offices in Exchange Place to look them over. Fully expecting her to approve the drawings and agree to have him proceed with the plans as a matter of course, the young architect was startled when she balked at paying the five-hundred-dollar fee he asked.

"If you'll pardon me for saying so, I consider that a very reasonable, almost modest, sum, Baroness," he said. "Especially when one considers that the project you propose will cost in excess of a quarter of a million dollars."

"*You* may consider that fee reasonable and modest Mr. Howard, but *I* consider it excessive," she protested. "You must bear in mind that not only have I given you Mr. Lynch's preliminary sketches, for which he has been paid by me, but I have contributed many of my own ideas as well, even to the dimensions of the various rooms."

"I do appreciate your suggestions, Baroness, but I

must remind you that you are hardly considered an architect in the professional sense."

"Nonsense! As far as I am concerned, degrees are worthless pieces of sheepskin. I am quite knowledgeable in the area of construction, as I believe I have demonstrated. After all, I built one of the finest homes in all of Paris. Building for me has been a lifelong passion."

"Yes, so I've heard."

"In any case, Mr. Howard, although I refuse to pay you the five-hundred-dollar fee for the plans, I will pay you for the expense of having them executed. However, these expenses must not exceed one hundred dollars."

"My costs are at least one hundred and fifty dollars."

"All right then, one hundred and twenty-five," she declared adamantly. "And not a penny more."

"Very well. You win, Baroness," he sighed. "One hundred and twenty-five it is."

Eventually Henry Howard completed plans that were satisfactory to Micaela, and she submitted them to the city council, which, in time, approved them. Only after the city council's approval, however, did Howard convince Micaela that she had to eliminate the graceful arcades that she especially loved.

"The cost of constructing such arches is prohibitive," he told her.

"If Henry the Fourth of France could do it, why can't I?" she demanded.

"I doubt if Henry the Fourth was quite as concerned with costs as you are, Baroness," Howard replied. "Besides, the actual construction is very complicated and difficult."

"What do you propose I add instead?" she asked. She was sure that Patrick would have found a way to construct the arcades that would be both reasonable in cost and technically feasible, but she restrained herself from saying this to Howard.

"My idea is that you ornament your new buildings with cast-iron galleries," he suggested.

"Cast-iron galleries?" she repeated with a puzzled frown.

The young architect nodded. "We can develop some very attractive designs for you. Your buildings will be the first in New Orleans to feature decorative cast-iron work. Once everyone sees how attractive ironwork is it will become the rage. Ironwork will grace every building here."

Micaela contemplated his suggestion, attracted by the thought of being the first with something new and different.

"Yes, decorative ironwork does sound rather nice," she admitted.

When the final edition of the plans was completed by Howard, Micaela gave the builder Stewart the go-ahead to erect the sixteen dwelling units on the St. Peter Street side of the Place d'Armes for a price of one hundred fifty-six thousand dollars. Shortly afterward, the actual work began.

Despite her excitement over the start of construction and her desire to monitor the daily progress of her buildings, Micaela had a morbid fear of yellow fever, which seemed to plague the city each summer. Since Alfred and Gaston had recently sailed from France to join her, she thought it best to move from Versailles to Pascagoula on the breezy Gulf coast for the summer months.

In a rented home in Pascagoula, they waited out the yellow-fever season, Alfred occupying himself by managing his mother's business affairs and corresponding faithfully with his father in Paris, Gaston working with Micaela on the design of a monogram that would be cast in iron and incorporated in the scheme of the decorative grille work fronting the galleries of each building.

"I want our monogram to be truly unique," Micaela said as they experimented with the various ways of combining the two letters A and P—signifying Almonester and Pontalba.

"If Papa were here, he might enjoy this," Gaston remarked as he carefully shaded in the intertwined A and P with India ink. "He likes to make original designs for his needlepoint. He's quite clever at that sort of thing."

"Yes, he is," Micaela conceded.

"I think you're very artistic, too, Mama," Gaston went on. "I'm sure your buildings will be the most attractive in the whole city."

"I hope so, dear," she sighed, gazing at the emerging monogram. "I certainly hope so."

From Pascagoula it was possible for Micaela to travel to New Orleans without great difficulty by a combination of train and boat, and she made regular trips to check on the progress of her buildings. On one of her visits she presented the final A-P monogram design to Stewart.

"I want you to insure that the French ornamental scrollwork is strictly followed in all castings, Mr. Stewart," she said.

"Yes, of course, Baroness," the builder agreed, rubbing his protruding stomach.

Turning her attention to other matters, Micaela asked, "Have you purchased the granite for the sills and lintels yet, Mr. Stewart?"

"Yes, Baroness," he replied. "They're coming from the finest quarries in Quincy, Massachusetts."

"Have you personally inspected this granite?"

"Personally, no. But I hear the quality of stone from those quarries is excellent."

"I want you to visit those quarries before the granite is shipped and be sure it is truly the finest," she directed.

Stewart was stunned by such a request. "Go to Massachusetts?" he said. "That's quite a journey."

"Yes, it is."

"And I suppose," he persisted sardonically, "that en route I am to stop in Baltimore and Philadelphia to see that the pressed bricks, the marble, the iron, the banisters, and the mahogany are the finest also?"

"Why not? Those cities are, as you say, sir, en route."

For the ironwork, Micaela personally called on Allen Hill, a New Orleans dealer, and was so pleased with his service that she chose the marble mantels and the ornate fireplace fronts either from designs in his catalogs or from samples in his showroom. However, it took four or five visits to Hill's establishment before she could reach a final decision.

"It's very difficult to make up my mind," she sighed. "I am so anxious for my buildings to be the finest in New Orleans."

"I am sure that if you are as meticulous about everything else as you are about the ironwork you are buying from me, they will be," the tactful and shrewd Hill commented.

At times Pierre, who was avidly following the progress of her building project, alluded to the possibility that perhaps she was taking out her frustrations in her excessive, almost obsessive, preoccupation with the construction.

"Stewart is telling everyone you are the most difficult woman he has ever met," Pierre said.

She shrugged indifferently. "Is he really?"

"And so is poor Mr. Howard."

"Everyone with high standards appears difficult to others at times," she remarked, refusing to acknowledge that he might have hit on the truth. She kept trying to convince herself that she had put Patrick out of her mind forever, but she was not at all sure that she truly had or ever could.

By October, Micaela decided it would be safe to leave Pascagoula and return to New Orleans with her sons, her buildings being well under way. She leased a home for them close to the construction site but vowed to stay away from there, hiring a man named Domingo to check on the work and protect her interests. However, she soon became dissatisfied with him and decided to oversee the job herself.

"But, Mama, you can't do that," Alfred objected.

"Why not?" she snapped.

"Because it means climbing up and down ladders, wading through the mud, being around workmen who use rough language. It's a man's job, not a woman's."

"It's my money that's paying for those buildings,"

she argued. "I have a perfect right to see how it's being spent."

"Alfred's right," Gaston chimed in. "No respectable woman would ever climb a ladder."

"It's absolutely unthinkable, Mama," Alfred protested. "To put it bluntly—and you must forgive me, Mama—the workmen will be able to look up your skirts."

"Well, then," she said after considering a moment, "I won't wear skirts."

Micaela paid a call on the leading mulatto seamstress of the city and had her execute several pairs of heavy cotton pantaloons designed by Micaela that would protect her modesty when she was climbing the ladders and scaffolding.

In her new and unique pantaloons, Micaela visited the building site nearly every day, often galloping through the city streets on horseback, too eager to see the day's progress to wait for her coachman to get the carriage ready. On the days she was forced to remain at home for one reason or another, she climbed to the topmost gallery, got her spyglass, and trained its lenses on the construction site. Even at a distance very little escaped her attention.

One afternoon when the project was nearly completed, a city inspector appeared and told her that the buildings did not conform to the original plans that had been approved by the city council.

Astonished by such news, Micaela indignantly demanded what he meant by such a statement.

"I mean, Baroness," the inspector, a rather stuffy man, answered, "that your buildings do not incorporate the arcades for which you were conceded the two-foot strip of ground by the city."

"It was necessary to change those plans," she explained.

"So I see," the inspector said dryly.

Almost at once the mayor and the city council, still smarting over the twenty-year tax exemption that Micaela had extracted from them, seized upon this deviation as an excuse to rescind the exemption, charging that she had violated the original agreement with the city.

"Technically, they're within their rights, you know," Pierre informed her after she had rushed to Versailles with the news.

"Of course they're within their rights," she conceded, still smarting with anger. "But you must admit that this is shabby treatment to accord one who is only trying to beautify and revitalize a part of the city which they themselves have shamefully allowed to decline."

Pouring himself a glass of bourbon, Pierre cocked his head and glanced at her quizzically. "And that is your only aim, dear Cousin?" he asked skeptically.

"Naturally, I shall receive rents from my buildings, but I was receiving rents from the old ones," she argued. "I had no obligation to do anything at all. I invested my money in this project because I love New Orleans and want it to be a beautiful, elegant city like Paris."

"You know what I think?" Pierre said after taking a large drink of his bourbon. "I think you've gotten into this whole business because you're frustrated and unhappy."

"Who cares what you think?" she lashed back at him. "Besides, you've said all that many times before!"

Deep within her, however, she suspected once more, that he might indeed be right.

49

MICAELA'S NEW BUILDINGS, when completed, were among the handsomest the citizens of New Orleans had ever seen. Built in twin rows of red brick, their design was basically Renaissance, but adapted to the Creole locale. Intricate ornamental ironwork extended from the street level to the third story. In keeping with the Continental tradition, the street floors were devoted to shops and commercial establishments, while the upper floors were divided into stylish family apartments. Micaela had very specifically designated the kinds of shops that could be located in her buildings. Cafes, cabarets, fruit stalls, and boarding houses were prohibited. She was equally particular about the tenants who would occupy the apartments and invited only the leading figures of New Orleans society to apply. Many accepted her offer, knowing instinctively that these luxurious homes, probably the first and certainly the most magnificent apartments in America at the time, would provide them with a most fashionable address. Micaela herself, together with Alfred and Gaston, moved into Number Five St. Peter Street, which occupied approximately the same site as her mother's original townhouse. All the apartments had large rooms with thick walls, deep doors, and high windows. Crystal chandeliers and marble fireplaces lent a graceful touch, as did the quiet yet picturesque interior courts. The elegant fittings from the Duc du Maine's mansion, which had been incorporated into her Paris home, had accustomed Micaela to the finest appointments, a tradition she wished to continue in her New Orleans residence. The front galleries, or balconies, extended the entire length of both upper floors, and the entwined letters A and P, in a design of which Micaela was very proud, were repeated in the ironwork at regular intervals. The fourth and topmost floor was intended for servants, and the windows there were decorated with simpler cast-iron grilles.

Micaela received much civic praise for her endeavors, and the venture proved successful with both the press and the public. The *Daily Delta* lauded her single-handed revitalization of the old heart of the city, calling it a remarkable undertaking and a labor of love.

Pleased with the results of what she had accomplished, Micaela, once she had established herself in her apartment, was not content to rest on her laurels. Anxiously she looked about for another project in which to immerse herself, occasionally wondering if her desire to keep herself occupied and create a swirl of activity around her wasn't simply a result of her unsuccessful marriage and her hopeless love affair with Patrick. Since that painful day in his office when she had dismissed him, she had tried to eradicate all memories of him from her mind, but it was impossible to overlook the strong desire she still harbored for the tall Irishman with his soft, deep voice and strong-fingered hands. A tiny shiver coursed through her as she recalled the heat within those hands when they had caressed her smooth body, the sweetness of his mouth when he had firmly pressed it over hers. Micaela shook her head violently, as if to dispel all thoughts of him from her brain, and forced herself to turn her attention to more productive matters.

Early one evening, as she and her two sons were sitting on the gallery sipping cool drinks, Micaela gazed at the Place d'Armes before her and realized she did not have far to look for her next project. It lay just beyond the edge of her gallery. Appraising the square's shabbiness, she was immediately stirred.

"How lovely the parks and squares in Paris were," she reminisced. "Do you recall?"

"Of course we do, Mama," Alfred laughed. "We haven't been away *that* long, you know."

"Then you must realize how ugly that square in front of us is," she continued.

"Yes, it's a disgrace," Alfred agreed. "A real eyesore."

"Lately it looks worse than usual," Gaston said. "No one's cut the weeds for months, and they've been allowed to grow quite wild."

"The sycamores, too, are shedding worse than usual and cry out for the pruner's shears," Alfred added.

"Or an ax," Micaela suggested.

"The paths are nothing but mud," Gaston complained. "I took a shortcut across the square, and my boots sank in nearly to the tops."

"I suppose you wish you were looking over a Parisian park instead, don't you, Mama?" Alfred said.

She nodded. "I'd much prefer it."

"Do you miss Paris, Mama?" Gaston asked.

"Yes and no," she answered thoughtfully. "I miss

the lovely parks, but America, after all, is the land of my birth."

"There's no reason why the Place d'Armes couldn't be turned into a Parisian park," Gaston observed. "With formal plantings and lovely, curving walks."

"Yes, it could be," Micaela said, a note of excitement rising in her voice.

"I suppose that will be your next project, won't it?" Alfred mused.

She considered a moment before answering. "Possibly. It's certainly a thought."

"You know how indifferent the city council is to aesthetics," Gaston said. "They must be, or they wouldn't permit such a shoddy, disgraceful public square to exist."

"You're probably right," she conceded, still smarting over the city's cancellation of the twenty-year tax exemption she had fought so hard to obtain. "But still, that doesn't discourage me from trying to change their thinking."

After having certain sketches drawn—some by Gaston—and organizing a definite campaign, Micaela went before the city council once more and proposed her plans for the beautification of the central square of the French Quarter. Initially, the council members were not enthusiastic, recalling how she had tried to wrangle the tax exemption from them. Wary, they fully expected a similar maneuver on this project as well and stubbornly refused to allocate funds for the improvement of the Place d'Armes, despite her pleas and cajoling.

Undaunted, Micaela stood before the city's distinguished governing body and said, "All right, then, gentlemen, since you choose not to release any funds for this project, I shall be forced to draw on my personal resources."

"That is your privilege, Baroness," a councilman replied.

"But in any case, I shall transform the Place d'Armes into a public square as fine as any in the world, no matter what it takes."

"You have our blessing, Baroness," another councilman offered.

"My only request is that I have your official permission and sanction for the undertaking."

"As long as it doesn't cost this city a cent, you have it, Baroness," the mayor assured her. "But you will receive nothing more—no payments, no exemptions. Nothing. You are on your own. Is that clear?"

"Yes, your Honor," she replied.

With that the mayor banged his gavel and suggested they go on to other business.

Later she related the results of the council session to Pierre during one of his visits to her apartment.

"My motives aren't as unselfish as I tried to make them sound," she admitted.

"Surely, dear Cousin, you don't think the honorable city councilmen have overlooked the fact that by improving the square, you greatly enhance the value of your real estate that fronts it, do you?" he said, sipping the frothy Ramos Gin Fizz that Binnie had brought him.

"Of course not," she answered. "But in the end the whole city will benefit. Don't you see?"

Once she had secured official approval of her plans, Micaela set about overhauling the square almost immediately. During the slack season she brought in slaves and overseers from the outlying sugar plantation she had inherited from her mother. They were put to work clearing away the grass, weeds, and debris that choked the muddy square. When that task was accomplished, she tackled a more controversial matter and ordered the removal of the double avenue of sycamores, the city's sole concession to any sort of beauty for its former military parade grounds. Despite their shedding bark and unruly branches, these trees were held in high regard by a great number of citizens. Thus, when they began crashing to the ground under the axes of Micaela's workmen, a great hue and cry arose against the Baroness de Pontalba and her aggressive beautification efforts. If having a new public square meant the loss of their beloved sycamores, the people wanted none of it.

The highly emotional tree lovers banded together and stormed the mayor's office, demanding that he put a stop to Micaela and her vandalism at once.

While the noisy protest was taking place at the city hall, Micaela was waiting impatiently in the patio of her home for the coachman to get her carriage ready for a trip to Versailles.

"Miss Micaela! Miss Micaela!" Binnie cried, bursting through the garden gate and running toward her mistress in an obviously agitated state.

"What is it?" Micaela demanded impatiently.

"I just got back from the French Market and I heard that the mayor and a bunch of folks is madder than a nest of hornets because you is choppin' down all the trees. They're headin' for the square."

"What for?"

"They is fixin' to stop you."

"They are, are they?" Micaela said, planting her hands indignantly on her hips. "Well, I intend to go on chopping down trees until every one of those disgraceful eyesores is gone. I also intend to remove Ruffignac's old fence and the ugly curfew cannon as well, whether anyone likes it or not."

"I hear that some of them folks is mighty vexed," the slave warned.

"Let them be." Micaela shrugged indifferently. "The city council has given me full permission to proceed as I choose—just so long as I don't ask them for any money or special privileges."

Changing her mind about journeying to her cousin's plantation that day, Micaela ordered her groom to saddle a single mount instead, and while he was doing that, she instructed Binnie to go into the house and bring her the shotgun Alfred used for duck hunting.

"A shotgun?" Binnie exclaimed, wide-eyed. "What is you gonna do with that?"

"Use it if I have to," Micaela replied.

"Have you done gone and lost your head, Miss Micaela?"

"Go and get it, I said. And hurry!"

When Micaela arrived at the Place d'Armes on horseback, shotgun in hand, she was confronted by a sea of angry protesters carrying placards that bore slogans protesting her plans for the square. Because of the demonstration, the slaves and other workers she had engaged were in a state of great agitation, fearful of the crowd and uncertain of what they might do to them.

"Go on with your work," Micaela directed the men from astride her horse. "There are still more trees to remove."

"We can't, ma'am," the overseer said. "That crowd will skin us alive."

"No, they won't," Micaela assured him. "Get the men back to work."

"They're scared of them people," the overseer insisted.

"You let me worry about them. Now get back to work."

While she was speaking to the overseer, the feisty mob began to close in on her, yelling their objections, waving the placards in her face, and chanting the popular song "Woodsman, Spare That Tree." Micaela raised her hand for silence and tried to address them, but their cries drowned her out. As they pressed closer, they began singing louder and striking her horse with the placards, frightening the normally calm animal so much that it reared and nearly threw Micaela. To stay in the saddle, she pressed her knees into its ribs and held tight to the reins.

"Back! Back!" she shouted, waving her arms. "All of you, back!"

When they showed no sign of withdrawing, she raised the shotgun to her shoulder and aimed it into the crowd.

"Back, I say. Back! Back, before somebody gets hurt!" she ordered.

"You have no right to order us off this land," a protest leader balked. "You don't own it. This is public property and we are citizens."

"I'm a citizen, too, sir," Micaela retorted. "And as long as I have this shotgun in my hand, I have any right I choose. I'm going to count to three, and by the time I do, I want all of you out of here."

At that the crowd jeered, and a few members picked up stones and lumps of dirt and started to pelt her. A stone struck her on the chest, just above the breast in which the bullet still lodged, and startled her so much that she accidentally pulled the trigger. Fortunately, the shot went over the heads of the hecklers. They reacted with surprise and realized that she had been serious when she told them to disperse.

Slowly they broke up, and the tumult gradually died down.

When most of the demonstrators had gone, Mayor Crossman appeared on the scene. Deciding it was to her advantage to talk with him, Micaela dismounted and greeted him.

"Good day, Mr. Mayor," she said.

"Well, now, I guess you know the public's feeling about these trees, Baroness?"

"Yes, I think they have done their best to make me aware of them."

He smiled smugly. "Good."

"But then, what does the public know? When I am finished with this square, they'll forget a few straggly sycamores. There will be other trees, new ones that will be far more beautiful and well cared for. There'll also be shrubs and plants of every description. This dismal parade grounds will be transformed into a jewel of a park, full of lush foliage and flowers of every color of the rainbow. Truly, sir, it will be the finest city square in all of America. But the people must give me a chance. I didn't disappoint the citizens of New Orleans with my buildings, and I won't disappoint them with the square, either. It will be a miniature of the gardens of the Palais Royal, with parterres of roses, lilies, oleander, myrtle, orange, pittosporum, magnolias, jasmine . . . The city will fall in love with it, and more than that, they will praise you for supporting me in my efforts, Mr. Mayor. Your term in office will be long remembered."

"At the moment, I am more concerned about you and that shotgun than about anything else." The mayor nervously eyed the weapon in her hands.

"Forgive me, sir," she said, laying the weapon across the saddle.

"Thank you, Baroness."

"Yes, sir, when the good people of this city see the new square, they'll forget about a few sorry sycamores, and I'll have no further need of this shotgun."

50

ONCE THE TREE-LOVING citizens of New Orleans had adjusted to the loss of their beloved sycamores, they accepted the newly transformed square and allowed it to capture their fancy, conceding that the gracefully curving flatstone paths and the formal plantings had converted the shabby parade grounds into an elegant showplace. Micaela herself had designed the cast-iron fence that surrounded the area; each individual picket was capped with the famous fleur-de-lis as a tribute to France, the country to which she owed the inspiration for the design of the park.

On Sundays the new square was filled with families who promenaded along its flower-bordered paths, greeting friends, stopping to chat with neighbors after Mass at the cathedral, enjoying the flowers and shrubs. On weekdays it served as a gathering spot for businessmen, young matrons and nursemaids with their charges, and an occasional courting couple. Micaela's two major stipulations were that the city keep the square free of vendors and that the panoramic view of the river remain forever unobstructed. The city council was so delighted by the success of the Baroness de Pontalba's projects and by the revival they spurred in the French Quarter, returning business, commerce, and tourism to the formerly blighted section, that it promptly adopted her stipulations into law.

Once again in the good graces of the mayor and the city council, Micaela decided to capitalize on her present position of favor and request that the square be given a new name, thinking that "Place d'Armes" no longer seemed suitable or appropriate.

One evening she gave an elegant dinner party for the mayor and his wife and several other prominent citizens, including Pierre and François LeBreton, at Number Five St. Peter Street. She would have liked to have invited Patrick, feeling that he deserved a place at such a gathering, but she could not face the prospect of seeing him with his new, young bride. During the course of the meal she proposed the matter of a new name to her guests.

"We simply must rechristen it," Micaela added, glancing up and down the table to see how much support such a suggestion would have.

"Have you any ideas, Baroness?" Mayor Crossman's wife asked, knowing perfectly well she had.

Smiling, Micaela said, "I've been thinking about 'Jackson Square.'"

A murmur went around the table, and soon several heads were nodding enthusiastically.

"Jackson Square," LeBreton mused, letting the words roll eloquently off his tongue. "Yes, that's interesting."

For days Micaela had been mulling over the matter, and of all the deserving and distinguished individuals she had considered, Jackson consistently remained her personal favorite and the one whom she most wanted to honor by bestowing his name on the square. Although he had been unable to help her obtain her divorce, the fiery Democrat had, nevertheless, made a strong impression on her during her trip to Washington. She could still recall his thick mane of silvery hair and his dynamic personality.

"Jackson . . . ?" Mayor Crossman repeated dubiously.

"Yes, why not?" Micaela challenged, prepared to defend her choice.

"It seems to me that's the least the city could do to honor a man who saved us all from destruction at the hands of the British thirty years ago," Pierre, staunchly on Micaela's side, reminded them.

Mayor Crossman leaned forward and looked directly at Micaela, who was seated at the head of the elegant table set with the finest china, crystal, and silver. "I find it most amusing, Baroness, that you have taken on the role of Mr. Jackson's champion," he said.

"Amusing, Mr. Crossman?" she replied. "Why is that?"

"Well, by marriage, you are a French noblewoman and quite, shall we say, affluent."

"I am *rich,* not merely affluent, Mr. Crossman," she subtly corrected him, "and an aristocrat as well. In the United States I am a loyal Jacksonian Democrat. I believe in a strong President who acts decisively and is not afraid of tangling with the Congress now and then. In France, of course, my politics are quite another matter. There I am a firm supporter of the monarchy and the aristocracy, but that is another country, another way of life."

"And you don't find these two quite opposite political positions difficult to reconcile, Baroness?" Mrs. Crossman asked.

"Not a bit." Micaela signaled to her butler to refill the wineglasses.

"And your sons, what positions do they take?" Le-Breton inquired, looking from Alfred to Gaston.

Micaela answered for them. "My sons are French, Monsieur LeBreton. Don't talk to them about democracy. The French know nothing of such a concept and could never comprehend it if they did. They are no more ready for democracy than a bunch of monkeys."

"Really, Mama . . ." Alfred protested.

"It's true," she asserted.

"Give us credit for more intelligence than that," Gaston said.

"It's not a question of intelligence," his mother replied. "It's a question of temperament."

Following the dinner party, the city council, at its next meeting, unanimously voted to adopt the name Jackson Square for the former Place d'Armes, much to Micaela's great satisfaction.

"My next move," she confided to Pierre on a visit to Versailles one day, "is to press for a statue of Pres-

ident Jackson in the center of the square. I have
learned that on a visit here in 1840 he had already
laid the cornerstone for such a monument in his honor,
but nothing further has been done since then. I consider
it disgraceful."

"Ah, dear Cousin, your energies are boundless,"
Pierre sighed.

"It's a good thing for this city that I have returned,"
she declared. "Otherwise nothing would be accomplished. The French Quarter would have been allowed
to decay, and Jackson Square would still be a weed-
covered mudhole."

"There is in existence a Jackson Monument Association, you know," Pierre told her.

"No, I didn't know that."

"It was formed some years ago but has probably
fallen into inactivity now."

"Then I must get in touch with it. We must revive
it."

The renaissance of building and general improvement in the French Quarter, stimulated by the
Pontalba Buildings and Jackson Square made the re-
institution of the Jackson Monument Association much
easier. With Micaela goading its members, the Association managed to obtain an appropriation of ten
thousand dollars from the state legislature toward the
erection of a statue. Then Micaela set about seeking
an appropriate monument. At her suggestion a competition was conducted, and the winner was a talented,
but rather inexperienced, sculptor by the name of
Clark Miller, who, like Micaela, cherished the memory of Old Hickory. The plaster model Miller submitted was an equestrian figure—Jackson seated on a
rearing mount.

When Mayor Crossman viewed it, he said, "It's
rather an exciting—if a little unnatural—pose for a
horse."

"I think it's quite dashing," Micaela remarked defensively.

"Dashing as it may be," Crossman replied, "I doubt
if, when cast in bronze, it can be made to stand without visible props or supports at strategic points."

"That is a problem Mr. Miller and the Association will solve," Micaela promised. She loved the statue and mere practical considerations were not going to dampen her enthusiasm.

"I wish you and Mr. Miller luck, Baroness," the mayor said.

Unfortunately, the inexperienced Miller could not solve the more fundamental aspects of his proposed statue, and feeling was mounting on the part of the Jackson Monument Association against adopting it, especially after a plaster mock-up of the equestrian figure crashed to the ground during a demonstration.

"We must abandon it and search for another, more feasible monument," one of the members of the Association proposed.

"Over my dead body," Micaela declared, rising to her feet.

"Well, Baroness, you must admit it certainly won't be much of a tribute to Mr. Jackson if his horse collapses under him," another member pointed out, and his remark was greeted with laughter all around.

"The horse will not collapse," Micaela assured them.

"But you just saw, Baroness . . ."

"I am certain there is a way of casting the statue so that the horse can rear up on its hind legs without falling. Someone in this city must have an answer."

"Who?" several members replied in unison.

Micaela pondered a moment, her mind racing to come up with a name that would satisfy her detractors. She knew of only one.

"Mr. Patrick Lynch," she asserted. "If anyone can find a way to make that statue stand satisfactorily, Mr. Lynch is the man."

The assembled group was dumbfounded by her suggestion. Certainly they would all agree that for many years Patrick Lynch had had an excellent reputation as a first-rate architect who had solved many sticky problems. It was he who had devised ways to prevent tall buildings from sinking into the Louisiana ooze and had designed chimneys for the special demands of the new sugar houses. Nevertheless, it was well known that his ability had declined the last few years, and recently he had retired completely from his practice, turning it over to his son.

"But Mr. Lynch is no longer at his office," one of the members said. "In fact, he has scarcely been seen at all lately. It's said he's become a virtual recluse."

"Just the same, I shall contact him on this matter," she promised.

Resolved to put aside whatever personal feelings she had toward the Irish architect for the sake of the statue, Micaela knew that once she had made the promise to the Association to consult Patrick, she was obliged to keep it.

Since Patrick no longer was available at his office, she directed her coachman to drive to his home in the Garden District, which turned out to be a stately residence fronted by the tall white columns of the Greek revival style he loved so much. A butler greeted her at the door and ushered her into a well-appointed parlor. For a moment Micaela wondered what it might be like if she were Patrick's wife and the mistress of this house, but she quickly dismissed such speculation at the appearance of an attractive young woman with a friendly smile who she was certain must be the new Mrs. Lynch.

"Baroness . . ." the woman said, extending her hand. She was small and fair and pretty, with tiny freckles across the bridge of her nose, and bore little or no resemblance to her mother. "How do you do? I'm Mrs. Lynch."

"I know who you are," Micaela snapped. Although it was the first time the two women had met face to face, Micaela wondered if Patrick had told this young woman about her and their affair, feeling certain he had. She believed that lovers eventually told each other everything. "I have come to see Mr. Lynch. I have a most pressing matter to discuss with him. A business matter," she added hastily.

"As you probably have heard, Mr. Lynch is now retired."

"Patrick retired? Nonsense," Micaela scoffed. "I know him much too well to believe that."

Rosine Wright Lynch continued to smile in a pleasant open fashion, which Micaela found most disconcerting. "I'm afraid it's true, Baroness," she replied. "I give you my word. Might I inquire as to the nature of the business matter you wished to consult with him about? Perhaps I can be of some assistance."

"I doubt if you could be of any assistance at all," Micaela retorted. "I would much prefer talking to Patrick himself."

"I'm sure you would, but Mr. Lynch sees almost no one these days. However, if you'll be kind enough to tell me about it . . ."

"Very well," Micaela agreed after a moment's hesitation. "I've come to see him about a certain monument—an equestrian statue of President Andrew Jackson—that we want to erect in Jackson Square."

"I'm afraid statues are a little out of Mr. Lynch's line, Baroness." The young woman laughed. "He's been quite versatile in the past, but not that versatile."

Micaela refused to be put off. "Our problem is how to execute this statue in bronze so that it stands as the sculptor intended it to. Patrick is very clever at such practical matters."

"Mr. Lynch no longer takes on any work."

Micaela was becoming rapidly impatient with Rosine's obstinacy. "This isn't *work* I care to discuss," she informed her. "I seek his advice, his counsel. Is he in, or isn't he? If he is, then I wish to speak to him."

"Yes, he's in, but—"

Micaela cut her off. "Where is he?"

"Upstairs in the sitting room . . ."

Without further discussion, Micaela brushed past her and headed for the stairs.

"Where are you going, Baroness?" Rosine anxiously called after her. "You can't go up there. He sees no one."

"He'll see me," Micaela snapped.

When she reached the top of the stairs, she glanced quickly about, trying to determine which room might be the second-story sitting room.

"Patrick!" she called out.

From a darkened doorway to her left she heard her name being uttered. "Micaela . . . is that you?" The soft, deep voice was unmistakably familiar and trembled with both joy and apprehension at her possible presence.

Instantly Micaela headed for the room from which the voice had come. She could hear Rosine coming up the stairs after her.

"Please, Baroness, don't go in there!" Rosine pleaded from below.

Ignoring her, Micaela entered the sitting room. Although the drapes were tightly drawn against the afternoon sun, she saw a figure seated in a horsehair easychair and knew without a doubt that it was Patrick. Her heart began to pound wildly, and her mouth became so dry she was afraid she would not be able to speak.

"Patrick . . . how are you?" she managed hoarsely, crossing the room toward him.

"Micaela, this is truly a surprise!" he exclaimed, holding out his arms to her. As he squeezed her hands tightly in his, she felt suddenly relieved. The tension began to leave her body, and she was calm again. "I wasn't expecting you. Rosine said nothing to me about this visit."

"Yes, I'm afraid it is a bit unexpected," she murmured. "I've come on a rather urgent matter."

"Urgent?" he repeated.

"Yes. It's about the statue of Andrew Jackson for the square. I need your help."

"My help? I'm afraid I'm not much good to anyone in my present condition," he said sadly.

Micaela stared at him. Even though the room was darkened and she could not see distinctly, she thought he seemed perfectly well.

"What are you talking about?" she asked. "Are you ill? You look perfectly well to me."

Rosine, having heard their conversation from the doorway, now entered the room.

"Mr. Lynch is not ill," she assured Micaela as she came over and stood behind his chair, placing her hands affectionately on his shoulders.

"Then what is this nonsense about?" Micaela demanded, irked by the air of mystery they seemed to be trying to create.

"Mr. Lynch can no longer see," Rosine announced, attempting to control her quavering voice.

Micaela was stunned. "You mean that Patrick is . . . ?" Her throat suddenly became choked.

"Yes, blind," Patrick admitted.

"Oh, my God, no!" Micaela cried.

"That's why I no longer practice," he said quietly. "I began losing my sight slowly at first. I fought it and tried to deny that it was happening to me, that it wasn't really serious or permanent. For a long time I was still able to perform my work, but gradually my condition deteriorated, perhaps from the strain of forcing myself to see, forcing myself to work. Soon things became intolerable. I sought out various cures . . . here and abroad . . . but none of them helped, at least not permanently. My vision grew steadily worse. In my work I was making too many mistakes, taking too long to complete jobs. My clients were growing impatient. Finally I had to give it all up and turn things over to my son."

"I had no idea," Micaela murmured.

Affectionately patting Rosine's hand, he went on. "Rosine's been so kind to me. She's done a wonderful job, not only of taking care of me but of saving me from my despair and self-pity. One could scarcely ask for a better daughter-in-law."

Micaela gasped audibly. "Daughter-in-law?" she repeated.

"She's been good for my son as well," Patrick chuckled. "Calmed his ways and straightened him out, even at his not-so-young age. I've finally been able to entrust the business to him."

Seeing Micaela's obvious amazement, Rosine laughed. "Good heavens, Baroness, you look as if you thought I was Mr. Lynch's wife instead of his son's!"

"I thought no such thing," Micaela lied with a self-conscious smile. How foolish she had been to assume that this dewy-eyed young woman was Patrick's bride instead of the bride of his son. How foolish and ridiculous!

However, the shock of this revelation was far exceeded by the news of Patrick's—*her* Patrick's—condition.

"You must forgive me for barging in this way today," Micaela apologized. "I had no idea . . ."

"How could you?" he replied. "I deliberately kept it from you. From everyone except my immediate family, which is Patrick Junior and Rosine. I wanted to tell you of my condition for a long time now, but somehow I couldn't bring myself to do it, perhaps because I've had such a hard time accepting it myself. Anyway, I'm glad you know now. I'm glad you came today."

"Oh, Patrick, I'm *so* sorry," Micaela whispered, tears beginning to fill her eyes as she knelt beside his chair and put her arms around him.

"Don't be. The last thing I want, lass, is pity. I'd much rather have your love."

On hearing those words, Rosine discreetly withdrew from the room.

When they were alone, Patrick cupped Micaela's face between his hands and kissed her tenderly. Clinging to him, she returned his kiss with all her pent-up ardor.

"Oh, Patrick . . . Patrick . . ." she murmured.

His fingers slipped inside the bodice of her emerald-green barège silk dress and slowly caressed her breasts, taking great care with the left one. Her nipples stiffened and throbbed in response to his familiar touch.

"My love, my love," he whispered, his lips moist against her ear.

Later, when they had expressed their longings for each other, he finally inquired about the matter she had originally come to discuss.

"What is the problem with this statue of yours which I heard you talking to Rosine about downstairs?"

Micaela explained the situation and he listened carefully. When she finished, he said, "Give me some time to think about it. I don't believe it's as hopeless as the city fathers say it is."

For the next few weeks Micaela conferred frequently with Patrick in his home, and together they worked to surmount the practical problems involved in the execution of the monument. In many ways their renewed association reminded her of the happy days they had spent together in Paris while he was working on her home on the Rue du Foubourg St. Honoré.

"The way I see it," Patrick explained, "the statue will have to be cast in thirteen separate sections. The tail and hind legs of the horse, on which all the weight of the statue rests, must be made of solid iron, but the remainder of the body will be bronze, one-half inch thick, as planned. The iron will have to be forged at the navy yard. That's the only place in New Orleans that can handle such a job. To anchor the figure, the rear hooves of the horse must be riveted solidly to an iron plate. Stones or cement or something else can be placed over the plate to conceal it. I'm giving you only a rough layman's idea of how it will be accomplished. There's one drawback to all of this, though, he cautioned. "It's going to be expensive."

"We've raised ten thousand dollars already," Micaela told him. "Isn't that enough?"

Patrick shook his head. "According to my calculations, that won't do. I'd estimate that it will cost thirty thousand dollars or more."

Considering a moment, Micaela took the news in stride. "Then we'll just have to get out and raise the difference!"

"That's my lass," he chuckled, throwing an arm around her and planting an affectionate kiss on her eager lips.

Patrick's estimate was correct, and just as she had promised, Micaela raised the money—well in excess of thirty thousand dollars—some of it from private donators, but the majority from her own personal funds.

The statue was cast in gleaming bronze and erected according to Patrick's specifications. Except for a few minor problems, it proved to be both stable and a great success. Neither Andrew Jackson nor his horse fell flat on their faces—nor did Micaela.

On the day that had been selected for the official unveiling, it seemed that all New Orleans turned out. Jackson Square was so crowded, Micaela worried that her beloved plants and shrubs might never survive the sheer numbers of people, but the municipal police did an excellent job of protecting the landscaping.

Mayor Crossman gave a long speech extolling Andrew Jackson and his contributions to the city. He also praised the citizens of New Orleans for their support of the beautification program, eventually citing the Baroness de Pontalba for her personal contributions and untiring efforts, omitting, of course, the incident of the sycamores. At the end of his speech, Micaela, seated on the dais to the left of the mayor, rose in response to the applause and cheers of the crowd.

"Thank you, thank you, my friends," she murmured. "Thank you for the opportunity of allowing me to repay this city in a small way for all it has given me."

Also seated on the dais, on the other side of her, was Patrick Lynch. Micaela had insisted that he be present, asserting that, in his way, he had contributed as much to New Orleans as she had. The city council readily acknowledged this fact, but Patrick himself was reluctant to appear in public in his handicapped state. Only through Micaela's persistent efforts did he finally capitulate and consent to appear.

At a signal from the mayor, workmen lifted the canvas dropcloth concealing the statue and exposed it to the public for the first time. Amid the elegant greenery and brilliantly colored flowers, General Jackson, astride his horse, tipped his cocked hat and saluted the crescent-shaped city.

The enthusiastic response of the crowd made Micaela's pulse race and her eyes fill with tears.

One of the onlookers released a large striped balloon; it floated above the gathered populace, higher and higher, until it was a mere speck in a blue sky filled with fluffy white clouds.

Gazing after the balloon, Micaela thought of her father and his love for this city. She felt certain that wherever he was, he would be very proud of her accomplishments in behalf of his beloved New Orleans.

All at once Micaela felt truly exalted, knowing she had carried out a dream that had begun more than a half century ago with Don Andrés.

While she turned her attention to the bronze statue gleaming in the bright sun, Patrick suddenly reached out and took Micaela's hand, holding it tight and giving it a squeeze, as he had done so often in the past. It was then that she could no longer contain the floodgates of emotion steadily rising within her, and allowed a stream of happy tears to roll down her cheeks.

About the Author

ROBIN JOSEPH was introduced to story-telling by his grandfather, who filled his childhood with colorful, exciting, and sometimes ribald tales that were continued serial fashion from day to day. Perhaps it was in admiration of him that he began to spin stories himself. His mother has saved a collection of these (some illustrated), which were created at the age of five.

Literary interests were temporarily sidetracked when he attended the University of Pennsylvania to pursue a degree in zoology. Medical school followed, and Robin became a physician.

While living in Texas and California, he began writing again, was successful in having a drama produced on *CBS Playhouse*, and has had three previous novels published: *Diva, Kate's Way,* and *Odile.* Robin has abandoned the medical field to devote full time to writing. He does most of his early drafts on isolated beaches with his dog, Lady, as a companion.

Robin Joseph is a person of varied interests, including year-round ocean swimming and history. In addition, he speaks five languages, enjoys music of all kinds, and has a love for dogs.